D1259213

SHADOWS OVER BAKER STREET

SHADOWS OVER BAKER STREET

Edited by Michael Reaves and John Pelan

BALLANTINE BOOKS
NEW YORK

A Del Rey® Book
Published by The Random House Publishing Group

Copyright © 2003 by John Pelan and Michael Reaves

Grateful acknowledgment to the Estate of Dame Jean Conan Doyle for the use of the Sherlock Holmes characters in these stories.

www.delreydigital.com

Library of Congress Cataloging-in-Publication Data is available upon request from the publisher.

ISBN 0-345-45528-2

Book design by Kris Tobiassen

Manufactured in the United States of America

First Edition: October 2003

10 9 8 7 6 5 4 3 2 1

As always, for Kathy . . .
And for Jennifer, thanks for making this happen.

—J. P.

For Art Cover and Lydia Marano.

—M. R.

"When you have eliminated the impossible, whatever remains, however improbable, must be the truth."

—Sir Arthur Conan Doyle,
"A Study in Scarlet"

"The most merciful thing in the world, I think, is the inability of the human mind to correlate all its contents."

—H. P. Lovecraft,
"The Call of Cthulhu"

CONTENTS

INTRODUCTION | xi

A STUDY IN EMERALD (1881) | Neil Gaiman | 1

TIGER! TIGER! (1882) | Elizabeth Bear | 25

THE CASE OF THE WAVY BLACK DAGGER
(1884) | Steve Perry | 48

A CASE OF ROYAL BLOOD (1888)
Steven-Elliot Altman | 60

THE WEEPING MASKS (1890) | James Lowder | 94

ART IN THE BLOOD (1892) | Brian Stableford | 116

THE CURIOUS CASE OF MISS VIOLET STONE (1894)
Poppy Z. Brite and David Ferguson | 138

THE ADVENTURE OF THE ANTIQUARIAN'S NIECE
(1894) | Barbara Hambly | 158

THE MYSTERY OF THE WORM (1894)
John Pelan | 189

THE MYSTERY OF THE HANGED MAN'S PUZZLE
(1897) | Paul Finch | 205

THE HORROR OF THE MANY FACES (1898)
Tim Lebbon | 243

THE ADVENTURE OF THE ARAB'S MANUSCRIPT
(1898) | Michael Reaves | 268

THE DROWNED GEOLOGIST (1898)
Caitlín R. Kiernan | 295

A CASE OF INSOMNIA (1899) | John P. Vourlis | 313

THE ADVENTURE OF THE VOORISH SIGN (1899)
Richard A. Lupoff | 342

THE ADVENTURE OF EXHAM PRIORY (1901)
F. Gwynplaine MacIntyre | 372

DEATH DID NOT BECOME HIM (1902)
David Niall Wilson and Patricia Lee Macomber | 392

NIGHTMARE IN WAX (1915) | Simon Clark | 420

CONTRIBUTORS | 439

INTRODUCTION

The deerstalker hat, the pipe, the tobacco-filled slipper on the mantel . . . the image conjured, whether of Basil Rathbone, Jeremy Irons, or the reader's own conception, is unmistakable. The most recognizable figure in English-language fiction is, without a doubt, that of Sherlock Holmes. For more than a hundred years the stories of the Great Detective using the razor-sharp blade of ratiocination against evil have captivated an enthusiastic readership throughout the world.

Numerous studies and related works, from biographies to encyclopedias that scrupulously list each minor character and setting, have been written over the decades. There have been films, radio dramas, plays, comic books, TV series, and even a couple of cookbooks. The number of unauthorized pastiches runs well into the hundreds. Holmes is one of the most fascinating characters in literature; the concept of a man solving the most difficult and challenging of puzzles by pure logic and deductive ability still strikes a chord with both writers and readers over a century after the character first appeared in *The Strand Magazine*. We can always count on Watson's chronicles of the world's first consulting detective to end with the comforting knowledge that all can be explained; there is no darkness too deep to be illuminated by the light of intellect and reason.

But what if . . .

What if Holmes and Watson were to be confronted by things *outside* the realm of human experience? What if the inconceivable proved to be true? What if there were places, entities, concepts in the cosmos that man not only did not, but could not, understand?

The "Cthulhu Mythos" cycle of H. P. Lovecraft is only a shade behind that of the Holmes canon in the number of adaptations and works that it has influenced. Ever since Lovecraft postulated the existence of Arkham, the *Necronomicon,* and the Great Old Ones in the pages of *Weird Tales,* scores of other writers have been inspired to compose their own visions of his outré mythology. The Mythos implies that the reality we know is narrow and constricted—that lurking just beyond the boundaries of sanity are beings of vast power and malice that ruled this world before mankind, and that intend to do so again. What strange events were caused by these powerful alien entities in the twilight days of the nineteenth century? How might the Great Detective fare as humanity's defender against beings of incalculable knowledge and might?

We asked eighteen of today's best mystery, fantasy, and science-fiction writers these questions. The answers are to be found in this book, which is the first such authorized by the Doyle Estate in many years. You may see slight differences in each author's perception of the characters. This is to be expected; we all, (as the Great Detective himself would attest) observe things a bit differently. We trust that ardent Holmesians will find no discrepancies in the chronology presented here. Are these tales all to be considered part of the official canon or merely loving tributes from modern scriveners? That's for you, the reader, to decide.

From the Far East to New York City to Holmes's own London, a new and terrifying game is afoot. Sherlock Holmes and his allies have had lengthy experience in confronting the mysterious and the unusual; now they must confront the unknowable and the unspeakable . . .

Here, then, is the world prophesied by the mad Arab Abdul al-Hazred as seen through the eyes of Dr. John H. Watson, Irene Adler, Professor James Moriarty, and others. From Watson's earliest adventures in Afghanistan to reminiscences written during the Great War after both men had retired, these stories are glimpses of a world where the impossible is real and terrifying.

Strange shadows lengthen over Baker Street, and in R'lyeh dead Cthulhu is stirring . . .

John Pelan and Michael Reaves
Seattle and Los Angeles, 2002

A Study in Emerald

NEIL GAIMAN

1. THE NEW FRIEND

———————◆━━◆━◆━━————————

Fresh *from Their Stupendous European Tour, where they performed before several of the* **CROWNED HEADS OF EUROPE,** *garnering their* plaudits *and* praise *with* magnificent dramatic performances, *combining both* **COMEDY** *and* **TRAGEDY,** *the* Strand Players *wish to make it known that they shall be appearing at the* Royal Court Theatre, Drury Lane, *for a* **LIMITED ENGAGE-MENT** *in April, at which they will present* "My Look-Alike Brother Tom!" "The Littlest Violet-Seller" *and* "The Great Old Ones Come" *(this last an Historical Epic of Pageantry and Delight): each an* entire play *in one act! Tickets are available now from the Box Office.*

———————◆━━◆━◆━━————————

It is the immensity, I believe. The hugeness of things below. The darkness of dreams.

But I am wool-gathering. Forgive me. I am not a literary man.

I had been in need of lodgings. That was how I met him. I wanted someone to share the cost of rooms with me. We were introduced by a mutual acquaintance, in the chemical laboratories of St. Bart's. "You have been in Afghanistan, I perceive"; that was what he said to me, and my mouth fell open and my eyes opened very wide.

"Astonishing," I said.

"Not really," said the stranger in the white lab coat who was to become my friend. "From the way you hold your arm, I see you have been wounded, and in a particular way. You have a deep tan. You also have a military bearing, and there are few enough places in the Empire that a military man can be both tanned and, given the nature of the injury to your shoulder and the traditions of the Afghan cave folk, tortured."

Put like that, of course, it was absurdly simple. But then, it always was. I had been tanned nut brown. And I had indeed, as he had observed, been tortured.

The gods and men of Afghanistan were savages, unwilling to be ruled from Whitehall or from Berlin or even from Moscow, and unprepared to see reason. I had been sent into those hills, attached to the —th Regiment. As long as the fighting remained in the hills and mountains, we fought on an equal footing. When the skirmishes descended into the caves and the darkness, then we found ourselves, as it were, out of our depth and in over our heads.

I shall not forget the mirrored surface of the underground lake, nor the thing that emerged from the lake, its eyes opening and closing, and the singing whispers that accompanied it as it rose, wreathing their way about it like the buzzing of flies bigger than worlds.

That I survived was a miracle, but survive I did, and I returned to England with my nerves in shreds and tatters. The place that leechlike mouth had touched me was tattooed forever, frog white, into the skin of my now-withered shoulder. I had once been a crack shot. Now I had nothing, save a fear of the world-beneath-the-world akin to panic, which meant that I would gladly pay six-pence of my army pension for a hansom cab rather than a penny to travel underground.

Still, the fogs and darknesses of London comforted me, took me in. I had lost my first lodgings because I screamed in the night. I had been in Afghanistan; I was there no longer.

"I scream in the night," I told him.

"I have been told that I snore," he said. "Also I keep irregular hours, and I often use the mantelpiece for target practice. I will need the sitting room to meet clients. I am selfish, private, and easily bored. Will this be a problem?"

I smiled and shook my head and extended my hand. We shook on it.

The rooms he had found for us, in Baker Street, were more than adequate for two bachelors. I bore in mind all my friend had said about his desire for privacy, and I forbore from asking what it was he did for a living. Still, there was much to pique my curiosity. Visitors would arrive at all hours, and when they did I would leave the sitting room and repair to my bedroom, pondering what they could have in common with my friend: the pale woman with one eye bone white, the small man who looked like a commercial traveler, the portly dandy in his velvet jacket, and the rest. Some were frequent visitors; many others came only once, spoke to him, and left, looking troubled or looking satisfied.

He was a mystery to me.

We were partaking of one of our landlady's magnificent break-fasts one morning when my friend rang the bell to summon that good lady. "There will be a gentleman joining us, in about four minutes," he said. "We will need another place at table."

"Very good," she said, "I'll put more sausages under the grill."

My friend returned to perusing his morning paper. I waited for an explanation with growing impatience. Finally, I could stand it no longer. "I don't understand. How could you know that in four minutes we would be receiving a visitor? There was no telegram, no message of any kind."

He smiled thinly. "You did not hear the clatter of a brougham several minutes ago? It slowed as it passed us—obviously as the driver identified our door—then it sped up and went past, up into the Marylebone Road. There is a crush of carriages and taxicabs letting off passengers at the railway station and at the waxworks, and it is in that crush that anyone wishing to alight without being observed will go. The walk from there to here is but four minutes . . ."

He glanced at his pocket watch, and as he did so I heard a tread on the stairs outside.

"Come in, Lestrade," he called. "The door is ajar, and your sausages are just coming out from under the grill."

A man I took to be Lestrade opened the door, then closed it carefully behind him. "I should not," he said. "But truth to tell, I have not had a chance to break my fast this morning. And I could certainly do justice to a few of those sausages." He was the small man I had observed on several occasions previously, whose demeanor was that of a traveler in rubber novelties or patent nostrums.

My friend waited until our landlady had left the room before he said, "Obviously, I take it this is a matter of national importance."

"My stars," said Lestrade, and he paled. "Surely the word cannot be out already. Tell me it is not." He began to pile his plate high with sausages, kipper fillets, kedgeree, and toast, but his hands shook a little.

"Of course not," said my friend. "I know the squeak of your brougham wheels, though, after all this time: an oscillating G-sharp above high C. And if Inspector Lestrade of Scotland Yard cannot publicly be seen to come into the parlor of London's only consulting detective, yet comes anyway, and without having had his breakfast, then I know that this is not a routine case. Ergo, it involves those above us and is a matter of national importance."

Lestrade dabbed egg yolk from his chin with his napkin. I stared at him. He did not look like my idea of a police inspector, but then, my friend looked little enough like my idea of a consulting detective—whatever that might be.

"Perhaps we should discuss the matter privately," Lestrade said, glancing at me.

My friend began to smile impishly, and his head moved on his shoulders as it did when he was enjoying a private joke. "Nonsense," he said. "Two heads are better than one. And what is said to one of us is said to us both."

"If I am intruding—" I said gruffly, but he motioned me to silence.

Lestrade shrugged. "It's all the same to me," he said, after a moment. "If you solve the case, then I have my job. If you don't, then I have no job. You use your methods, that's what I say. It can't make things any worse."

"If there's one thing that a study of history has taught us, it is that things can always get worse," said my friend. "When do we go to Shoreditch?"

Lestrade dropped his fork. "This is too bad!" he exclaimed. "Here you are, making sport of me, when you know all about the matter! You should be ashamed—"

"No one has told me anything of the matter. When a police inspector walks into my room with fresh splashes of mud of that peculiar yellow hue on his boots and trouser legs, I can surely be forgiven for presuming that he has recently walked past the diggings at Hobbs Lane in Shoreditch, which is the only place in London that particular mustard-colored clay seems to be found."

Inspector Lestrade looked embarrassed. "Now you put it like that," he said, "it seems so obvious."

My friend pushed his plate away from him. "Of course it does," he said, slightly testily.

We rode to the East End in a cab. Inspector Lestrade had walked up to the Marylebone Road to find his brougham, and left us alone.

"So you are truly a consulting detective?" I said.

"The only one in London, or perhaps the world," said my friend. "I do not take cases. Instead, I consult. Others bring me their insoluble problems, they describe them, and, sometimes, I solve them."

"Then those people who come to you . . ."

"Are, in the main, police officers, or are detectives themselves, yes."

It was a fine morning, but we were now jolting about the edges of the Rookery of St. Giles, that warren of thieves and cutthroats which sits on London like a cancer on the face of a pretty flower seller, and the only light to enter the cab was dim and faint.

"Are you sure that you wish me along with you?"

In reply, my friend stared at me without blinking. "I have a feeling," he said. "I have a feeling that we were meant to be together. That we have fought the good fight, side by side, in the past or in the future, I do not know. I am a rational man, but I have learned the value of a good companion, and from the moment I clapped eyes on you, I knew I trusted you as well as I do myself. Yes. I want you with me."

I blushed, or said something meaningless. For the first time since Afghanistan, I felt that I had worth in the world.

2. THE ROOM

———————————◆————◆————◆————————————

Victor's "Vitae"! An electrical fluid! Do your limbs and nether regions lack life? Do you look back on the days of your youth with envy? Are the pleasures of the flesh now buried and forgot? Victor's "Vitae" will bring life where life has long been lost: even the oldest warhorse can be a proud stallion once more! Bringing Life to the Dead: from an old

family recipe and the best of modern science. To receive signed at-
testations of the efficacy of Victor's "Vitae" write to the V. von F.
Company, 1b Cheap Street, London.

It was a cheap rooming house in Shoreditch. There was a policeman at the front door. Lestrade greeted him by name and made to
usher us in, but my friend squatted on the doorstep and pulled a
magnifying glass from his coat pocket. He examined the mud on
the wrought-iron boot scraper, prodding at it with his forefinger.
Only when he was satisfied would he let us go inside.

We walked upstairs. The room in which the crime had been
committed was obvious: it was flanked by two burly constables.

Lestrade nodded to the men, and they stood aside. We walked in.

I am not, as I said, a writer by profession, and I hesitate to describe that place, knowing that my words cannot do it justice. Still,
I have begun this narrative, and I fear I must continue. A murder
had been committed in that little bedsit. The body, what was left of
it, was still there on the floor. I saw it, but at first, somehow, I did
not see it. What I saw instead was what had sprayed and gushed
from the throat and chest of the victim: in color it ranged from bile
green to grass green. It had soaked into the threadbare carpet and
spattered the wallpaper. I imagined it for one moment the work of
some hellish artist who had decided to create a study in emerald.

After what seemed like a hundred years I looked down at the
body, opened like a rabbit on a butcher's slab, and tried to make
sense of what I saw. I removed my hat, and my friend did the same.

He knelt and inspected the body, examining the cuts and
gashes. Then he pulled out his magnifying glass and walked over
to the wall, investigating the gouts of drying ichor.

"We've already done that," said Inspector Lestrade.

"Indeed?" said my friend. "What did you make of this, then? I
do believe it is a word."

Lestrade walked to the place my friend was standing and looked up. There was a word, written in capitals, in green blood, on the faded yellow wallpaper, some little way above Lestrade's head. *"Rache . . . ?"* he said, spelling it out. "Obviously he was going to write *Rachel*, but he was interrupted. So—we must look for a woman . . ."

My friend said nothing. He walked back to the corpse, and picked up its hands, one after the other. The fingertips were clean of ichor. "I think we have established that the word was not written by His Royal Highness."

"What the devil makes you say—"

"My dear Lestrade. Please give me some credit for having a brain. The corpse is obviously not that of a man—the color of his blood, the number of limbs, the eyes, the position of the face—all these things bespeak the blood royal. While I cannot say *which* royal line, I would hazard that he is an heir, perhaps—no, second to the throne—in one of the German principalities."

"That is amazing." Lestrade hesitated, then he said, "This is Prince Franz Drago of Bohemia. He was here in Albion as a guest of Her Majesty Victoria. Here for a holiday and a change of air . . ."

"For the theatres, the whores, and the gaming tables, you mean."

"If you say so." Lestrade looked put out. "Anyway, you've given us a fine lead with this Rachel woman. Although I don't doubt we would have found her on our own."

"Doubtless," said my friend.

He inspected the room further, commenting acidly several times that the police had obscured footprints with their boots and moved things that might have been of use to anyone attempting to reconstruct the events of the previous night. Still, he seemed interested in a small patch of mud he found behind the door.

Beside the fireplace he found what appeared to be some ash or dirt.

"Did you see this?" he asked Lestrade.

"Her Majesty's police," replied Lestrade, "tend not to be excited by ash in a fireplace. It's where ash tends to be found." And he chuckled at that.

My friend took a pinch of the ash and rubbed it between his fingers, then sniffed the remains. Finally, he scooped up what was left of the material and tipped it into a glass vial, which he stoppered and placed in an inner pocket of his coat.

He stood up. "And the body?"

Lestrade said, "The palace will send their own people."

My friend nodded at me, and together we walked to the door. My friend sighed. "Inspector. Your quest for Miss Rachel may prove fruitless. Among other things, *Rache* is a German word. It means 'revenge.' Check your dictionary. There are other meanings."

We reached the bottom of the stair and walked out onto the street.

"You have never seen royalty before this morning, have you?" he asked. I shook my head. "Well, the sight can be unnerving, if you're unprepared. Why my good fellow—you are trembling!"

"Forgive me. I shall be fine in moments."

"Would it do you good to walk?" he asked, and I assented, certain that if I did not walk I would begin to scream.

"West, then," said my friend, pointing to the dark tower of the palace. And we commenced to walk.

"So," said my friend, after some time. "You have never had any personal encounters with any of the crowned heads of Europe?"

"No," I said.

"I believe I can confidently state that you shall," he told me. "And not with a corpse this time. Very soon."

"My dear fellow, whatever makes you believe—?"

In reply he pointed to a carriage, black-painted, that had pulled up fifty yards ahead of us. A man in a black top hat and a greatcoat stood by the door, holding it open, waiting silently. A coat of arms familiar to every child in Albion was painted in gold upon the carriage door.

"There are invitations one does not refuse," said my friend. He doffed his own hat to the footman, and I do believe that he was smiling as he climbed into the boxlike space and relaxed back into the soft leathery cushions.

When I attempted to speak with him during the journey to the palace, he placed his finger over his lips. Then he closed his eyes and seemed sunk deep in thought. I, for my part, tried to remember what I knew of German royalty, but apart from the Queen's consort, Prince Albert, being German, I knew little enough.

I put a hand in my pocket, pulled out a handful of coins— brown and silver, black and copper green. I stared at the portrait of our Queen stamped on each of them, and felt both patriotic pride and stark dread. I told myself I had once been a military man, and a stranger to fear, and I could remember a time when this had been the plain truth. For a moment I remembered a time when I had been a crack shot—even, I liked to think, something of a marksman—but now my right hand shook as if it were palsied, and the coins jingled and chinked, and I felt only regret.

3. THE PALACE

---

*At **Long Last** Dr. Henry Jekyll is proud to announce the general release of the world-renowned "Jekyll's Powders" for popular consumption. No longer the province of the privileged few. **Release the Inner You!** For Inner and Outer Cleanliness!* **TOO MANY PEOPLE,** *both men and women, suffer from* **CONSTIPATION OF THE SOUL!** *Relief is immediate and cheap—with Jekyll's powders! (Available in Vanilla and Original Mentholatum Formulations.)*

The Queen's consort, Prince Albert, was a big man, with an impressive handlebar mustache and a receding hairline, and he was undeniably and entirely human. He met us in the corridor, nodded to my friend and to me, did not ask us for our names or offer to shake hands.

"The Queen is most upset," he said. He had an accent. He pronounced his *S*s as *Z*s: *Mozt. Upzet.* "Franz was one of her favorites. She has many nephews. But he made her laugh so. You will find the ones who did this to him."

"I will do my best," said my friend.

"I have read your monographs," said Prince Albert. "It was I who told them that you should be consulted. I hope I did right."

"As do I," said my friend.

And then the great door was opened, and we were ushered into the darkness and the presence of the Queen.

She was called Victoria because she had beaten us in battle seven hundred years before, and she was called Gloriana because she was glorious, and she was called the Queen because the human mouth was not shaped to say her true name. She was huge—huger than I had imagined possible—and she squatted in the shadows staring down at us without moving.

Thizsz muzzst be zsolved. The words came from the shadows.

"Indeed, ma'am," said my friend.

A limb squirmed and pointed at me. *Zstepp forward.*

I wanted to walk. My legs would not move.

My friend came to my rescue then. He took me by the elbow and walked me toward Her Majesty.

Isz not to be afraid. Isz to be worthy. Isz to be a companion. That was what she said to me. Her voice was a very sweet contralto, with a distant buzz. Then the limb uncoiled and extended, and she touched my shoulder. There was a moment, but only a moment, of pain deeper and more profound than anything I have ever experienced, and then it was replaced by a pervasive sense of well-being. I could feel the muscles in my shoulder relax, and for the first time since Afghanistan, I was free from pain.

Then my friend walked forward. Victoria spoke to him, yet I could not hear her words; I wondered if they went, somehow, directly from her mind to his, if this was the Queen's counsel I had read about in the histories. He replied aloud.

"Certainly, ma'am. I can tell you that there were two other men with your nephew in that room in Shoreditch, that night—the footprints, although obscured, were unmistakable." And then, "Yes. I understand . . . I believe so . . . yes."

He was quiet when we left and said nothing to me as we rode back to Baker Street.

It was dark already. I wondered how long we had spent in the palace.

Upon our return to Baker Street, in the looking glass of my room, I observed that the frog white skin across my shoulder had taken on a pinkish tinge. I hoped that I was not imagining it, that it was not merely the moonlight through the window.

4. THE PERFORMANCE

LIVER COMPLAINTS?! BILIOUS ATTACKS?! NEUR-ASTHENIC DISTURBANCES?! QUINSY?! ARTHRI-TIS?! *These are just a handful of the* complaints *for which a professional EXSANGUINATION can be the* remedy. *In our offices we have sheaves of* **TESTIMONIALS** *which can be inspected by the public* at any time. *Do not put your health in the hands of amateurs!! We have been doing this for a very long time:* **V. TEPES— PROFESSIONAL EXSANGUINATOR.** *(Remember! It is pronounced* Tzsep-pesh!*)* Romania, Paris, London, Whitby. You've tried the rest—**NOW TRY THE BEST!!**

That my friend was a master of disguise should have come as no surprise to me, yet surprise me it did. Over the next ten days a strange assortment of characters came in through our door on

Baker Street—an elderly Chinese man, a young roué, a fat, red-haired woman of whose former profession there could be little doubt, and a venerable old buffer, his foot swollen and bandaged from gout. Each of them would walk into my friend's room, and with a speed that would have done justice to a music-hall "quick-change artist," my friend would walk out.

He would not talk about what he had been doing on these occasions, preferring to relax and stare off into space, occasionally making notations on any scrap of paper to hand—notations I found, frankly, incomprehensible. He seemed entirely preoccupied, so much so that I found myself worrying about his well-being. And then, late one afternoon, he came home dressed in his own clothes, with an easy grin upon his face, and he asked if I was interested in the theatre.

"As much as the next man," I told him.

"Then fetch your opera glasses," he told me. "We are off to Drury Lane."

I had expected a light opera, or something of the kind, but instead I found myself in what must have been the worst theatre in Drury Lane, for all that it had named itself after the royal court—and to be honest, it was barely in Drury Lane at all, being situated at the Shaftesbury Avenue end of the road, where the avenue approaches the Rookery of St. Giles. On my friend's advice I concealed my wallet, and following his example, I carried a stout stick.

Once we were seated in the stalls (I had bought a threepenny orange from one of the lovely young women who sold them to the members of the audience, and I sucked it as we waited), my friend said quietly, "You should only count yourself lucky that you did not need to accompany me to the gambling dens or the brothels. Or the madhouses—another place that Prince Franz delighted in visiting, as I have learned. But there was nowhere he went to more than once. Nowhere but—"

The orchestra struck up, and the curtain was raised. My friend was silent.

It was a fine-enough show in its way: three one-act plays were performed. Comic songs were sung between the acts. The leading man was tall, languid, and had a fine singing voice; the leading lady was elegant, and her voice carried through all the theatre; the comedian had a fine touch for patter songs.

The first play was a broad comedy of mistaken identities: the leading man played a pair of identical twins who had never met, but had managed, by a set of comical misadventures, each to find himself engaged to be married to the same young lady—who, amusingly, thought herself engaged to only one man. Doors swung open and closed as the actor changed from identity to identity.

The second play was a heartbreaking tale of an orphan girl who starved in the snow selling hothouse violets—her grandmother recognized her at the last, and swore that she was the babe stolen ten years back by bandits, but it was too late, and the frozen little angel breathed her last. I must confess I found myself wiping my eyes with my linen handkerchief more than once.

The performance finished with a rousing historical narrative: the entire company played the men and women of a village on the shore of the ocean, seven hundred years before our modern times. They saw shapes rising from the sea, in the distance. The hero joyously proclaimed to the villagers that these were the Old Ones, whose coming was foretold, returning to us from R'lyeh, and from dim Carcosa, and from the plains of Leng, where they had slept, or waited, or passed out the time of their death. The comedian opined that the other villagers had all been eating too many pies and drinking too much ale, and they were imagining the shapes. A portly gentleman playing a priest of the Roman god tells the villagers that the shapes in the sea are monsters and demons, and must be destroyed.

At the climax, the hero beat the priest to death with his own crucifix, and prepared to welcome Them as They come. The heroine sang a haunting aria, whilst in an astonishing display of magic-lantern trickery, it seemed as if we saw Their shadows cross the sky at the back of the stage: the Queen of Albion herself, and the Black One of Egypt (in shape almost like a man), followed by the Ancient Goat, Parent to a Thousand, Emperor of all China, and the Czar Unanswerable, and He Who Presides over the New World, and the White Lady of the Antarctic Fastness, and the others. And as each shadow crossed the stage, or appeared to, from out of every throat in the gallery came, unbidden, a mighty "Huzzah!" until the air itself seemed to vibrate. The moon rose in the painted sky, and then, at its height, in one final moment of theatrical magic, it turned from a pallid yellow, as it was in the old tales, to the comforting crimson of the moon that shines down upon us all today.

The members of the cast took their bows and their curtain calls to cheers and laughter, and the curtain fell for the last time, and the show was done.

"There," said my friend. "What did you think?"

"Jolly, jolly good," I told him, my hands sore from applauding.

"Stout fellow," he said with a smile. "Let us go backstage."

We walked outside and into an alley beside the theatre, to the stage door, where a thin woman with a wen on her cheek knitted busily. My friend showed her a visiting card and she directed us into the building and up some steps to a small communal dressing room.

Oil lamps and candles guttered in front of smeared looking glasses, and men and women were taking off their makeup and costumes with no regard to the proprieties of gender. I averted my eyes. My friend seemed unperturbed. "Might I talk to Mr. Vernet?" he asked loudly.

A young woman who had played the heroine's best friend in the first play, and the saucy innkeeper's daughter in the last, pointed us to the end of the room. "Sherry! Sherry Vernet!" she called.

The man who stood up in response was lean; less conventionally handsome than he had seemed from the other side of the footlights. He peered at us quizzically. "I do not believe I have had the pleasure . . . ?"

"My name is Henry Camberley," said my friend, drawling his speech somewhat. "You may have heard of me."

"I must confess that I have not had that privilege," said Vernet.

My friend presented the actor with an engraved card. The man looked at it with unfeigned interest. "A theatrical promoter? From the New World? My, my. And this is . . . ?" He looked at me.

"This is a friend of mine, Mr. Sebastian. He is not of the profession."

I muttered something about having enjoyed the performance enormously, and shook hands with the actor.

My friend said, "Have you ever visited the New World?"

"I have not yet had that honor," admitted Vernet, "although it has always been my dearest wish."

"Well, my good man," said my friend, with the easy informality of a New Worlder, "maybe you'll get your wish. That last play. I've never seen anything like it. Did you write it?"

"Alas, no. The playwright is a good friend of mine. Although I devised the mechanism of the magic-lantern shadow show. You'll not see finer on the stage today."

"Would you give me the playwright's name? Perhaps I should speak to him directly, this friend of yours."

Vernet shook his head. "That will not be possible, I am afraid. He is a professional man, and does not wish his connection with the stage publicly to be known."

"I see." My friend pulled a pipe from his pocket and put it in his mouth. Then he patted his pockets. "I am sorry," he began. "I have forgotten to bring my tobacco pouch."

"I smoke a strong black shag," said the actor, "but if you have no objection—"

"None!" said my friend heartily. "Why, I smoke a strong shag myself," and he filled his pipe with the actor's tobacco, and the two men puffed away while my friend described a vision he had for a play that could tour the cities of the New World, from Manhattan Island all the way to the farthest tip of the continent in the distant south. The first act would be the last play we had seen. The rest of the play might tell of the dominion of the Old Ones over humanity and its gods, perhaps imagining what might have happened if people had had no royal families to look up to—a world of barbarism and darkness. "But your mysterious professional man would be the play's author, and what occurs would be his alone to decide. Our drama would be his. But I can guarantee you audiences beyond your imaginings, and a significant share of the takings at the door. Let us say fifty percent?"

"This is most exciting," said Vernet. "I hope it will not turn out to have been a pipe dream!"

"No, sir, it shall not!" said my friend, puffing on his own pipe, chuckling at the man's joke. "Come to my rooms in Baker Street tomorrow morning, after breakfast time, say at ten, in company with your author friend, and I shall have the contracts drawn up and waiting."

With that, the actor clambered up onto his chair and clapped his hands for silence. "Ladies and gentlemen of the company, I have an announcement to make," he said, his resonant voice filling the room. "This gentleman is Henry Camberley, the theatrical promoter, and he is proposing to take us across the Atlantic Ocean, and on to fame and fortune."

There were several cheers, and the comedian said, "Well, it'll make a change from herrings and pickled cabbage," and the company laughed. It was to the smiles of all of them that we walked out of the theatre and onto the fog-wreathed streets.

"My dear fellow," I said. "Whatever was—"

"Not another word," said my friend. "There are many ears in the city."

And not another word was spoken until we had hailed a cab and clambered inside and were rattling up the Charing Cross Road.

And even then, before he said anything, my friend took his

pipe from his mouth and emptied the half-smoked contents of the bowl into a small tin. He pressed the lid onto the tin and placed it into his pocket.

"There," he said. "That's the Tall Man found, or I'm a Dutchman. Now, we just have to hope that the cupidity and the curiosity of the Limping Doctor proves enough to bring him to us tomorrow morning."

"The Limping Doctor?"

My friend snorted. "That is what I have been calling him. It was obvious, from footprints and much else besides when we saw the prince's body, that two men had been in that room that night: a tall man, who, unless I miss my guess, we have just encountered, and a smaller man with a limp, who eviscerated the prince with a professional skill that betrays the medical man."

"A doctor?"

"Indeed. I hate to say this, but it is my experience that when a doctor goes to the bad, he is a fouler and darker creature than the worst cutthroat. There was Huston, the acid-bath man, and Campbell, who brought the Procrustean bed to Ealing . . ." and he carried on in a similar vein for the rest of our journey.

The cab pulled up beside the kerb. "That'll be one and ten-pence," said the cabbie. My friend tossed him a florin, which he caught and tipped to his ragged tall hat. "Much obliged to you both," he called out as the horse clopped out into the fog.

We walked to our front door. As I unlocked the door, my friend said, "Odd. Our cabbie just ignored that fellow on the corner."

"They do that at the end of a shift," I pointed out.

"Indeed they do," said my friend.

I dreamed of shadows that night, vast shadows that blotted out the sun, and I called out to them in my desperation, but they did not listen.

5. THE SKIN AND THE PIT

———————◆·◆·◆———————

This year, step into the Spring—with a spring in your step! **JACK'S.**
Boots, Shoes, and Brogues. Save your soles! Heels our speciality.
JACK'S. *And do not forget to visit our new clothes and fittings*
emporium in the East End—featuring evening wear of all kinds, hats,
novelties, canes, swordsticks &c. **JACK'S OF PICCADILLY.**
It's all in the Spring!

———————◆·◆·◆———————

Inspector Lestrade was the first to arrive.

"You have posted your men in the street?" asked my friend.

"I have," said Lestrade. "With strict orders to let anyone in who comes, but to arrest anyone trying to leave."

"And you have handcuffs with you?"

In reply, Lestrade put his hand in his pocket and jangled two pairs of cuffs grimly.

"Now, sir," he said. "While we wait, why do you not tell me what we are waiting for?"

My friend pulled his pipe out of his pocket. He did not put it in his mouth, but placed it on the table in front of him. Then he took the tin from the night before, and a glass vial I recognized as the one he had had in the room in Shoreditch.

"There," he said. "The coffin nail, as I trust it shall prove, for our Mr. Vernet." He paused. Then he took out his pocket watch, laid it carefully on the table. "We have several minutes before they arrive." He turned to me. "What do you know of the Restorationists?"

"Not a blessed thing," I told him.

Lestrade coughed. "If you're talking about what I think you're talking about," he said, "perhaps we should leave it there. Enough's enough."

"Too late for that," said my friend. "For there are those who do not believe that the coming of the Old Ones was the fine thing we all know it to be. Anarchists to a man, they would see the old ways restored—mankind in control of its own destiny, if you will."

"I will not hear this sedition spoken," said Lestrade. "I must warn you—"

"I must warn you not to be such a fathead," said my friend. "Because it was the Restorationists who killed Prince Franz Drago. They murder, they kill, in a vain effort to force our masters to leave us alone in the darkness. The prince was killed by a *rache*—it's an old term for a hunting dog, Inspector, as you would know if you had looked in a dictionary. It also means 'revenge.' And the hunter left his signature on the wallpaper in the murder room, just as an artist might sign a canvas. But he was not the one who killed the prince."

"The Limping Doctor!" I exclaimed.

"Very good. There was a tall man there that night—I could tell his height, for the word was written at eye level. He smoked a pipe—the ash and dottle sat unburned in the fireplace, and he had tapped out his pipe with ease on the mantel, something a smaller man would not have done. The tobacco was an unusual blend of shag. The footprints in the room had for the most part been almost obliterated by your men, but there were several clear prints behind the door and by the window. Someone had waited there: a smaller man from his stride, who put his weight on his right leg. On the path outside I had seen several clear prints, and the different colors of clay on the boot scraper gave me more information: a tall man, who had accompanied the prince into those rooms and had later walked out. Waiting for them to arrive was the man who had sliced up the prince so impressively . . ."

Lestrade made an uncomfortable noise that did not quite become a word.

"I have spent many days retracing the movements of His Highness. I went from gambling hell to brothel to dining den to madhouse looking for our pipe-smoking man and his friend. I made no progress until I thought to check the newspapers of Bohemia, searching for a clue to the prince's recent activities there, and in them I learned that an English theatrical troupe had been in Prague last month, and had performed before Prince Franz Drago."

"Good Lord," I said. "So that Sherry Vernet fellow . . ."

"Is a Restorationist. Exactly."

I was shaking my head in wonder at my friend's intelligence and skills of observation when there was a knock on the door.

"This will be our quarry!" said my friend. "Careful now!"

Lestrade put his hand deep into his pocket, where I had no doubt he kept a pistol. He swallowed nervously.

My friend called out, "Please, come in!"

The door opened.

It was not Vernet, nor was it a Limping Doctor. It was one of the young street Arabs who earn a crust running errands—"in the employ of Messieurs Street and Walker," as we used to say when I was young. "Please, sirs," he said. "Is there a Mr. Henry Camberley here? I was asked by a gentleman to deliver a note."

"I'm he," said my friend. "And for a sixpence, what can you tell me about the gentleman who gave you the note?"

The young lad, who volunteered that his name was Wiggins, bit the sixpence before making it vanish, and then told us that the cheery cove who gave him the note was on the tall side, with dark hair, and, he added, had been smoking a pipe.

I have the note here, and take the liberty of transcribing it.

My Dear Sir,

I do not address you as Henry Camberley, for it is a name to which you have no claim. I am surprised that you did not announce yourself under your own name, for it is a fine one, and one that does you credit. I have read a number of your papers, when I have been able to obtain them. Indeed, I corresponded with you quite profitably two years ago about certain theoretical anomalies in your paper on the Dynamics of an Asteroid.

I was amused to meet you yesterday evening. A few tips which might save you bother in times to come, in the profession you currently follow. Firstly, a pipe-smoking man might possibly have a brand-new, unused pipe in his pocket, and no tobacco, but it is exceedingly unlikely—at least as unlikely as a theatrical promoter with no idea of the usual customs of recompense on a tour, who is accompanied by a taciturn ex–army officer (Afghanistan, unless I miss my guess). Incidentally, while you are correct that the streets of London have ears, it might also behoove you in the future not to take the first cab that comes along. Cabdrivers have ears, too, if they choose to use them.

You are certainly correct in one of your suppositions: it was indeed I who lured the half-blood creature back to the room in Shoreditch. If it is any comfort to you, having learned a little of his recreational predilections, I had told him I had procured for him a girl, abducted from a convent in Cornwall where she had never seen a man, and that it would only take his touch, and the sight of his face, to tip her over into a perfect madness.

Had she existed, he would have feasted on her madness while he took her, like a man sucking the flesh from a ripe peach, leaving nothing behind but the skin and the pit. I have seen them do this. I have seen them do far worse. It is the price we pay for peace and prosperity.

It is too great a price for that.

The good doctor—who believes as I do, and who did indeed write our little performance, for he has some crowd-pleasing skills—was waiting for us, with his knives.

I send this note, not as a catch-me-if-you-can taunt, for we are gone, the estimable doctor and I, and you shall not find us, but to tell you that it was good to feel that, if only for a moment, I had a worthy adversary. Worthier by far than inhuman creatures from beyond the Pit.

I fear the Strand Players will need to find themselves a new leading man.

I will not sign myself Vernet, and until the hunt is done and the world restored, I beg you to think of me simply as,
    Rache

Inspector Lestrade ran from the room, calling to his men. They made young Wiggins take them to the place where the man had given him the note, for all the world as if Vernet the actor would be waiting there for them, a-smoking of his pipe. From the window we watched them run, my friend and I, and we shook our heads.

"They will stop and search all the trains leaving London, all the ships leaving Albion for Europe or the New World," said my friend, "looking for a tall man and his companion, a smaller, thick-set medical man, with a slight limp. They will close the ports. Every way out of the country will be blocked."

"Do you think they will catch him, then?"

My friend shook his head. "I may be wrong," he said, "but I would wager that he and his friend are even now only a mile or so away, in the Rookery of St. Giles, where the police will not go except by the dozen. They will hide up there until the hue and cry have died away. And then they will be about their business."

"What makes you say that?"

"Because," said my friend, "if our positions were reversed, it is what I would do. You should burn the note, by the way."

I frowned. "But surely it's evidence," I said.

"It's seditionary nonsense," said my friend.

And I should have burned it. Indeed, I told Lestrade I *had* burned it, when he returned, and he congratulated me on my good sense. Lestrade kept his job, and Prince Albert wrote a note to my friend congratulating him on his deductions while regretting that the perpetrator was still at large.

They have not yet caught Sherry Vernet, or whatever his name really is, nor was any trace found of his murderous accomplice, tentatively identified as a former military surgeon named John (or perhaps James) Watson. Curiously, it was revealed that he had also been in Afghanistan. I wonder if we ever met.

My shoulder, touched by the Queen, continues to improve; the flesh fills and it heals. Soon I shall be a dead shot once more.

One night when we were alone, several months ago, I asked my friend if he remembered the correspondence referred to in the letter from the man who signed himself *Rache*. My friend said that he remembered it well, and that "Sigerson" (for so the actor had called himself then, claiming to be an Icelander) had been inspired by an equation of my friend's to suggest some wild theories furthering the relationship between mass, energy, and the hypothetical speed of light. "Nonsense, of course," said my friend, without smiling. "But inspired and dangerous nonsense nonetheless."

The palace eventually sent word that the Queen was pleased with my friend's accomplishments in the case, and there the matter has rested.

I doubt my friend will leave it alone, though; it will not be over until one of them has killed the other.

I kept the note. I have said things in this retelling of events that are not to be said. If I were a sensible man I would burn all these pages, but then, as my friend taught me, even ashes can give up their secrets. Instead, I shall place these papers in a strongbox at my bank with instructions that the box may not be opened until long after anyone now living is dead. Although, in the light of the recent events in Russia, I fear that day may be closer than any of us would care to think.

S—— M—— Major (ret'd)
Baker Street
London, Albion, 1881

Tiger! Tiger!

ELIZABETH BEAR

What of the hunting, hunter bold?
  Brother, the watch was long and cold.
What of the quarry ye went to kill?
  Brother, he crops in the jungle still.
Where is the power that made your pride?
  Brother, it ebbs from my flank and side.
Where is the haste that ye hurry by?
  Brother, I go to my lair—to die!

—RUDYARD KIPLING

It was in India, on the high Malwa Plateau in July of 1882, that I chanced to make the acquaintance of an American woman whom I have never forgotten and undertake an adventure which I have long waited to recount. The monsoon was much delayed that hot and arid summer, and war raged between the British and the Russians in nearby Afghanistan—another move on the chessboard of the "Great Game." No end was yet in sight to either problem when I, Magnus Larssen, *shikari,* was summoned to the village of Kanha to guide a party in search of tiger.

My gunbearer (who was then about fifteen) and I arrived some ten days before the shooters, and arranged to hire a cook, beaters, and *mahouts* and prepare a base of operations. On the first full day of our tenancy, I was sitting at my makeshift desk when "Rodney" came into my tent, ferment glistening in his brown eyes. "The villagers are very excited, sahib," he said.

"Unhappy?" I felt myself frown.

"No, sahib. They are relieved. There is a man-eater." He danced an impatient jig in the doorway.

I raised an eyebrow and stretched in my canvas chair. "Driven to it by the drought?"

"The last month only," he answered. "Three dead so far, and some bullocks. It is a female, they think, and she is missing two toes from her right front foot."

I sipped my tea as I thought about it, and at last I nodded. "Good. Perhaps we can do them a favor while we're here."

After some days of preparation, we took transportation into Jabalpur to meet the train from Bhopal. The party was to be seven: six wealthy British and European men and the woman, an American adventuress and singer traveling in the company of a certain Count Kolinzcki, an obese Lithuanian nobleman.

The others consisted of a middle-aged, muttonchopped English gentleman, Mr. Northrop Waterhouse, with adolescent sons James and Conrad; Graf Baltasar von Hammerstein, a very Prussian fellow of my long acquaintance, stout in every sense of the word; and Dr. Albert Montleroy, a fair-haired Englishman, young around the eyes.

As they disembarked from the train, however, it was the lady who caught my attention. Fair-haired, with a clean line of jaw and clear eyes, she was aged perhaps twenty-two, but her beauty was not the sort that required youth to recommend it. She wore a very practical walking dress in sage green, fashionably tailored, and her gloves and hat matched her boots very well. I noticed that she carried her own gun case as well as her reticule.

"Ah, Magnus!" Von Hammerstein charged down the iron steps from the rail coach and clasped my hand heavily, in the European style. "Allow me to present your charges." Remembering himself, he turned to the American, and I saw that she was traveled enough to recognize his courtesy. "Fraulein, this gentleman is the noted author and hunter of heavy game, Mr. Magnus Larssen. Magnus, may I present the talented contralto, Miss Irene Adler."

"So what is this I hear about a mankiller, *shikari?*" The older Waterhouse boy, James, was talking. "On the train, we heard a rumor that a dozen men had been found mauled and disemboweled!"

"Lad," his father warned, with a glance to the woman. She looked up from her scarcely touched sherry.

I think Miss Adler winked. "Pray, sir, do not limit the conversation on my behalf. I am here to hunt, just as the rest of you, and I have visited rougher surroundings than this."

Montleroy nodded in the flicker of lantern light. The boys had collected the supper dishes, and we were each relaxing with a glass. "Yes, if we're to have a go at this man-eater, let's by all means hear the details. It's safest and best."

"Very well," I allowed, after a moment. "There have been three victims so far, and a number of cattle. It seems that the tigress responsible is wounded and taking easy prey. All of the bodies have been mauled and eaten; that much is true. The details are rather horrible."

Horrible indeed. The eyes had been eaten out of their heads, and the flesh off the faces. The bodies had been dismembered and gnawed. If it had not been for the fact that the only prints close to the bodies were those of the wounded tiger, I might have been tempted to think of some more sinister agency: perhaps agents of a Thuggee cult. I was not, however, about to reveal those facts in mixed company, Miss Adler's high opinion of her own constitution notwithstanding.

Across the room, I saw the younger Waterhouse boy, Conrad, shudder. I shook my head. Too young.

Thick leaves and fronds brushed the flanks of our elephants as they stepped out of the cool of the jungle and into more dappled shade. The ground cover cracked under their feet as we emerged from the sal trees into a small meadow. From there, we could catch a glimpse of the grasslands sweeping down a great, horseshoe-shaped valley to the banks of the Banjar River.

"This heat is beastly, Mr. Larssen!" the count complained.

I glanced across the red-and-gold knotted carpets spanning the broad back of the elephant we shared with Miss Adler. I sweated even in my shaded perch, and I did not envy the *mahouts* perched astride the beasts' necks in the brutal light of the sun, but I presumed they must be more accustomed by blood and habituation to this barbarous calescence. "It is India, Count," I replied—perhaps more dryly than necessary.

"And the insects are intolerable." Kolinzcki's humor did not seem to extend to irony. I raised an eyebrow and returned my attention to the trail, keeping my pot gun to hand and an eye out for edible game, as the beaters took a large portion of their pay in meat.

My mind drifted as I sought any spoor or scat of our quarry. A strange, oppressive silence hung on the air, and there was no trace of moisture upon the breeze. I felt a chill of unease upon my neck—or perhaps it was only the shade of the trees as our mounts carried us back down the jungle trail.

I felt the need to break the uncanny quietude. "The tiger," I said to Miss Adler and her companion, "is the true king of the jungle. No mere lion can compare to him for ferocity, intelligence, or courage. He fears nothing and will easily turn the tables on a hunter."

"That is why we ride elephants?" The Lithuanian's accent could have been better, but his speech was comprehensible.

I nodded. "Tigers respect elephants, and the reverse is true as well. One will not trouble the oth—"

A great outcry among the monkeys and the birds in the jungle on our left ended my lecture. I heard an intermittent crashing in the bamboo as an antelope sprinted away. Our tiger was on the move.

Our beaters fanned toward the jungle, several of them disappearing from sight among the trees. One or two glanced back at us before vanishing into the brush, understandably apprehensive: there was at least one tiger in that cover who had learned the taste of man.

I directed the *mahouts* back to the clearing, where we could intercept the line of beaters. The good doctor and von Hammerstein were mounted on the second beast, and Mr. Waterhouse with his two sons rode the final one. Rodney walked alongside with a cargo of rifles. Count Kolinzcki fumbled with his gun, and I made a note to myself to keep an eye on the Lithuanian, in case he should require assistance. Miss Adler quietly and efficiently broke her under/over Winchester and made it ready on her own.

We reached the clearing in good order and took a moment to array ourselves. The cries of the beaters rang out—*"bAgha! bAgha!"*—"Tiger! Tiger!"

She was within their net and moving toward us. Miss Adler drew a deep breath to steady herself, and I restrained myself from laying a hand on her shoulder to calm her. A glance at her lovely face, however, showed only quiet resolve.

Von Hammerstein also readied his gun, as did the Waterhouses and the doctor. Not intending to shoot, I foolishly failed to exchange the bolt-action .303 Martini-Lee for my double rifle.

The moment stretched into silence. I found myself counting my breaths, gaze fixed on the wall of brush. *"Mir Shikar,"* von Hammerstein began—luckily, for as I turned toward my stout and stalwart old friend, I saw the tigress lunge.

The tricky old killer had somehow doubled back and come up upon our flank. She was too close, perhaps a stride away. She made one gigantic bound out of the brush and was airborne even as I whipped my rifle around.

In that instant, my eye photographed her—the twisted fore-foot, the sad traces of mange and hunger, the frantic golden eye—and my finger tightened on the trigger.

To no avail. With a hollow click, the rifle failed to discharge. It seemed an eon as I worked the bolt—jammed—and tossed it aside, extending my hand down to Rodney for the .534 Egyptian. In the instant before my fingers closed on the warm Turkish walnut of the stock, I heard two weapons roar and sudden plumes of acrid white smoke tattered in the hot breeze. The shots caught the ti-gress in side and breast, tumbling her over and backward.

She dragged herself upright, and Mr. Waterhouse fired as well, squinting along the barrel like a professional as he put a third and final bullet into the defiant cat. She made a little coughing sound and expired, her body going fluid in each joint.

I glanced around before sliding off my elephant. Miss Adler had broken her Winchester and was calmly replacing the cartridge she had expended into the creature's breast. Von Hammerstein was also dismounting his beast, keeping his weapon at the ready in case he was forced to fire again.

I bent over to examine the kill, and found myself straightening abruptly, scanning the jungle for any sign of movement. I saw only our returning beaters.

Von Hammerstein saw it and laid a questioning eye on me.

"Her teeth," I said thickly. "There must be a second cat. This one might bring down a man, but she could never manage a bull-ock. Not with that crippled foot, and the ruined teeth."

It was then that I heard a sound like a throbbing drumbeat, dis-tant but distinct. I did not know what made it, and my curiosity was piqued.

I would give anything to have remained so ignorant.

Three of the beaters did not come out of the woods, nor were their bodies found.

A search until nightfall failed to turn up the men—or, in fact, any trace of a second tiger. Reluctantly, we reunited and turned for the camp, our beaters muttering in dissatisfaction. We resolved to resume the hunt in the morning, and hopefully find traces of the victims and whatever cat had taken them. Dr. Montleroy did get a lucky shot at a leopard, and brought it down, so we had two trophies: the elderly tigress, and a beautiful spotted cat perhaps seven feet in length.

Dinner that night was a somber affair, despite the excellent food: bread of a flat sort stuffed with potato, vegetables curried with tomato and onion, mutton spiced and baked in a clay pot. It was a great relief when the Lithuanian Count pressed Miss Adler to entertain us by singing, and she obliged. Even without accompaniment, her contralto was superb and much relieved our heavy hearts.

My sleep, when it came, was troubled by the sounds of a quiet argument nearby—the voice of Miss Adler demanding, "But you must give it back to me!" And a male rumble—stubborn, I thought—replying. A lovers' quarrel, perhaps.

I am not sure what brought me from my cot, other than the sort of prurience that a man does not like to admit. I wondered what he had of hers, of course, and a gentleman does not leave a lady alone in a tight spot, even when that lady is an adventuress.

It was Kolinzcki whom she argued with, for I recognized his voice as I moved closer to the wall of my tent, feeling my way barefoot in the unrelieved darkness. He switched languages, and she followed. I was surprised to be able to understand them somewhat, for I speak no Lithuanian. But the disagreement they conducted in low tones was in Russian, and that language I have a fair command of.

"It was not yours to take," Miss Adler whispered, urgency

resonating in her trained voice. "Do you know what you'll be unleashing?"

"It is unleashed already," Kolinzcki replied. "I merely bring our noble friends the means to control it."

She sighed, the harsh Russian tongue taking on a certain fluidity when she spoke it. "It is not so simple as that, and you know it. It will be a great embarrassment for my friends in Prague if I cannot return their property. If it seems they are cooperating with the Tsar, it will go hard for them."

He was silent, and she continued in a voice I barely heard under the sawing of insects. "Have I not done everything you asked?"

It was obvious to me that the Count was blackmailing the lovely singer, and I made up my mind to intervene. But as my hand was on the tent flap, I heard again the low, resonant throbbing that had so startled us in the afternoon. Outside, Miss Adler gave a little cry of surprise, and as I came around the corner to confront them, I heard him say in English, "And that is the reason why I cannot oblige you, my dear, as well you know. Perhaps when we are back in civilized lands, we can discuss this again."

She stepped close to him and laid her hand on his arm. "Of course, darling."

Then perhaps a lovers' quarrel after all, and already made up for. Silent in bare feet, I returned to my sleepless bed, unaccountably disappointed, and harboring suspicions I did not care to address. Who was I, a Norwegian, to care what alliances and wars the Tsar and the British Queen make against and upon each other? They seemed determined to tear Afghanistan in two between them, in their so-called Great Game: an endless series of imperialist intrigues and battles. A game, to my eye, whose chiefest victims were simple folk like my Rodney. The best the rest of us—I thought then—could manage was a sort of detached distaste for the whole proceedings.

The morning found us all awake early and unsettled. It was bold young James Waterhouse who sought me out before we mounted our elephants. *"Shikari,"* he said—they had picked up the usage from von Hammerstein and thought it delightfully quaint. "Did you hear that noise again last night?"

I hesitated. "The drumming? I did indeed." I said no more, but he must have noted my frown.

He pressed me. "That wasn't an animal noise, was it? I heard it when we killed the tiger."

It had absorbed my thoughts through the night, when I wasn't distracted by the implications of the argument between the Lithuanian—or perhaps not Lithuanian—Count and the fair Miss Adler. It wasn't quite exactly a drumming: it was more a . . . heartbeat. It was true; it didn't sound like an animal noise. But it didn't sound precisely like a human noise either.

"I don't know," I answered uncomfortably. "I haven't heard it before." I turned to aid Miss Adler in climbing the rope ladder to our elephant. Truthfully, the count required more assistance, and as I helped him up, his waistcoat gaped and I noticed the golden hilt of a dagger secreted within it. Great-grandfather's hunting knife, no doubt: too showy, but not a bad precaution. He rose a bare notch in my estimation.

There were some clouds on the horizon, and I thought the wind might carry a taint of moisture. I was eager to find the second cat and travel deeper into the jungle, perhaps to seek a third. We were past due for weather, and monsoon would mean the end of our hunt.

My party were on edge, made nervy no doubt both by the loss of the beaters the day before and by the close call with the tiger. Still no sign had been found of the missing men—even of a scuffle—and I found myself tending toward the explanation that they had deserted. Conrad seemed spooked, and I permitted the brothers to ride my elephant while Miss Adler and her escort traveled with Mr. Waterhouse.

Instead of skirting the forest, we resolved to plunge into it, and search among the bamboo and the sal trees for the second man-eater. I found myself eager as a young man, and by the time we broke for luncheon we had covered some miles into the thicker part of the forest. We found a little clearing in which to enjoy our cold curry and venison with the native bread. I sat beside von Hammerstein, while noting that Miss Adler had taken a place some distance from her Count. I wondered.

I kept the Egyptian close to hand, in case our man-eater should be drawn out by the scent of food or prey, but lunch passed uneventfully. We resolved to take a short siesta on the grass in the appalling heat of the afternoon with some of the beaters standing guard.

I again caught a glimpse of clouds massed on the horizon, but they seemed no closer than they had been in the morning, so I determined that we should press on after resting, but I must have dozed. I was awakened with a start by the sound of crashing in the brush—something sprinting straight for us. I scrambled to my feet, clutching my rifle. I noticed that the rest had dozed as well—except Miss Adler, who was on her feet, straightening from adjusting the Count's jacket, and loyal Rodney, who was chatting with one of the beaters in their native Hindi.

I brought my weapon to bear on the sound. The beaters moved rapidly out of the line of fire, and I did not spare a glance for the others.

It was no tiger that broke the screen of trees, but a man, ragged and hungry looking, on the verge of exhaustion, bare feet bloodied as if from some long journey. He did not look Indian but rather Arab—Afghan, perhaps? I cautiously lowered my rifle, and he collapsed at my feet with a cry.

He babbled a few words in a tongue I did not understand. I again shifted my estimation of Count Kolinzcki, as I noticed it was he who first came to the man's side, bending over him. I watched warily for a moment. The Arab seemed no threat, however, and I gestured Rodney to bring water as I crouched beside him as well. My bearer had just begun to cross the clearing, leaving his post at my shoulder, when the eldest elephant threw up her trunk and trumpeted in alarm.

A stray breeze brought a whiff of scent to my nostrils: char and hot metal. I cast about for any sign of smoke and noticed the elephants rocking nervously. It seemed obvious to me at that time that they had scented fire, for I knew then of no beast that could so disturb them.

I was both right and wrong.

"Mount!" I cried. The Waterhouses began immediately to move toward the elephants while Dr. Montleroy and von Hammerstein helped the beaters grab up our possessions. I reached down with some thought of assisting the prostrate Arab, but Kolinzcki was already dragging him to his feet.

The Arab grabbed Kolinzcki by the collar, and the fat Count knocked his grubby hand aside. And then, looking startled and sick, the Count pressed his right hand to his breast, with the expression of a man who realizes that his watch has gone missing from his waistcoat.

I remembered the argument of the night before, and Miss Adler bent over his supine form as he slept, but the rush of events did not permit me to inquire.

I barely caught a glimpse of it before it was among us: it came silent as a wisp of smoke, disturbing the vines and brush not at all. It glowed, even in the incandescence of the afternoon, with a light like a coal, and across the back it bore stripes like char. It possessed the rough form of a tiger, but it stank like a forest fire and its maw was a lick of flame.

It sprang to the back of the smallest elephant with an easy leap, transfixing Conrad Waterhouse with its burning gaze. Even as the elephant panicked, he froze like a bird charmed by a snake. The Creature's blazing claws scorched down her sides, leaving rents in her thick hide that I wouldn't have credited to an ax. She screamed and reared up, ponderously reaching over her shoulder in an attempt to dislodge the predator. Her panic knocked Conrad from his feet, and I did not see him move again. His brother lunged across the path of the Creature to shield the fallen boy with his body: a brave and futile gesture.

The Creature avoided the elephant's wild blows contemptuously, plunging to the soft earth like a cannonball as all three of our mounts stampeded and the injured elephant's foot struck James.

The beaters and *mahouts* scattered. The Creature casually disemboweled the closest man: it never even turned its head, already gathering itself for another pounce. Even as I leveled my weapon I knew it was hopeless. I squeezed the trigger and the rifle hammered my shoulder once, and again. Rodney sprinted back to me, my Purdey clutched in his hand. He had two cartridges between his fingers, drawn from the loops on his vest, and he had the rifle broken, loading both barrels simultaneously as he ran.

The good doctor stood rooted in shock. I heard the report of von Hammerstein's gun and, a second later, that of Miss Adler's. I released my empty weapon as Rodney, spitting fragments of words in his excitement, smoothly handed me the replacement. Mr. Waterhouse was turning to cover the beast with shaking hands, unable to fire as long as we stood behind it, craning his neck in an attempt to see both the quarry and his two sons.

The animal stalked forward, opening its flame-rimmed maw, and I heard again the sound I had compared to the pounding of drums or the throb of a mighty heart. The roar went on and on, and my heart quailed and my hands shook as it slunk one padfooted step forward.

I readied my useless weapon, determined to die fighting, and Miss Adler loosed her second shot. The bullet ruptured the hide of the beast and a ripple shuddered across its surface as if she had tossed a rock into water. A few spattering droplets of fire shot up, falling to the grass, where they smoked and vanished.

Count Kolinzcki staggered back, down on one knee in fright and despair, his hand dropping from his breast to fumble with his weapon. Von Hammerstein held his fire. I knew he would be waiting for a shot at the eye—a forlorn hope, but the one I clung to as well.

The thunder of hooves spoiled my aim. I raised my gaze from my gun sight to witness the arrival of the proverbial cavalry. A lathered bay gelding—of Arab stock, to guess by its small stature and luxurious mane—charged out of the bamboo in full flight. Its flanks heaved and blood-flecked foam flew from its bit. On its back was a mustachioed officer, who hauled up short on the reins and virtually lifted his mount into the air.

It was a prodigious leap: the little horse's hindquarters bunched and released, and it sailed up and over the back of the Creature. The tigerlike thing twisted in a fruitless attempt to score the horse with its claws, and then recoiled as the rider hurled some sort of pouch at its face. Whatever it was, it hurt! The Creature throbbed again, searing the depths of my ears, and turned and bounded away.

The officer hauled his horse to a stop and whirled it about on its haunches—an unequaled display of horsemanship. The little bay half reared in protest of the hard handling, and then settled down, pawing and snorting.

The officer gentling it with a hand on its neck was a man of middle years, his hair iron gray as was his copious mustache. He had a high forehead and a sensual twist to his mouth, and his eyes glittered still with the excitement of the hunt.

At the appearance of the officer, the Arab turned as if to flee, and almost ran directly into me. He still wove on his feet, and I detained him easily enough.

"Sir," Miss Adler said, first in command of her wits, "we are indebted to you beyond any repayment."

"Miss," he replied, "it is my privilege to serve. And now we must be away, before it returns."

I identified the British insignia upon his uniform. "Colonel, I thank you as well. I am Magnus Larssen, these good people's guide. We have wounded." The beater who had been disemboweled by the Creature was dead or dying quickly, but I could see James picking himself up painfully, his father crouching beside him with an expression of terrible grief. Dr. Montleroy was already trotting to their side.

"Colonel Sebastian Moran, Her Majesty's First Bengalore Pioneers," he said. I noticed that in addition to a sidearm and saber, there was an elephant gun sheathed on his saddle in much the fashion that the Americans carry their buffalo rifles.

Von Hammerstein and Rodney were crouched where the Creature had been. Rodney held up a burst leather water bottle: the object that the colonel had thrown in its face.

"There's no spoor, sahib," Rodney said. "It leaves no marks in the grass. Like smoke. There are"—a silence—"specks of molten lead." *Bullets,* he did not say.

I felt a cold, thickening sensation in my belly: fear.

"Shikari," began the colonel, but then he hesitated with a glance to the grief-stricken father, and began to dismount and unlimber his gun. "The young man looks well enough to ride. Have him sling the boy over my saddle. We must make it to the river by nightfall."

He spared a glance for the Arab, and another caress for the exhausted horse. "This man is my prisoner. I pursued him from the border, and I will be bringing him back with me."

Kolinzcki, rising to his feet, seemed about to protest, but something in the glitter of the colonel's eyes silenced him. For myself, I merely nodded, and went with von Hammerstein to collect the casualties.

The events of that afternoon return to me now only as a heat-soaked blur. We walked only when we could run no longer. Waterhouse clung to the stirrup of the colonel's horse, trotting alongside it as he steadied his sons. Conrad still breathed, but he had not regained consciousness, and I believed James was suffering an internal injury: he grew ever whiter and more silent, and most of our water went to him.

I knew the Creature stalked us, as wounded cats will, for every so often I caught a taste of its red scent upon the breeze, and the gelding was hot-eyed and terrified. I feared the poor beast's wind was broken: it wheezed through every breath and staggered under its double burden, but it kept up gamely.

The colonel had bound the Arab's hands before him with a leather strap. Through this means, Moran contrived to keep the prisoner upright and moving, although he was staggering from exhaustion.

I came up beside him when we had not been moving long and leaned into his ear. "The Arab is a Tsarist agent?"

"Of a sort," he said, one wary eye on the individual in question. "A tribal shaman. A personage. And an Afghan, not an Arab." He raked me with a sidelong glance and I nodded to encourage his discourse. "He was traveling to India with an entourage. We stopped the rest at the border, but this one got through. Fortunately, I've apprehended him before . . ." His voice trailed off. "What are your politics, Larssen?"

"I haven't any."

He grunted. "Get some." And walked away.

My especial burden was the fat Count, who staggered along in our wake and complained. Miss Adler kept along nicely, bearing her own distress very well, despite suspicious looks from the Count. Almost, I thought he was about to break into open argument with her, but he directed a hard look at Moran and kept his comments to the heat.

Finally, in the haze of heat and despair, Moran turned on the Count. "If you don't stop whining, I'll send you back in pieces!" he snapped, shaking his gun for emphasis.

The Count halted. "A common Englishman does not call me a fool!" he replied sharply. "I am accustomed to a dignified pace, and

if this Norwegian idiot had not led us into the lair of monsters"—
a rude gesture in my direction—"we'd all be bathed and fed by
now!"

The colonel's prisoner chose this moment to break in, gesticu-
lating and seeming to berate the Count, shrieking in anger. The
Count listened for a moment, and shook his head. He glanced
around in appeal. "Do any of you understand this barbarian?" he
asked, glancing from one to another.

None answered, but Moran's eyebrow rose in silent speculation.

Night came on more quickly than I could have imagined. My feet
were bloody in my boots, and sun blisters rose along the length of
my nose where my helmet did not shade it. I grew deaf to the
hum of insects, the chatter of monkeys and birds. The sole promise of relief was the black storm front piling up on the horizon:
the long-overdue monsoon, racing northward to greet us. Whenever I found the strength to raise my head, I glanced at those
bulging clouds, prayerful, but they never seemed closer. As if some
invisible army held them besieged, they roiled and tore, but could
not advance.

Dr. Montleroy sought me out as the afternoon waned into
evening. "I'm going to lose James unless I can get him to help, and
quickly. I may anyway, but there's still time to try."

"What does his father say?" I croaked.

"He knows," Montleroy answered, with a glance over his shoulder to the white-faced man. "It is one son or neither."

I nodded once. "Take all the water. Go."

We pulled Conrad down off the exhausted gelding over James's
feeble protests, and the good doctor swung up behind. Moran
poured water for the horse into his hat, and the animal sucked it
up in a single desperate draft. "Go like the wind," he said to it, and
slapped it hard across the flank. It startled and bolted, Montleroy
and James bent low over its neck.

"Godspeed," said Miss Adler from beside me. I glanced around in surprise. It was then that I noticed that the Count was missing.

No one had seen him fall behind, and we could not turn back. Mr. Waterhouse, von Hammerstein, and I took turns carrying Conrad, who drifted in a fever. He mumbled strange phrases in a language I had never heard, but which seemed to discomfit Moran's prisoner greatly.

The prisoner attempted to speak to me, but I could only shake my head at his foreign tongue. He tried von Hammerstein as well, to equally little avail, and Moran did not interfere. I had the distinct impression that the colonel watched out of the corner of his eye, as if observing our faces for any sign of comprehension, but the chattering of the monkeys meant more, at least to me.

With her paramour gone, Miss Adler stalked up to the front of the group. It was she who first identified the clearing where we had killed the tigress. We paused for breath, and the prisoner threw himself down in the long grass and panted.

"Two more miles to the river," she said, in a flat and hopeless tone, resting the Winchester's stock on the ground. Moran glanced from her to the rapidly darkening sky and grunted. Waterhouse's face clenched in terror and I knew it was not for himself that he feared.

"We could try to run it," offered von Hammerstein. He shifted the still form of Conrad Waterhouse on his shoulder and stared out toward the grasslands, a calculating look on his face. "Could you keep up, miss?"

The woman frowned. "I daresay." She bent down to unlace her boots while Rodney held the Winchester. She stepped out of them and knotted them over her shoulder.

The monkeys fell silent. The prisoner started up, eyes staring, and he cried aloud—*"Ia! Ia Hastur cf'ayah 'vugtlagln Hastur!"*—and then, in mangled Hindi, "The burning one comes!" His eyes shimmered insanely. His voice was exultant. I wondered why he had not spoken Hindi before, at least to myself or Rodney.

"Run," Moran shouted, yanking on the leather strap, and we ran.

The six of us, Moran dragging his captive, pelted out of the sal and down the slope of the land toward the riverbank. Around us the grass burned from gold to bloody in the light of the sunset. An enormous orb, already half concealed by the horizon, lit the scene like the plains of hell.

I ran with my hand clenched on my rifle, heedless of clutching grasses. Rodney darted ahead with one hand on von Hammerstein's arm, nearly dragging the laden man. Conrad bounced on his back, voice raised in a peculiar shriek, raving a string of words that pained my ears.

The ground blurred under my feet, and as I passed Miss Adler I caught her elbow and dragged her along—she was running well, but my legs were longer. Ahead of me, I saw Moran give an assisting shove to Waterhouse and turn around to yank the leather strap again. His prisoner simply piled into him, swinging his hands like a club, teeth bared to bite.

"The dagger!" he shrieked in broken Hindi, foam flying from his teeth. "You fool, or it will have us all!"

Moran moved with the speed of a man half his age. "Go on," he yelled at me as I moved to help him. He ducked under the prisoner's swing and brought his gun butt up under the man's jaw. As I pelted past, the Arab tumbled boneless to the ground, and Moran raised his weapon.

I flinched, expecting a shot, but Moran snarled as he hauled the prisoner to his feet.

I caught my breath in my teeth. It hurt. "Not . . . going to make it," Miss Adler groaned between breaths.

A lone tree rose before us as I stole a glance over my shoulder. We were less than halfway to the river, and I could see the red glow of the sunset matched by an answering inferno only yards behind.

Von Hammerstein and Waterhouse had reached the same con- clusion, for as we drew up we saw them crouched in the grass. Rodney stood just behind them, his eyes very white and wide in his mahogany face. He clapped my shoulder as I passed him, and I realized that he was younger than Conrad Waterhouse, over whose raving form he stood guard.

"Good lad," I said to him, which seemed wholly inadequate, and I came and stood beside him. I remembered that we had given all our water to James, and nevertheless I found my fear lifting. I was resigned.

Moran came up to us and took in the situation with a nod. We turned at bay, the devil before us and the sunset at our backs.

It let us see it coming—a glowing specter in the darkness, a de- mon of flame and fear. It leaped through the tall grass toward me—a bound of perhaps forty feet. I caught a very clear view of it as it gathered itself. Flaming eyes glittered at me with unholy intel- ligence in the moment before it leaped.

I felt something rise in my heart under that regard, an an- tique horror such as I had never known, and I heard Waterhouse whimper—or perhaps I myself moaned aloud in fear. Words seemed to form in my mind, words of invocation that I both knew and did not know, powerful and ancient and evil as maggots in my soul: *"Iä! Iä Hastur . . ."*

I emptied the .534 at it, to no effect. Beside me, I heard von Hammerstein's gun choke and roar twice. He reached for a second one. The reek of powder hung thick upon the air.

The beast was in midair—it was among us—Conrad had risen to his feet with madness on his face and thrown himself at Rod- ney. Waterhouse caught the blow, staggered, and bore the boy over onto the ground, kneeling on his chest and bearing his hands down only with great difficulty. Rodney never flinched.

I dropped the empty weapon. "Boy. *Gun!*"

Rodney snapped the Purdey into my hand, and I aimed along the barrel with a prayer to Almighty God on my lips. Moran was distracted from his prisoner, shaking his weapon loose and raising it in a futile and beautiful gesture. His luxurious mustache draped across the scrollwork on the gun as he sighted, and he placed two shots directly into the beast's eye as it lunged.

The flaming paw hurt not at all. It struck me high on the thigh, and I felt a distinct shattering sensation, but there was no pain. I lost the Purdey, and I saw poor Rodney hurled aside by a second thunderous blow. He fell like a broken doll, and he did not rise. Mr. Waterhouse started up to defend his boy, and was knocked backward fifteen feet into the tree before its next blow crushed von Hammerstein against the earth. I felt the impact from where I lay.

Moran turned with his gun, coolly tracking the Creature. He did not see his prisoner rise up from the ground clutching a rock in his bound hands, and my shout came too late. Even as he spun, the villain laid him out.

Then, suddenly, Miss Irene Adler was standing behind the prisoner, something glittering in her hand. She drew her arm back, and with a Valkyrie shout she plunged the Count's dagger deep into the Arab's back. The man stiffened, shuddered, and clawed, tied hands thrust into the air as if to drag Miss Adler off his back. I was eerily reminded of the poor, wounded elephant.

He sagged to his knees as the Creature snarled its throbbing snarl and spun about on its haunches. It took a step toward Miss Adler and screamed as only a cat can scream.

The prisoner fell to the ground dead, and Miss Adler stood defiant and braced behind the corpse, ready for whatever death might find her. Seeming unaffected by the death of the Arab, the Creature crouched to leap. Pain grinding in my broken leg, I started to drag myself upright with some futile idea of hurling myself on the thing.

At that moment, the rain came.

The monsoon was upon us like a wall of glass, and the Creature screamed again—this time, in agony. It turned this way and that, frantic to escape the raindrops, like a dog that seeks to elude a beating. Each drop sizzled and steamed as it struck, and with each drop the devil's light flickered, spots appearing on its hide like the speckles on a coal sprinkled with water.

It twisted about itself, shrieking, and finally seemed to collapse. A sickening scent of char rose from the wet ashes that were all that remained.

My leg flared at last into agony, and a black tunnel closed upon my sight.

I groaned and opened my eyes on a vision of bedraggled and ineffable beauty tucking a jeweled dagger into her reticule. There was a tarpaulin under me—wet, but drier than the ground—and another one hung over the branches of the tree to shield me from the worst of the rain. I recognized it as gear Rodney had carried. Moran lay beside me, under a blanket, quite still.

She laid a damp cloth on my forehead and smoothed back my hair before she stood. "Your leg is broken. I beg you to forgive me for leaving you in such straits, Mr. Larssen. I assure you I will send help, but I must leave at once: it is a delicate matter, and vital to the security of a certain Baltic nobleman that the theft of this dagger from his household never be proven—either by the English or the Russians."

"Wait," I cried. "Miss Adler—Irene—"

"You may certainly call me Irene," she replied, something like amusement in her voice. I saw that her gloves were burned through, and the palms of her hands were blistered.

I tried for a moment to formulate a question, but words failed me. "What has happened here?" I finally asked her, trusting that she would understand.

"I am afraid you have been rather overtaken by events, my dear Mr. Larssen . . . Magnus. As have we all. I came here to retrieve this dagger, which was stolen from a friend of mine. The rather vile Mr. Kolinzcki, whom I fear is neither a Count nor a Lithuanian but an agent of the Tsar, stole it and brought it here with the intention of providing it to this Afghan sorcerer."

She spurned the corpse with her toe.

"For all I know, he intended some foul ritual of human sacrifice, which may have greatly discomfited the British army. At the very least, it seems to have had the power to control that." She gestured expressively to the pile of ashes. "A pity I had to kill him. I imagine he would have befuddled British intelligence greatly, if they had the chance to interrogate him. But once I understood that he was somehow holding back the storm . . ."

"Monsoon. If I may be so bold as to correct a lady."

"Monsoon." She smiled.

"But how? You cannot tell me how?" I wished I could grit my teeth against the pain in my leg, but they chattered so that I could not manage it. I did not look to where Rodney lay, out in the cold rain.

"It seems that there are things in heaven and earth that lie beyond our ken as Western minds of scientific bent."

I nodded and a wave of pain and nausea threatened to overwhelm me. "The Count?" I asked.

She lifted her strong shoulders and let them drop, her expression dark. "Left behind and eaten, I presume. I assure you that your assistance has been invaluable, and that the war in Afghanistan may now come to a close."

She set a pan of rainwater and a loaded pistol close by my hand. "The colonel is alive but unconscious—it seems the blow rendered him insensate." A final hesitation, before she turned to go.

She turned back, and seemed to study my face for a moment. I hoped I saw something like affection there. "I am also very sorry about Rodney."

It was a very long, cold night then, but the villagers and Dr.

Montleroy came for me in the morning. We did not speak, then or ever, of the thing we had seen.

James survived, although Conrad never regained himself. I had occasional dealings after with Colonel Moran, until he left the region for cooler climes. I understand he has come to a very bad end.

As for Miss Adler—her, I never saw again. But my dreams are haunted to this day by her face and, less pleasantly, by those eerie words—*Iä! Iä Hastur cf'ayah 'vugtlagln Hastur!*—and I have never since been able to take up a gun for sport.

The Case of the Wavy Black Dagger

STEVE PERRY

Holmes sat in the overstuffed leather chair, making ready his briar pipe. The room was more or less quiet. A small coal fire burned in the iron stove set upon on the brick in front of the fireplace, the stove's metal creaking slightly from the heat; two oil lamps with well-trimmed wicks provided enough light to read by, and with the window open but a tiny crack, the winter winds and cold were kept more or less at bay. A woolen shawl about his shoulders finished the battle against whatever slight chill might whisper its way into the room. From the adjoining chamber, the door of which had been left ajar, came Watson's snores, not so loud as to impede Holmes's concentration, but enough to mark the doctor's position precisely.

It was not as comfortable as 221B Baker Street, but it was sufficient shelter for their brief visit to New York City. He had certainly stayed in worse places.

Holmes packed a goodly pinch of moist tobacco into the bowl of his briar. It wasn't his favorite meerschaum, grown golden with the years, but that beauty was too good to risk loss or damage to on a trip to the wilds of America. He compacted the tobacco, using for this purpose a solid gold tamper presented to him by Her Royal Majesty Victoria Regina years past for his invaluable assistance in the affair of the purloined love letters. When satisfied it would produce a proper smoke, he struck a match, allowed the vapors to rise from the stinking sulfur's ignition, then carefully lowered the flame into the bowl, inhaling until he produced a cheery glow and a cloud of fragrant bluish smoke that enveloped his face.

Ah.

He took another puff, exhaled the smoke, and nodded.

Now the night would become interesting.

"Good evening," he said, looking at the pipe. "I know you're hiding there. Won't you come and join me?"

Two seconds passed. Then, from out the dark shadow of the tall wooden chifforobe that held his traveling clothes, stepped a woman.

She was tall, willowy, and like the stained oaken chifforobe, her skin was dark. She wore a green long-sleeved wool blouse and a black wool skirt whose hem brushed the tops of sensible shoes. Her shining jet hair was pinned on top of her head. Let down, it must reach nearly to her waist, Holmes estimated. When she smiled, her teeth flashed pure and white against her café au lait features. Though he had never been one for the sensual pleasures to be found in most female company, he had to admit she was a handsome woman—strikingly handsome.

"Good evening, Mr. Holmes," she said.

He took another deep draft of the pipe smoke and allowed it to tendril out from his thin nose and lips, wreathing his head. "Shall we get on with it?" he asked. He waved his free hand at the chair across from his own, one that would put her face toward the nearer lamp.

She nodded and moved toward the chair. She had the feline grace of a tigress.

"There is a decanter of port, and one of whiskey there on the sideboard; please feel free to help yourself."

"Thank you, but I don't indulge in those kinds of spirits."

He smiled. Sometimes they made it almost criminally easy for him.

This was a test of his abilities, of course, and save for the sneaking in and skulking in the shadows, not that unusual. He had grown accustomed to such small adventures. They happened with more frequency since Watson's cataloging of his cases, and he had to confess to himself—even if he would never let Watson know it—that he enjoyed these little challenges.

Wits, like a razor, needed to be honed to stay sharp. The pity was there were so few people who could serve as proper strops for a mind such as his. Mycroft was never around when he needed him. The woman was hardly a threat, and had he felt any worry on that score, he had at hand a Webley revolver, one of several Watson owned, tucked into the pocket of his smoking jacket. This was America, after all.

Holmes took yet another draft of the pipe's nicely scented mix. They did have good tobacco here, he had to admit.

Now to the business at hand.

"Let me see. You are . . . a priestess of an exotic faith, and you have come here from far away. The tropics, I'd say—the Spice Islands—on a mission of great importance. To recover a lost—no, a *stolen* item. This item is not in and of itself extremely valuable, though it is certainly not a trifle, but instead has great religious worth, and is necessary for some important ritual. You were chosen for this role because you are an adept in physical and mental disciplines, and you wish my help in recovering the lost treasure. There is some danger in this quest, and while danger per se does not frighten you, you are being cautious because you know a misstep can be fatal."

That amused smile shined brightly in her face again, even in the dim light. He suppressed his own smile. He knew that such offhand and confident recitations always impressed those who sought to test him. He inclined his head in a short military bow, acknowledging her smile. They always asked at this point, and this would be his moment to give her a clever, if elementary, reconstruction of the clues that had provided his deductive reasoning.

He drew breath to speak, but she surprised him: "Well-spoken, sir, but not really *that* impressive, is it?"

The pipe threatened to go out. Holmes frowned, tamped the tobacco again, drew more air through it, brightening the glow in the bowl.

"I can offer two trains of thought that would explain how you know these things," she continued. "First, my appearance. Even though I am dressed as a local woman, it is obvious from my complexion and features that I am of Indian and not European or African descent. My English, while quite good, carries a trace of my native accent, and a man such as yourself would surely be familiar with the Malay tongue, so it is no great stretch to hazard a broad guess at my place of origin. The Spice Islands cover a long swath of ocean, Mr. Holmes. Would you care to localize it a bit more?"

Holmes considered it a moment. "Bali," he said. He allowed his face to reveal nothing.

"Indeed, that is so. But again, not that difficult a deduction, is it? The Balinese accent is detectable to a trained ear. Although that is not the only reason you called it thus."

He nodded, growing even more intrigued. "Go on."

"You watched me walk to the chair, and from a place where I had been concealed for some time before you noticed me—despite your pretense to have known I was there all along—so you realize I have some training in physicality and matters of . . . stealth."

He nodded again. She was fascinating. "Please—continue, continue."

"Since ninety percent of the civilized residents of the Spice

Islands are of the Islamic faith, and women are not traditionally counted among Muslim clerical circles, then it would be likely that with such training I would be from some other religion, one that allows women adepts. Bali still admits to more followers of the Buddhist and the Hindu persuasion than Java, not to mention some pockets of animism here and there."

He sucked in more smoke. He was much enjoying this conversation. What a magnificent creature she was!

"And the easiest part, of course, is the reason that I am here. Why else would I approach the renowned Sherlock Holmes if not to garner his help regarding some matter only he could solve? It would involve some criminal behavior, a missing person or thing, and were it merely misplaced, it would hardly have made its way halfway around the world, would it? And if I were seeking a person of my persuasion, such as would be likely, a man or woman of the Indian race would certainly stand out and be more readily identifiable in the United States than in most other countries—in which case, why would I need a great detective? Thus, I must be seeking some harder-to-find item, and one stolen."

"You, madam, are a woman after my own heart," he said, realizing it was true.

She inclined her head, still smiling. "Such parlor games are amusing, but prove little."

Holmes raised an eyebrow. "Indeed, madam, ah—?"

"Sita Yogalimari," she said. At his questioning look, she added, "My grandparents were Javanese."

"Ah." She had known he would recognize that the names were not Balinese. What a wondrous creature to realize he would immediately comprehend that! She had his full attention in a way no woman, with the possible exception of Irene Adler, ever had. Mycroft would love her. Perhaps it was best if he never mentioned her to his brother for that very reason . . .

"Can you tell me anything more, Mr. Holmes?"

"The final test, Miss Yogalimari?" He looked into the pipe's bowl. Gone out. He turned it over, knocked the dottle into the ashtray, set the briar precisely in its stand. He knew what she wanted, and, of course, he knew more than he let on. "You have a rather large knife hidden under your clothes." He considered it for a moment, then could not resist: "A . . . kris, I believe."

Again, the flash of perfect teeth. She reached behind her back and did something to the hem of her skirt. When her hand returned to view, she held gripped in it a knife in an intricately carved wooden scabbard with a silver tube covering much of the more than foot-long length. The top portion of the weapon and carved sheath looked somewhat like a high-prowed boat.

She arose, stepped across the short distance, and offered it to him.

Holmes took the weapon, careful to collect it with both hands. He withdrew the blade, a wavy affair, and raised it to touch it against his forehead lightly, the majority of the asymmetrical steel crosspiece above the pistol-shaped grip pointed to his right side. The scent of sandalwood oil rose from the metal, pungent and sharp.

"Interesting, Mr. Holmes. One would not expect an Englishman to know the proper ritual salute when drawing and inspecting a *keris.*"

He shrugged. "A simple thing, Miss Yogalimari, for anyone who reads even a little Dutch. They have written extensively about these things. Even Governor Raffles mentioned them in his excellent history of the islands." He looked at the blade. The steel was "watered," stained a dark black, with a Damascus pattern of shiny nickel threads twisted and running aslant through the iron. *"Pamor,"* he said. "Is that not what they call the pattern in the steel?"

"Yes."

"And the dark color comes from a wash made of lemon juice and arsenic."

"Dried under the tropical sun. The nickel does not take the stain, hence the patterns. Your knowledge is indeed formidable,

Mr. Holmes. There are hundreds of *pamor* patterns, each imbued with its own special magic. This one, of the twisted variety, is called *buntel mayit*—the 'death shroud.' Very powerful."

He nodded, holding the blade up to the light to examine the pattern more closely. There were five waves in the knife—a dagger—which narrowed from handle to point, and was sharp on both sides. A small symbol was incised into the steel at the base, and he recognized this as the Malay symbol for *dexter*—the right hand. He nodded. Of course. But let it play out—it was too delicious. He looked at her again.

"This *keris* is one of a matched pair," she said. "Made a hundred and fifty years ago by a master *empu*, a smith in Bali, from magic iron that fell from the sky."

"A meteorite."

"Yes." She paused. When she spoke again, her voice was lower. "Have you heard of . . . the Old Ones, Mr. Holmes?"

A chill frosted his shoulders, even under the shawl.

She instantly discerned this. "I see that you know the stories. No doubt a man of your erudition has some knowledge of ancient and forbidden texts. There are many of these creatures of legend—among them, one who arose in Bali eons before man came to live there. His true name may not be spoken aloud, but he is sometimes known as the Eater of Souls, sometimes as the Devourer of Children, and sometimes simply as Black Naga. The legend says that Black Naga awakens every thousand years to eat, and before he sleeps again, hundreds will have become his meals. He seeks only the fairest of the fair upon whom to dine, and any man who tries to stay his path will be destroyed, for it is said that Black Naga has six arms and nine legs, and that he breathes a noxious vapor so foul that its touch instantly fires wood and melts even rock. His teeth are longer than the fingers of a man, a hundred in number, and he can bite a man's arm off quick as a wink." She paused for a moment, then: "And it is said that he has two hearts."

Holmes said nothing, but his glittering gaze was fixed on her face.

"Yes, I see you understand. This is the reason for the two *kerises*. Both his hearts must be struck at once to effect the True Death. Though the *kerises* were prepared and made a century and a half ago, Black Naga's next hour has only just begun to come 'round. A month or more, a year or less, and he will shake the earth and cobwebs from his body and rise, coming forth from his hidden cave to kill and dine on his victims."

"And you believe in this monster." It was not a question.

"I do."

"But who would dare *face* such a fearsome creature, did one actually exist, Miss Yogalimari?"

"Only one trained from birth for that very confrontation, sir. Trained rigorously in the Malay and Balinese arts of *pukulan*, and *pentjak silat*, and an expert in the indigenous Chinese boxing system called *kun-tao*."

"And such a person could hope to defeat Black Naga?"

"If armed with the magical *kerises* designed and enchanted specifically for that purpose, yes, such a person could hope for that victory. Though it would by no means be a certain thing."

"This man would have to be most formidable."

He hardly saw her move. Of a moment, she was in the chair, smiling benignly at him, and in the next breath she stood next to him, one hand lightly touching his head, and what felt like a sharp fingernail pressed ever so gently against the side of his neck.

"Before you could draw your revolver, Mr. Holmes, I could, if I so desired, slice your carotid arteries in such a manner that Dr. Watson and a host of England's best battlefield surgeons could not stanch the flow of blood in time to save your life."

Beyond an initial stiffening of surprise, Holmes made no reaction to her sudden threat. She stepped back a short distance, and what he thought was a fingernail turned out to be a short, hook-shaped knife no longer than a finger.

His composure at least outwardly unruffled, he reached again for his briar and tobacco pouch. As he set about repacking the bowl, he noticed that a few strands of her hair were out place, and deduced where she had kept the blade hidden. He pursed his lips, amazed, but not afraid. She was magnificent! Such a mind, and in such a body—it was hard to believe.

He would definitely have to revise his opinion of women.

She returned to her chair, moving with the grace of an acrobat, and reseated herself.

Holmes got his pipe going again, and drew in a meditative lungful. Calmly—at least he thought he sounded so to his own ears—he said, "But you spoke of *two* trains of thought, madam."

He looked for the smile, and was not disappointed.

"Oh, yes. The second way you could have so quickly offered up your expository revelation is much simpler, even though I will grant that your skills of observation are as keen as any *man's*."

He heard the accent on that final word, and knew he was meant to hear it.

"And that way would be . . . ?" he prompted, gesturing gently with the briar, even though he knew what she was going to say. What a wonderful game this was! He had never played a more intriguing one.

Again he was not disappointed. "You *expected* someone like me, sir. Because you have seen the mate to the *keris* designed to slay Black Naga. And in fact, you have that weapon in your possession. Once I arrived and made myself known, you knew immediately who I was and why I was here."

Holmes felt a smile as genuine as any he had ever mustered rise to shape his face. "Bravo, Miss Yogalimari, bravo! How did you come to me?"

She leaned forward slightly, and he was aware for the first time that her breasts strained against the fabric of her blouse. She said, "The thief was Setarko, a Malay with connections in Hong Kong. He stole the pair of daggers nearly twenty years past.

"Those responsible for their care searched far and wide for two decades. The right-hand blade was finally found tucked away in a back room in the Royal Dutch Museum, in Batavia." She pointed at the dagger in Holmes's lap. "The other blade, the one marked *sinister*, remained missing.

"But before he . . . passed away, it was learned that the thief Setarko had had dealings with the late Professor Moriarty, who was a collector of such items. Setarko admitted to having sold one of the blades to your nemesis. When Moriarty died, many of his holdings were sold off, but such collectibles did not come to light."

"And you assumed that I had it?"

"I considered the possibility."

"But you could hardly be certain."

"Not until tonight."

"And what business assured that for you?" He knew, but he wished to hear her say it.

"A man expert enough to see I carried a hidden dagger under my skirt would also be expert enough to know I carry other weapons hidden upon my person. You did not know about the *kerambit*—the tiger's claw—I use as a hair fastener."

True. But he said, "You cannot be certain of that."

"I can. A fighter trained enough to see what weapons I carry would not have allowed me to get within striking range with those weapons, for he would also know I can use them with deadly expertise. You are not a skilled fighter, Mr. Holmes, save with your wits. Therefore the only way you could have known I had the *keris* is if you already suspected I had the one that is mate to yours. A man who has a *keris* as finely crafted as these, marked with the Malay word for *sinister*, a man of your caliber of intellect? He would certainly suspect there existed a *dexter* somewhere. When you saw me, a Balinese woman, you made the connection. It was quite clever of you, that leap. Almost femininely intuitive."

"I did not think a woman could be so brilliant," Holmes admitted, perhaps somewhat gracelessly. "To have followed such a long trail, to have found me, and to have learned what you wanted, as well as knowing what I knew—all in so short a time. I am amazed."

"I am counted least among my sisters in intellect, Mr. Holmes. My talents lie primarily in more brutal skills."

"So I have seen," he said, "though I suspect you are too modest." She smiled slightly at the compliment. Holmes arose. "Well, let me get the *keris* for you." He went to the wooden box where the relic was kept and opened it. He lifted out the weapon, wrapped in a piece of black silk, crossed the room, and presented it to her.

She took it reverently, bowed to him.

"Aren't you going to examine it?"

"There is no need. You are a man of honor, are you not?"

He nodded, pleased by her use of the term. "And what will you do after you dispatch this Black Naga, Miss Yogalimari? When your lifetime of deadly training is no longer necessary? Assuming, of course, that you survive?"

"I will return to my sisters and instruct younger ones in my art. There will ever be a need for women to have such skills. And I shall see what life brings me."

He weighed his next words very carefully. "And are you allowed to have visitors there?"

She gave him that smile again, and it quite warmed him to see it. "Not usually. But exceptions can be made. I needn't tell you of all people where to find me, should you ever travel that way, should I, Mr. Holmes?"

He smiled. Another test.

"It has been my pleasure to have made your acquaintance, madam. I expect we shall see each other again someday." He bowed. There was no need to wish this woman safety in her journey—she carried her own well enough.

She nodded. "Until we meet again, Mr. Holmes, farewell."

She slipped out of the room like a shadow, like a wraith, and was gone.

Holmes sat back in his chair and attempted to return to his reading of crop statistics in South Africa, but his concentration was less than it should be. After a moment, he heard Watson's snoring stop abruptly. A few seconds later, his friend padded into the doorway, dressed in his nightcap and gown, ratty slippers shuffling over the wooden floor. He stuck his head into the room, glanced about, and frowned.

"I say, Holmes, did I hear you talking to someone in here?"

He tugged the shawl about his shoulders again; despite the fire, the room had grown much chillier. There were a few adventures—a very few—over the years that had not found their ways into Watson's catalogs. Usually for reasons of national security, for the safety of the realm. And, even more rarely, for the safety of mankind.

He answered his old friend's question. "Only the woman of my dreams, Watson."

"Humph." Watson eyed him a moment, then yawned, turned, and shuffled back to his bed. "Well, good night, then, Holmes."

Holmes smiled. Yes. A very good night, indeed.

A Case of Royal Blood

STEVEN-ELLIOT ALTMAN

It all began with a curious cable that found me one damp February evening as I lounged at my favored haunt, the Turkish baths at 33 Northumberland—one of the city's more discreet and solicitous establishments. Instructing the valet to fetch my clothes, summon my coach, and remove a shilling from my coat for his service, I towelled off and reread the cable, striving to believe its content and origin. It read:

> Dear Mr. Wells,
>
> Your attendance is requested in an investigation of grave importance to the Royal Family of the Nederlands. Please consult S. Holmes posthaste regarding your willingness to participate.
>
> Sec. to H.M. Emma of Waldeck-Pyrmont

As we rumbled across the poorly tended stones toward Regent's Park, in the flickering glow of the gaslight, I read the note yet again, wondering what could possibly require *my* attentions in relation to the notorious Mr. Sherlock Holmes, a man famed throughout Europe for his keen investigative prowess. I, a mere teacher and author of fiction, barely knew the man, save for the few occasions on which we'd suppered together with our mutual friend, John Watson, and the knowledge I shared with all Londoners regarding his casework as detailed in the *Daily Press*. Watson's recent marriage and homeownership had demanded he take up his civil practice once more, and I wondered if Holmes was simply desirous of company—the cable a mere fabrication.

The coach ground to a halt before the illustrious lodging at 221B Baker Street and I leaped out with a wave to my man to await my return. I rang the bell and was admitted by Holmes's housekeeper, who'd been informed of my probable arrival. She led me to the study, where I warmed my hands by the fire and took note of the man's desk, cluttered to the point of overflow. The room held the stale scent of pipe smoke and the heavy drapes gave one the impression of a funeral parlor. On the table by an armchair, beneath a precariously balanced candle, was a bound edition of my latest novel, satisfyingly dog-eared and well thumbed— placed to flatter and conciliate, I suspected, but not distastefully so.

A light footstep announced the arrival of my host: gaunt of frame, hair tousled, adorned in a purple dressing gown and Persian bedroom slippers. The keen eyes and sharp features of his face were exactly as I'd recalled, though there was now a weariness about him I attributed to a lack of sleep. "Wells," he exclaimed, in a tone at once familiar and matter-of-fact, "it's quite good of you to come 'round so quickly at such a late hour." He shook my hand firmly, then drew forth a case of Burns & Hill and offered one to me.

"What the devil is going on, Holmes?" I demanded, accepting the offer.

"Come, come, Wells," he responded, striking a match and lighting both our cigars. "I know you well enough; you must be brimming with curiosity. And it may be the devil indeed. Please sit."

He pulled his armchair to face mine and, with the firelight flickering across his brow, grinned a sardonic smile. "I see you've been hard at work on your next novel, and well paid on the last. You've also been to the baths on Northumberland within the hour."

"Talking to my publisher, I assume? And employing your usual network of irregulars?"

"No," he replied. "I simply took note of the fresh ink on your shirt cuff and the Glenfiddich on your breath. Not a poor man's drink. I've only smelled that brand of talcum used in two places here in London: one a brothel in Camden—the sort you'd steer clear of—and the baths at 33 Northumberland. Your fingernails are impeccably clean."

He retrieved two short glasses and a silver flask from the mantel and placed them on the table between us. I motioned my disinterest, as I'd already imbibed my fair share for that hour and expected soon to be in the company of my wife.

"I'm adequately impressed, Holmes. Now do please explain the contents of the cable before I burst into flame with anticipation."

Holmes sat back and steepled his fingers. "As I'm sure you're aware from Watson's rather elaborate dramatizations of my casework, I do not accept cases which do not fit my own personal criteria. They must be of an unusual or fantastic circumstance not readily solvable by even the most experienced investigator, and the nature of the crime must fall within the higher order of darkness. Petty crimes are always tediously boring to solve, and invariably commence from poverty, greed, or unrequited love. I am only interested in purer evils, the ones that at first appear to defy logic or morality, crimes that trickle down from an arcane, yet quite *mortal* source, that I've yet to unmask."

"I applaud your purpose, Holmes. And I presume that this business in Holland presents such a case?"

"Yes," Holmes replied.

"And what is the crime?" I asked.

"Attempted murder on a member of the royal family, reportedly facilitated by a poltergeist."

I sat forward in my chair and requested the drink I'd refused. Holmes poured a double scotch. "Poltergeist, you say? Do tell me you disbelieve in such things."

He fixed me with a sobering stare. "Do *you* believe in such things, Wells?"

"No, I do not, though as you know well from our conversations, the study of occult sciences and myths constitutes the foundation for much of my fiction."

"Ah!" Holmes exclaimed, the firelight dancing across his gray irises. "Exactly the point, my dear Wells, and the first on the long list of the reasons I wish to recruit you: your thorough knowledge on the subject matter and your simultaneous skepticism as to its validity. I do believe, from the details I've received thus far, that a murder has been attempted and a second attempt is imminent. All participants believe a haunting is involved—and that belief is enough to color every aspect of the aforementioned crime. Our job is to expose and undermine the falsehood of the claim and apprehend those responsible. Not to mention, the young Princess Wilhelmina is apparently a fan of yours. Will you come to Holland?"

"Are you quite sure that my knowledge will be of use?"

"What is a poltergeist, Wells?"

"As I'm sure you're aware by picking up your *Britannica*, *poltergeist* is a German term, *polter* meaning 'noise' and *geist* meaning 'ghost.' A poltergeist is a disembodied spirit with malicious intent. However, your studied occultist would find this an appallingly meaningless and generic term, with little use for taxonomic purposes and of no use whatsoever in application. I myself could list over two dozen varieties of dark denizens specific to the mythos of Holland, but first I'd need to know a great deal more regarding the events witnessed. What did they see? Who saw it and when? Could be anything from a mischievous *Kobold* to a charnel-house *Fetch*. What events were recorded prior to—"

"Yes," he said, cutting short my explanation. "I'm quite sure you'll be of use. Pack enough for no less than a week. And be sure to bring rain gear; the weather in Holland makes London look positively balmy. We depart tomorrow morning from the port of Harwich for Rotterdam."

And with that he rose, shook my hand vigorously, added, "Thank you, Herbert. I believe you shall find this a most inspirational journey," and bid me good night.

Upon reentering my coach, I glanced back toward his window as someone began playing the violin with tremendous fervor—a somber work by Liszt. My coachman snapped the reins and we careened east toward Whitechapel. I had little time to contrive how I'd explain this sudden venture to my wife.

The captain of the Dutch steamship *Dordrecht* gave us free run of the vessel, assuring us his personal service. The pound sterling was then high against the gulden, but the discrepancy was of small consequence, for we were now guests of the Crown, and I had to prod Holmes to allow us to be treated as such. Holmes appeared to know little of earthly pleasures, and to be disinterested in the fineries that wealth could provide. I envied him his bourgeois contentment. The trip across the Channel was calm-weathered and uneventful, leaving us a good deal of time to lounge on deck and discuss a host of Dutch political intrigues.

"Holmes, I must admit that I'm not at all familiar with the current royal family, aside from King Willem and his—ahem—somewhat younger bride, Emma," I admitted with some embarrassment. "Please do identify the players."

"Understandable, Wells—it's not until the world is at war that we look past our own doorstep. Her Majesty Emma of Waldek and Pyrmont, our gracious host, is indeed forty-one years the king's junior, and she is in fact his second wife."

"Ah yes, the first one was Sofia. Rumor had it he beat her," I said.

"Never trust conjecture, my dear Wells, especially with the Dutch. They're a proud and protective lot." He motioned me to observe an elderly couple who had overheard my comment and now proceeded to cast angry glances our way.

"Point taken, do carry on," I said.

"Queen Sofia bore Willem three sons: Prince Nicolaas, Prince Frederik, and Prince Alexander. Frederik died at age seven—meningitis. He was reportedly misdiagnosed by the court physician, and when Sofia requested a second opinion the king refused her. When the child died, Sofia left the king quite hastily and returned to her native Württemberg."

"Bully for her," I cheered. "But surely there must have been some reconciliation—there was a third child."

"Indeed, Wells, there was: Alexander, one year later. Her Majesty was known to be rather ill-tempered, vengeful, and capricious, alienating the children from their father. It's also a little-publicized fact that she was King Willem's first cousin."

"Scandalous," I said, a trifle louder than necessary, to Holmes's chagrin.

"The surviving princes gave Holland their fair share of scandal as well," he continued, "before their mother died of an undiagnosed illness in the summer of seventy-seven. Then the king took up with young Emma, which deepened the rift between himself and his sons. Nicolaas took up residence in Paris and Alexander left for Switzerland. A year later, Emma gave birth to a daughter."

"Pretty little Princess Wilhelmina. Must be eight or nine by now."

"See that, Wells—you're not as uninformed as you've let on."

"And it is this young princess who is the subject of our attempted murder and alleged haunting."

I rose and stood by the ship's railing, rows of windmills now apparent in the distance like blackened pinwheels lined along the shore. I recalled from my grammar-school lessons that over half the country lay curiously below sea level; the Dutch engineers having masterminded the colossal system of canals, dikes, and mills to bleed the excess water from the pilfered soil and raise the sunken earth. Now they waged constant war to keep the sea from reclaiming the country.

"All right, Holmes, I'll take the bait and surmise that it's one of the princes who has promulgated this fictitious haunting, the obvious motives being jealousy and revenge."

"And you'd be quite wrong, my dear Wells." Holmes joined me at the railing. "At least in the choice of culprit. Both the princes are already dead—Nicolaas in a duel over a woman and Alexander of typhoid fever."

Arriving in Holland was like stepping backward in time some ten years, both in the fashion and the overall lack of facilities. Of Dutch culture I knew little, save they were known to breed the shrewdest businessmen and they purchased a great deal of English literature at bulk discount. Though Holmes spoke a fair amount of Dutch, it became clear that the majority of locals were quite fluent in the Queen's English and, unlike the French, were willing to exercise this facility in our presence.

A first-rate coach with an armed escort of five men awaited us at the docks. Holmes was immediately recognized and greeted by a giant of a man, nearly seven feet tall and nineteen stone, called Jan Gent, with a short beard and a short line of patience. Although Captain Gent was the very pinnacle of military courtesy, it was clear by his tone and manner that he was distressed. "Welcome to the Nederlands. Your presence is immediately requested at the palace. Please come this way," (my approximation of his full greeting to Holmes). Our luggage transferred, we clambered into the coach and were away from the port in minutes with the soldiers seated at their stations above. Passersby stopped and stood agape in wonderment; I deduced that soldiers bearing rifles were not usually seen in the thoroughfare.

"Captain, is the general public aware that the princess has been threatened?" Holmes inquired of Gent.

"We have done our best to keep the information close," he replied in his coarse English. "However, I must assume there are rumors. Over half a dozen servants have quit the employ of the palace since this began."

Holmes nodded. "I'll need a list of their names and particulars."

"Of course. Do you wish them all brought in for questioning?"

"Bit premature for that," Holmes said. "But I'll keep that possibility in mind."

Holmes directed my attention to several key landmarks as the pungent wharf odor and rough cobblestones of Rotterdam quickly transformed into the pristine and well-manicured architecture of Den Haag, or The Hague, as we Englishmen call it. Noordeinde Palace, current home to the royal family, appeared on the terminus of a beautiful length of road, and rivaled the monumental splendor of any British royal's accommodations. Huge arches of marble, fashioned in the style of the Romans, served to support the structure, while shielding the men and women who scurried below them from a cluster of gray-black clouds looming threateningly above.

The coach ground to a halt at the front gate, and as the good captain unlatched the door for Holmes, a young girl of perhaps twelve broke away from the shadows and dashed toward us, a bundle of something outstretched in one small hand. In an instant our guards cocked their rifles, ready to discharge, and the captain drew his saber and held its blade edge threateningly close to the child's throat. Dropping the bundle, the child burst into tears and lamentation. Holmes knelt, and retrieved a bouquet of tulips wrapped in linen. Once the guns were down, the saber sheathed, and the apologies made, the child was led away.

"Certainly on edge," Holmes whispered as Gent brought us up through the gates. At each twist and turn through the building, guards snapped to attention at our passing, their eyes fierce and weary from what Holmes surmised to be a lack of sleep, admitting he was well aware of the symptoms.

Our quarters were two adjoining rooms, the splendor and finery of which you can well imagine. We freshened ourselves and prepared for our audience with the queen. Gent reappeared soon after to convey us through the royal hall to the tearoom—a plush chamber unlike any other I'd spied as we passed, with fine European silk carpets, bookcases filled with well-worn volumes, a fireplace, crystal chandelier, and several comfortable chairs and settees. While we waited, the captain posting additional guards at each end of the hallway, Holmes and I silently observed the room.

"Quite the atmosphere for a haunting, eh, Holmes?"

"Indeed," came a soft, commanding voice from behind us. We turned to face H.M. Emma of Waldek-Pyrmont, a raven-haired beauty of some thirty years, with rose cheeks and sensitive green eyes, adorned in a timeless gown that bespoke great wealth. She seemed to glide, not walk, as she came to stand before us.

"Forgive us if we do not bend our knees, Your Majesty," Holmes said respectfully.

"No apologies," she responded graciously, apparently pleased by the presence of Holmes. "You are subjects of an English queen. And now our honored guests."

"*Dankuwel.*" Holmes kissed her hand. "*Wij zijn hoogst vereerd.*"

"*U bent meer dan welkom,* Mr. Holmes," the queen replied. "*Uw Nederlandsch es uitstekend.*" Then, seamlessly switching to English, she added, "But do let us include your countryman, Mr. Wells. Sir, you are also quite welcome. And as you'll soon see, my daughter is a tremendous admirer of your tale of *The Chronic Argonaut*. And as to our haunted atmosphere, I quite agree. Please sit."

Holmes and I sat in opposing chairs. The queen stepped before the fireplace, leaving her back to us, as if the story she was about to relate had offered her a sudden chill.

"It was in this very room, gentlemen, that my daughter, Mina, was attacked. It was just past nightfall and she sat in the exact chair you've selected, Mr. Wells, reading alone by candlelight. The door was locked from the inside."

Holmes nodded to himself, his gaze sweeping to survey the door.

"A noise caught her attention, and she looked up. She was no longer by herself. There was—*the* girl."

"The girl?" I questioned, my interest piqued by the emphasis she placed on the phrase.

"Yes, Mr. Wells, that's how we refer to this invading, and most assuredly malicious, intruder."

"So I take it this girl has been sighted on more than one occasion?" Holmes asked.

The queen turned back to us, her face drained now of its color. "Seven sightings to date since the attack."

"Hence the pervading suspiciousness of your guardsmen and a rather overzealous incident we witnessed at your gate involving a young girl," Holmes noted.

"Have you seen *the* girl yourself?" I inquired.

She nodded, with evident trepidation. "Once, upon awaking in my bedchamber."

"Will you describe her for us, please?"

The queen began to wring her hands. "Her appearance is that of a dark-haired young woman of perhaps sixteen years. Her skin is a bleached white, her eyes dark. She is gowned in white linen and she moves with unnatural grace. She . . ."

"Please, spare no detail," Holmes directed at her pause. "I assure you there's no cause to hold back anything, be it for reasons of disbelief or of discretion."

The queen nodded and said, "In all honesty, she bears a striking resemblance to Mina herself . . ." then paused again.

Holmes signaled me to continue. "Please, Your Majesty, do go on," I said.

The queen took a deep breath. "Mina quite innocently asked for her name and the girl refused to answer, simply wetting her lips and whispering Mina's name back to her. Somehow Mina assumed she was in danger and began crying out, hurling books at the girl and racing about the room to keep her distance. Captain Gent heard Mina's screams and broke the door in . . ."

"Carry on, Your Majesty. What did the captain see upon entering?"

"He found Mina unconscious, with bloodied marks about her throat and upon her nightgown," she said bravely.

Holmes and I rose and went to the door. He examined the slot where the bolt would secure the frame. "This door has been forced, by several kicks, I assume. See there, the large heel indentations in the wood."

My attention had been drawn elsewhere, to a singular stain—a handprint, visible only from a particular angle because of the near-matching color and texture of the wood, located about chest level upon the outside surface of the door. "Look at this, Holmes," I said.

Holmes drew his magnifying lens as the queen came quickly to observe our findings. "It is most certainly blood," he said.

"Seems as if this bloodied print was created upon arrival, not departure," I said.

"Please place your hand upon the door for us to examine, Your Majesty," Holmes requested, and she placed her own delicate hand near to the print.

Holmes lowered his lens. "It seems the size of a young girl's hand. Certainly not made from the giant paw of your man Gent."

"Could it be Mina's print," I suggested, "made after the attack?"

"But she was unconscious when Gent carried her from the room," the queen said.

"How tall is Mina?" Holmes inquired.

"Barely one meter."

"Just over three feet, not tall enough to have made this print. The uniformity of the blood mark clearly suggests a forward thrust made by a girl no taller than five foot two inches and no less than four foot nine inches."

"Most curious," I said. Then, turning to the queen, I asked, "Where did the blood on Mina come from? What was the wound?"

The queen looked to us with confusion. "There was no wound upon Mina that I found, though her neck was badly bruised. I bathed her myself."

"Well, someone was bleeding from somewhere," Holmes surmised. "Any mythos surrounding the woundless extraction of blood, Wells?"

"None I'm familiar with," I replied. "Save for *Nachzerer*, the German equivalent of the Romanian vampire. But there would be exit wounds, bite marks of some sort, as the legend goes."

"Right," Holmes agreed. He addressed the queen again. "You say you examined your daughter quite thoroughly and found no such wounds?"

"None, Mr. Holmes, I assure you."

"Forgive me a delicate question, Your Majesty. Has your daughter begun *menstrueren*?"

"*Nee, Mr. Holmes. Nacht neet.*"

Holmes made a keening noise under his breath, then said, "We must assume that the bloodprint here and that which was found upon the princess resulted from wounds unknown, prior to the attack. May I request now, Your Majesty, an interview with your daughter?"

"Certainly, I shall take you to her," she replied.

★   ★   ★

We then trailed down the corridor, preceded by guards, to the princess's rooms. The queen entered alone, leaving us to wait outside as the guards took up their posts. I seized the moment to ask Holmes, "Do you suspect Captain Gent of some treachery? He was certainly willing to strike down that girl with the tulips."

"True," Holmes replied, "but he stayed his hand."

"Perhaps due to our presence?"

"An interesting line of thought, Wells, and he was handily present on both occasions; however, I do find him lacking in motivation. If he meant the princess even the slightest harm, this keen mother would sense it. No, my observation of him reveals he is simply a man of action, fiercely loyal though a bit hot-tempered. An honest man."

I nodded my compliance.

"Look to draw the princess out on any details you feel appropriate, won't you, Wells? Proceed as if trying to prove that this is a true haunting."

"Done," I replied. "I shall play the believer."

Her Majesty's voice from within bade us enter.

The princess's bedchamber was every child's dream, fitted out with every plaything imaginable, each in its prescribed cubbyhole. The princess herself was propped up on no fewer than half a dozen pillows on a four-poster bed, draped with sheer linen, enjoying her supper on a silver tray. The child positively beamed as we were introduced, kicking her covers away and alighting at the foot of her bed to greet us.

"My daughter, Wilhelmina," the proud mother presented.

"The pleasure is mine, Mr. Holmes and Mr. Wells," Mina offered in a voice that should have belonged to a girl twice her age. "Oh, this is a joyous day. I do proclaim, Mother, that I am cured this very moment!"

"Now, Mina," the queen said. "The doctors have demanded you keep to your bed for at least three more days."

"Yes, Mother," the princess acquiesced. Then she turned and dug through a pile of books beneath her sheets and raised a familiar volume. "Look, Mr. Wells, I have *The Chronic Argonaut* right here with me."

"I am honored, Your Highness," I replied.

"We must hear of the danger that befell you," said Holmes, bringing us back to our mission at hand. "Of the girl who tried to hurt you."

Mina offered no resistance, or trace of fear, in recounting the attack, her story identical to her mother's, a result, no doubt, of the fact that the queen had related it with a meticulous accuracy.

"Did you notice any blood on the hands of the girl?" I asked when she concluded.

"No," she replied.

"Any peculiar smells in the air?"

She considered the question a moment, then answered. "Yes, I believe I *did* smell something strange—it made me look up from my book. She smelled like pine trees. Like the forest."

"How unusual," I replied. "And what was it about her that first made you realize that you were in danger?"

Again she carefully considered before revealing, "It was how she whispered my name. It was not a regular-sounding voice."

"How so?"

"It was angry, and not at all hers," Mina answered.

"And pray tell me, what had you been reading before she appeared?"

The child hesitated, almost imperceptibly. "It was a book of fairy tales," she replied in a softer voice, "by Hans Christian Andersen."

"Thank you, Your Highness. We'll leave you to your supper now," Holmes said, concluding our interview.

"But wait, I have something for you both, a gift," she said. "Mother, will you please bring me my jewelry box?"

The queen went to a bureau and did as requested, placing the box upon Mina's tray. The child rummaged through the box, producing a small pouch from which she removed two sparkling prizes. "Here they are!" she announced.

Upon seeing the twin silver rings, the queen chastised her daughter in Dutch: *"Mina, dat zijn ringen van je grootmoeders erfgoed!"* ("The rings were gifts from her grandmother," Holmes translated in my ear.)

"Can I not do with them as I please, Mother?"

The queen deferred to the princess, whether from pride in our presence or inability to deny her child, we shall not venture to guess. Holmes would have spoken up to refuse the gifts had I not grasped his shirt cuff at that precise moment.

"We'd be honored," I said, extending my hand to receive both rings and passing one to Holmes. I slid the beautiful gem on my right ring finger and admired its radiance. Holmes slid his on with mock gratitude.

"They were blessed by His Holiness, Pope Gregory, in Rome, weren't they, Mother?"

The queen nodded, and Mina raised her tiny frame up on her knees and whispered in my ear.

"I shall treasure it always," I pronounced before the room, my hand on my heart, as we left the young princess to her books.

In the hallway, the queen offered, "As you can see, the child has a flair for the dramatic, which she has inherited from her father."

Missing no opportunity, Holmes responded, "Might I inquire, Your Majesty, as to the whereabouts of King Willem?"

"The king is on the grounds at present, Mr. Holmes. If you like, I shall petition him to grant you an audience. Though I warn you, he shares not my dire concern for these events, dismissing any talk of the supernatural entirely."

"Would you describe your husband's current relationship with your daughter?" Holmes asked.

"Adoration from a distance," the queen answered after careful consideration. She called for a lady-in-waiting and gave her instructions in Dutch, then turned back to Holmes. "I've sent word to my husband of your request, though it may be some time before we receive his reply."

Holmes wasted no time. "Thank you, Your Majesty. May we now speak with the other members of the household who have observed the apparition?"

One by one, guardsmen, handmaids, valets, and kitchen staff were summoned before us and we conducted our interviews in her presence—only to find that the queen recollected events far better than those who'd experienced them firsthand, that she remembered details that they had forgotten with astoundingly vivid accuracy—who had seen what and when, every creaking floor plank and flickering light. It was evidence of a diligence that only a mother truly in fear for her child's safety could produce.

We dined with the queen in splendor, the details of which I shall not render, though suffice to say it was one of the best meals of my life. Afterward, we were granted an audience with the king in his private office.

King Willem III, a gentleman in his early seventies, was tall, like the majority of his subjects, balding slightly, with a white tuft of beard, an aquiline nose, and ruddy cheeks. His eyes possessed a disarming quality and his manner bespoke an impatience with nonsense. It was difficult to match him with the young queen—although it has been my observation that these things tend to work differently with royalty. He complimented Holmes on his high reputation amongst the European law enforcement communities, for which praise Holmes thanked him.

"Mr. Holmes, I am a tired man," he professed. "I've outlived one wife and three sons. It is only of late that I've brought the nation into some semblance of economic balance. I'm looking forward to a time, hopefully near at hand, when I can sit by the shoreside and fish. Her Majesty and the princess have been my second chance in life, and I mean to keep them protected."

"We are your servants on that mission," Holmes affirmed.

"Much to my appreciation," the king replied. "There is some dark intent running under my roof, and I mean to expunge it. Therefore, fire off your questions."

"Are there political enemies of your royal house that we should suspect?"

"None, sir," the king replied. "At present the Nederlands holds no open disputes."

"What about personal enemies, Your Majesty?"

The king considered long and hard, then said, "This house was once divided against itself, I sadly admit. My late wife, Sofia, poisoned my sons against me; the announcement of Princess Mina's birth was not received well by either of them. However, this feud was settled when Prince Alexander passed away."

"He was head of the Freemasons for a time, was he not?" asked Holmes.

"That is correct, though with them, as in most diversions my sons engaged in, the time was short before there was a parting of the ways. In that case in particular, the way was parted quicker than most. Alexander was too passionate and quick-tempered for the Masons."

At the mention of the Freemasons I wanted desperately to inquire further, their sometime involvement with unnatural arts demanding the very attention I was recruited for. But Holmes's quick signal stayed my voice.

"*Dankuwel, zijne Majesteit,*" Holmes concluded, inclining his head in respect. "We shall leave you to govern your country."

It had been a long day, full of strange tales and foreign sights. When we returned to our rooms, I sat on the edge of my bed and observed my tired reflection in the ornate mirror. Holmes was still bristling with energy; I wondered what sorcery he employed that kept him so finely tuned.

"Don't prepare to retire just yet, my dear Wells; I've one more task for you before this day's out."

I sighed. "Right, Holmes, ever at your service."

"I'd like you to pop 'round and offer our young princess a bed-time story."

"You're joking. It would be highly improper to do so without royal permission."

"Nevertheless, I'm quite serious," Holmes replied. "And do give her a choice—one tame story and one dreadful."

"I'm sure that I don't see the point."

"At the very least you'll gain her favor, Wells. She will be queen someday."

I looked at him solemnly, trying to gauge his true intent. "And you'll be off—"

"Attending to other things. By the way, what was it the princess whispered to you after presenting us with these?" he asked, display-ing the remarkable brilliant on his finger.

"She told me that they should protect us from the devil." Holmes arched an eyebrow. "You don't suppose this whole business is merely a child's method of drawing us here, do you?"

Holmes leaned his thin frame against the doorway and consid-ered. "Wells, this whole family is trying to tell us something, not just the princess," he said. "But they are not sure what it is that they're trying to tell. It's something they all intuit—the king with his guilty conscience, the queen with her suspicions, and the princess with her gifts to protect us. The entire household is gripped by chimera—it's an uncanny display of transcendent cognition." As I digested his words, he straightened and added, "Now do go tell the princess a story. We'll meet back here by ten bells."

I watched Holmes slink off, so silent and deft that the guards down the hall took no notice. I approached them moments later and asked to be escorted to the princess's room, which to my surprise they did without hesitation. The princess seemed delighted to see me.

"I have a few stories I'm concocting, Your Highness," I said, as if confiding a trusted secret. "One regards a fantastic journey by men shot out of a cannon to land on the moon; the other concerns a mad scientist who transforms animals into half-human creatures."

"Do tell me about the mad scientist if you please, Mr. Wells," she eagerly responded.

I returned to our rooms to find Holmes lying, fully dressed, on his bed, fingers clasped behind his head, awaiting my return. "Which did she choose?" he asked, rather smugly.

"The most terrifying story I've ever dreamed up," I told him. "Nearly frightened myself."

"Not surprising," Holmes replied, "considering what she's been reading." Sitting up, he recited to me his past hour.

"Two things bothered me regarding Princess Mina. One: The fact that she had supposedly locked herself within the tearoom to read—why do that unless you're reading something that you fear might be objectionable? Two: She hesitated briefly when you asked what she'd been reading prior to the attack."

"Her mother was present," I offered.

"Indeed," Holmes replied. "So I examined the contents of the bookshelves at some length, finding nothing queer, then sat in the very chair and allowed myself to observe. There I saw it—a length of molding, set forward at unequal length to the opposing wall, which quickly revealed a hidden shelf."

Buttoning on my nightshirt, I demanded, "The contents, man, if you please."

Lowering his voice, he said, "Have you ever heard of an ancient text called the *Necronomicon*?"

"Holmes, do say you're joking," I whispered. "The book's

fictitious—a rumored work. The title translates from the Greek as 'Book Concerning the Dead.' "

Holmes nodded gravely. "Yes, Wells, though its content suggests even more arcane purposes. A compendium of rituals pertaining to the manifestation of demons. Look for yourself."

From his travel case he drew forth and handed over a dark ledger-sized volume that was bound in uncured leather and bore a musty odor. I opened to a random page and beheld a nonsensical incantation; scrawled in tedious longhand and accompanied by a cryptic diagram upon the yellowed parchment. I wanted to denounce its authenticity at once; however, the *peculiarity* of the thing in my hands prevented me from voicing my doubt.

"Holmes, it is preposterous to think that the princess—"

"Calm yourself, man," Holmes said, and I lowered my voice. "I believe that she merely discovered the book, which I suspect belonged to her half brother Alexander. There were other books cached there; including Von Junzt's despicable *Nameless Cults* and certain texts possessed only by high-order Freemasons."

"Then she's only guilty of hiding it again." I sighed, quite relieved.

"Yes, Wells—though I pray her innocent young mind cannot grasp the dark implications of whatever she's read so far. But the fact remains—the book *is* here, and that raises the stakes considerably, in my estimation. I found also a collection of correspondence from a woman named Elisabeth Cookson, who was illicitly involved with one if not both of the princes, and quite possibly with the king himself."

"Do you have those letters with you as well?"

"No, I replaced them. And in any event, they were penned in Dutch. She'll be the subject of tomorrow's delicate inquiry." At this, Holmes outstretched his hand to retrieve the book and I handed it back, somewhat disturbed by the intensity he displayed.

"Now sleep, Herbert. I'm on tonight's ghost watch."

"Holmes, does nothing tire you?" I asked, dazzled by his vigor.

Holmes got up and moved for the door, answering, "Not while such devilry may be afoot." Extinguishing the room's single candle, he left me to my troubled slumber.

Owing perhaps in equal parts to my natural wanderings, the horrific tale I'd offered the princess, the eldritch atmosphere surrounding the palace, and the profane sickness contained within the pages of that evil book, I fell prey to the most elaborate nightmare.

It began with a lone meteorite that came streaking earthward from the outer cosmos—crash-landing in some barren, uninhabited place, displacing tons of sand and gravel for miles about. It was nowhere on earth that I could readily identify; though I shuddered to think what would happen were such a rock to fall upon an inhabited city like our London. As I moved closer, I saw bits of debris crumbling away to reveal the thing's true nature—not a meteor at all, but a cylindrical canister of sorts, some thirty yards in length, composed of a metal I could not distinguish and a color that defied comparison.

I was both rapt and unnerved when the circular top of the cylinder began to rotate and I realized there was life aboard the thing that had fallen from the stars! I floated there, transfixed, dreading what damaged thing might emerge—then willed myself awake to no avail as the first grisly tentacle came slithering from the wreckage. Then, to my horror, it was succeeded by several more flailing appendages—their number difficult to gauge because of their lashing, billowing movements—each terminating in something roughly akin to eyes. Then came a grayish rounded bulk of enormous size, rising slowly and painfully out of the cylinder. The Dark Thing was gruesome and certainly not of this earth.

I was repeatedly startled as dozens more of these cylinders rocketed down in like manner, and soon there was assembled no less than a battalion of the loathsome creatures. As I observed them in their makeshift settlement, I became aware that their alien intelligence and ability far exceeded that of mankind. These Dark Things had language I could not decipher, composed of high-pitched wailing, each utterance giving rise to primal fear within me.

Time flashed by me in terrible increments and I came to realize, quite thankfully, that this vision was not of earth's future, but of its distant past, as I observed the creatures colonizing and taming the primordial wilderness that surrounded them.

Life on Earth had not yet developed past rudimentary multicelled organisms and early vegetations, but the Dark Things utilized techniques I could not fathom to induce and persuade this indigenous life to evolve as they required. From the oceans they raised and fused together great protoplasmic globules, and from the newly risen tree life they incubated pulpy, bulbous bipedal creatures, experimenting upon each by molding their tissues into all sorts of temporary organs.

Bred as slaves, these mindless elementals worked tirelessly by night and were penned like cattle during daylight, wholly mistreated and controlled by some sort of telepathic bond to their masters. The Dark Things used these slaves, engineered with limbs more suitable than their own, capable of hauling and manipulating tremendous weights, to build their city and perform all manner of tasks. It brought to mind the impossible pyramids of the Egyptians, though their scale was paltry when compared to the mammoth spires of the emerging city of Dark Things.

Millennia passed and the slave things began to develop periodic rebellious tendencies, most prominent during specific phases of the stars. The trouble apparently stemmed from the fact that these slaves were now hunting and feeding off several new species of earth life that had begun to evolve unchecked by their masters. They'd acquired a taste for blood and it began to alter them in subtle ways. The bothersome ones were disciplined by the use of an alien alloy, closely resembling silver, that when brought to bear would somehow numb the things back to submission. The dangerous ones were exterminated by various means; those from the sea by sonic dismemberment, and those from the land by curious handheld incendiary devices.

Then some unseen grand disaster rocked and hammered our prehistoric world, so great that it burned away the atmosphere and ripped the very moon into existence. The Dark Things survived, though their great city was plunged many leagues beneath the sea. They were forced to observe helplessly as their entire colonization process came undone beneath the advance of great sheets of ice that spread and shackled the earth.

The sunken, star-born Dark Things sealed themselves into cocoons and fell into deathlike slumber in the lower depths.

Eons passed and slowly the world began to thaw, eventually giving rise to all manner of races and civilizations, while the Dark Things remained trapped beneath the sea. Epochs passed again before mankind finally walked erect upon dry land, and then somewhere—a Dark Thing stirred. For some reason, those primitive Cro-Magnon brains were susceptible to the telepathic communications of the entombed Dark Things, who called to them in their dreams, manifesting most unnatural behaviors that stunted their evolution. Secret rites were transmitted to these early men, of methods lost in ages past; and mankind was divided between those tribes that heeded the call of the Dark Things and those which remained deaf to their influence. I watched, horrified, as this very division introduced the concept of murder to our predecessors.

The Dark Things whispered to their faithful that someday, when the earth had sufficiently warmed, their great city would rise again from the depths, rejoining the coastline from which it broke free, and I was . . .

Thankfully startled awake from the dreadful slumber by Holmes's insistence that we take our breakfast before embarking on the workday he'd mapped out.

I dressed hastily as the nightmare waned, offering little by way of conversation during our meal together; perplexed by my own heightened level of grotesque imagination.

★   ★   ★

By the time I'd finally shed the dream, I found myself being jostled about in a coach, with Captain Gent seated across from me and Holmes to my left. "Where are we off to exactly?" I demanded.

"The public sanatorium in Leiden," Gent said.

"Which one of us is that far gone? It must be me."

"Quite comedic, Wells," Holmes said. "This morning, when I explained to Captain Gent that His Majesty had confided the name Elisabeth Cookson to us as a possible suspect, I found, much to my surprise, that he was already acquainted with her."

"Aye," Gent replied. "I brought her from the palace to the sanatorium myself not six months back. The very route you both are taking now."

"What exactly do you know about this woman?" I asked, playing along with Holmes's ruse.

"Under strict confidence, I tell you that she was a prostitute, involved for a time with young Prince Alexander. After his death she came demanding recompense from His Majesty, spouting all sorts of theatrical nonsense, the last time with a concealed dagger on her person. I assure you, she's quite mad."

"Odd that the king allowed an audience to a prostitute," I remarked.

"Our good king makes himself available to his subjects," Gent responded, defending his sovereign.

"Of course," Holmes said.

The sanatorium gates swung wide on rusted hinges and we entered hurriedly. An attendant accompanied us to Miss Cookson, heaping accolades upon the captain all the while. To describe the barbarism glimpsed from cell to filth-strewn cell in our passing would be an exercise in the repulsive with which I will not burden the reader of this tale.

Elisabeth Cookson was a disheveled woman whose age was indeterminate because of a lack of proper hygiene. Hard to imagine her once capable of eliciting the desire of a nobleman. Her dark hair was cut short, doubtless to minimize lice and other infestations. Barefoot she trod, dressed in a simple gown of burlap, wringing her hands and whispering incessantly. One look at the captain and she began shrieking, the corridors echoing with her cries.

"Captain, do please remove yourself," Holmes requested, and Gent left us alone with her. Immediately, she grew calm and resumed her pacing.

"*Vrouw* Cookson," Holmes entreated in Dutch, which I here shall translate. "Please tell us of your claim upon the royal family. We are here to help set things right."

With alarming speed, she turned and grasped Holmes by his cloak, dragging him close. "The servant of *Het Duivelsche Volk,* of the Dark Things," came her cracked and unsettling growl. "It comes to call. We are owed. We are owed at a terrible price!"

At her mention of the Dark Things, I was taken aback, first considering, then abandoning, the idea that she'd entertained dreams similar to my own.

"Who owes you?" Holmes cooed in a settling voice.

She released him and threw her arms in the air, raving, "They all do, the whole lot! Promises broken and blood let!"

"What promises, Miss Cookson? Whose blood let?"

"Yes, yes—she'll come then. Blood from royal blood."

Holmes took her roughly by the arm and twirled her toward him. "Who is *she*? I demand that you tell me!"

The old courtesan cackled. "Yes, she will be blood."

It was then I took note of the object hanging round the woman's neck, and shouted, "Holmes, the locket!"

Holmes grasped the thin cord and tore it from her throat, sending the madwoman into a swinging rage that forced us to withdraw from the room. The waiting Captain Gent slammed and bolted the door. Her face against the viewing grate, contorted to violent proportions, Cookson cried out, "*Geef het Terug!* Give it back! Give it back!"

Gent slammed the grate with his great fist, yelling, "Stand back or forfeit your life!"

"Outside," Holmes ordered. "This hysteria's contagious; we need to remove ourselves."

We left swiftly, fleeing her taunting scream, "We're promised she's dead!" I was glad of daylight as we reached the sanatorium steps and regained our composure.

"Forgive me my outburst, Mr. Holmes," the captain said.

"Understandable, Captain," Holmes assured him, snapping open the locket and examining the villainess's photograph within. We looked over his shoulders to view the image of a young girl. Although the quality was poor, her resemblance to the royal family was clear.

Gent's ruddy cheeks went white. "That's her," he exclaimed. "*Godverdomme,* she's real!" He stormed back into the building, returning minutes later with the attendant in tow.

"Do you know this girl?" Gent demanded. Holmes brought the photograph up for inspection.

"Yes," the man replied, still on edge from Miss Cookson's outburst. "It's the daughter, Sarah. She visits her mother from time to time, the poor soul."

"And where might we find her?" Holmes asked.

The orderly shrugged his shoulders. "Perhaps the red-light district in Utrecht or Den Haag?"

"The apple falls close to the tree," Gent said. "Come along, we shall find this young villainess!"

We sped back toward The Hague, where, with picture in hand and guldens to follow, we were soon directed to a guest house on red-light row. Gent entered the house with us tight on his heels. We whisked past enraged bruisers, held back by their distraught madame, to the rooms above, where Gent began kicking in doors and accosting each occupant as to the girl's whereabouts. Scantily dressed women and their clients vacated the premises by all possible routes. Minutes later, Gent found her, alone and asleep. He barreled through the room, rousing her roughly.

It was indeed the girl in the photograph; as she rose up, struggling to retrieve her thin wrist from the captain, her resemblance to Princess Mina was unmistakable.

"What have I done, what's the meaning of this?" she cried out, in obvious pain.

"Let her go, Captain," Holmes insisted. "At least till we've made our inquiry."

Gent grunted and released the girl. She rubbed her injured wrist and began to weep. "What have I done?" she repeated.

"Are you Sarah Cookson, daughter to Elisabeth Cookson?" Holmes asked.

"I am, sir," she sobbed, her pale skin luminescent. I found myself taken with her.

"Have you been visiting the Palace Noordeinde?"

"Of course she has," Gent answered for her. "I've seen her there with my own eyes."

"Please, sirs," the girl entreated, looking at us with tearful eyes that beamed, "I assure you I've never stepped foot in Noordeinde. I have no idea what you want of me."

"Liar!" Gent shouted. "You are a whore and a murderer!"

That she was dumbfounded at his assertion was revealed in her breathtaking body, every inch of which trembled. She rose unsteadily from her bed and reached out clumsily to touch my hand. *"Een Moordenaar?"* she whispered. "I assure you, kind sir—though I am shamed by my profession, I—have never hurt a living soul."

In that instant I believed her innocent with every fiber of my being.

"Save your charms, temptress," Gent said, seizing her once more by the wrist and dragging her from the room in her bedclothes, ignoring Holmes's entreaty that he stay his hand. Turning back, he called, "Gentlemen, I trust you'll find your way to Noordeinde. The culprit is apprehended. I'm taking her to the guard-house for questioning. Your service is much appreciated."

We followed them out of the brothel as Gent coerced the girl into the coach and drove off.

As Holmes and I walked the cobblestones, asking directions, it began to rain, and for a time neither of us spoke. I broke the silence with, "Holmes, that girl was of royal descent or I'll lay down my life."

"Agreed, Wells—the resemblance is uncanny."

"And here in this country it seems as if guilt is presumed without trial."

"So it would seem," Holmes agreed. "Though the man's a reputed eyewitness."

"Circumstance and convenience is all—" I stopped then, astonished by the implication of his statement, rain coursing down my face. "Then the case is concluded?" I asked.

Holmes lowered his head. "It would appear so."

"Then an innocent girl is to be imprisoned and subjected to who knows what tortures, as a result of our diligence and your grave misjudgment of Jan Gent's character. Blast it, Holmes, at this moment I'm quite sorry I joined you!"

Holmes said nothing as we packed our bags, save "Thank you" to the servant who attended us, and, "Do come along, Wells," when we were summoned by the queen. So incensed was I at the conclusion to our investigation that I pleaded sudden indisposition and told Holmes to beg the queen's pardon for my absence.

Once Holmes was gone, I cursed the captain and the royal family, sure in my belief that the poor sobbing girl was incapable of infiltrating these halls and perpetrating such crimes. Parting the curtains, I watched the rolling clouds submerge the final daylight in darkness. Surely there was foul intent amidst these walls, and I was powerless against it.

Suddenly a gentle footfall and an odd smell, like woodlands, caught my attention. I turned, and was astounded to behold the girl, Sarah Cookson. Her bare feet left dark tracks on the marble as she stepped before me, gowned in translucent white fabric, her cheeks ruddy, her dark eyes radiating youthful abandon. So excited was I by her presence, unshackled, that I failed to consider the absurdity of the situation. Before I could speak, she pressed one finger to her crimson mouth to gain my silence, then twirled about, displaying her charms. I watched her, transfixed, overcome by desire. Then, in a movement so swift it brought wind through my hair, she was in my arms, her lips against mine.

A kiss unlike any other; sweet at first, then impassioned, then nearly overwhelming, then a taste in my mouth, not unfamiliar, startled me to my senses. It was blood. I looked at the two of us reflected in the mirror—and caught my breath. This was not Sarah Cookson in my arms but a hideous and shocking creature carved in slick, black, whalelike flesh, a face devoid of features save a gaping mouth hole, entangling me now with several writhing coiled limbs.

I hurled the awful thing away and again it was Sarah; her beauty restored, but now tarnished by a most disturbing grimace. She reached for me; I raised my hands in defense. Upon contact with the silver band across my finger she recoiled, shrieking, and fled from the room with netherworldly speed.

I shouted an alarm, then rushed headlong toward Princess Mina's room, my heart pounding with each pace, fearing I might be too late. From down the corridor, I heard Mina issue one terrified and prolonged scream. I arrived in time to find *the* girl caught between a menacing, flaming-candelabra-wielding Holmes and an open window. Holmes forced her backward toward the ledge, where she dove outward and disappeared from view.

Peering down, we saw no evidence of her landing. Princess Mina crouched beneath her bed, apparently unharmed.

★　★　★

An extensive search of the grounds provided no further clues. Holmes sent a messenger to Captain Gent announcing there had been another attack and requesting he meet us back at the sanatorium as quickly as possible. Leaving the princess with her mother under guard, Holmes commandeered a coach and lashed the horses forward as I scrambled aboard, still shaken with disbelief. (To think I had actually *embraced* the bloody thing!) We rode like the devil through the deserted streets. Arriving at our destination, Holmes pushed the night clerk aside and we raced to Miss Cookson's cell.

She chuckled nervously as Holmes slammed the door.

"Your daughter Sarah has been arrested and charged with the attempted murder of the Princess Wilhelmina," Holmes told her. "If you would save her—I'd have you call off that creature this instant!"

Her humor quickly left her. "You must release my daughter; she's no part of this!" she pleaded.

"That's up to you now," Holmes replied, unmoved.

"But—I have no power to halt what's begun!"

"Then instruct us," I said, stepping forward.

"It were the princes, not I, that planted the damned thing. Sarah knew nothing of it, she was but a child," she moaned, quaking.

"Planted? Do explain!" Holmes demanded.

"No, I mustn't! *Het wordt mij verboden!*"

"Forbidden by whom?" At this, Holmes drew forth the locket, unclasped it, and held it forth. "Take this back as a token of my word that you'll be protected. And think now of Sarah above yourself!"

She grasped the locket and gazed upon the photograph, quieting. "When they received word that Mina was born, they were furious. Alexander was schooled in the Pnakotic ways and damned his knees at the altar of Yog-Sothoth, invoking the forbidden rites from the stolen book and setting the thing to grow. He took my Sarah's blood from her against my wish."

"Blood, you say? How much blood was taken?"

"A pint," the crone whispered. "One pint per month for a year from my dear one. Siphoned with the cruelest of tools. She were helpless, sir!"

"To what purpose was this blood put?"

"So the Shoggoth might grow to bear her likeness—this slave of their revenge."

The strange word birthed terror within me, for I knew it to be coupled to the dream.

"How might this Shoggoth be stopped?" Holmes demanded, his voice tripping on the alien word, confirming my dread that it was not of Dutch origin. "Speak now. I hear the captain's coach approaching!"

The woman shriveled up against the stone in the corner as Holmes's broad cloak enveloped her.

"Find the root. Sever the thing at the root, lest it grow back, *God allemachtig!*"

"Where do I find it?"

"Where it was begun," she whispered hoarsely. "The southernmost tip of De Veluwe." At the last she collapsed, blathering. We left her there, staring into the locket, to join Captain Gent.

We took Gent's coach, as it was more fortified, and we three, accompanied by five guardsmen, sped off for the Veluwe, a dense wooded area several hours' journey east. The sheer insanity of all that had transpired nearly overwhelmed me, and I struggled to keep my wits, saying little, but fearing much.

"I trust Sarah Cookson's name will be cleared," Holmes said to Gent, "seeing that this last attack came whilst she was held in your custody."

"The girl will be released, Mr. Holmes, when I'm sure that the princess is safe, not before."

The damp and evil sounds of the night increased tenfold as the road gave way to forest trails. The hooting of several large gray owls announced our passage as if telegraphing danger, and Gent's men began preparing their rifles with ammunition.

"If this is a trick of the old woman, she shall pay dearly," Gent said.

The southernmost tip of the Veluwe was an odd bit of woodland. We stepped from the coach in silence, enthralled by the milky-black stillness. The captain's men used kerosene lamps to light torches, and passed one to me.

"See how the trees grow so densely in that patch," Holmes directed our attention. "Most unnatural."

We approached the cluster of trees and circled its perimeter. "Holmes," I said, clasping his elbow as we moved, "Do you smell that? The same scent as from the palace."

He nodded affirmation as I supressed my urge to run.

Holmes was correct: this was no natural formation of trees. The trunks were gnarled with great tumors, their limbs woven together like incestuous lovers, the flaking bark of the wood cold and slick to the touch, like the skin of a reptile. The thorned branches thrust sharply outward like claws, and the whole growth gave one the impression of many black entities congealed into a single one. Each step I took was laborious, each outthrust root a cause for alarm.

Holmes beckoned me with a wave of his torch to a dark cavity carved in the wood.

"An orifice," he whispered, reaching out to touch the lip of the opening. His hand came back wet. He brought down my torch to inspect the viscous red fluid on his fingers, then called out, "Captain, come at once!"

All torches were brought to bear; we gazed into the hole and beheld the unspeakable.

There, burrowed in the wet wood, entwined with bloodied vines like throbbing veins, *the* girl was nestled. A perfect doppelgänger of Sarah in every detail, save the insidious expression on its carved face as it slumbered.

"God allemachtig!" Gent cried out, visibly shaken.

"The Shoggoth," I whispered with twin dread and awe at the alien word on my lips. "Holmes, touch your ring to the wood."

Holmes touched his left hand to the trunk for a moment. The girl-thing writhed.

"Wells, how do we kill this thing?" Holmes asked, deferring to my sudden display of intuition.

All eyes fell on me as I shivered and surrendered myself to details of my dangerous vision—how the Dark Things would exterminate their land-born slaves. "It's fire," I proclaimed. "Burn the tree and *it* dies along with it!"

"Are you quite sure, Wells?"

"How can I be sure, Holmes? But it's clear that this tree is the nest."

Captain Gent stood guard before the hole as his men retrieved kerosene from the coach whilst Holmes and I dragged up huge mounds of dead needles and dry twigs to ring the base of the tree. Then Holmes pulled his pipe, struck a match, took a draw, and knelt to light the kindling.

We stepped back and watched the tree catch fire and burn as hideous, soul-wrenching screams emanated from the very wood itself—screams that would haunt me the rest of my days.

"We've saved the princess, Holmes," I said.

Holmes nodded and drew at his pipe. "Indeed, Wells, though I fear this particular evil is but one severed tentacle heralding much darker forces to come."

I pulled my cloak tightly about my shoulders as the sun began filtering through the trees.

Holmes was correct: the journey had been inspirational, in a most horrific manner. The girl, Sarah Cookson, was released and provided a modest endowment for her silence. Upon the king's subsequent death, the Princess Wilhelmina did indeed ascend the throne, at age ten, and conduct her country admirably through the

Second World War. I can only assume that Holmes confiscated and destroyed the evil *Necronomicon*, though I have never dared to broach the subject. For when social occasions brought the two of us together, he refused to speak openly of the matter—though I observed that the silver ring, twin to my own, remained always upon him.

The Weeping Masks

JAMES LOWDER

In looking back over the accounts I have written about the singular exploits of Mr. Sherlock Holmes, and remembering all those cases which I never set down upon paper, I recognize only now how foolish I was to deny him the chance to solve the greatest mystery I ever encountered. He would have welcomed the challenge, of course. His keen mind would have pierced the veil of strangeness surrounding those awful events in Afghanistan, and focused upon the true cause of the things I witnessed there. Then, with a glitter in his eyes akin to boyish mischief, he would have explained away the horrors, made them vanish under the intensity of his intellect like so much moor mist before a bright morning sun.

Now that sun has set, its fires doused by the torrent of the Reichenbach Falls, I am left to wonder why I did not allow its light to shine upon the darkness secreted within me while I had the chance. He recognized its presence; it was impossible to hide anything from Holmes completely. I suspect he saw the telltale signs of habitual dread upon me even at our initial meeting. "You have been in Afghanistan, I perceive," he noted after he shook my hand that very first day. He later revealed the details about my manner and appearance that had led him to that conclusion— my medical knowledge, military air, tanned face, and stiff, obviously wounded left arm. But those things might just as well have marked me as an army doctor come from the Sudan or Zululand. No, he observed something else in my haggard face: The stunned stare common to those who serve in Afghanistan. No British soldier leaves that desolate land without it. And my features were all the more blasted for the extraordinary things I had witnessed in that hellish place.

In those early days of my friendship with Holmes, I sometimes hinted at the reason for my disquiet. The prompts were obscure and offered halfheartedly, I must admit. But the awful events were still fresh in my mind, and both my composure and my trust of Holmes too tentative to inspire a more direct disclosure.

The reason why Holmes never pursued the matter still eludes me. Perhaps he did not question me out of courtesy. He could be surprisingly kind at times, especially to me, and he often made it clear that he respected my privacy, beyond what his powers of observation made obvious to him. Or perhaps he never gave the subject a second thought, once he had correctly deduced the origins of my wound and my military bearing. He could be oblivious to such human concerns as fear and despair, too, even when they impacted on his tight circle of friends.

The rest of humanity is not so well armored against the more baneful emotions, and we must deal with them as best we can. Some transmute them into rage and lash out at the world. Others attempt escape. Memories of those Afghan experiences proved so insistent in their companionship, even after my return to England, that I myself took refuge in the bottle. Had Stamford not happened upon me at the Criterion Bar and taken me that same afternoon to meet Holmes—a meeting that resulted in adventures all but guaranteed to reassure me of the supremacy of reason over mystery—I would today be well along the path to gin-fueled dissolution. My only brother followed that same sad road to its inevitable terminus. When I learned of his death, just a year before I shipped out for the East, I could not understand how things could get so bad as to push a sane and well-to-do man to such an end. I pray now that whatever overwhelming unhappiness goaded him to self-destruction was born of more mundane hardships than the ones I faced in Afghanistan.

Maiwand provided me reason enough to take to the bottle. I was but a newly minted soldier when I took my place in the field as assistant surgeon for the Berkshires. I had traveled the East extensively in my younger days, so that I expected the conditions in Afghanistan to be far from inviting. Still, I was unprepared for the long marches across miles of barren ground, with temperatures reaching nearly 120 degrees Fahrenheit in the shade, were any such luxury to be had.

"Let this heat serve as a caution against an intemperate life," noted Murray, my orderly, as we trudged toward our fateful meeting with Ayub Khan's army. "If this weather strikes you as unbearable, imagine what the furnaces of hell are like."

"Can you be so certain we are not there already?" I replied, hoping the scowl in my voice conveyed the expression my lips were too sun-seared to frame.

Murray gave me a look that surely has passed between veteran and green trooper on every battlefield since time began. "Begging your pardon, sir, but you'd be safer to reserve judgment about hell until after your first battle."

"Have no fear for me, Murray. I shall acquit myself with distinction when the shooting starts."

"No doubt, sir, no doubt. But the fighting will be unlike anything the officers described in your training or even the firsthand accounts published in the newspapers back home."

He paused to swipe away a large swarm of sand flies that had gathered around one of the wounded litters close by in the column. It was a seemingly pointless bit of kindness—the flies buzzed everywhere, and hung especially thick among the pack animals and the wounded—but an act typical of Murray. He went nowhere without pausing to do some little bit of good. He was a veteran of some years, but had long ago rejected the hardness of heart that so characterized the medical personnel drawn to the Queen's service. To them, suffering was a fact of camp and campaign to be accepted or, worse still, ignored. Murray regarded all hardship as a test of character. To surrender to callousness or despair in the face of such sorrow was to be revealed as its accomplice.

"There's just no way for anyone to explain what a battle is like," he continued after he had more securely fixed the netting over the unconscious man. "The words don't exist to describe the vastness and weight of even the smallest skirmish—not ones that can do it justice. You'll find that out for yourself, if you're ever called upon to describe one."

As he was with so many things, Murray was correct about this. When I attempt to relate the events of that fateful day, the resulting narrative either scuffs along with the parched precision of our column on the way to the fight that morning, or swirls out of control, like the retreat of the survivors from the field a scant four hours later. Only fragments can be made clear—the awful shriek of the cavalry horses when a shell landed in their midst; the unearthly sight of a lone Afghan woman, veiled and ghostlike, moving among the massed enemy, exhorting the warriors to vengeance and glory; the palpable feeling of hatred that enwrapped the battlefield as each side did its utmost to annihilate the other.

Positioned as we were on the right flank, the Berkshires confronted the enemy in the form of Ghazis. Thousands of these religious zealots had joined with Ayub Khan in hopes of driving the hated British from the land or, failing that, hastening their own trip to the afterlife. To this end, they came to the fighting ready-clad in shrouds. Some even charged at us unarmed, so eager were these madmen to gain whatever eternal reward their mullahs had promised them. I still see them in my nightmares: fearsome white-wrapped figures emerging from the dry riverbed that ran alongside our position. Brilliant bit of strategy that, using the ditches to hide an advance. Their abrupt appearance had added impact in that it resembled nothing so much as shrouded corpses scrabbling up from some mass grave.

We did our best to put the Ghazis back in that hole as actual corpses. A blizzard of Martini-Henry rounds mowed them down by the score. For two hours we stood our ground, and might have held out all day had the British left flank not been overrun. The retreating infantry and artillery rolled into us like a wave, and we broke, too.

How I got cut off from the Sixty-sixth I cannot recall, at least not clearly. One moment I stood next to Murray; the next I found myself alone and surrounded by a small mob of zealots. The earlier fighting was orderly, well mannered even, when compared to the chaos that descended after the lines broke. It was no longer army against army, but man against man, a thousand savage brawls occurring within a stone's throw of one another, but isolated by a choking soup of smoke and dust. Shrieks of victory commingled with the cries of the wounded, the thunder of onrushing Afghans with the clatter of the British retreat, until a single sound— a deafening, skull-shaking din—overhung all. Little wonder, then, that neither I nor my would-be murderers discerned the crash of the oncoming artillery limber until it was almost upon us. The galloping horses appeared as if from nowhere, scattering ally and enemy alike. Crazed Ghazis hung from the wagon in a dozen places, while the driver and a gunner, armed only with handspikes and Khyber knives, hacked madly at their hands and arms, anything to loosen their hold and keep them from the gun.

The passing of the limber broke up the mob. I escaped, only to find myself a moment later at the edge of the dry watercourse the enemy had used to such good effect. The haze was not so thick here, though that was nothing to be cheered. Bodies lay two and three deep at the bottom of the steep-sided ravine, men and animals together, as far as the eye could trace the rift. Here were the Ghazis we had cut down, and the British who had been slaughtered as they abandoned the field. Most were still. A few raised trembling hands to the sky or tried in vain to free themselves from the bloody tangle. A camel with shattered forelimbs thrashed about, moaning like a damned soul—which was appropriate, as the scene resembled nothing so much as an illustration of Dante.

I stood on the brink of the ravine, frozen by fear or mesmerized by the horrific scene before me—I cannot now say which—until a figure on the opposite bank drew my attention. Dazedly I noted that he wore an obsolete British uniform, the familiar red cloth tunic and dark blue trousers of our soldiers in the first Afghan war. But atop his head rested a turban, and the twin rifles slung across his shoulder were not Enfields or Sniders, but *jezails*. My own rifle was gone, fumbled and dropped in my scramble away from the runaway artillery wagon. I reached for my service revolver. Before my fingers even touched the holster, the Afghan soldier raised one of his long-barreled flintlocks and fired.

The bullet bit into my left shoulder, spun me around so that I fell into the ravine backward. Chest aflame with pain, I slid down the embankment and came to rest atop the corpse river. The mass of bodies shifted slightly at my arrival. Cradled there among the dead and near dead, I felt the hot, wet mark of my wound spread. Feebly I tried to stanch the flow, all the while staring up at the red-coated assassin. Calmly he dropped his first rifle and raised the second. The *jezail* takes so long to reload that experienced Afghan warriors carry more than one, ready to fire, for just such eventualities.

But the fatal shot never came. The soldier suddenly threw his arms out. His mouth framed a startled gasp that never escaped his throat, and then he toppled, already lifeless, into the ravine. Standing in his place atop the embankment was Murray, a bloody Khyber knife in his hand. I gestured to him, called out weakly, anything to let him know I still lived. To my horror, he hurtled forward and tumbled down as if he, too, had been stabbed in the back. But it was haste that drove him on, not steel, and he quickly made his way to my side.

"Don't try to move," he said, taking in my condition at a glance. "Keep your hand in place on the wound. Stay still."

Without another word, he lay down beside me, the Khyber knife clutched to his chest, then pulled the corpse of a Ghazi so that it rested atop us both. "Only until the stragglers pass," he said, by way of an explanation.

I soon understood the meaning of that cryptic comment. From the din on the plain, it sounded as if the fighting had moved to the southwest. The Afghans were hard on the heels of our troops, even as they fell back upon the little villages of Mundabad and Khig to make their final stand. This left us rather far behind the enemy line.

From time to time a scavenging tribesman picked his way across the corpse river. The body of the Afghan atop us shielded us from the blows these savages sometimes dealt the British dead they encountered. So long as we remained still, the stragglers passed us by. Eventually we could hear shouting up on the plain, and then that, too, receded, until it became quiet enough for me to hear the steady buzzing of the sand flies over the distant clash of arms.

"Someone's put them to collecting their dead farther up the riverbed," Murray whispered. "Organizing them for burial."

He shrugged off our fleshy shield and placed strong hands on me. "This will hurt, I'm afraid, but we'd best move. I'll find some-place for us to hide. We'll keep to the riverbed, head northeast—"

"Away from the regiment?" I asked weakly.

"It's our only chance, sir," he said as he did his best to secure a bandage in place over my shattered shoulder. Then he heaved me onto his back, adding, "I suspect that there's little enough left of the Sixty-sixth for us to rejoin anyway."

I recall only parts of our journey along the ravine. By then I was delirious from the pain and loss of blood. The hours passed as a series of half-understood incidents, dream melding with reality. The dead seemed to reach for us. Gray hands snatched at Murray's boots until they tripped him, and we both fell onto the corpse river. Later, a shrouded figure rose up from the rest. Gore stained his clothes so completely that they might as well have been dyed crimson. His face, too, was smeared with it. And as I watched, that face contorted, mouth stretching impossibly wide to loose a shriek of alarm. Murray let me fall and, drawing his Khyber knife, buried the blade in the man's throat. But that did not silence the cry, at least to my addled brain. The wound on his neck opened and, like a second mouth, added to the alarm. Even after the Afghan collapsed, his cry continued—only now from the lips of my orderly.

At last Murray let that wailing end. "I've countermanded that fellow's alarm," he said as he approached me. I shrank back, and received in return a kind, weary smile. "It helps to know a little of the enemy's tongue, sir, but that doesn't make me one of them."

My head cleared enough then for me to recognize my friend. "Of course not," I said. "Sorry. I thought I saw—thought that you—"

"No need to explain," Murray interrupted. "The mind plays tricks under these circumstances." Before he lifted me again, he removed a thin chain from his pocket and wrapped it around my right hand. In my palm rested the silver disk of a Saint Christopher medal. "If it's not imposing, perhaps you might find this of help . . ."

" 'Marvel thou nothing, for thou hast borne all the world upon thee,' " I quoted, hearing the voice of my father as he told the story of the saint carrying the child Jesus safely across the brook. I closed my eyes and tried to hold on to that memory, long forgotten until that moment. I must have passed out then, for the next thing I knew a trio of Afghan villagers was hauling me into a barren orchard, the parched trees looking dead and withered. I struggled for a moment, until Murray laid a calming hand on me.

"Where—?" I croaked

"Safe," he said. "I left the watercourse when it reached the foothills, and came across these fellows searching for some goats that had wandered off. Their headman fought on our side in the last war."

"You help our sick," one of the tribesmen interrupted in heavily accented, but comprehensible English. "No more weep."

Murray nodded and said something in Persian. Then he turned to me and explained: "When we first met up, I managed to get them to understand we're medical staff. They'll hide us from Ayub Khan's followers, if we help them with some sickness that's got their families by the throat. I can't quite understand what he means by 'weep,' though. Tears for the dead, perhaps. Or running sores. It's a symptom common to a half-dozen native maladies."

I marveled at the equanimity my friend displayed in discussing this unpleasantness, even as I wondered at his strength and stamina. He had carried me for miles in that unbearable heat, yet walked beside me then as if it were still the calm hours before the battle. His military experience, or his faith, or a combination of the two had so well prepared him that no trial seemed beyond his capabilities. I would learn how wrong I was about that later, but at that moment, as we made our way to the largest of the grim, mud-walled houses in that Afghan village, I believed Murray a match for anything we might encounter.

A wizened old man met us at the door. He was clad in typical native dress, save for his ancient Western-style boots, which looked as if they had not left his feet since they were issued to him during the last war. At his side was a small boy, who snapped Murray a salute. The elder slapped the boy's arm down and growled something in Persian.

"You are right to correct him," Murray said. "We come as guests, not conquerors."

The old man eyed Murray, as if he could discern the sincerity of a stranger by look alone. Finally he nodded. "As guests be welcome, then."

He directed the villagers to carry me to a communal sickroom at the back of the house. The long, low-ceilinged room stank of disease and despair. Two men occupied mats on the floor. Despite the stifling heat, they were wrapped in blankets. Places for three more lay ready for the newly afflicted or abandoned by the recently dead. It was hard to tell which.

They placed me at the opposite end of the room from the door and, at the prompting of the old man, hung a ragged, gauzy sheet to separate me from the others. Murray immediately stripped away the makeshift bandage from my shoulder. *Jezail* bullets are often composed of bent nails, bits of silver, and any other metal scrap to hand, so that the wounds they create fester quickly. Such was the case with my shoulder. Though the bullet had passed right through my collarbone and out my back, infection had already set in.

Murray had managed somehow to hold on to his field medical kit, and he attended to the wound and the infection as best he could. "You're going to have to carry on the fight from here, sir," he said after he had finished his work.

I nodded and let him guide a cup to my lips. After a swallow of tepid water, I opened my right hand. The Saint Christopher medal shone dimly in the light of the candle by my sleeping mat, for night had come while Murray bled away what he could of the infection and closed as much of the gash as he dared. "You can carry me no farther," I whispered. "Take it, in case you need someone to shoulder your burdens awhile."

He took the chain from my hand. "If you want it back, just say the word. In the meantime, try to get some rest." After one final check on the new bandage, Murray carefully lifted the candle and pushed through the curtain.

Several times that night I awoke to find my friend close by, either at my side or tending to the others in the room. Even when he was kneeling by the natives, his shadow on the curtain seemed to be ministering to me, a hunched and wavering form that hovered like some guardian angel. His voice filled the dead hours of the night as he offered gentle words to quiet the ranting of the sick men. I heard the old Afghan in the gray time before dawn, too. He spoke with Murray about the nature of the disease that had swept through the village, all the time using English. He hoped, no doubt, to keep the gravity of the situation from his people.

My fever rallied with the sun, and by noon I became as incoherent as the shivering natives. As with our trek from the corpse river, the days and nights that followed reside in my memory as fragments only: Murray as shadowy protector; the awful heat that washed over me, wave upon wave; the moans and shrieks of the sick Afghans. The latter remain especially vivid, as the incessant chattering of their teeth gave their cries an inhuman, almost insect-like quality.

It was that eerie sound which woke me on the night I first saw the masked priests.

I came awake slowly, but soon realized that my fever had broken. The throbbing ache in my shoulder had lessened, and I could actually feel the chill of the evening air on my sweat-soaked skin. The respite from the fever heat was most welcome, but any relief I felt turned to panic after I thought to call out to Murray and found myself unable to speak or move. I could only stare at the curtain, now a sickly yellow green from some strange light on the other side, and at the tall, unfamiliar shadow that loomed, dark as a mine pit, at its center.

The figure was certainly not Murray. It was taller and thinner, with a vague outline that suggested robes, not a British uniform. Where my friend had knelt close to the sick men, this visitor stood with a straight back, aloof and disdainful. Where Murray had answered their cries with kind words, the stranger remained silent as he stood near first one bawling invalid, then the other. Over each he leaned forward slightly and bowed his head, as if in prayer, all the while keeping his arms rigid at his side.

Finally the shadow on the curtain grew larger, and I knew that the silent visitor was coming for me. Again I tried to call out. Again my shout died, stillborn, in my throat. The shadow now filled the curtain. A hand gloved in bleached leather drew back the ragged cloth, revealing a tall, solemn figure dressed in white robes and a turban. I assumed him to be male from his build, for his dress concealed his gender utterly, just as a porcelain mask hid his features. The mask was plain, the nose and mouth suggested by curves, not revealed by details. A small arcane symbol, yellow against the winter white of the porcelain, lay upon each cheek. Of human features, only his eyes were visible.

Those dark orbs seemed lifeless at first, as if they, too, were part of the mask. The illusion fell away when the silent stranger tilted his head. Only then did I see the tears. So copious were they that the liquid welled up at the bottom of each eyehole until it was ready to spill over the rim. Then, as he had done with the two natives, the masked priest leaned forward. I braced inwardly for those tears to fall on me. Somehow I knew even then to dread their touch.

"Get away from him!"

Murray followed this shout with words in Persian. The first command had been enough to startle the priest, though. The silent figure straightened and turned away, so that his tears spattered the yellow sigils upon his mask and not me. I found myself able to move, too. A long-suppressed cry of horror escaped my lips as I sat up and pushed the curtain aside.

A second masked priest stood near the door. He held an oddly shaped lantern, the source of the weird yellow-green light that suffused the room. Murray strode past him, toward the priest who had loomed over me. He got halfway to his goal when he noticed that the two natives had fallen silent. The men lay still upon their mats, staring up at the ceiling, eyes fixed upon something we could not see.

Murray pointed to the sick men, then asked the priest a question. The masked figure remained silent, but an answer came nonetheless: "What have they done? They've prayed for these men to be cured by sunset tomorrow or released from their suffering," growled the village elder, now standing framed by the doorway. "I welcomed you as guests, even tolerated your failure to help our sons. But I will not allow you to insult these holy men."

Murray apologized, but the priests did not respond. Still silent, they crossed to the door. There, each took one of the old man's hands in his own, then bowed over it. Though he tried, the elder could not hide his discomfort. Again, the priests appeared not to notice. They passed from the sickroom, the old man trailing in their wake, surreptitiously wiping his hands on his cotton trousers.

"The villagers fear the priests," Murray noted as he cleaned my wound and set a new bandage. " 'The Weeping Ones,' they're called. The natives think of them as harbingers of bad luck. But their own mullah was one of the first carried off by the plague, so—"

"Plague? Is it that serious?"

"It's claimed at least three nearby villages in the past year or so."

I glanced in the direction of the two natives. Murray had thrown the curtain back; we could see the two men shivering under their heavy blankets and staring up at the ceiling. "What of them?"

Murray rubbed his eyes, red-rimmed from lack of sleep. "Dead before morning," he said. "At least, that's been the pattern every other time the priests have come. I would suspect them of poisoning the poor fellows, but their presence alone seems sufficient to frighten them over the brink." He settled me back on my sleeping mat. "We'll need to move on tomorrow, sir. You should get as much rest as you can tonight."

"And you?"

"No rest for me." That familiar, kind smile flashed across his face. "If those poor souls are going to die, they should pass their last hours without pests hovering about."

"Those priests aren't sand flies," I said. "You can't just brush them away. Besides, there's something uncanny about them. Something . . . unnatural."

The dismissive laugh that comment elicited from Murray, gentle though it was, alarmed me. I could not put into words the specific cause of my unease, but I knew better than to deny so cavalierly what I had just witnessed. Yet Murray would not admit even the genuine weirdness of the priests. He cast them as unsavory mystics or dubious fakirs, as common in the East as fleas on a camel. He could not imagine the Weeping Ones as anything more sinister. His view of the world simply did not admit such possibilities. While I took some comfort from his certainty, I drifted off to sleep that night troubled by more than my wound or our immediate plight.

The sun was well up in the sky when I awoke the next day. Murray was gone, and in his place a pair of women tended to the natives. The two men lay uncovered, still staring heavenward. Dead, I realized. The women sobbed quietly beneath their veils, while outside, the more traditional keening for the departed could be heard in the distance. The smell of rosewater permeated the room.

I wanted to help them, but knew so little of their rituals that I feared offending them. The villagers were already angry with us for failing to save the young men. So I simply watched as the women first bathed the dead men, then, with heavily scented water, anointed the welts and oozing sores that covered the bodies. What I had taken for sobbing was, in fact, a prayer for the dead. They repeated the words over and over as first they cleansed the corpses, then dressed them from head to foot in new white clothes.

No sooner had they finished dressing the second figure than one of the masked priests entered. The village elder followed a few paces behind, the distance not born of respect, but exhaustion. As the priest signaled for the women to depart, the old man slouched against the wall. He shivered, despite the heavy winter clothes he wore. Now and then, the sudden chattering of his teeth interrupted his recitation of the simple prayer for the dead. I knew then that he would soon be confined to the sickroom himself, awaiting with dread the final visit of the Weeping Ones.

A full dozen more of the masked priests came in to retrieve the bodies. They hoisted the corpses onto litters and carried them from the room with the same cold efficiency displayed by the priest visiting the sick men the night before. For all their silent tears, they did not act like sorrowful men. If the weight of those deaths pressed heavy upon their hearts, it did not show in their bearing. They were interchangeable in appearance save for the yellow symbols upon the mask of their leader and the silver chain he now wore wrapped around his wrist. I thought nothing of that detail then, though its significance came clear to me soon after the Weeping Ones departed with the dead and someone finally answered my calls for Murray.

"The other soldier left?" I repeated, incredulous. The elder was even then being made comfortable in one of the sickroom beds, his thin form so racked with shivering that he could not speak to me. That left the villager who, in his broken English, had asked Murray that first day to stop the weeping. The meaning of that phrase was chillingly clear to me now.

"He go last night," the young man said. "Not come back."

I could not imagine Murray deserting me. Neither would he leave without some explanation. I remembered his comments about keeping the pests from bothering the dying men. Had he gone to the Weeping Ones to convince them to stay away? It seemed a foolhardy thing to do, but on reflection, so did carrying a wounded and possibly dying comrade along the corpse river after Maiwand.

It was at that moment I recalled the silver chain. It had not been there the previous night, and seemed out of place on the priest's person. Even so, it looked familiar.

The Saint Christopher medal. If Murray had left to confront the Weeping Ones, he would have taken it with him . . .

The natives looked on in puzzled amusement when I pushed myself out of bed and struggled into my clothes. It proved a difficult task, my left arm still all but useless to me. But I managed somehow to dress, rig a sling, and check to see that my service revolver was fully loaded. If the priests held Murray hostage, I would free him. If they had murdered him, I would recover his body for Christian burial. I never bothered to consider how either task might be accomplished by one man with an Adams .450 and a wound that threatened to reopen at any moment. After all that Murray had done, the obligation was upon me to do for him anything, everything that I could.

The only directions I could extract from the young man were rudimentary. He pointed down a path that led toward the mountains, and said only "cave" and "golden sign." I secured a torch, which I carried as a cudgel during my long walk, and hoped to catch up with the Weeping Ones on the road.

Despite the burdens in their care, the priests managed to stay so far ahead of me that I never caught them. Fortunately, the road proved easy to follow. Even the weather cooperated, with a thick, steel-gray blanket of clouds covering the sky from horizon to horizon. The heat remained oppressive, of course, but without the lash of the sun, it was almost bearable.

Full dark was upon the world when I found the entrance to the cave. I knew it to be the correct one by the yellow sigil engraved in the stone to either side. I lingered at the mouth, staring into the maw and squinting at the gloom within. Oddly, the darkness of the cavern was less absolute than that of the land beneath the moonless, cloud-choked night sky. Far into the mountain, at the limits of my vision, a faint luminescence lit the interior. This was not the wavering light of torches, but a steady glow. Still, I set fire to my torch before venturing inside, and felt the more secure for doing so.

The source of the light proved to be a dripping, noisome mold, which grew in patches at irregular intervals all along the course of the cavern. The yellow-green glow it produced was identical to that of the strange lanterns the Weeping Ones carried. Despite the eerie natural lighting, I was still glad for my torch. In many places the mold light shone only weakly. In others, where the priests had harvested the slime, darkness reigned.

The tunnel twisted and turned, but never forked, as if it had been excavated for the sole purpose of leading men to the huge central chamber into which 'it emptied. I soon found myself on the brink of that vast room, at the top of a broad stair that descended to a floor patterned with shattered and gouged mosaics. Towering walls hemmed in the chamber on all sides, with the stone made to resemble the facades of some ancient city. These carvings might have been beautiful once, but now mold obscured their magnificence. For three stories or more the walls stretched up, to where my eye should have met a ceiling or a dome, but instead found the night sky.

Far below this expanse of star-dotted emptiness, at the very center of the chamber, a group of altars squatted on the floor like mushrooms. Twoscore or more of the Weeping Ones stood amongst the altar stones, their attention focused on their leader and the two corpses that had been carried from the village that afternoon. The dead men were laid out on their backs so that their scabrous faces stared up into the night. And as I watched, the head priest rested a porcelain mask upon each of those disease-ravaged faces and began to chant.

Voices unused to speech took up the prayer, until they filled the chamber with a horrible wailing, like the cries of drowned men at the bottom of a lake. I dropped my torch and covered my ears in hopes of blocking out the sound. But the prayer of the Weeping Ones rang clear, scoring itself upon my memory as indelibly as the sight of those two dead villagers even then rising up and adding their voices to the chorus.

"They were never dead," I whispered, my mind struggling to maintain its hold on sanity. "Only catatonic, or mesmerized . . ."

I did not have time to decide which, for at that instant a gloved hand closed over my right shoulder and pushed me, face first, into the wall. The grip was firm, yet somehow also disgustingly soft, as if the flesh yielded too much when I pushed back against it. I tore myself free and turned on my attacker. The masked priest leaned close, tears brimming in his eyes.

I lashed out with a fist, possibly the worst thing I could have done at that moment. The sudden exertion ripped open my wound, while the blow tore the porcelain mask from the face of the priest. The mask did not fall, though. It hung at his chest, suspended on clear, ropy strands that secured it to the remains of what had once been a human face.

Staggering back, I managed somehow to draw my revolver and fire three times. The bullets bit into his body. Clear stains spread out from each impact, but the bullets, though well placed for such hasty shooting, seemed to do him no serious harm. It was as if his entire form were gelatinous beneath those robes.

My own wound had driven me to the ground, and in the fall, I lost my revolver. I slid my back to the wall, tried to push myself to my feet, but it was useless. I could only watch in horror as the priest pressed his mask back into place with a wet sound, then advanced upon me with that unhurried, mechanical gait.

He stood over me, tilting his head so that the ooze of his decaying face welled up under his eyes like tears. I knew then how the plague was spread from village to village, knew, too, that I would not let him infect me. I felt the ground around me for anything I might employ as a weapon. My fingers closed upon the abandoned torch.

The blow I struck was feeble, hardly enough to make him

stagger a step. But the dying torch did the work neither my arm nor my revolver could complete. The flame leaped up the white robes and engulfed the priest as if his decaying flesh were oil. He screamed only once with that terrible, liquid voice of a drowned man, then collapsed into a still-burning heap.

My victory was short-lived. From within the temple came the sounds of movement, the slow, steady approach of the fifty or more Weeping Ones gathered there. I thought to escape back down the tunnel. Even if my wound had not prevented me from putting that desperate plan into action, the commotion that echoed along the stony corridor dashed any hopes I had of retreat. They had caught me. I wiped my blood-slicked fingers on my jacket and re-trieved my revolver, ready to fight to the end.

It is fortunate I lacked the strength to pull the trigger when the first figures rushed toward me from the tunnel. It was not more priests that were arriving from the direction of the cave entrance, but a small band of Ghurkas led by my orderly, my friend, Murray.

The Ghurkas carried torches of their own, and even an oil lantern or two. Once they knew what to do, the lads made short work of the priests. As Murray field-dressed my shoulder, we saw the smoke from their burning bodies rise up through the open roof of the chamber into the starry night sky. After that, we left the cave in silence.

Murray later explained that he had indeed gone off from the village, but only after hearing one of the goatherds tell of spotting a small British expeditionary force the previous day. Given the mood of the natives and the trouble with the masked priests, Mur-ray knew we had to depart as soon as possible. He could not pass up a chance to secure some assistance for us, uncertain as he was of my ability to make the long trek back to Kandahar on my own. The village elder would have been able to explain where Murray had gone, had the old man not been struck down by the plague.

And the silver medal that prompted my foolhardy assault on

the temple of the Weeping Ones? Murray had left it with one of the sick men before he went to search out patrol. The priest must have taken it from the unfortunate fellow before his corpse was prepared for burial.

The simplest explanation for the medal ending up in the hands of the priest eluded me; that is hardly a surprise. Even now, after all my lessons in deductive reasoning from the one true master of that science, I cannot claim with any confidence that, given the same evidence, I would not reach the same wrong conclusion, or perhaps a different, but equally faulty one. Still, I trust in logic. With it I can explain away the masked priests as victims of some rare form of leprosy, as damaging to the mind as it is to the body. The rites I saw enacted did not raise the dead, merely roused the sick men from a catatonic state, one rather similar to the sleep paralysis I myself suffered the night I first saw the priests. These are explanations of which Holmes would have approved. And if I cannot imagine how he would have explicated what I saw through the roof of the temple chamber, it is because I lack his talent for deduction.

I wonder now more than ever how he would have explained it: a roof opening onto a clear night sky when clouds were all anyone could observe outside the cave. The scene might have been painted on the rock, and yet I witnessed the smoke from the burning priests curl up and out of the chamber, not gather at the roof as it surely must do were the sky mere decoration. Or perhaps the cloudless vista seen by the visitors to that chamber resulted from some freak weather condition, like the eye of a hurricane, only lacking the storm. I can almost bring myself to believe those explanations. What I cannot describe away is the thing that I saw move against that starry sky: a mammoth . . . *being,* all boneless limbs and writhing darkness, with a face more horrible than the decaying visages of its priests. Even as the last of the Weeping Ones fell, I lay on the cold stone floor at the entrance to the chamber, staring up at the sky much like the initiates did from their position on the altars. I watched the thing blot out Aldebaran and, turning, the constellation of Taurus. And in that same instant, I knew that it was looking back at me.

"The unspeakable one," the priests called him. "He Who Is Not to Be Named." At least that is how the scholars at the British Museum translated the parts of the prayer I could pronounce. Again, Murray was correct: it helps to know a little of the enemy's tongue. But a little is enough. Although I remember the entire incantation, I have no desire to make my mouth pliable enough to form the other blasphemous words, even if it will help those scholars to recover a language that was old when the Pharaohs ruled Egypt.

What name would Holmes have given the beast? I will never know now, and I suspect that is for the best. I had opportunities enough to tell him about the thing in the night sky, to make him understand that it was not my experiences at Maiwand or the enteric fever I contracted in hospital at Peshawur, after my escape from the Weeping Ones, that forced me to be shipped back to England. So why did I hesitate?

The answer to that is simple enough, even for my flawed powers of deduction: *Elementary, my dear self. You do not wish to end up like Murray.*

He might have pulled through if he had not asked me to confirm what he, too, saw that night. So long as he could tell himself that it was a delusion, like the screaming wound I saw on the Ghazi he killed during our escape from the battlefield, he could bear the burden. He could dismiss it, then, or ignore it, and keep his too-rigid view of the world intact. The moment I confirmed his fears, though, he was undone. And when the Catholic priest at Peshawur could not frame that impossible experience within the tenets of the Church, Murray walked to the most isolated part of the hospital, so as to disturb as few people as possible, and shot himself through the heart.

Yes, that is why I never shared this tale with Mr. Sherlock

Holmes. After I described the awful events, he might have leaned back in his chair, steepled his fingers, and solved the mystery. Or perhaps there are things logic cannot conquer. Holmes knows the truth or falsity of that, now that he has taken that fateful plunge at the Reichenbach Falls. Reason tells me that the very fact of his death provides my answer: The thing in the Afghan caves remains, while Holmes is gone, all hope with him. Then again, I could be coming to the wrong conclusion. I have been known to be wrong before. In this case, I am counting on it.

Art in the Blood

BRIAN STABLEFORD

"Art in the blood is liable to take the strangest forms."
—A. CONAN DOYLE, "THE ADVENTURE OF
THE GREEK INTERPRETER"

It was not yet five o'clock; Mycroft had barely sunk into his nook and taken up the *Morning Post* when the secretary appeared at the door of the reading room and gestured brusquely with his right hand. It was a summons to the Strangers' Room, supplemented by a particular curl of the little finger which told him that this was no casual visitation but a matter in which the Diogenes Club had an interest of its own.

Mycroft sighed and hauled his overabundant flesh out of his armchair. The rules of the club forbade him to ask the secretary what the import of the summons was, so he was mildly surprised to see his brother Sherlock waiting by the window in the Strangers' Room, looking out over Pall Mall. Sherlock had brought him petty puzzles to solve on several occasions, but never yet a matter of significance to any of the club's hidden agendas. It was obvious from the rigidity of Sherlock's stance that this was no trivial matter, and that it had gone badly thus far.

There was another man in the room, already seated. He seemed tired; his gray eyes—which were not dissimilar in hue to those of the Holmes brothers—were restless and haunted, but he was making every effort to maintain his composure. He was obviously a merchant seaman, perhaps a second mate. The unevenness of the faded tan that still marked his face—the lower part of which had long been protected by a beard—testified that he had returned to England from the tropics less than a month ago. The odors clinging to his clothing revealed that he had recently visited Limehouse, where he had partaken of a generous pipe of opium. The bulge in his left-hand coat pocket was suggestive of a medicine bottle, but Mycroft was too scrupulous a man to leap to the conclusion that it must be laudanum. Mycroft judged that the seaman's attitude was one of reluctant resignation, that of a man determined to conserve his dignity even though he had lost hope.

Mycroft greeted his brother with an appropriate appearance of warmth, and waited for an introduction.

"May I present John Chevaucheux, Mycroft," Sherlock said, immediately abandoning his position by the window. "He was referred to me by Dr. Watson, who saw that his predicament was too desperate to be salvageable by medical treatment."

"I'm pleased to meet you, sir," the sailor said, coming briefly to his feet before sinking back into his chair. The stranger's hand was cold, but its grip was firm.

"Dr. Watson is not here," Mycroft observed. It was not his habit to state the obvious, but the doctor's absence seemed to require explanation; Watson clung to Sherlock like a shadow nowadays, avid to leech yet another marketable tale from his reckless dabbling in the mercurial affairs of distressed individuals.

"The good doctor had a prior engagement," Sherlock reported. His tone was neutral, but Mycroft deduced that Sherlock had taken advantage of his friend's enforced absence to carry this particular inquiry to its end. Apparently, this was one "adventure" Sherlock did not want to read in *The Strand*, no matter how much admiring literary embellishment might be added to it.

Given that Chevaucheux's accent identified him as a Dorset man, and that his name suggested descent from Huguenot refugees, Mycroft thought it more likely that the seaman's employers were based in Southampton than in London. If the man had come to consult Watson as a medical practitioner rather than as Sherlock's accomplice, he must have encountered him some time ago, probably in India—and must have known him well enough to be able to track him down in London despite the doctor's retirement. These inferences, though far less than certain, became more probable in combination with the ominous news—which *was* ominous news, although it had not been reported in the *Post*—of the sudden death, some seven days ago, of Captain Pye of the S.S. *Goshen*. The *Goshen* had dropped anchor in Southampton Water on the twelfth of June, having set out from Batavia six weeks before. Captain Pye was by no means clubbable, but he was known to more than one member of the Diogenes as a trustworthy agent.

"Do you know how Dan Pye died, Mr. Chevaucheux?" Mycroft asked, cutting right to the heart of the matter. Unlike Sherlock, he did not like to delay matters with unnecessary chitchat.

"He was cursed to death, sir," Chevaucheux told him bluntly. He had obviously been keeping company with Sherlock long enough to expect that Holmesian processes of deduction would sometimes run ahead of his own.

"Cursed, you say?" Mycroft raised an eyebrow, though not in jest. "Some misadventure in the Andamans, perhaps?" If Pye had been about the club's business—although he would not necessarily have known whose business he was about—the Andamans were the most likely spot for him to run into trouble.

"No, sir," Chevaucheux said gravely. "He was cursed to death right here in the British Isles, though the mad hatred that activated the curse was seething for weeks at sea."

"If you know the man responsible," Mycroft said amiably, "where's the mystery? Why did Watson refer you to my brother?" The real puzzle, of course, was why Sherlock had brought the seaman here, having failed to render any effective assistance—but Mycroft was wary of spelling that out. This could be no common matter of finding proofs to satisfy a court of law; the secretary's little finger had told him that. This mystery went beyond mere matters of motive and mechanism; it touched on matters of blood.

Sherlock had reached into his pocket while Mycroft was speaking, and produced a small object the size of a snuffbox. His expression, as he held it out to Mycroft, was a study in grimness and frustration. Mycroft took it from him, and inspected it carefully.

It was a figurine carved in stone: an imaginary figure, part human—if only approximately—and part fish. It was not a mermaid such as a lonely sailor might whittle from tropic wood or walrus ivory, however; although the head was vaguely humanoid, the torso was most certainly not, and the piscine body bore embellishments that seemed more akin to tentacles than fins. There was something of the lamprey about it—even about the mouth, which might have been mistaken for human—and something of the uncanny. Mycroft felt no revelatory thrill as he handled it, but he knew that the mere sight of it was enough to feed an atavistic dream. Opium was not the best medicine for the kind of headaches that Chevaucheux must have suffered of late, but neither he nor Watson was in a position to know that.

"Let me have your lens, Sherlock," Mycroft said.

Sherlock passed him the magnifying glass, without bothering to point out that the lamplight in the Strangers' Room was poor, or that the workmanship of the sculpture was so delicate that a fine-pointed needle and the services of a light microscope would be required to investigate the record of its narrow grooves. Mycroft knew that Sherlock would take some meager delight in amplifying whatever conclusions he could reach with the aid of the woefully inadequate means to hand.

Two minutes' silence elapsed while Mycroft completed his superficial examination. "Purbeck stone," he said. "Much more friable than Portland stone—easy enough to work with simple tools, but liable to crumble if force is misapplied. Easily eroded, too, but if this piece is as old as it seems, it's been protected from everyday wear. It could have been locked away in some cabinet of curiosities, but it's more likely to have been buried. You've doubtless examined the scars left by the knives that carved it and the dirt accumulated in the finer grooves. Iron or bronze? Sand, silt, or soil?" He set the object down on a side table as he framed these questions, but positioned it carefully, to signify that he was not done with it yet.

"A bronze knife," Sherlock told him, without undue procrastination, "but a clever alloy, no earlier than the sixteenth century. The soil is from a fallow field, from which hay had been cut with considerable regularity—but there was salt, too. The burial place was near enough to the sea to catch spray in stormy weather."

"And the representation?" Mycroft took a certain shameful delight in the expression of irritation that flitted across Sherlock's finely chiseled features: the frustration of ignorance.

"I took it to the museum in the end," the great detective admitted. "Pearsall suggested that it might be an image of Oannes, the Babylonian god of wisdom. Fotherington disagreed."

"Fotherington is undoubtedly correct," Mycroft declared. "He sent you to me, of course—without offering any hypothesis of his own."

"He did," Sherlock admitted. "And he told me, rather impolitely, to leave Watson out of it."

"He was right to do so," Mycroft said. *And to notify the secretary in advance,* he added, although he did not say the words aloud.

"Excuse me, sir," said the sailor, "but I'm rather out of my depth here. Perhaps you might explain what that thing is, if you know, and why it was sent to Captain Pye . . . and whether it will finish me the way it finished him. I have to admit, sir, that

Rockaby seemed to have near as much hatred of me as he had of the captain toward the end, even though we were friends once and always near neighbors. I don't mind admitting, sir, that I'm frightened." That was obvious, although John Chevaucheux was plainly a man who did not easily give in to fear, especially of the superstitious kind.

"Alas, I cannot give you any guarantee of future safety, Mr. Chevaucheux," Mycroft said, already fearing that the only guarantees to be found were of the opposite kind, "but you will lose nothing by surrendering this object to me, and it might be of some small service to the Diogenes Club if you were to tell me your story, as you've doubtless already told it to Dr. Watson and my brother."

Sherlock shifted uneasily. Mycroft knew that his brother had hoped for more even if he had not expected it—but Sherlock and he were two of a kind, and knew what duty they owed to the accumulation of knowledge.

The seaman nodded. "Telling it has done me good, sir," he said, "so I don't mind telling it again. It's much clearer in my head than it was—and I'm less hesitant now that I know there are men in the world prepared to take it seriously. I'll understand if you can't help me, but I'm grateful to Mr. Sherlock for having tried."

Anticipating a long story, Mycroft settled back into his chair—but he could not make himself comfortable.

"You'll doubtless have judged from my name that I'm of French descent," said Chevaucheux, "although my family have been in England for a century and a half. We've always been seafarers. My father sailed with Dan Pye in the old clippers, and my grandfather was a middy in Nelson's navy. Captain Pye used to tell me that he and I were kin, by virtue of the fact that the Normans who came to England with William the Conqueror were so called because they were descended from Norsemen, like the vikings who colonized the north of England hundreds of years earlier. I tell you this because Sam Rockaby was a man of a very different stripe from either of us, although his family live no more than a day's ride from mine, and mine no more than an hour on the railway from Dan Pye's.

"Captain Pye's wife and children are lodged in Poole, my own on Durlston Head in Swanage, near the Tilly Whim caves. Rockaby's folk hail from a hamlet south of Worth Matravers, near the western cliffs of St. Aldhelm's Head. To folk like his, everyone's a foreigner whose people weren't clinging to that shore before the Romans came, and no one's a true seaman whose people didn't learn to navigate the Channel in coracles or hollowed-out canoes. Dr. Watson tells me that every man has something of the sea in his blood, because that's where all land-based life came from, but I don't know about that. All I know is that the likes of Rockaby laugh into their cupped hands when they hear men like Dan Pye and Jack Chevaucheux say that the sea is in our blood.

"Mr. Sherlock tells me that you don't get about much, sir, so I'll guess you've never been to Swanage, let alone to Worth Matravers or the sea cliffs on the Saint's Head. You're dead right—and then some—about the way the local people work the stone. They used Portland stone to make the frontage of the museum Mr. Sherlock took me to yesterday, but no one has much use for Purbeck stone because it crumbles too easily. These days, even the houses on the isle are mostly made of brick—but in the old days stone was what they had in plenty, and it was easily quarried, especially where the coastal cliffs are battered by the sea, so stone was what they used. They carved it, too, though never as small and neat as that *thing*, and you'll not see an old stone house within ten miles of Worth Matravers that hasn't got some ugly face or deformed figure worked into its walls. Nowadays it's just tradition, but Sam Rockaby's folk have their own lore regarding such things. When Sam and I were boys he used to tell me that the only *real* faces were those that kept watch on the sea.

" 'Some'll tell ye they're devils, Jacky boy,' Sam told me once,

'an' some'll tell ye they're a-meant for the scarin' away of devils—
but they ain't. The devils in hell are jest fairy tales. Mebbe these
are the Elder Gods, and mebbe they're the *Others*, but either way
they're older by far than any Christian devil.' He would never tell
me exactly what he meant, though, so I always figured that he was
teasing me. It was the same with the chapels. All along that coast
there are little chapels on the cliff, where whole villages would go
to pray when their menfolk were caught at sea by a storm. Even
in Swanage the rumor was that it wasn't just for the safe return
of fishermen that Rockaby's folk prayed, for they were wreckers
even before they were smugglers, but Sam sneered at that kind of
calumny.

" 'They rearranged the stones to build the chapels,' he told me,
'An' threw away the ones that scared 'em—but the stone knows
what it was before your Christ was born, an' fer what its eyes were
set to watch. The Elders were first, but their watchin' did no
good. The Others came anyway, an' printed their own faces in the
stone.' He was always a little bit crazy—but harmless, I thought,
until the fire got him.

"Rockaby's father and mine sailed together once or twice. So
far as I know, they got on well enough with Dan Pye and each
other. When I first signed on the *Goshen* Sam's dad was still on the
sailing ships, and I reckon Sam would have followed him if the age
of sail wasn't so obviously done. Sam never liked steam, but you
can't hold back the tide, and if you want to work you have to go
where the work is. He was a seaman through and through, and if
going under steam was the price of going to sea, he'd pay it. I
don't think he was resentful of my having got my mate's papers by
the time he joined the *Goshen*, even though he was older by a year
or two, because he didn't have an ounce of ambition. He was a
good seaman—and the most powerful swimmer I ever saw—but
he wasn't in the least interested in command. I always wanted to
be master of my own ship, but he never wanted to be master of
anything, not even his own soul.

"I can't put my finger on any one incident that first set Rockaby and Captain Pye at odds. It's in the nature of seamen to grumble, and they always find a scapegoat on the bridge. I wasn't aware that anything new had crept into the scuttlebutt when the *Goshen* set out, although the talk grew dark soon enough when the weather wouldn't let up. Landlubbers think that steam's made seafaring easy, but they don't know what the ocean's like. A steamship may not need the wind for power, but she's just as vulnerable to its whims. Sometimes, I could swear that the wind tries twice as hard to send a steamship down, purely out of pique. We had a rough ride out, I can tell you. I never saw the Mediterranean so angry, and no sooner were we through the canal and into the Red Sea than the storms picked us up again. Rockaby was the only man in the crew who wasn't as sick as a pig—and that, I suppose, might be why things between him and Dan Pye began to get worse. Rockaby said he was being picked on, given more than his fair share of work—and so he was, because he was sometimes the only man capable of carrying out the orders. The captain did more than his own share, too, and I tried, but there were times when we were all laid low.

"There's nothing to be ashamed of in being sick at sea. They say Nelson took days to find his sea legs. But the ordinary kind of seasickness was only the beginning—laudanum got us through the fevers and the aches, until we were far enough east to buy hashish and raw opium. You might disapprove of that, Mr. Mycroft, but it's the way things work out east, at least among seafaring men. You have bad dreams, but at least you can bear to be awake. Or so it usually goes. But this time was different; the ocean seemed to have it in for us. We were carrying mail for the company, so we had to make a dozen stops on the Indian mainland and the islands, and somewhere along the way we picked up the fire. St. Anthony's fire, that is.

"Dr. Watson told that he'd encountered similar cases while he was in India—I first met him in Goa thirteen years ago, while I was an able seaman on the *Serendip*—and that the cause was bad bread, contaminated with ergot. Maybe he's right, but that's not what seamen believe. To them, the fire is something out of hell. The men who took it worse said they felt as if crabs and snakes were crawling under their skin, and they had blinding visions of devils and monsters. This time, Rockaby was affected just as badly as anyone else, and he took it very bad indeed. He began blaming Dan Pye, saying that the captain had ridden him too hard, and brought the affliction on the ship by the insult to his blood.

"We lost two more men before we made port in Padang and laid in fresh supplies. That was when Rockaby disappeared—overboard, we thought, though he was too strong a swimmer to drown so close to shore, raving or not. We nearly shipped out without him, but he got back to the ship just in time, unfortunately. He was over the fire, didn't seem any worse for wear than the rest of us, physically speaking—quite the reverse, in fact—but we soon found out that his mind hadn't made the same recovery as his body. No sooner were we under way that he began twitching and jabbering away, sometimes mumbling away as if in a foreign language, stranger than any I'd ever heard. He did his work, mind—there was no lack of strength in him—but he was a changed man, and not for the better. Captain Pye said that his mumbling was nonsense, but it really did sound to me like a language, though maybe one designed for other tongues than human. There were names that kept cropping up: Nyarlathotep, Cthulhu, Azathoth. When he did speak English, Rockaby told anyone who would listen that we didn't understand and couldn't understand what the world was really like, and what it will become when the *Others* return to claim it.

"Captain Pye could see that Sam was ill, and didn't want to come down hard on him, but ships' crew are direly superstitious. That kind of ill-wishing can make any trouble that comes along a thousand times worse. No one likes to be part of a jittery company even at the best of times, and when a ship's already taken a battering and there are typhoons to be faced and fought . . . well, a captain has no alternative but to try to shut a Jonah up. Dan tried, but it only made things worse. I tried to talk some sense into Sam myself, but nothing anyone could say had any effect but to make him crazier. Perhaps we should have dropped him off in Madras or Aden, but he was a Purbeck man when all was said and done, and it was our responsibility to see him safely home. And we did, though I surely wish we hadn't.

"By the time we came back into Southampton Water, Rockaby seemed a good deal better, though we'd dosed him with opium enough to keep an elephant quiet and maybe taken any un- healthy amount ourselves. I thought he might make a full recovery once he was back home, and I traveled with him on the train to Swanage to make sure that he got back safely. He was calm enough, but he wasn't making much sense. 'Ye're a fool, Jacky,' he said to me, before we parted. 'Y' think you can make it right but y' can't. The price has to be paid, the sacrifice made. The Others never went away, y' know, when they'd seen off the Elder Gods. They may be sleeping, but they're dreaming, too, and the steam fil- ters into their dreams the way sails never did, stirrin' an' simmerin' an' seethin'. Ain't no good hopin' that they'll let us all alone while there's tides in the sea an' the *crawlin' chaos* in our blood. Y' can throw away the faces but y' can't blind the eyes or keep the ears from hearin'. I know where the curses are, Jacky. I know how Dan Pye'll die, an' how it has to be done. Cleave to him an ye're doomed, Jacky. List to me. I know. I've the *old blood* in me.'

"I left him at Swanage station, waiting for a cart to take him home, or at least as far as Worth Matravers. He was still mumbling to himself. I heard no more from or about him—but less than two weeks later I got a letter from Dan Pye's wife begging me to come to their house in Poole. I caught the first train I could.

"The captain was confined to his bed, and fading fast. His doc- tor was with him, but didn't have the faintest idea what was wrong with him, and had nothing to offer by way of treatment save for laudanum and more laudanum. I could see right way that it wouldn't be enough. All laudanum can do is dull the pain while your body makes its own repairs, and I could tell that the captain's body was no longer in the business of making repairs. It seemed to me that his flesh had turned traitor, and had had enough of being human. It was changing. I've seen men with the scaly disease, that makes them seem as if they're turning into fish, and I've seen men with gangrene rotting alive, but I never saw anything like the kind of transformation that was working in Dan Pye. Whatever kind of flesh it was that he was trying to become, it was nothing that was ever ancestor to humankind, and no mere decay.

"He had breath enough left in him to tell me to get rid of the doctor and to send his wife away, but when we were alone he talked fast, like a man who didn't expect to be able to talk for long. 'I've been cursed,' he told me. 'I know who did it, though he isn't entirely to blame. Sam Rockaby never had the least vestige of any power to command, though he's a good follower if you can get mastery over him, and a powerful swimmer in seas stranger than you or I have ever sailed. Take this back to him, and tell him that I understand. I don't forgive, but I understand. I've felt the crawling chaos and seen the madness of darkness. Tell him that it's over now, and that it's time to throw it off the Saint's Head, and let it go forever. Tell him to do the same with all the rest, for his own sake and that of his children's children.' The thing he gave me to give back to Rockaby was that thing your brother just gave you.

"He said more, of course, but the only thing relevant to the story was about the dreams. Now, Dan Pye was a seaman for forty years, and no stranger to rum, opium, and hashish. He knew his dreams, Dan did. But these, he said, were different. These were real visions: visions of long-dead cities, and creatures like none that Mother Earth could ever have spawned, whether she's been four thousand or four thousand million years in the making. And there were words, too: words that weren't just nonsense, but parts of a language human tongues were never meant to speak. 'The

Elder Gods couldn't save us, Jack,' he said. 'The Others were too powerful. But we don't have to give ourselves up—not our souls, not our will. We have to do what we can. Tell Rockaby that, and tell him to throw the lot into the sea.'

"I tried to do what Dan asked me to, but when I went to Worth Matravers I found that Rockaby had never arrived home after I left him at Swanage station. I didn't throw the stone off the cliff because I found out that the curse that killed Dan had already started in me, and I thought it best to show it to whoever might be able to help me. I knew Dr. Watson from before, as I said, and I knew he'd been in India. I wasn't certain that he'd be able to help, but I was sure that there wasn't a doctor in Dorset who could, and I knew that any man who's been long in India has seen things just as queer and just as bad as whatever has its claws in me. So I found Dr. Watson through the Seamen's Association in London, and he sent me to see Mr. Sherlock Holmes—who has promised to find Sam Rockaby for me. But he wanted to come here first, to ask your advice about the cursing stone, because of what this chap Fotherington told him at the museum. And that's the whole of it—apart from this."

While he completed this last sentence John Chevaucheux had unbuttoned his coat and the shirt he wore beneath it. Now he drew back the shirt to display his breast and abdomen to Mycroft's gaze. The seaman's eyes were full of horror as he beheld himself, and the spoliation that had claimed him.

The creeping malaise appeared to have commenced its spread from a point above Chevaucheux's heart, but the disfiguration now extended as far as his navel and his collarbone, and sideways from one armpit to the other. The epidermal deformation was not like the scaly patina of icthyosis; it seemed was more akin to the rubbery flesh of a cephalopod, and its shape was slightly reminiscent of an octopus with tentacles asprawl. It was discolored by a multiplicity of bruises and widening ulcers, although there seemed to be no sign yet of any quasi-gangrenous decay.

Mycroft had never seen anything like it before, although he had heard of similar deformations. He knew that he ought to make a closer investigation of the symptoms, but he felt a profound reluctance to touch the diseased flesh.

"Watson has no idea how to treat it," Sherlock said unnecessarily. "Is there any member of the Diogenes Club who can help?"

Mycroft pondered this question for some moments before shaking his head. "I doubt that anyone in England has a ready cure for this kind of disease," he said. "But I will give you the address of one of our research laboratories in Sussex. They will certainly be interested to study the development of the disease, and may well be able to palliate the symptoms. If you are strong, Mr. Chevaucheux, you might survive this, but I can make no promises." He turned to Sherlock. "Can you honor your promise to find this man Rockaby?"

"Of course," Sherlock said stiffly.

"Then you must do so, without delay—and you must persuade him to lead you to the store of artifacts from which he obtained this stone. I shall keep this one, if Mr. Chevaucheux will permit, but you must take the rest to the laboratory in Sussex. I will ask the secretary to send two of the functionaries with you, because there might be hard labor involved and this is not the kind of case in which Watson ought to be allowed to interest himself. When the artifacts are safe—or as safe as they can be, in human hands—you must return here, to tell me exactly what happened in Dorset."

Sherlock nodded his head. "Expect me within the week," he said, with his customary self-confidence.

"I will," Mycroft assured him, in spite of his inability to echo that confidence.

Sherlock was as good as his word, at least in the matter of timing. He arrived in the Strangers' Room seven days later, at four-thirty in the afternoon. He was more than a little haggard, but he had summoned all his pride and self-discipline to the task of maintaining his image as a master of reason. Even so, he did not rise from his seat when Mycroft entered the room.

"I received a telegram from Lewes this morning," Mycroft told him. "I have the bare facts—but not the detail. You have done well. You may not think so, but you have."

"If you are about to tell me that there are more things in heaven and earth than are dreamed of in my philosophy . . ." Sherlock said, in a fractured tone whose annoyance was directed more at himself than his brother.

"I would not presume to insult you," Mycroft said, a trifle dishonestly. "Tell me the story, please—in your own words."

"The first steps were elementary," Sherlock said morosely. "Had Rockaby been in London, the irregulars would have found him in a matter of hours; as things were, I had to put the word out through my contacts in Limehouse. Wherever Rockaby was, I knew that he had to be dosing himself against the terrors of his condition, and that was bound to leave a trail. I located him in Portsmouth. He had gone there in search of a ship to carry him back to the Indian Ocean, but no one would take him on because he was so plainly mad, and he had given up sometime before, in favor of drinking himself into oblivion. Chevaucheux and I went down there posthaste, and found him in a wretched condition.

"There were no signs of Captain Pye's disease on Rockaby's body—which gave me some confidence that the stone was not carrying any common or garden-variety contagion—but his mind was utterly deranged. My questions got scant response, but Chevaucheux had slightly better luck. Rockaby recognized him, in spite of his madness, and seemed to feel some obligation to him, left over from a time when they were on better terms. 'I shouldn't of done it, Jacky,' he said to Chevaucheux. 'It warn't my fault, really, but I shouldn't of. I shouldn't of let the blood have its way—an' I'm damned now, blood or no blood. Won't die but can't live. Stay away, lad. Go away and stay away.'

"Chevaucheux asked him where the remainder of the stones

could be found. I doubt that he would have told us, had he been well, but his condition worked to our advantage in that matter. Chevaucheux had to work hard, constantly reminding Rockaby of the ties that had bound them as children and shipmates, and in the end he wormed the location out of him. The place-names meant nothing to me, and probably meant nothing to anyone who had not roamed back and forth across the isle with the child that Rockaby once was, but Chevaucheux knew the exact spot near the sea cliffs that Rockaby meant. 'Leave 'em be, Jacky,' the madman pleaded. 'Don't disturb the ground. Leave 'em be. Let 'em come in their own time. Don't hurry them, no matter how you burn.' We did not take the advice, of course."

Mycroft observed that Sherlock seemed to regret that now. "You went to St. Aldhelm's Head," he prompted. "To the sea cliffs."

"We went by day," Sherlock said, his eyes glazing slightly as he slipped back into narrative mode. "The weather was poor—gray and drizzling—but it was daylight. Alas, daylight does not last. Chevaucheux led us to the spot readily enough, but the old mine where the stoneworkers had tunneled into the cliff face was difficult to reach, because the waves had long since carried away the old path. The mine entrance was half blocked, because the flat layers of stone had weathered unevenly, cracking and crumbling— but Rockaby had contrived a passage of sorts, and we squeezed through without disturbing the roof.

"When your clubmen set to work with a will, one plying a pickax and the other a miner's shovel, I was afraid the whole cliff might come down on us, but we were forty yards deep from the cliff face, and the surrounding rock had never been assailed by the waves. I never heard such a sound, though, as the wind got up and the sea became violent. The crash of the waves seemed to surge through the stone, to emerge from the walls like the moaning of a sick giant—and that was before your men began pulling the images out and heaping them up.

"You studied the one that Chevaucheux gave you by lamplight, and magnified its image as you did so, but you can't have the least notion of how that crowd of faces appeared by the light of *our* lamps, in that godforsaken hole. More than a few were considerably larger than the one Rockaby sent to Captain Pye, but it wasn't just their size that made them seem magnified: it was their malevolence. They weren't carrying a disease in the same way that a dead man's rags might harbor microbes, but there was a contagion in them regardless, which radiated from their features.

"Chevaucheux had shown me the stone faces built into the houses in Worth Matravers, but they'd been exposed for decades or centuries to the sun and the wind and the salt in the air. They had turned back into mere ugly faces, as devoid of virtue as of vice. These were different—and if they had stared at me the way they stared at poor Chevaucheux . . ."

Mycroft knew better than to challenge this remarkable observation. "Go on," he prompted.

"Reason tells me that they could not really have stared at Chevaucheux—that he must have imagined it, in much the same way that one imagines a portrait's gaze following one around a room—but I tell you, Mycroft, *I imagined it, too.* I did not perceive the eyes of those monsters as if they were looking at me, but as if they were *looking at him* . . . as if they were accusing him of their betrayal. Not Rockaby, although he had told Chevaucheux where to find them, and not you or I, although we were the ones who asked him to locate them on behalf of your blessed club, but him and him alone. Justice, like logic, simply did not enter into the equation.

" 'Do you see it, Mr. Holmes?' he asked me—and I had to confess that I did. 'It is in my blood,' he said. 'Sam was wrong to think himself any more a seaman than Dan Pye or Jacky Chevaucheux. There are stranger seas, you see, than the seven on which we sail. There are greater oceans than the five we have named. There are seas of infinity and oceans of eternity, and their salt is the bitterest brine that creation can contain. The dreams you know are but phantoms . . . ghosts with no more substance than rhyme or reason . . . but there are dreams *of the flesh*, Mr. Holmes. I have done nothing of which I need to be ashamed, and yet . . . *I cannot help but dream.*'

"All the while that he was speaking, he was moving away, toward the narrow shaft by which we had gained entry to the heart of the mine. He was moving into the shadows, and I assumed that he was trying to escape the light because he was trying to escape the hostile gaze of those horrid effigies—but that was not the reason. You saw what was happening to his torso when he was here, but his face was then untouched. The poison had leached into his liver and lights, but not his eyes or brain . . . but the bleak eyes of those stone heads were staring at him, no matter how absurd that sounds, and . . . do you have any idea what I am talking about, Mycroft? Do you understand what was happening in that cave?"

"I wish I did," Mycroft said. "You, my dear brother, are perhaps the only man in England who can comprehend the profundity of my desire. Like you, I am a master of observation and deduction, and I have every reason to wish that my gifts were entirely adequate to an understanding of the world in which we find ourselves. There is nothing that men like us hate and fear more than the *inexplicable*. I do not hold with fools who say that there are things that man was not meant to know, but I am forced to admit that there are things that men are not yet in a position to know. We have hardly begun to come to terms with the ordinary afflictions of the flesh that we call diseases, let alone those which are extraordinary. If there are such things as curses—and you will doubtless agree with me that it would be infinitely preferable if there were not—then we are impotent, as yet, to counter them. Did Chevaucheux say anything more about these *dreams of the flesh*?"

"He had already told me that Dan Pye had been right," Sherlock went on. "They were more than dreams, even when they were phantoms. Opium does not feed them, he said, but cannot suppress them. He had told me, very calmly, that he had already seen the deserts of infinity, the depths within darkness, the horrors that lurk on reason's edge . . . and that he had heard the mutterings, the discordance that underlies every pretense of music and meaningful speech . . . but when he moved into the shadows of the cave . . ."

Sherlock made an evident effort to gather himself together. "He never stopped talking," the great detective went on. "He wanted me to know, to understand. He wanted *you* to know. He wanted to help us—and, through us, to help others. 'The worst of it all,' he said, 'is what I have *felt*. I have felt the *crawling chaos*, and I know what it is that has me now. St. Anthony's fire is a mere caress by comparison. I have felt the hand of revelation upon my forehead, and I feel it now, gripping me like a vise. I know that the ruling force of creation is blind, and worse than blind. I know that it is devoid of the least intelligence, the least compassion, the least *artistry*. You may be surprised to find me so calm under such conditions as this, Mr. Holmes, and to tell you the truth I am surprised myself—all the more so for having seen Dan Pye upon his deathbed, and Sam Rockaby on a rack of his own making—but I have learned from you that facts must be accepted as facts and treated as facts, and that madness is a treason of the will. You might think that you and your brother have not helped me, but you have . . . in spite of everything. Take these monstrous things away, and study them . . . learn what they have to teach you, no matter what the cost. That's better by far than Sam Rockaby's way, or mine . . ." Sherlock trailed off again.

"Mr. Chevaucheux was a brave man," Mycroft said, after a moment's pause.

Sherlock met his eyes then, with a gaze full of fear and fire. "Am I damned, Mycroft?" he demanded harshly. "Is the disease incubating in me, as it was in him? Are my own dreams worse than dreams?"

Mycroft had no firm guarantees to offer, but he shook his head. "There was something in Chevaucheux, as there was in Pye, which responded to the curse. You and I are a different breed; the art in our blood is a different kind. I cannot swear to you that we are immune, or will remain so, but I am convinced that we are better placed to fight. Those effigies you took to Lewes may have the power to make some men see a terrible truth, and to make some human flesh turn traitor to the soul, but they are not omnipotent, else the human race would have succumbed to their effect long ago. At any rate, there is no safety in hiding them, or in hiding from them. Whatever the risk, they must be studied. Such studies are dangerous, but that does not excuse us from our scholarly duty. We must try to understand what they are—what *we* are—no matter how hateful the answer might be."

"You believe that we are safe from this contagion, then—you and I?"

Mycroft had never seen Sherlock so desperate for reassurance. "I dare to hope so," he said judiciously. "The Diogenes Club has some experience in matters of this sort, and we have survived thus far. The entities that men like Rockaby term the *Others* have proved more powerful in the past than those he calls the Elder Gods, but the blood of Nodens is not extinct; it flows in us still and it has its expression. The gift that was handed down to men like us is not to be despised. You sometimes suspect that I think less of you because you have become famous instead of laboring behind the scenes of society, as I do, but I am glad that you have become a hero of the age because the age is direly in need of your kind of hero. Our art is in its infancy, and many more confrontations such as this one will expose our incapacity in years—perhaps centuries—to come, but we must nurture it regardless, and store its rewards. What else can we do if we are to be worthy of the name of humankind?"

Sherlock nodded, seemingly satisfied.

"Tell me, then," Mycroft said, "what happened in the cave. I know that you and my faithful servants succeeded in taking the artifacts to Lewes, but I know that Chevaucheux was not with you. Rockaby has been committed to a lunatic asylum, where an agent of ours will be able to interrogate his madness, but I gather from the tone of your account that Chevaucheux will not be available for further study. Do you feel able now to tell me what became of him?"

"What became of him?" Sherlock echoed, fear flooding his eyes again. "What *became*? Ah . . ." As he paused, he put his hand into his pocket and took out a bottle. Mycroft had no way to be sure, but it seemed to him to be an exact match to the outline he had observed in John Chevaucheux's clothing a few weeks before. The label on this bottle, scrawled in a doctor's unkempt hand, confirmed that it was laudanum.

Sherlock put his hand to the cork, but then he stopped himself and put the unopened bottle down on the side table. "It does no good," he said. "But they are only dreams, are they not? Mere phantoms? There is no necessity that will turn them into dreams of *my* flesh. That is what Chevaucheux told me, at any rate, when he reached forward to give me the bottle, before he ran away. I think that he was trying to be kind—but he might have been kinder to remain in the shadows. He had faith in me, you see. He thought that I would want to *see* what he had *become* . . . and he was right. He ought to have been right, and he was. Before he ran to the end of that makeshift corridor of stone, and hurled himself into the thankless sea, where I hope to God that he died . . .

"That brave man wanted me to see what the crawling chaos had done to him, as it turned his flesh into a dream beneath the evil eyes of those *creatures* we had excavated from their hiding place . . .

"And I did see it, Mycroft."

"I know," Mycroft answered. "But you must tell me what it was you saw, if we are ever to come to terms with it." And he saw his brother respond to this appeal, seeing its sense as well as its necessity. All his life, Sherlock Holmes had believed that when one had eliminated the impossible, whatever remained—however improbable—must be the truth. Now he understood that when the impossible was too intractable to be eliminated, one had to revise one's opinion of the limits of the possible; but he was a brave man, in whom the blood of Nodens still flowed, after a fashion, still carrying forward its long and ceaseless war against the tainted blood of the *Others*.

"I saw the flesh of his face," Sherlock went on, stubbornly bringing his tale to its inevitable end, "the texture of which was like some frightful, pulpy cephalopod, and the shape of which was dissolving into a mass of writhing, agonized worms, every one of them suppurating and liquefying as if it had been a month decaying . . . and I met his eyes . . . his glowing eyes that were blind to ordinary light . . . which were staring, not at me, but into the infinite and the eternal . . . *where they beheld some horror so unspeakable that it required every last vestige of his strength to pause an instant more before he hurled himself, body and soul, into the illimitable abyss.*"

The Curious Case of Miss Violet Stone

POPPY Z. BRITE AND
DAVID FERGUSON

I came down to breakfast one morning and found Sherlock Holmes still in his dressing gown, contemplating a note written in a large, straggling hand. He waited for me to pour my first cup of coffee, then passed the note across the table to me.

Mr. Holmes:

Please, sir, may I come and see you. I fear for the life of my dear sister. I will come after luncheon today. Please, Mr. Holmes, I do not know where else to turn.

Thomas Stone

"What do you make of it, Watson?" he asked when I had had time to peruse the childish scrawl.

"Not much. I suppose you already know all about him, though."

"No more than appears in the note," Holmes said, though I was well aware that even such a short note might speak volumes to his practiced eye. "A fact or two, nothing more. Let us wait and see what the man himself has to say."

The morning had dawned clear and mild, but by midday a loathsome yellow fog rolled through Baker Street, pressing like a greasy face against the windows and filling our cozy rooms with a damp chill. Holmes was stoking the fire when the bell rang and Mr. Thomas Stone was shown in.

I could not determine his age at once, for he was a young man who seemed somehow old. His features did not appear particularly aged—in fact, he was fair-haired and handsome, with dark determined eyes and a set to his jaw that suggested a tendency toward stubbornness. His shoulders were broad, but something in his posture and bearing made me think at first glance that he might almost be a pensioner. Then I looked again and determined that he could not be more than twenty-five. The cuffs of his trousers were dark with some grime heavier than that of the London streets.

"Thank you kindly for letting me come on such short notice," he said as he shook our hands.

"I have no doubt that it was necessary," Holmes said. "Watson, permit me to introduce you to Thomas Stone, apprentice cook at the Grand Hotel."

"The two of you have already met, then?" I asked, but one glance at our guest's astounded face told me that it was not so.

"I never laid eyes on the gentleman until this very moment. But I suspected he was in the restaurant business when I read the note, and I knew I was correct the moment he came in."

"I can't imagine how you knew it, sir," said the awed young man.

"You used the word *luncheon* in your note. Most people would say *midday*, unless they had reason to measure out the day in meals. As well, the note was written on a scrap of invoice from a Dover fish merchant. On the reverse of the paper I found the letters *TEL* and the word *sole*. What sort of establishment would receive such an invoice? The restaurant in a fine hotel. I heard no cab outdoors before you entered, and there is no mud on your shoes, so I deduced that you came from nearby. The Grand's restaurant is the only one in the area fine enough to serve Dover sole."

"But surely he might have come from somewhere other than his workplace!" I ejaculated.

"Observe the stains on his trouser cuffs, Watson. Traces of grime from the kitchen, and a fragment of fresh parsley there in his boot lace. As for his position, observe the heavy callus on the second joint of his right forefinger. That sort of callus comes from a long acquaintance with a knife, though perhaps not quite long enough to become the head chef. And his eyes lack the chef's tyrannical gleam. No, he must be the apprentice. If I am wrong, I shall cook supper for him with my own two hands. Am I wrong, Mr. Stone? For the sake of your digestion, I hope I am not."

"Not at all, sir. I been apprentice cook at the Grand for two years under Chef John Sutcliffe. But that's not why I come."

"No," I recalled, "your note said you feared for your sister's life. Whatever is wrong with the girl?"

"Ah, my poor Violet," Stone began. But he got no further, for Holmes shot out of his chair and snatched up a newspaper from the table. "Your sister is Violet Stone?" Holmes demanded.

"Who on earth is Violet Stone?" I said.

"Forgive me, Watson. I forget that you read no part of the dailies save the financial news. You might do well to take a closer interest in the doings of your fellow citizens!"

I began to sputter, for Holmes had always spoken contemptuously of human-interest stories, claiming the minutiae of people's lives were inconsequential unless he could study them with his own keen eyes. Holmes handed me the newspaper, pointing out a story, and I subsided as I scanned the headlines.

GIRL HAS EATEN NOTHING FOR THREE YEARS
Mother tells reporter, "She subsists on air and faith"
AN ANOMALY OF NATURE

PHYSICIANS SAY "PREPOSTEROUS!"
BUT CAN FIND NO EVIDENCE OF IMBIBITION

I read the accompanying feature and learned that Miss Violet Stone of 10 Percy Lane, Highgate, had become ill three years before on holiday in Greece. She had swum in an island pond and taken a chill, after which her family reported she was never the same. Gradually she ate less and less until she could be made to swallow nothing; she would retch and choke when food was pressed upon her, and reject whatever was forced down her throat. Recently a charwoman had left the family's employ and reported the strange case to the newspapers.

"I agree with my colleague, whoever he may be," I said. "The story is preposterous. If Miss Stone had truly stopped eating and drinking, she would have expired after thirty or forty days at the outside. You see, the human body is like that fire there." I pointed at the grate, where a few logs were blazing merrily. "It burns because it has fuel. Take away the logs and you have no more fire."

"A pretty analogy," said Holmes, "but the fire is also fed by oxygen. Smother it and you will extinguish it. Yet you cannot see the oxygen, and if you were not a learned man, you would have no evidence that oxygen existed at all."

"Are you suggesting that Miss Stone subsists on something unknown to science?"

"Not at all," said Holmes, who had begun to pare his nails with a Malay kris. "I was merely pointing out a flaw in your analogy."

"If you please, sirs," said Stone timidly. Holmes and I looked at him, surprised; we had become so interested in the tale of his sister that I believe we had both half forgotten he was there.

"Forgive us," said Holmes. "We are a pair of old pedants, nothing more. Because your family name is a common one, I failed to connect your note with the newspaper article until you told us your sister's Christian name was Violet. Pray go on."

"Well, it is true that she never eats, at least not that I can tell. My hours at the Grand are long and I only see my family in the early mornings, and sometimes if Chef gives me a day off. But neither she nor Mother has ever told a falsehood that I know of. And why would she lie? Why would she suffer deliberately?"

"Is she suffering, then?" Holmes asked.

"Her body is thin and twisted, but she claims no hunger. She says she takes her sustenance from other realms and needs no food on this earth. That's a bit of a blow to me, as you might imagine— I used to cook little things for her when she first became ill. Custards and the like. Now she says swallowing one of my custards would be as painful as swallowing hot coals."

"Indeed! And she has been so ever since taking a swim on holiday?"

"Oh, yes, sir. Three years ago our great-aunt died and left some money to our mother. Our father's been dead since I was small, you see, and he left us comfortable, but there was never any money for extras. My mother had always wanted to stand among Grecian ruins and feel the ancient wind blowing through her hair—that was how she put it, like. She's got a bit of a poetic soul. I couldn't leave the kitchen, but I insisted she and Violet use the money for a holiday.

"They were picnicking on the isle of Knoxos one day when Violet saw a clear pond and went for a swim. She wasn't usually the swimming sort, but Mother says she saw something glimmering on the bottom and wanted to dive for it—thought it might be a coin of antiquity or some such. It was nothing, Violet said, only a trick of the sunlight on the water—but that night she took ill, and they had to sail for home a fortnight earlier than they'd intended. Mother thought she would improve once they reached London, but she took to her bed and hasn't got up since."

"What are her symptoms?"

"While still on Knoxos, she suffered amnesia—though it was almost as though she tried to hide it. She pretended to know Mother, but could not answer the simplest questions about our lives back in London. When she returned I could see she didn't know me either. I sat with her whenever I had a moment, telling her tales of our childhood, often reading to her. She dotes on being read to. It's queer, though—before the accident she used to enjoy newspapers and modern novels. Now she prefers tomes I scarcely understand the like of, myself. Not long ago she asked me to bring her something called the *Necronomicon*, but I've not been able to find it in any of the high-street bookshops."

"The *Necronomicon*!" Holmes murmured. "What could a young English lady want with that moldy bit of occult trash?"

"Many nights she stays up scribbling in a little book. It is one of the few tasks she can still make herself do. She's recovered from her amnesia, or at any rate she knows us, even if she had to relearn everything like a newborn babe. But she never recovered from her physical illness. First her body burned with fever. She would rave and screech in a tongue no one could understand. I don't mind telling you the sound of it gave me a nasty turn, and it nearly shattered my poor mother's nerves altogether.

"When the fever finally passed, Violet's limbs began to wither and draw up like those of an old woman. Finally she stopped eating or drinking altogether, and we thought she would leave us then, but she lives yet. Sometimes she says she wishes to die, yet she still has this thirst for knowledge."

Holmes had perched on the edge of his chair listening to Stone's tale. Now he stood and reached for his hat. "Well, Watson, there's nothing else for it—we must see Miss Violet Stone."

Knowing there would be no rest for myself, Holmes, or the

unfortunate Mr. Stone until we had, I donned my greatcoat and followed Holmes and the younger man out to the street. A cab was summoned and our trio rode over London's slick gray cobbles into the dim afternoon.

Holmes produced from his waistcoat his faithful pipe and a pouch of tobacco. Meditatively tamping the bowl and gazing out the window of the carriage, he queried, "Pray, Mr. Stone, is there anything further you can tell us about your sister's condition? Watson is quite a fine physician. Perhaps he can glean something from your description."

The courteous lad inclined his head to me before saying, "I hardly know where to begin, sir."

"I should say that of all places, the beginning would be the best place to begin. Wouldn't you agree, Watson? Tell us what you observed of her initial symptoms, and of the amnesia that afflicted your poor sister."

Puffing small plumes of blue smoke, Holmes leaned back against the cushions. His eyelids drooped, as they tended to do when he was listening to something with his peculiar powers of attention. When Holmes's senses were most alive, his narrow frame always gave an impression of deep lassitude. Many a careless liar had allowed himself to be tripped up by the seeming inattention of this posture.

Young Stone, however, hardly seemed the sort who would have any reason to lie to us. His solemn face clouded as he cast his mind back to the time three years before. "It was like our Violet was gone altogether, sir," he said. "Her voice was musical before, and her laugh like a bird singing. She was full of life, and when she talked, she would always move her hands, like. It was as if she was drawing pictures in the air of what she was telling you. When the awful fever finally passed and she could speak again without raving, all the light in her was gone out."

The young man paused to take a deep breath and wipe at his eyes, stubbornly blinking at tears. Clearly, he was deeply affected by the tragic change wrought in his sister. Although he had years since reached his majority, for a moment the exhausted young cook before us was gone and we saw an overtired little boy struggling to keep his feelings in check.

"She's different now. She never laughs. Her voice is flat, no spark anymore. Honestly, sir, it's like she's a different girl." He sighed heavily and wiped at his eyes again. "And I fear that she'll pass away anytime. How can she not eat, sir? How can she not eat and stay alive?"

"I hope to discern that, young man," replied Holmes.

The cab had entered the sleepy terraces of Highgate and pulled up to the address Stone had provided. To all externals, the house was normal enough, another tall narrow building among many, each with its own gate and patch of yard. But Stone's despair had communicated itself to me sufficiently that I could not look upon the Stones' house with an objective eye: its half-shrouded windows became drooping eyes, its sooty walls the dull complexion of the sickbed.

Fog pressed moist fat lips to our faces as Stone led us up to the door. We were greeted by an emerald-eyed young maid who accepted our coats. "I'll go tell the mistress you're in, Mr. Stone," she said, a mild Irish burr in her voice.

All was as the young man had described. The Stones appeared to be comfortable, but not among London's elegant upper tiers of families. The house was decorated comfortably, but the occasional carpet edge was frayed, and the drawing-room chairs gave testament to many hours of use.

"Tom, who are these gentlemen?" said a voice from the hallway, and thusly we made the acquaintance of Mrs. Stone, a matronly widow swathed in a dress of figured bombazine. Her face was kind but careworn, and faint purplish smudges around her eyes spoke of anxious hours and lost sleep.

"This is Sherlock Holmes, Mum," said Thomas. "And Dr. Watson is a physician."

"Ah, yes," replied Mrs. Stone. "I have read your names in the *Times*. It is a pleasure to make your acquaintance. I will have Anna bring us some tea, or perhaps a bit of claret?"

"Mum," said Stone, "I've brought them to see Violet. Mr. Holmes is quite learned, as you might know."

At the mention of her daughter's name, Mrs. Stone's shoulders fell as if a great weight had fallen on them. "Oh, my poor Violet," she said, "I know not how she continues to draw breath in this world."

"Is it true, madam, that she has taken no food or drink in three years?" Holmes inquired.

"Yes, sir, it is quite true. She has wasted away to almost nothing, and yet she continues to thrive, after a fashion. We have done everything we can to keep her comfortable, but as Tom must have told you, she hardly seems the same girl at all."

"Well, then, claret will have to wait," Holmes said. "If it is not too much trouble, may we see her at once?"

"The present moment is as good as any other," said the weary mother, "for she is at all hours much the same. She hardly seems to sleep. Her eyes never close. There are times when she speaks less and goes entirely still in the bed, her breathing the only sign of life, but we have never known her to sleep as others do since all this began."

We were led up the stairs and to a narrow hall where three doors led, doubtless, to the respective bedchambers of the Stone family. A faint redolence of jasmine hovered in the hall, a sachet perhaps.

Mrs. Stone turned to the leftmost door and silently opened it. The lamps in the bedchamber were turned low, and the murky dimness of the afternoon reached through the windows and sank the corners in gloom. When first I observed the maid kneeling at the foot of the bed, I thought she was performing some service for the bedridden girl. It was only upon closer inspection that I discerned the Catholic rosary beads dangling from the maid's clasped hands.

"Anna!" barked Mrs. Stone. "How could you?"

The poor maid clutched the beads to her bosom, and it was then that I noticed her cheeks were streaked with tears.

"B-but, ma'am," she protested, "surely 'tis a miracle! She is a saint!"

"I have told you before, Anna," said Mrs. Stone, storm clouds collecting on her brow, "we'll have none of that Papist claptrap in this house! Captain Stone was a Protestant like myself, and that is how I have raised our children!"

"Please, Mum," interrupted young Mr. Stone. "Our guests . . ."

"Indeed," replied the widow, regaining her composure. "Anna, wait for me downstairs. These gentlemen are here to see Violet."

"Yes, ma'am," replied the frightened maid, who then hurriedly left the room.

It was then that we beheld the stricken girl for the first time. Drawing aside one of the hangings around the narrow bed, the mother gestured us forward.

"Here she is," said the mother, "my poor dear."

The girl, perhaps seventeen, huddled in an implausibly small bundle beneath the coverlet. Her arms were mere sticks, her fingers small twigs scratching weakly at her lace-trimmed pillow. Her face may at one time have been quite comely, but the visage now was sunken, cheeks drawn in, complexion the pearly blue white of the recently departed. If I am to be wholly honest, she looked like something I would have expected to see on a mortuary table, not in a shabbily genteel Highgate bedchamber. Only the blazing eyes set in that livid face gave any indication of life.

"Mother?" she said softly, her voice barely more than a rasp.

"Yes, dear, and Tom is here early today. He has brought a doctor and another friend." With one hand, Mrs. Stone urged us to come closer.

"Another doctor?" the wraithlike girl asked in a tone of resignation. Over time, she had doubtless come to associate the visits of physicians with gropings of her fragile limbs, tests of the blood, and other discomforts.

"Miss Stone," said Holmes, bowing to the girl, "I am Sherlock Holmes. This is my—"

But before Holmes could finish his introductions, the girl lunged forward in the bed and seized Holmes's right arm by the wrist. *"You!"* she cried, her bright eyes burning with that eerie, maniacal fire. Her tiny hand was withered almost to a claw, but her grip on my friend's arm must have been preternaturally strong, for Holmes did not pull away. Never had I known him to bear unexpected physical touch with anything like equanimity. However, in this instance, he stood quite still, nor did he speak or betray any emotion whatsoever.

"You can help me," gasped the girl. "Yes, you. You have the necessary mental capacities."

"What's this?" I demanded, edging forward even as both the Stones took involuntary steps back from the suddenly animated girl.

"I have come here by mistake. It has all gone quite badly. We are new to this science of replacement. I am trapped here in the body of this girl child and I must return. There have been errors in the process. We are imperfectly joined." The girl seemed quite out of her mind.

"I see," said Holmes, his face a curious blank mask.

"You have access to a lens grinder? A metallurgist? Perhaps the shop of a machinist?" The girl's pale eyes were desperate. All the life essence in her form seemed concentrated in those eyes. Her skin, hair, even the grayish bedclothes pooling at her waist seemed drained of any spark or color, but her eyes were as bright as those of the unfortunate lunatics I had been called upon to treat in London's sanatoriums.

"Yes, all of those," Holmes replied, still oddly blank of aspect and strangely passive before this wild-eyed wraith of a girl.

"You must help me," the girl reiterated. "Tom?"

"Yes, Violet?" answered Stone after a pause, still recovering from the shock of his sister's sudden animation.

"Where is my book of notes?" she asked him.

From a chest by the bed, Stone withdrew a small flowered notebook of the kind young English ladies are encouraged to keep as diaries. "It is here, sister," he said, laying it beside her on the coverlet.

Releasing Holmes's wrist, she pressed it into his large, dexterous hands. "All of the instructions are here," she told him. "Follow them to the letter. Please do not fail me, Mr. Holmes!"

"Yes, Miss Stone," said the still curiously passive Holmes. "I will endeavor to do my best." And with that, he tucked the diary into his waistcoat and left the bedside without another word. I remained there with the equally startled Stones. Violet Stone settled back against the bedclothes and let her eyes drift shut.

After explaining to the Stones that surely my friend had excellent reasons for his abrupt departure from the room, I conducted a brief physical examination of Miss Stone. Failing to detect any immediate threat to her life, I followed the Stones back downstairs to the drawing room.

We found the detective's lanky form folded into a chair, his long nose buried in the girl's diary. "Fascinating," he muttered, fishing a cigarette from his pocket and lighting it with a wooden match. "Utterly amazing."

"What is it, Holmes?" I asked him, as anxious as the Stones for some explanation.

"Ah!" said Holmes, arising from the chair and closing the little book with a snap. "Mr. Stone, madam, we shall return in a few days' time, when I hope we shall set things to rights."

And saying little more, we retrieved our coats and made our way back out to the waiting hansom.

On the return trip to Baker Street, Holmes continued to peruse the young girl's diary. I wondered what on earth could command such rapt attention from my friend, but many years of Holmes's caprices and occasional erratic behavior had taught me to wait, for he would answer no questions but in their hour.

Burning with curiosity, however, I did contrive to steal a look at the pages. I do not know what I expected, but what met my questioning eyes was a complete shock. Rather than pages of a schoolgirl's neat hand, the diary seemed full of highly technical drawings and schemata. While most of the letters and symbols I glimpsed were familiar, there were several lines of a flowing script that vaguely resembled Arabic, and on one page a shape that appeared to twist itself into eldritch configurations before my very eyes. If I were a superstitious man, I suspect the sight of that shape would have made me seize the book and hurl it out of the cab. Instead I averted my gaze until Holmes turned the page.

Finally, I could bear it no longer. "What has she written there, Holmes?"

"Instructions, Watson," Holmes answered vaguely, and it was then I noted the queer expression in his eyes. It was as if he were not entirely there with me in the coach. He looked vastly preoccupied, as if even as he spoke, the wheels of his mind were already turning and he was buried in some faraway set of problems and calculations. "Miss Violet Stone has provided me with a very detailed list of instructions."

Upon our arrival back to our rooms, Holmes prepared himself an especially large dose of cocaine. As he rolled up his sleeve, he said to me, "I shall be spending a great deal of the next few days in private, in my study. Pray do not interrupt me except in the direst emergency."

"I wouldn't dream of it," I said as he carefully found a site for the injection and released the cocaine into his bloodstream. "But I have never known you to take cocaine at a time like this, Holmes."

"Ahhhhhhhhhh . . ." he sighed. Instantly his head lolled on his shoulders as the powerful drug coursed through him. "Normally

cocaine sends me to a drowsy land of dissociated dreams." He
chuckled softly. "But today's events have left me believing that I
may be lost in one of those dreams and only dreaming that I am
awake and aware."

With infinite care, he extracted the gleaming hypodermic syringe from his arm. After a moment of reverie, he leaped from his
chair and began to pace the room. "Watson, I am going to tell you
this now. The drug has loosened my tongue, but we shall never refer to it again, because I fear I would feel a fool."

I waited silently in my chair by the fire. Rarely have I seen my
dear friend in the throes of the drug, and certainly not at such a
copious dosage. His eyes were as fever bright as those of Violet
Stone. His stately forehead gleamed with a sheen of sweat, and a
vein pulsed ominously at his temple. He hastily poured himself a
whiskey from the sideboard and, seizing a poker, began to jab sav-
agely at the fire.

"Watson, what is the earliest record of a sentient race on this
planet?"

"The Sumerians, I believe, from approximately 4000 B.C."

"What if I told you that this was a gross instance of humanity's
shortsightedness? That a much wiser race preceded us?"

"I would ask you what evidence you have to support this
claim."

"Ah, dear Watson, ever the pragmatic scientist." He downed
the whiskey in two neat swallows and returned to the sideboard
for another. "Cigarette?" he asked me, proffering the gilt box. I
stated that at this hour I would prefer a cigar, with which he gladly
provided me.

"Watson, my old friend, something singular occurred in that
house today. When young Miss Stone seized my wrist, it was as if,
as if . . ." He downed the second whiskey and took a chair in order to prepare his syringe for a second injection.

"Please, Holmes," I said. "As a gentleman, I would never

presume to tamper with your pleasures. But as a physician, I feel obliged to inform you that a second dose of cocaine at that volume could seriously—"

"Doctor," he interrupted, "I do appreciate your concern." But he continued nonetheless. When he had finished his preparations, he glanced up at me. "I wish I could even begin to convey what I experienced at that moment by the bedside," he said.

Sliding the needle in and driving the plunger home, he groaned aloud at the waves of pleasure that assailed him. Then he began to laugh a giddy madman's laugh. Seconds later, a stillness came over him. The drug was accelerating his moods, or perhaps just jangling them into an inchoate frenzy.

He lit another cigarette, clearly having forgotten the one he had left smoldering in the mantel ashtray. "If I attempt to explain it, you must give me your word we shall never speak of the matter again."

I freely gave it, and waited.

"Watson, a race of sentient beings inhabited this planet millennia before humans arrived. And as preposterous as it may seem, they have discovered the means of moving their souls backward and forward through time."

"Good Lord, Holmes! What on earth are you suggesting?"

Holmes held up a patient, silencing hand. He drew hard on his cigarette before continuing. "At a single touch of her hand, she was able to communicate this to me. She has confided to no one else, but the consciousness inhabiting the body of Miss Violet Stone is in truth a traveler from this time before man, come to gather the information and lore of our age."

I was mute, stupefied. And yet Holmes, in spite of his mischievous nature, had never once told me anything other than the truth of his perceptions. During the whole of our acquaintance he had never deceived me, misled me, or informed me of anything with any other principle at heart other than my own enlightenment. As discordant a note as it struck in my own rational nature, I had no choice other than to believe that this was the truth.

"This race refer to themselves as the Great Ones. Though you might not recognize them as sentient beings, were you to lay eyes on one—they are rather like enormous limpets as far as I can gather—they possess a body of knowledge unrivaled by anything in our history. Alexandria was but a village lending library by comparison.

"They require a living host, and the consciousness of the person they inhabit is in turn spirited back to their own time, between the ending of the Mesozoic and the beginning of the Palaeolithic period. This traveler inside Miss Stone is inexperienced, and something has gone dreadfully wrong in the process. Miss Stone's body has rebelled. She will not take sustenance, and as a result is too weak to move. The traveler has kept her alive as best it can, but in order to reverse the process, a special device is required. And that, Watson, is what these instructions are for."

He sat upright in his chair, cigarette in hand, face gleaming.

I have known madmen, treated them, done what I could to help with their sufferings. A person off the street might at that moment have looked upon the countenance of Sherlock Holmes and declared him mad, irrevocably insane. And yet through our years of acquaintance I had learned that what might look like one thing in the mien and deportment of a normal personage, on Holmes tended to indicate the exact opposite.

"I shall be very busy for the next few days. Send away any callers. I am not to be disturbed. We must hope I shall find myself equal to the task before me." He rose, ascended the stairs, and shut his study doors with a bang.

True to his word, Holmes remained sequestered for three days. Meals sent up to him were largely ignored. Requests came for cups of tea and coffee and pitchers of water for drinking, and on three occasions, Holmes abruptly quit Baker Street, twice in the first day and once again late at night on the second. He returned with oddly shaped parcels, greeted no one, and again disappeared into the study.

Finally, on the morning of the third day, he emerged, somewhat wild-eyed and with an air of disorder about him. I was just waking, and through eyes still slightly bleary from sleep, I watched as he blithely tossed Violet Stone's notebook onto the fire crackling in the grate.

"Great Scott, Holmes!" I said, returning my coffee cup to its saucer. "What are you doing?"

"It is finished, Watson. The instructions were to be destroyed when the task is complete." He settled into a chair opposite me.

"The device is finished? What the devil does it do?"

"Were I to explain it to you, Watson, you would think I had utterly taken leave of my senses. I scarcely understand it myself." He stretched and yawned like a great cat. "We shall pay a visit to the Stones before the morning is out. And after that, I shall greatly enjoy myself resting. This has been most taxing indeed."

A message was sent to the Stone house to expect us within the hour. At the appointed time, Holmes emerged from his rooms every bit as fresh and crisp as if he had just returned from a seaside holiday. A queerly shaped bundle draped in black cloth was tucked beneath his arm.

I was barely able to restrain my curiosity about this bundle. What bizarre machine could help to alleviate the suffering of Miss Violet Stone? What could be the actual cause of this suffering? Could it truly be as Holmes had explained? As a medical doctor, I had seen nothing in my own patients that seemed to fit the history of the case. As I had done so many times before, I wordlessly followed Holmes out to a cab in the gray London morning and trusted that all would be revealed to me in time.

We found Mrs. Stone sitting anxiously in her front room, twisting a sodden handkerchief between her white-knuckled fists. "Good morning, gentlemen," she greeted us. "Tom should be along shortly. He sent word that he would come when the chef permits him." She quickly tucked the handkerchief away, and again I caught a faint whiff of jasmine as I leaned down to clasp her hand.

"Ah, good," said Holmes, taking a seat and setting the draped bundle next to his feet. "I hope this morning's events will bring the business to a satisfactory conclusion."

"Mr. Holmes, it is so strange," said Mrs. Stone.

"What is that, madam?" asked Holmes, raising a quizzical eyebrow.

"This morning, when I went in to see her, Violet told me that you would return before noon today. She asked Tom to put off going to work, but he went anyway. How could she have known the hour of your visit before I knew it myself?"

But before Holmes could venture to answer the lady, Mr. Thomas Stone bustled in. "I came as fast as I could," he said breathlessly.

"Ah, good," said Holmes, rising. "Now that we are all present, I will require a moment or two alone with Miss Stone. May I show myself up to her room?"

Mrs. Stone and Thomas exchanged a baffled look, but gave no protest as Holmes once again tucked the mysterious (but apparently quite heavy) machine under his arm and made his way up the stairs. I endeavored to make polite conversation with the Stones in his absence, but anxiety pinched their features and I was considerably preoccupied with my own bafflement. Our conversation proceeded only in fits and starts as a quarter of an hour passed, then twenty-five minutes.

At last, just as my watch declared that Holmes had been gone for the better part of an hour, his voice summoned us from the top of the stairs. The Stones and I rose with one motion, and were I not a gentleman, I would attest that Mrs. Stone sharply elbowed me out of the way at the bottom of the stairs.

We found Holmes grinning to himself at the bedside of Miss Stone. The lamps in the room were turned up bright and the fire had been stoked in the grate. The chest by the bed had been moved, and I noted briefly that its surface looked to have been recently marred and scratched by the weight of some heavy, sharp-edged object. But such thoughts were driven from my mind only to be puzzled over in later days, for when my eyes bore witness to the transformed girl on the bed, I could think of nothing else.

"Mummy! Tom!" she cried. "I had the strangest dream! I was swimming in a pool on the isle of Knoxos. And then I woke up here! I must be so excited about going on holiday that I'm dreaming of it in advance." And then she laughed, a merry bell-like laugh every bit as musical as Thomas had described to us in the hansom cab. Though still terrifyingly gaunt, Violet Stone appeared a wholly different person. Light danced in her eyes. It was a warm light, though, entirely unlike the hideous gleam of three days before. And just as Mr. Stone had said, her restless hands carved graceful gestures from the air as she spoke.

"Violet?" queried Mrs. Stone, and then rushing to her daughter with a mother's instinct, she cried, "Dear, dear Violet!" She threw her arms about the girl and burst into a violent fit of weeping.

"Mummy, what is it?" the girl asked anxiously. "What's wrong?"

"Nothing is wrong, Violet," said Holmes, patting the lady on her shoulder. "Absolutely nothing is wrong."

Moments later, when the smiling girl announced that she was hungry, absolutely *dying* for one of her brother's delicious custards, we knew it was time to withdraw. Holmes slumped in the leather seat of the cab back to our rooms, exhausted. I noticed that the mysterious device he had brought on our journey was now missing, as was the black cloth he had draped it in. When I remarked on this, Holmes looked at me as if I were thoroughly out of my mind and said nothing.

I felt so full of questions as we ascended the stairs at Baker Street that my head seemed about to burst, but it was apparent that my old friend was in no way disposed to explain. He cordially bid me good morning and disappeared into his room without another word.

I spent many hours of the following days struggling in vain to come up with some sort of explanation for the whole business. When a grateful letter arrived containing a generous check and the heartfelt thanks of the Stone family, I endeavored to pry some sort of explanation from the closed lips of my friend, only to be wordlessly repelled once again.

To this day, I have never been able to explain the case to myself, and true to our agreement, no further attempts to explain it to me have been forthcoming. I must, as a last recourse, trust in the account given to me by Holmes. As much as this record may stray beyond the bounds of credulity, such is the sum and the entirety of what I know of the curious case of Miss Violet Stone.

The Adventure of the Antiquarian's Niece

BARBARA HAMBLY

In my career as the chronicler of the cases of Mr. Sherlock Holmes, I have attempted (his assertions to the contrary) to present both his successes and his failures. In most instances his keen mind and logical deductive facility led him to the solutions of seemingly insoluble puzzles. Upon some occasions, such as the strange behavior of Mrs. Effie Munro, his conclusions went astray because of unknown and unforeseen facts; on others, such as the puzzle of the dancing men or the horrifying contents of the letter received by Mr. John Openshaw, his correct assessment of the situation came too late to save the life of his client.

In a small percentage of his cases, it was simply not possible to determine the correctness or incorrectness of his reasoning because no conclusion was ever reached. Such a case was that of Mr. Burnwell Colby and his fiancée, and the abominable inhabitants of Depewatch Priory. Holmes long kept the singular memento of his investigation in a red cardboard box in his room, and if I have not written of these events before, it is because of the fearful shadow which they left upon my heart. I only write of them now in the light of the new findings of Mr. Freud concerning the strange workings of the human mind.

Burnwell Colby came to the lodgings that I shared with Holmes in Baker Street in the summer of 1894. It was one of those sticky London afternoons that make one long for the luxury of the sea-shore or the Scottish moors. Confirmed Londoner that Holmes was, I am sure he was no more aware of the heat than a fish is of water: whatever conditions prevailed in the city, he preferred to be surrounded by the noise and hurry, the curious street scenes and odd contretemps engendered by the close proximity of over a million fellow creatures, than by any amount of fresh air. As for my-self, the expenses incurred by my dear wife's final illness prevented me from even thinking of quitting the metropolis—and the de-pression of spirits that had overtaken me from the same source sometimes prevented me from thinking at all. While Holmes never by word or look referred to my bereavement, he was an aston-ishingly restful companion in those days, treating me as he always had instead of offering a sympathy which I would have found unendurable.

He was, as I recall, preparing to concoct some appalling chemi-cal mess at the parlor table when Mrs. Hudson's knock sounded at the door. "A Mr. Burnwell Colby to see you, sir."

"What, at this season of the year?" Holmes thumbed the card she handed him, angled it to the window's glaring light. "Heavy stock, one and six the hundred, printed in America in a typeface of a restraint generally found only in the most petrified of dip-lomatic circles but smelling of—" He broke off, and glanced at Mrs. Hudson with eyes suddenly sharp with wary interest. "Yes," he said. "Yes, I shall see this gentleman. Watson, if you would re-main, I would much appreciate an outsider's unbiased view of our guest."

For I had folded together the newspaper, which for the past hour I had stared at, unseeing, preparatory to making a retreat to my bedroom. To tell the truth I welcomed the invitation to remain, and helped Holmes in his rapid disposal of alembic and pipettes into his own chamber. As I reached down for the card, still lying on the much scarred rosewood, Holmes twitched it from my fingers and slipped it into an envelope, which he set in an obscure corner of the bookcase. "Let us not drip premature surmise into the distilled waters of your observation," he said with a smile. "I am curious to read what would be writ upon a tabula rasa."

"Behold me unbesmirched," I replied, throwing up my hands, and settled back onto the settee as the door opened to admit one of the most robust specimens of American manhood that it has ever been my privilege to encounter. Six feet tall, broad of shoulder and chest, he had dark eyes luminous with intelligence under a noble brow in a rather long face, and by his well-cut, if rather American brown suit and gloves of fawn kid, he clearly added material wealth to the blessings of kindly nature. He held out his hand to Holmes and introduced himself, and Holmes inclined his head.

"And this is my partner and amanuensis, Dr. Watson," said Holmes, and Mr. Colby turned unhesitatingly to shake my hand. "Anything that may be said to me may be said in his presence as well."

"Of course," said Colby, in his deep, pleasing voice, "of course. I have no secrets—that's what gravels me." And he shook his head with a ghost of a chuckle. "The Colbys are one of the wealthiest families in New England: we've traded with China for fifty years and with India for twice that, and our railroad interests now will better those profits a thousand percent. I've been educated at Harvard and Oxford, and if I may say so without tooting my own horn, I'm reasonably good to look on and I don't eat with my knife or sleep in my boots. So what would there be about me, Mr. Holmes, that would cause a respectable girl's guardians to reject my suit out of hand and forbid me to exchange a word with her?"

"Oh, I could name a dozen commonplace possibilities," replied Holmes, gesturing him to a chair. "And a score more if we wished to peruse a catalog of the outré. Perhaps you could tell me, Mr. Colby, the name of this unfortunate young lady and the circumstances under which you were so rudely ejected from her parents' favor?"

"Guardians," corrected our visitor. "Her uncle is the Honorable Carstairs Delapore, and her grandfather, Gaius, Viscount Delapore, of Depewatch Priory in Shropshire. It's a crumbling, moldering, Gothic old pile, sinking into decay. My family's money could easily rescue it—as I've said to Mr. Delapore, any number of times, and he agrees with me."

"A curious thing to do, for a man rejecting your suit."

Colby's breath gusted again in exasperated laughter. "Isn't it? It isn't as if I were a stranger off the street, Mr. Holmes. I've been Mr. Delapore's pupil for a year, have lived in his household on weekends, eaten at his table. When I first came to study with him I could have sworn he approved of my love for Judith."

"And what, precisely, would you say is the nature of Mr. Delapore's teaching?" Holmes leaned back in the basket chair, fingertips pressed lightly together, closely watching the young American's face.

"I guess you'd say he's . . . an antiquarian." Colby's voice was hesitant, as if picking his words. "One of the most remarkable students of ancient folklore and legend in the world. Indeed, it was in the hopes of studying with him that I came to Oxford. I am—I guess you might call me the intellectual black sheep of the Colby family." He chuckled again. "My father left the firm to my brothers and myself, but on the whole I've been content to let them run it as they wished. The making of money . . . the constant clamor of stocks and rail shares and directors . . . From the time I was a small boy I sensed there were deeper matters than that in the world, forgotten shadows lurking behind the gaslights' artificial glare."

Holmes said nothing to this, but his eyelids lowered, as if he were listening for something behind the words. Colby, hands clasped, seemed almost to have forgotten his presence, or mine, or the reality of the stuffy summer heat. He went on, "I had corresponded with Carstairs Delapore on . . . on the subject of some of the more obscure Lammastide customs of the Welsh borderlands. As I'd hoped, he agreed to guide my studies, both at Oxford and, later, among the books of his private collection—marvelous volumes that clarified ancient folkloric rites and put them into contexts of philosophy, history, the very fabric of time itself! Depewatch Priory . . ."

He seemed to come to himself with a start, glanced at Holmes, then at me, and went on in a more constrained voice, "It was at Depewatch Priory that I first met Mr. Delapore's niece, Judith. She is eighteen, the daughter of Mr. Delapore's brother Fynch, a spirit of light and innocence in that . . . in that dreary old pile. She had just returned from finishing school in Switzerland, though plans for her come-out into London society had run aground on the family's poverty. Any other girl I know would have been pouting and in tears at being robbed of her season on the town. Not she! She bore it bravely and sweetly, though it was clear that she faced a lifetime of stagnation in a tiny mountain town, looking after a decrepit house and a . . . a difficult old man."

From his jacket pocket Colby withdrew an embossed cardboard photograph case, opening it to show the image of a most beautiful young lady. Thin and rather fragile looking, she wore her soft curls in a chignon. Her eyes seemed light, blue or hazel so far as I could tell from the monotone photograph, her hair a medium shade—perhaps red, but more likely light brown—and her complexion pale to ghostliness. Her expression was one of grave innocence, trusting and unselfconscious.

"Old Viscount Delapore is a grim old autocrat who rules his son, his niece, and every soul in the village of Watchgate as if it were 1394 instead of 1894. He owns all of the land thereabouts—the family has, I gather, from time immemorial—and so violent is his temper that the villagers dare not cross him. From the first moment Judith declared her love for me, I offered to take her away from the place—to take her clean out of the country, if need be, though I hardly think he would come after her, as she seems to fear."

"Does she fear her grandfather?" Holmes turned the photograph thoughtfully over in his hands, examining the back as well as the front most minutely.

Colby nodded, his face clouding with anger. "She claims she's free to come and go, that there's no influence being brought to bear upon her. But there is, Mr. Holmes, there is! When she speaks of Viscount Delapore she glances over her shoulder, as if she imagines he could hear her wherever she is. And the look in her lovely eyes . . . ! She fears him, Mr. Holmes. He has some evil and unwholesome hold upon the girl. He's not her legal guardian—that's Mr. Carstairs Delapore. But the old man's influence extends to his son as well. When I received this"—he drew from the same pocket as the photograph a single sheet of folded paper, which he passed across to Holmes—"I begged him to countermand his father's order, to at least let me present my case. But this card"—he handed a large, stiff note to Holmes—"was all I got back."

The letter was dated August 16, four days ago.

My best beloved,

My heart is torn from my breast by this most terrible news. My grandfather has forbidden me to see you again, forbidden even that your name be mentioned in this house. He will give no reason for this beyond that it is his will that I remain here with him, as his servant—I fear, as his slave! I have written to my father, but fear he will do nothing. I am in despair! Do nothing, but wait and be ready.

Thine only,

Judith

The delicate pink paper, scented with patchouli and with the faint smoke of the oil lamp by which it must have been written, was blotted with tears.

Her father's card said merely:

Remove her from your thoughts. There is nothing which can be done.

Burnwell Colby smote the palm of one hand with the fist of the other, and his strong jaw jutted forward. "My grandfather didn't let the mandarins of Hong Kong chase him away, and my father refused to be stopped by Sioux Indians or winter snows in the Rockies," he declared. "Nor shall this stop me. Will you find out for me, Mr. Holmes, what vile hold Lord Gaius has upon his granddaughter and his son, that I may free the gentlest girl that ever lived from the clutches of an evil old man who seeks to make a drudge of her forever?"

"And is this all," asked Holmes, raising his eyelids to meet the American's earnest gaze, "that you have to tell me about Carstairs Delapore and his father? Or about these 'lurking shadows' that are Delapore's study?"

The young man frowned, as if the question took him momentarily aback. "Oh, the squeamish may speak of decadence," he said after a moment, not offhandedly, but as if carefully considering his words. "And some of the practices which Delapore has uncovered are fairly ugly by modern standards. Certainly they'd make my old pater blink, and my poor hidebround brothers." He chuckled, as if at the recollection of a schoolboy prank. "But at bottom it's all only legends, you know, and bogies in the dark."

"Indeed," said Holmes, rising, and held out his hand to the young suitor. "I shall learn of this what I can, Mr. Colby. Where might I reach you?"

"The Excelsior Hotel in Brighton." The young man fished from his vest pocket a card to write the address upon—he seemed to carry everything loose in his pockets, jumbled together like cabbages in a barrow. "I always stay there," he explained as he scribbled. "It was how Miss Delapore knew where to reach me.

How you can abide to remain in town in weather like this beats me!" And he departed, apparently unaware that not everyone's grandfather rammed opium down Chinese throats in order to pay the Excelsior's summer-holiday prices.

"So what do you think of our American Romeo?" inquired Holmes as the rattle of Colby's cab departed down Baker Street. "What sort of man does he appear to be?"

"A wealthy one," I said, still stung by that careless remark about those who remained in town. "One not used to hearing the word *no*. But earnest and good of heart, I would say. Certainly he takes a balanced view of these 'decadent' studies—to which the Delapores can scarcely object, if they share them."

"True enough." Holmes set letter and note upon the table, and went to the bookcase to draw out his copy of the *Court Gazette*, which was so interleaved with snipped-out society columns, newspaper clippings, and notes in Holmes's neat, strong handwriting as to bulge to almost double its original size. "But what are the nature of these folkloric 'practices' which are 'fairly ugly by modern standards'? Ugliness by the standards of a world which has invented the Maxim gun can scarcely be termed bogies in the dark.

"Carstairs Delapore," he read, opening the book upon his long arm. "Questioned concerning his whereabouts on the night of the twenty-seventh August, 1890, when the owner of a public house in Whitechapel reported her ten-year-old son Thomas missing; a man of Delapore's description—he is evidently of fairly unforgettable appearance—seen speaking with the boy that evening. Thomas never found. I thought I recognized the name. Delapore was also questioned in 1873 by the Manchester police—he was in that city, for no discernible reason, when two little mill girls went missing . . . I must say I'm astonished that anyone reported their disappearance. Mudlarks and street urchins vanish every day from the streets of London and no one inquires after them any more than one inquires the whereabouts of butterflies once they flitter over the garden fence. A man need not even be very clever to kidnap children in London." He shut the book, his eyes narrowing as he turned his gaze to the endless wasteland of brick that lay beyond the window. "Merely careful to pick the dirtiest and hungriest, and those without parents or homes."

"That's a serious conclusion to jump to," I said, startled and repelled.

"It is," Holmes replied. "Which is why I jump to nothing. But Gaius, Viscount Delapore, was mentioned three times in the early reports of the Metropolitan police—between 1833 and 1850—in connection with precisely such investigations, at the same time that he was publishing a series of monographs on 'Demonic Ritual Survivals Along the Welsh Borders' for the discredited Eye of Dawn Society. And in 1863, an American reporter disappeared while investigating rumors of a pagan cult in western Shropshire, not five miles from Watchgate village, which lies below the hill upon which Depewatch Priory stands."

"But even so," I said, "even if the Delapores are involved in some kind of theosophistic studies—or white slaving, for that matter—would they not seek rather to get an outsider like Delapore's niece out of the house, rather than keeping her there as a potential source of trouble? And how would the old man use a pack of occult rubbish to dominate his granddaughter and his son against their will?"

"How indeed?" Holmes went to the bookcase again, and took down the envelope in which he had bestowed Burnwell Colby's card. "I, too, found our American visitor—despite his patent desire to disown association with his hidebound and boring family—an ingenuous and harmless young man. Which makes this all the more curious."

He held out the envelope to me, and I took it out and examined it as he had. The stock, as he had said, was expensive and the typeface rigidly correct, although the card itself bore slight traces of having been carried about loose in Mr. Colby's pockets with pens, notes, and photographs of his beloved Judith. Only when I brought it close to examine the small dents and scratches on its surface was I conscious of the smell that seemed to imbue the thick, soft paper, a nauseating mix of frankincense, charred hair, and . . .

I looked up at Holmes, my eyes wide. I had been a soldier in India, and a physician for most of my life. I knew the smell.

"Blood," I said.

The note Holmes sent that afternoon received an answer within hours, and after we had finished our supper he invited me to accompany him to the home of a friend on the Embankment near the Temple: "A curious customer who may fill in for you some hitherto unsuspected colors in the palette of London life," he said. Mr. Carnaki was a thin young man of medium height and attenuated build, whose large gray eyes regarded one from behind thick spectacle lenses with an expression it is hard to define: as if he were always watching for something that others do not see. His tall, narrow house was filled with books, even lining the walls of the hallways on both sides, so that a broad-built man would have been obliged to sidle through crabwise, and through the darkened doorways I glimpsed the flicker of gaslight across what appeared to be complex chemical and electrical apparatus. He listened to Holmes's account of Burnwell Colby's visit without comment, his chin resting on one long, spidery hand, then rose from his chair and climbed a pair of steps to an upper shelf of one of the many bookcases that walled the small study at the back of the house to which he'd led us.

" 'Depewatch Priory,' " he read aloud, " 'stands on a cliff above the village of Watchgate in the wild hill country on the borders of Wales, where in 1215 King John confirmed the appointment of an Augustinian prior over an existing "hooly howse" of religion said to date back to foundation by Joseph of Arimathea. It appears from its inception to have been the center of a cycle of legends and whispers: indeed, the king's original intent was apparently to have the place pulled down and salt strewn on its foundations.

One Philip of Mundberg petitioned Edward IV, describing the monks there engaged in "comerce wyth daemons yt did issue forth from Hell, and make knowne theyr wants by means of certain dremes," but he apparently never reached the king himself and the investigation was dropped. There were repeated accusations of heresy involving the transmigration of the souls of certain priors, rumors which apparently transferred themselves to the Grimsley family, to whom Henry VIII presented the priory in 1540, and surfaced in the 1780s in connection with the Delapores, who succeeded them through marriage.'

"William Punt"—he tapped the black leather covers of the volume as he set it on the table beside Holmes—"in his *Catalogue of Secret Abominations* described the place in 1793 as being a 'goodly manor of gray stone' built upon the foundations of the Plantagenet cloister, but says that the original core of the establishment is the ruin of a tower, probably Roman in origin. Punt speaks of stairs leading down to a subcrypt, where the priors used to sleep upon a crude altar after appalling rites. When Lord Rupert Grimsley was murdered by his wife and daughters in 1687, they apparently boiled his body and buried his bones in the subcrypt, reserving his skull, which they placed in a niche at the foot of the main stair in the manor house itself, 'that evil dare not pass.' "

I could not repress a chuckle. "As protective totems go, it didn't do Lord Rupert much good, did it?"

"I daresay not," returned Holmes with a smile. "Yet my reading of the 1840 Amsterdam edition of Punt's *Catalogue* leads me to infer that the local population didn't regard Rupert Grimsley's murder as particularly evil; the villagers impeded the Metropolitan police in the pursuit of their duties to such effect that the three murderesses got completely away."

"Good heavens, yes." Carnaki turned, and drew out another volume, more innocuous than the sinister-looking tome of abominations: this one was simply a history of West Country families, as heavily interleaved with clippings and notes as was Holmes's *Gazette*. "Rupert Grimsley was feared as a sorcerer from Shrewsbury to the Estuary; he is widely reputed to have worked the roads as a highwayman, carrying off not valuables but travelers, who were never seen again. Demons were said to come and go at his command, and at least two lunatics from that section of the Welsh border—one in the early part of the eighteenth century and one as recently as 1842—swore that old Lord Rupert dwelled in the bodies of all the successive Lords of Depewatch."

"You mean that he was being constantly reincarnated?" I admit this surfacing of this Tibetan belief in the prosaic hill country of Wales startled me considerably.

Carnaki shook his head. "That the spirit—the consciousness—of Rupert Grimsley passed from body to body, battening like a parasite upon that of the heir and driving out the younger man's soul, as the human portion of each Lord of Depewatch died."

The young antiquarian looked so serious as he said this that again I was hard put to suffocate a laugh; Carnaki's expression did not alter, but his eyes flicked from my face to Holmes's. "I suppose," said the young man after a moment, "that this had something to do with the fact that each of the gentlemen in question were rumored to be involved with mysterious disappearances among the coal miners of the district: Gerald, Viscount Delapore, who is reputed to have undergone so terrifying a change in personality at his accession to the title that his wife left him and fled to America . . . with the young Gaius Delapore himself."

"Indeed?" Holmes leaned forward eagerly in his chair, his hand still resting on the *Catalogue*, which he had been examining with the delighted reverence of a true lover of ancient volumes. He had hardly taken his eyes from the many tomes that were stacked on every table and most of the corners of Carnaki's little study, some of them the musty calf or morocco of Georgian bookbinders, others the heavier, more archaic black-letter incunabula of the early days of printing, with not a few older still, handwritten in Latin upon parchment or vellum and illuminated with spidery marginalia that even at a distance disturbed me by their anomalous *bizarrerie*. "And what, precisely, is the evil that is ascribed by legend to Depewatch Priory, and for what purpose did Rupert Grimsley and his successors seek out those who had no power, and whom society would not miss?"

Carnaki set aside his history and seated himself on the oak bookcase steps, his long, thin arms resting on his knees. He glanced again at me, not as if I had offended him with my earlier laughter but as if gauging how to phrase things so that I would understand them; then his eyes returned to Holmes.

"You have heard, I think, of the six thousand steps, that are hinted at—never directly—in the remote legends of both the old Cymric tribes that preceded the Celts, and of the American Indian? Of the pit that lies deep at the heart of the world, and of the entities that are said to dwell in the abysses beyond it?"

"I have heard of these things," said Holmes quietly. "There was a case in Arkham, Massachusetts, in 1869 . . ."

"The Whateley case, yes." Carnaki's long, sensitive mouth twitched with remembered distaste, and his glance turned to me. "These legends—remembered only through two cults of quite shockingly degenerate Indian tribes, one in Maine and the other, curiously, in northeastern Arizona, where they are shunned by the surrounding Navajo and Hopi—speak of things, entities, sentient yet not wholly material, that have occupied the lightless chasms of space and time since the days before humankind's furthest ancestors first stood upright. These elder beings fear the light of the sun, yet with the coming of darkness would creep forth from certain places in the world to prey upon human bodies and human dreams, through the centuries making surprising and dreadful bargains with individuals of mankind in return for most hideous payment."

"And this is what Gaius Delapore and his son believe they have in their basement?" My eyebrows shot up. "It should make it easy enough for us to assist young Mr. Colby in freeing his fiancée from the influence of two obvious lunatics."

Holmes said softly, "So it should."

We remained at Carnaki's until nearly midnight while Holmes and the young antiquarian—for so I assumed Carnaki to be—spoke of the appalling folkloric and theosophical speculations that evidently fueled Viscount Delapore's madness: hideous tales of creatures beyond human imaginings or human dreams, monstrous legends of dim survivals from impossibly ancient eons, and of those deluded madmen whose twisted minds accepted such absurdities for truth. Holmes was right in his assertion that the visit would supply the palette of my knowledge of London with hitherto unsuspected hues. What surprised me was Holmes's knowledge of such things, for on the whole he was a man of practical bent, never giving his attention to a subject unless it was with some end in view.

Yet when Carnaki spoke of the abomination of abominations, of the terrible amorphous shoggoths and the Watcher of the Gate, Holmes nodded, as one does who hears familiar names. The shocking rites engaged in by the covens of ancient believers, whether American Indians or decayed cults to be found in the fastnesses of Greenland or Tibet, did not surprise him, and it was he, not our host, who spoke of the insane legend of the shapeless god who plays the pipe in the dark heart of chaos, and who sends forth the dreams that drive men mad.

"I did not know that you made a study of such absurdities, Holmes," I said, when we stood once more on the fog-shrouded Embankment, listening for the approaching clip of a cab horse's hooves. "I would hardly have said theosophy was your line."

"My line is anything that will—or has—provided a motive for men's crimes, Watson." He lifted his hand and whistled for the jehu, an eerie sound in the muffled stillness. His face in the glare of the gaslight seemed pale and set. "Whether a man bows down to God or Mammon or to Cthulhu in his dark house at R'lyeh is no affair of mine . . . until he sheds one drop of blood not his own in his deity's name. Then God have mercy upon him, for I shall not."

All of these events took place on Monday, the twentieth of August. The following day Holmes was engaged with turning over the pages of his scrapbooks of clippings regarding unsolved crimes, seeming, it appeared to me, to concentrate on disappearances during the later part of the summer in years back almost to the beginning of the century. On Wednesday Mrs. Hudson sent up the familiar elegantly restrained calling card of the American folklorist, the man himself following hard upon her heels and almost thrusting her out of the way as he entered our parlor.

"Well, Holmes, it's all settled and done with," he declared, in a loud voice very unlike his own. "Thank you for your patience with old Delapore's damned rodomontade, but I've seen the old man myself—he came down to town yesterday, damn his impudence— and made him see reason."

"Have you?" asked Holmes politely, gesturing to the chair in which he had first sat.

Colby waved him impatiently away. "Simplest thing in nature, really. Feed a cur and he'll shut up barking. And here's for you." And he drew from his pocket a small leather bag which he tossed carelessly onto the table. It struck with the heavy, metallic ring of golden coin. "Thank you again."

"And I thank you." Holmes bowed, but he watched Colby's face as he spoke, and I could see his own face had turned very pale. "Surely you are too generous."

" 'S blood, man, what's a few guineas to me? I can tear up little Judi's poor letter, now we're to be wed all right and tight . . ." He winked lewdly at Holmes and held out his hand. "And her old dad's damned impudent note as well, if you would."

Holmes looked around him vaguely and picked up various of

his scrapbooks from the table to look beneath them: "Didn't you tuck it behind the clock?" I asked.

"Did I?" Holmes went immediately to the mantel—cluttered as always with newspapers, books, and unanswered correspondence—and after a brief search shook his head. "I shall find it, never fear," he said, his brow furrowing. "And return it, if you would be so kind as to give me your direction once more."

Colby hesitated, then snatched the nearest piece of paper from the table—a bill from Holmes's tailor, I believe it was—and scribbled an address upon it. "I'm off to Watchgate this afternoon," he said. "This will find me."

"Thank you," said Holmes, and I noticed that he neither touched the paper, nor came within arm's reach of the man who stood before him. "I shall have it in the post before nightfall. I can't think what can have become of it. It has been a pleasure to make your acquaintance, Mr. Colby. My felicitations on the happy outcome of your suit."

When Colby was gone Holmes stood for a time beside the table, looking after him a little blankly, his hands knotted into fists where they rested among the scrapbooks. He whispered, "Damn him," as if he had forgotten my presence in the room. "My God, I had not believed it . . ."

Then, turning sharply, he went to the mantelpiece and immediately withdrew from behind the clock the note which Carstairs Delapore had sent to Colby. This he tucked into an envelope and sealed. As he copied the direction he asked in a stiff, expressionless tone, "What did you make of our guest, Watson?"

"That success has made him bumptious," I replied, for I had liked Colby less in his elevated and energized mood than I had when he was merely unthinking about his own and other people's money. "Holmes, what is it? What's wrong?"

"Did you happen to notice which hand he wrote out his direction with?"

I thought for a moment, picturing the man scribbling, then said, "His left."

"Yet when he wrote the address of the Hotel Excelsior the day before yesterday," said Holmes, "he did so with his right hand."

"So he did." I came to his side and picked up the tailor's bill, and compared the writing on it with that of the Excelsior address, which lay on the table among the scrapbooks and clippings. "That would account for the hand being so very different."

Holmes said, "Indeed." But he spoke looking out the window onto Baker Street, and the harsh glare of the morning sunlight gave his eyes a steely cast, faraway and cold, as if he saw from a distance some terrible event taking place. "I am going to Shropshire, Watson," he said after a moment. "I'm leaving tonight, on the last train; I should be back—"

"Then you find Viscount Delapore's sudden capitulation as sinister as I do," I said.

He looked at me with blank surprise, as if that construction of young Colby's information had been the farthest thing from his mind. Then he laughed, a single sharp mirthless breath, and said, "Yes. Yes, I find it . . . sinister."

"Do you think young Colby is walking into some peril, returning to Depewatch Priory?"

"I think my client is in peril, yes," said Holmes quietly. "And if I cannot save him, then the least that I can do is avenge."

Holmes at first refused to hear of me accompanying him to the borders of Wales, sending instead a note to Carnaki with instructions to be ready to depart by the eight o'clock train. But when Billy the messenger boy returned with the information that Carnaki was from home and would not return until the following day, he assented, sending a second communication to the young antiquarian requesting that he meet us in the village of High Clum, a few miles from Watchgate, the following day.

It puzzled me that Holmes should have chosen the late train, if he feared for Colby's life should the young man return to fetch his fiancée from the hands of the two monomaniacs at Depewatch Priory. Still more did it puzzle me that, upon our arrival at midnight in the market town of High Clum, Holmes took rooms for us at the Cross of Gold, as if he were deliberately putting distance between us and the man he spoke of—when he could be induced to speak at all—as if he were already dead.

In the morning, instead of attempting to communicate with Colby, Holmes hired a pony trap and a boy to drive us to the wooded ridge that divided High Clum from the vale in which the village of Watchgate stood. "Queer folk there," the lad said as the sturdy cob leaned into its collars on the slope. "It's only a matter of four mile, but it's like as if they lived in another land. You never do hear of one of their lads come courtin' in Clum, and the folk there's so odd now none of ours'n will go there. They come for the market, oncet a week. Sometimes you'll see Mr. Carstairs drive to town, all bent and withered up like a tree hit by lightnin', starin' about him with those pale eyes: yellow hazel, like all the Delapore; rotten apples my mum calls 'em. And old Gaius with him sometimes, treatin' him like as if he was a dog, the way he treats everyone."

The boy drew his horse to a halt and pointed out across the valley with his whip: "That'll be the priory, sir."

After all that had been spoken of monstrous survivals and ancient cults, I had half expected to see some blackened Gothic pile thrusting flamboyant spires above the level of the trees. But in fact, as Carnaki had read in William Punt's book, Depewatch Priory appeared, from across the valley, to be simply a "goodly manor of gray stone," its walls rather overgrown with ivy and several windows broken and boarded shut. I frowned, remembering the casual way in which Colby had thrown his sack of guineas onto Holmes's table: feed a cur and he'll shut up barking . . .

Yet old Gaius had originally turned down Colby's offer to help him bring the priory back into proper repair.

Behind the low roofline of the original house I could see what had to be the Roman tower Carnaki had spoken of—beyond doubt the original "watch" of both priory and village names. It had clearly been kept in intermittent repair up until the early part of this century, an astonishing survival. Beneath it, I recalled, Carnaki had said the subcrypt lay: the center of that decadent cult that dated to pre-Roman times. I found myself wondering if old Gaius descended the stairs to sleep on the ancient altar, as the notorious Lord Rupert Grimsley had been said to do, and if so, what dreams had come to him there.

After London's stuffy heat the thick-wooded foothills were deliciously cool. The breezes brought the scent of water from the heights, and the sharp nip of rain. Perhaps this contrast was what brought upon me what happened later that day, and that horrible night—I know not. For surely, after I returned to the Cross of Gold, I must have come down ill and lain delirious. There is no other explanation—I pray there is no other explanation—for the ghastly dreams, worse than any delirium I experienced while sick with fever in India, that dragged me through abysses of horror while I slept and have for years shadowed not only my sleep, but upon occasion my waking as well.

I remember that Holmes took the trap to the station to meet Carnaki. I remember, too, sitting by the window of our pleasant sitting room, cleaning my pistol, for I feared that, if Holmes had in fact found some proof that the evil viscount had kidnapped beggar children for some ancient and unspeakable rite, there might be trouble when we confronted the old autocrat with it. I certainly felt no preliminary shiver, no premonitory dizziness of fever, when I rose to answer the knock at the parlor door.

The man who stood framed there could be no one but Carstairs Delapore. "Withered all up like a tree hit by lightnin'," the stable lad had said: had his back been straight, he still would not have been as tall as I, and he looked up at me sideways, twisting his head upon a skinny neck like a bird's.

His eyes were a light hazel, almost golden, as the boy had said. They are my last memory of the waking world that afternoon.

I dreamed of lying in darkness. I ached all over, my neck and spine pinched and stiff, and from somewhere near me I heard a thin, harsh sobbing, like an old man in terror or pain. I called out, "Who is it? What is wrong?" and my voice sounded hoarse in my own ears, like the rusty caw of a crow, as alien as my body felt when I tried to move.

"My God," sobbed the old man's voice, "my God, the pit of six thousand stairs! It is Lammastide, the night of sacrifice—dear God, dear God save me! Iä! Shub-Niggurath! It waits for us, waits for us, the Goat with Ten Thousand Young!"

I crawled across an uneven floor, wet and slimy, and the smells around me were the scents of deep earth, dripping rock, and far off the terrible fetors of still worse things: corruption, charred flesh, and the sickeningly familiar scent of incense. My hands touched my companion in this darkness and he pulled away: "No, never! Fiends, that you used poor Judith as bait, to bring me to you! The Hooded Thing in the darkness taught you how, as it taught others before you—showed you the passages in the *Book of Eibon*—told you how to take the bodies of others, how to leave their minds trapped in your old and dying body . . . the body that you then sacrificed to them! A new body, a strong body, a man's body, healthy and fit . . ."

"Hush," I whispered, "hush, you are raving! Who are you, where is this?"

Again I touched his hands, and felt the sticklike bones and flaccid, silky flesh of a very old man. At the same moment those frail hands fumbled at my face, my shoulders, in the dark, and he cried out: "Get away from me! You weren't good enough for him, twisted and crippled and weak! And your daughter only a woman, without the power of a man! It was all a trap, wasn't it? A trap to lure me, thinking it was *she* who sent for me to set her free . . ." His thin voice rose to a shriek and he thrust me from him with feeble hysteria. "And now you will send me down to the pit, down to the pit of the shoggoths!" As his sobs changed to thin, giggling laughter, I heard a stirring, far away in the darkness; a soughing, as if of the movement of things infinitely huge, and soft.

I staggered to my feet, my legs responding queerly; I reeled and limped like a drunken man. I followed the wall in darkness, feeling it to be, in places, ancient stones set without mortar, and, in others, the naked rock of the hill itself. There was a door, desiccated wood strapped with iron that grated, rusty and harsh, under my hands. I stumbled back into the darkness, and struck against something—a stone table, pitted with ancient carvings—and beside it found the only means of egress, a square opening in the floor, in which a flight of worn, shallow steps led downward.

Gropingly I descended, hands outstretched on either side to feel the wet rock of the wall that sometimes narrowed to the straightest of seams: terrified of what might lie below me, yet I feared to be in the power of the madmen I knew to be above. I was dizzy, panting, my mind prey to a thousand illusions, the most terrifying of which was that of the sounds that I seemed to hear, not above me, but below.

In time, the darkness glowed with thin smears of blue phosphor, illuminating the abyss below me. Far down I could descry a chamber, a sort of high-roofed cave where the niter dripped from the walls and showed up a crumbling stone altar, ruinously ancient and stained black with horrible corruption. There was an obscene aberration to the entire geometry of the chamber, as if the angles of floor and walls should not have met in the fashion they appeared to; as if I viewed an optical illusion, a trick of darkness and shadow. From the innermost angle of that chamber darkness issued, like a thicker flow of night, blackness that seemed one moment to congeal into discrete forms which the next proved to be only inchoate stirrings. Yet there was something there, something the fear of which kept me from moving on, from making a sound—from breathing, even, lest the gasp of my breath bring upon me some unimaginably nightmarish fate.

My fellow captive's high, hysterical giggling on the stair above me drove me into a niche in the wet rock. He was coming down—and he was not alone. Pressed into the narrow darkness, I only heard the sounds of bodies passing on the stair. A moment later others followed them, while I crouched, praying to all the gods ever worshiped by fearful man to be spared the notice of anything that walked that eldritch abyss. At the same moment sounds rose from below, a rhythmless wailing or chittering that nevertheless seemed to hold the form of music, underlain by a thick lapping or surging sound, as if of thick, unspeakably vile liquid rising among stones.

Looking around the sheltering coign of rock, I saw by the growing purplish hell glare below me the tall figure of Burnwell Colby, standing beside the altar, an unfleshed skull held upraised in his hands. Darkness ringed him, but it seemed almost as if the skull itself gave light, a pulsing and horrible radiation that showed me—almost—the shapes of which the utter blackness was composed. I bit my hand to keep from crying out, and wondered that the pain of it did not wake me; an old man lay on the altar, and by his sobbing giggles I knew him to be he who had been shut into the stone crypt above with me. Colby's deep voice rang out above the strident piping: *"Ygnaiih . . . ygnaiih . . . thflthkh'ngha . . ."*

And the things in the darkness—horrible half-seen suggestions of squamous, eyeless heads, of tentacles glistening, and of small round mouths opening and closing with an appalling glint of teeth—answered with a thick and greedy wail.

"H'ehye n'grkdl'lh, h'ehye . . . in the name of Yog-Sothoth I call, I command . . ."

Something—I know not what nor do I dare to think—raised itself behind the altar, something shapeless that glowed and yet seemed to swallow all light, hooded in utter darkness. The old man on the altar began to scream, a high thin steady shriek of absolute terror, and Colby shouted, "I command you . . . I command . . . !" Then it seemed to me that he gasped, and swallowed, as if his breath stopped within his lungs, before he held up the skull again and cried, "*Ngrkdl'lh y'bthnk,* Shub-Niggurath! In the name of the Goat with Ten Thousand Young I command!"

Then the darkness swallowed the altar, and where a moment before I could see the old man writhing, I could see only churning darkness, while a hideous fetor of blood and death rolled up from the pit, nearly making me faint. "Before the Five Hundred," cried Colby . . . then he staggered suddenly, nearly dropping the skull he held. "Before the Five Hundred . . ."

He gasped, as if struggling to speak. The thing upon the altar lifted its hooded head, and in the sudden silence the dreadful lapping sound of the deeper darkness seemed to fill the unholy place, and the far-off answering echo of the now-silenced pipes.

Then with a cry Colby fell to his knees, the skull slipping from his hands. He choked, grasping for it, and from the darkness of the stair behind him another form darted forward, small and slim, and stooped to snatch up the talisman skull of the terrible ancestor who had ruled this place.

"*Ygnaiih, ygnaiih* Yog-Sothoth!" cried a woman's voice, high and powerful, filling the hideous chamber, and the darkness that had surged toward her seemed for a moment to close in as it had closed around the old man on the altar, then to fall back. By the queer, actinic luminosity of the skull I could see the woman's face, and recognized her as Judith Delapore, niece and granddaughter of the madmen who ruled Depewatch. Yet how different from the sweet countenance painted on Colby's miniature! Like the ivory mask of a goddess, cold and lined with concentration, she bent her eyes on the heaving swirl of nightmare that surrounded her, not even glancing at her lover, who lay gasping, twisting in convulsions at her feet. In a high, hard voice she repeated the dreadful words of the incantations, and neither flinched nor wavered as the dreadful things flittered and crawled and quivered in the darkness.

Only when the hideous rite was ended, and the unspeakable congregation had trickled away through the blasphemous angle of the inner walls, did the young woman lower the skull she held. She stood in her black gown, outlined in the gleam of the niter on the walls, staring into the abyss from which those dreadful unhuman things had come, barely seeming to notice me as I stumbled and staggered down the last of the stairs.

Of the old man's body that had lain upon the altar, nothing whatsoever remained. A thick layer of slime covered the stone and ran down onto the floor, which was perhaps half an inch deep in a brownish liquid that glistened in the feeble blue gleam of the niter. Having seen Burnwell Colby engulfed by that wriggling darkness, I staggered to where he had lain with some confused idea of helping him, but as I dropped to my knees I saw that only a lumpy mass of half-dissolved flesh and bones remained. The bones themselves had the appearance of being charred, almost melted. I looked up in horror at the woman with the skull, and her eyes met mine, clear golden hazel, like other eyes I could not quite recall. Her eyes widened and filled with anger and hate.

"You," she whispered. "So you did not take him after all?"

I only shook my head, her words making no sense to me in my shaken state, and she went on, "As you have seen, Uncle, it is I, now, and not Grandfather—Grandfather who has not existed for over fifty years—who rules now here." And to my horror she held out her hand toward that hideously anomalous angle of the walls where the darkness lay waiting. *"Y'bfnk—ng'haiie . . ."*

I cried out. At the same instant light blazed up on the stairway that led to the upper and innocent realms of the ignorant world: blue-white incandescence, like lightning, and the crackle of ozone filled the reeking air.

"My dear Miss Delapore," said Holmes, "if you will pardon my interruption, I fear you are laboring under a misapprehension." He came down the last of the stairs, bearing in one hand a metal rod, from which a flickering corona of electricity seemed to sparkle, flowing back to a similar rod held up by Carnaki, who followed him down the stairs. Carnaki wore a sort of pack or rucksack upon his back, of the kind one sees porters in Constantinople carrying; a dozen wires joined it to the rod in his hand, and lightnings leaped from that rod to Holmes's, seeming to surround the two men in a deadly nimbus of light. The cold glare blanched all color from Holmes's face, so that his eyebrows stood out nearly black, like a man who has received a mortal blow and bleeds within.

Looking down at me, he asked, as if we shared a cup of tea at Baker Street, "What was your wife's favorite flower?"

Miss Delapore, startled, opened her mouth to speak, but I cried in a convulsion of grief: "How can you ask that, Holmes? How can you speak of my Mary in this place, after what we have seen? Her life was all goodness, all joy, and it was for *nothing*, do you understand? If this—this blasphemy—this monstrous abyss underlies all of our world, how can any good, any joy, exist in safety? It is a mockery—love, care, tenderness . . . it means nothing, and we are all fools for believing in any of it . . ."

"Watson!" thundered Holmes, and again Miss Delapore turned her eyes to him in astonishment.

"Watson?" she whispered.

His gaze held mine, and he asked again: "What was Mrs. Watson's favorite flower?"

"Lily of the valley," I said, and buried my face in my hands. Even as I did so I saw—such was the horror and strangeness of my dream—that they were the hands of an elderly man, thin and twisted with arthritis, and the wedding band that I had never ceased to wear with my Mary's death was gone. "But none of it matters now, nor ever will again, knowing what I now know of the true nature of this world."

Through my weeping I heard Carnaki say softly, "We'll have to switch off the electrical field. I don't think we can get him up the stairs."

"You will be safe," said Miss Delapore's voice. "I command Them now—as did my grandfather, or the thing that for so many years passed itself off as my grandfather. I knew his goal—its goal—was to take over Burnwell's body, as it had taken over my grandfather's fifty years ago. He despised my uncle, as he despised my father, and as he despised me as a woman, thinking us all too weak to withstand the power raised by the Rite of the *Book of Eibon*. Why else did he bring me home from school, save to lure that poor American to his fate?"

"With a letter blotted with tears," said Holmes dryly. "Even in the margins, and the blank upper portion by the address. Hardly the places where a girl's tears would fall while writing, but it's difficult to keep drops from spattering there when they're dipped from a bedroom pitcher with the fingers."

"Had I not written that letter," she replied, "it would be I, not Grandfather, who was given to the Hooded One tonight. At least by luring Burnwell to me I was able to give him poison—brown spider mushroom, that does not take effect for many days. Grandfather would have had him, one way or another—he does not give up easily."

"And was it you who sent for him, to meet your grandfather in Brighton?"

"No. But I knew it would come. When Grandfather—when Lord Rupert's vampire spirit—entered poor Burnwell's body, that body was already dying, though none knew it but I. I knew Uncle Carstairs had mastered the technique, too, of crossing from body to body—I assume it is you who were his target, and not your friend."

"Even so," said Holmes, and his voice was quiet and bitterly cold. "He underestimated me—and both underestimated you, it seems."

And there was the smallest touch of defiance in her voice as she replied, "Men do. Yourself included, it seems."

The snapping hiss of the electricity ceased. I opened my eyes to see them kneeling around me, in the horror of that nighted cavern: Holmes and Carnaki, holding their electrical rods to either of my hands, and Miss Delapore looking into my eyes. Somehow, despite the darkness, I could see her clearly, could see into her golden eyes, as one can in dreams. What she said to me I do not remember, lost as it was in the shock and cold when Carnaki touched the switch . . .

I opened my eyes to summer morning. My head ached; when I brought my hand up to touch it, I saw that my wrists were bruised and chafed, as if I had been bound. "You were off your head for much of the night," said Holmes, sitting beside the bed. "We feared you would do yourself an injury—indeed, you gave us great cause for concern."

I looked around me at the simple wallpaper and white curtains of my bedroom at the Cross of Gold in High Clum. I stammered, "I don't remember what happened . . ."

"Fever," said Carnaki, coming into the room with a slender young lady whom I instantly recognized from the miniature Burn-well Colby had showed us as Miss Judith Delapore. "I have never seen so rapid a rise of temperature in so short a time; you must have taken quite a severe chill."

I shook my head, wondering what it was about Miss Delapore's haggard calm, about her golden-hazel eyes, that filled me with such uneasy horror. "I remember nothing," I said. "Dreams . . . Your uncle came here, I believe," I added, after Holmes had intro-duced the young lady. "At least . . . I believe it was your uncle . . ." Why was I so certain that the wizened, twisted little man who had come to my room—whom I believed had come to my room—yesterday had been Carstairs Delapore? I could recall nothing of what he had said. Only his eyes . . .

"It was my uncle," said Miss Delapore, and as I looked at her again I realized that she wore mourning. "You remember nothing of why he came here yesterday? For before he could mention the visit to anyone at the priory"—and here she glanced across at Holmes—"he fell down the stairs there, and died at the bottom."

I expressed my horrified condolences while trying to suppress an inexplicable sense of deepest relief that I somehow associated with dreams I had had while delirious. After inclining her head in thanks, Miss Delapore turned to Holmes, and held out to him a box of stout red cardboard, tied up with string. "As I promised," she said.

I lay back, overcome again by a terrible exhaustion—as much of the spirit, it seemed, as of the body. While Carnaki prepared a sedative draft for me Holmes walked Miss Delapore out to our mutual parlor, and I heard the outer door open.

"I have heard much of your deductive abilities, Mr. Holmes," said the young woman's voice, barely heard through the half-open bedroom door. "How did you know that my uncle, who must have come here to take you as my grandfather took Burnwell, had seized upon your friend instead?"

"There was no deduction necessary, Miss Delapore," said Holmes. "I know Watson—and I know what I have heard of your uncle. Would Carstairs Delapore have come down into danger to see what he could do for an injured man?"

"Do not think ill of my family, Mr. Holmes," said Miss Delapore, after a time of silence. "The way which leads down the six thousand stairs cannot be sealed. It must always have a guardian. That is the nature of such things. And it is always easier to find a venal successor who is willing to trade to Them the things They want—the blood They crave—in exchange for gifts and services, than to find one willing to serve a lonely guardianship solely that the world above may remain safe. They feared Lord Rupert—if the thing that all knew as Lord Rupert was in fact not some older spirit still. His bones, buried in the subcrypt, shall, I hope, prove a barrier that They are unwilling to cross. Now that the skull, which was the talisman that commanded Their favors, is gone, perhaps there will be less temptation among those who study in the house."

"There is always temptation, Miss Delapore," said Holmes.

"Get thee behind me, Mr. Holmes," replied the woman's voice, with a touch of silvery amusement far beyond her years. "I saw what that temptation did to my uncle, in his desperate craving to snatch the rule of the things from my grandfather. I saw what my grandfather became. These are things I shall remember, when the time comes to seek a disciple of my own."

I was drowsing already from Carnaki's draft when Holmes returned to the bedroom. "Did you speak to Colby?" I asked, struggling to keep my eyes open as he went to the table and picked up the red cardboard box. "Is he all right?" For my dreams as to his fate had been foul, terrible, and equivocal. "Warn him . . . prevent the old viscount from doing harm?"

Holmes hesitated for a long time, looking down at me with a concern that I did not quite understand in his eyes. "I did," he replied at length. "To such effect that Viscount Delapore has disappeared from the district—for good, one hopes. But as for Burnwell, he, too, has . . . departed. I fear that Miss Delapore is destined to lead a rather difficult and lonely life."

He glanced across at Carnaki, who was packing up what appeared to be an electrical battery and an array of steel rods and wires into a rucksack, the purpose of which I could not imagine. Their eyes met. Then Carnaki nodded, very slightly, as if approving what Holmes had said.

"Because of what was revealed," I asked, stifling a terrible yawn, "about this . . . this blackmail that was being practiced? The young hound, to desert a young lady like that." My eyelids slipped closed. I fought them open again, seized by sudden panic, by the terror that I might slide into sleep and find myself again in that dreadful abyss, watching the horrible things that fluttered and crept from those angles of darkness that should not have been there. "Did you learn . . . anything of these studies they practiced?"

"Indeed we did," said Carnaki. And then, a little airily, "There was nothing in them, though."

"What did Miss Delapore bring you, then?"

"Merely a memento of the case," said Holmes. "As for young Mr. Colby, do not be too hard on him, Watson. He did the best he could, as do we all. I am not sure that he would have been entirely happy with Miss Delapore in any event. She was . . . much the stronger of the two."

Holmes never did elucidate for me the means by which he bridged the gap between his supposition that Viscount Delapore was engaged in kidnapping children for the purposes of some vile cult centered in Depewatch Priory, and evidence sufficient to make that evil man flee the country. If he and Carnaki found such evidence at the Priory—which I assume was the reason he had asked the young antiquarian to accompany us to Shropshire—he did not speak to me of it. Indeed, he showed a great reluctance to refer to the case at all.

For this I was grateful. The effects of the fever I had caught were slow to leave me, and even as much as three years later I found myself prey to the sense that I had learned—and mercifully forgotten—something that would utterly destroy all my sense of what the world is and should be; that would make either life or sanity impossible, if it should turn out to be true.

Only once did Holmes mention the affair, some years later, during a conversation on Freud's theories of insanity, when he spoke in passing of the old Viscount Delapore's conviction— evidently held by others in what is now termed a *folie à deux*—that the old man had in fact been the reincarnated or astrally transposed spirit of Lord Rupert Grimsley, once Lord of Depewatch Priory. And then he spoke circumspectly, watching me, as if he feared to wake my old dreams again and cause me many sleepless nights.

I can only be sorry that the case ended without firm conclusion, for it did, as Holmes promised me that night on the Embankment, show me unsuspected colors in the spectrum of human mentality and human existence. Yet this was not an unmixed blessing. For though I know that my fever dream was no more than that—a fantastic hallucination brought on by illness and by Carnaki's own curious monomania about otherworld cults and ancient writings—sometimes in the shadowland between sleep and waking I think of that terrible blue-lit abyss that lies beneath an old priory on the borders of Wales, and imagine that I hear the eerie piping of chaos rising up out of blasphemous angles of night. And in my dreams I see again the enigmatic Miss Delapore, standing before the chittering congregation of nightmares, holding aloft in her hands the skull of Lord Rupert Grimsley: the skull that now reposes in a corner of Holmes's room, wrapped in its red cardboard box.

The Mystery of the Worm

JOHN PELAN

I have reviewed the remarkable facts of this narrative and conclude that even now, in a world where air travel is considered unremarkable and engines of war can spit death from the skies, the world is not yet ready for the truths exposed in it. The events of that awful night in 1894 shall remain chronicled in these pages, safely among my other papers until such a time as our world is prepared to learn great and terrifying truths.

Over the years my friend Sherlock Holmes has had his share of odd visitors, from women of the hysterical type in various sorts of distress to members of the royal family, ludicrously disguised in an effort to maintain a degree of anonymity. Whatever the nature of the errand, whatever the request for aide, Holmes has, as may be expected, remained the perfect gentleman and treated one and all with courtesy and aplomb. The unusual sequence of events culminating in the affair that I have previously referred to as "The Case of the Remarkable Worm Said to be Unknown to Science" began in the late spring of 1894, some mere weeks after the conclusion of the business with the ferocious Colonel Moran.

Holmes and I were both in the sitting room, reading; Holmes, a monograph on Egyptology by Professor Rockhill, and I indulging in a weakness for the sensational with Dick Donovan's latest mystery novel. I knew Donovan slightly from the Savage Club and had always needed to be discreet within earshot, lest references to friends' cases should find their way in fictionalized form into one of his lurid shockers.

We were startled from our reading by the sudden rap at the door. An unexpected guest! Holmes rose quickly and showed our visitor in with all due courtesy. The man was perhaps thirty, tall and lean but moving with a grace that belied his size and athletic build. He had with him a small bag, which he placed carefully on the table before taking the seat that Holmes indicated.

He looked at my friend. "You would be Sherlock Holmes, the consulting detective?" At Holmes's nod, he turned to me. "Thus making you Dr. John Watson?"

"Yes."

Satisfied that he was in the correct apartment, our guest withdrew a small wooden case and handed us each a card, on which was printed:

DR. ROBERT BEECH
Entomologist

"I am engaged in the study of insects; those that are native to Africa and the Far East are my area of specialty. I have come to you gentlemen with a bit of a problem that has me perplexed and I have hopes that Mr. Holmes can perhaps be of assistance."

Holmes said nothing, but steepled his hands and looked at our visitor with his full measure of attention.

"On a recent trip to Egypt, I found some rather unusual items in proximity to one another. I am afraid that the relationship of these items is too far beyond my rather specialized area of study for me to discern any clear sort of meaning. But you, Mr. Holmes, are famous for solving puzzles; would you mind very much having a look at what I have brought along? Your assessment of these items would be most appreciated."

Holmes nodded and our visitor opened his bag, carefully taking out three very peculiar items. The first was a cylinder of metal, rather greenish in hue, with an intricate pattern of markings that seemed to me to be completely devoid of any possible meaning. The thing itself was about a foot in length by four inches in width and a thickness of about half that. The markings apparently covered all the surfaces and were a chaotic mélange of whorls, slashes, and geometric shapes. As I peered at the object a pattern of sorts seemed to emerge, but my eyes must have suffered some strain from my recent reading, as the inscriptions seemed to shimmer and shift as I stared at them. Blinking, I turned my attention to the other items on the table.

The second was a crudely carved stone that looked like nothing so much as a starfish hewn from common quarry rock. While this may have been of some interest to an archaeologist, I could not fathom what possible relationship it had to the metal cylinder or to the repulsive third item.

The third item was much more in keeping with Dr. Beech's vocation. It was a large glass vial, which he carefully unwrapped from a thick cloth, revealing the contents: a singularly repulsive worm floating in formaldehyde. The creature was about an inch long and resembled a centipede, though with a good deal fewer legs. The head of the beast displayed nasty-looking mandibles surrounding what appeared to be a stinger or proboscis of some sort. I shuddered involuntarily.

While many of the lower forms of life seem strange or even repellent to us, there was something about this *thing* that went beyond physical repugnance. It felt unclean somehow. I was somewhat gratified that the creature was quite dead and at no risk of escaping to go burrowing about in our apartments.

"The worm," our guest went on, "is of singular interest, being found in arid deserts in a solitary state with no visible source of nutrients. The other objects are interesting curios, but of no great import, though I thought that, with your knowledge of cryptograms and the like, you might be able to translate the markings on the cylinder."

During the whole of this narrative, Holmes's eyes had darted quickly from the worm to the cylinder to the carved stone. Suddenly he sprang to his feet.

"Sir, I'll ask you to leave now. You are no more a professor of entomology than am I. You are a common fraud, and these things you have brought along are of no more interest than the sort of curios that Barnum displayed in his museum. Good day to you."

For a moment I thought the stranger would attempt to strike my friend, as he fairly trembled with rage at Holmes's accusations. But he regained his composure, silently gathered up his things, and left without another word.

I looked at Holmes quizzically, awaiting some sort of explanation for his uncharacteristic behavior.

There was a twinkle in his eye as he turned to look at me. "Good old Watson. You think I've gone mad from cocaine, that I am addled and cantankerous as the result of the drug. No, no, don't deny it, old man—it's plain in your expression. I assure you, I haven't gone mad, nor was I being any more discourteous than was mandated by the situation. These are deep waters, Watson, deep waters indeed! Our 'guest' is a very dangerous man, and I would not have behaved as I did were I not certain that he had only a sword and knife upon him and that your revolver was near at hand."

"Great heavens, Holmes, I saw no such devices, though I applied your methods as best I could . . ."

"Well then, Watson, what did you make of our visitor and his bag of gewgaws? The situation was very transparent."

I summarized my observations as I recalled them: "Our man was considerably above average height and athletically built, which, while unusual for a scientist, is not unheard of, particularly as his branch of study calls for a good bit of fieldwork. He was dressed well and carried a walking stick, certainly more as a fashionable accessory than from any physical need. Again, not the usual affectation of a man of science, but again, not unheard of. He was perhaps thirty years of age, young for his profession, but of an age where he would be more likely to be pursuing fieldwork than molding young minds in the halls of academe. All in all, nothing to contravene his story."

"Splendid!" Holmes clapped his hands and leaped to his feet, beginning to pace back and forth. "Watson, you have learned my methods well! Everything you say is accurate and plausible upon the surface. However, you saw only what our visitor wanted you to see and did not truly observe what was there to be observed.

"The walking stick he carried concealed a sword blade—I have seen its type many a time. You failed to note the unusual head of the cane that provides for a guard and grip necessary for combat. That in itself is not damning, but taken with the other evidence, it is clear that our man is not who he claims to be.

"Did you not take note of his wrists? His right was at least an inch or more thicker in diameter than the left. This, coupled with the calluses on his right hand, is indicative of a man who spends a good deal of time handling a sword—which, in turn, is suggestive of a duelist. Further, I noted his tendency to place his weight on the balls of his feet; again, the mark of a man who spends no little time in practicing swordplay."

"Holmes!" I exclaimed. "That's astonishing. You could not possibly have had more than a slight glimpse of his wrists."

My friend smiled and continued his explanation. "Did you not note his curious tan?"

"Of course I did—he looks like he has recently been burned red as an Indian."

"Precisely, Watson; and that is exactly what I found curious about it. A man who truly spent a good deal of time out of doors would display a much deeper and more even sort of coloring, consistent with frequent exposure to the sun over a prolonged period. Our man has the appearance of your average Londoner after his first trip to a sunny clime; hardly likely if he were telling us the truth about his occupation. Further, his calling card gave no address; a common enough practice of the world traveler, but, taken with the intensity of his tan, it immediately suggested fraud. Our man is most emphatically not accustomed to any location more exotic than our own coast.

"No, Watson; there is an odd game afoot here and I would like to be sure of the identity of our opponent. I suspect that we shan't have long to wait."

The timing of Holmes's remarks was uncanny; even as he spoke a hansom cab stopped at the curb and a lone passenger disembarked.

"Watson, fetch your revolver from the drawer and keep it close at hand. Unless I am very much mistaken, the gentleman you see approaching is dangerous on an order of magnitude that makes our previous guest seem an unruly urchin. I will show him in."

"Holmes, if he is as dangerous as you say, what purpose can possibly be served by inviting him inside, other than to put ourselves at peril?"

"Come now, Watson." Holmes's eyes held a twinkle indicative of his investigative instincts having been fully aroused. "Are you not the least a bit curious as to why such a man would seek out the world's foremost consulting detective?"

The man that Holmes ushered into the room was unusual, though certainly no more so than our earlier visitor. A youngish man of possibly Mediterranean descent, he was as immaculately dressed as any of the indolent scions of the Empire's wealthiest families. His height was about average, and he seemed from his carriage to be in fine physical trim. There was nothing odd about him at all until one took into account the large black cat perched on his shoulder and his oddly piercing eyes. They were, without a doubt, the eyes of a mesmerist.

"Mr. Holmes, Dr. Watson, I am Dr. Nikola," he said, taking the chair that Holmes indicated. All the while his feline companion eyed us with a baleful, unwinking stare. "I must first apologize for sending Persano to see you. I needed to be certain if your mental resources merited the accolades that have been bestowed. Persano's subterfuge would be discernible to a superior mind, but might well have passed muster with a lesser intellect.

"I sent Persano because, of all my assistants, his aspect is the least likely to cause alarm. But enough of that. My purpose in visiting you, Mr. Holmes, is quite simple. While I may well be the greatest intellect of this age, my studies are limited to certain fields of inquiry, just as your studies are focused on certain other disciplines. Allow me to explain the conundrum that confronts me and I am most certain that you will agree to lend assistance in a most worthy endeavor."

To say that the man was arrogant would be a gross understatement. He was clearly mad—and Holmes had invited him in! Our guest took no note of my expression of incredulity as he uttered his preposterous statements. Holmes merely nodded, listening carefully and keeping his gaze fixed on the cat, which sat there motionless save for a rhythmic lashing of its tail. He did not speak until our guest had concluded.

"Perhaps, Doctor, you had best begin at the beginning and explain why it is you think I can shed some small light on this enigma that confronts you."

Nikola inhaled deeply as though preparing for a great physical exertion. The cat remained still, save for its tail. "Mr. Holmes, I have recently returned from Egypt; to be more precise than that is not in my best interests to reveal. Suffice to say there is an ancient city, long thought to be lost, that my studies were able to locate.

"I am, as you no doubt know, a scientist. I have dedicated my rather long life to establishing a perfect world, one that shares the advantages to be offered by all the sciences, both the known and the arcane. To that end it is necessary that I live an extraordinarily extended length of time, and that others able to contribute measurably to my Utopia of Science are gifted with similar longevity. But I am getting ahead of myself . . ."

"Just a moment, sir." I could not countenance listening to any more of this madness without comment. "You talk of your years as though you were a senescent oldster. You cannot possibly be more than thirty-five at the oldest."

Holmes said nothing, but the glance he flashed in my direction was more than adequate to convey that I had said more than was prudent. Our guest seemed to take no offense at my challenge, but went on as though he were a professor lecturing to a particularly obtuse class of students.

"For what it is worth, I believe my physical condition to be that of a man of thirty, not thirty-five. It may interest you to know that I appeared much the same as this when your Duke of Wellington overcame the French monster. There are certain compounds known to a few that greatly prolong the human life span. For many years I have been engaged in a mutually beneficial correspondence with a Chinese gentleman who I have every reason to believe was young when the pyramids of Giza were being constructed. Our communication has resulted in my sampling a certain compound, many years ago, with obvious beneficent effects. However, my colleague has been somewhat reticent about giving me enough information to reconstruct his formula."

Holmes finally spoke. "I am very familiar with your reputation as a vivisectionist, but now the purpose behind your experiments becomes only too clear. You're after eternal life! You believe that your colleague has found a chemical key to immortality and you mean to replicate it."

"Quite right. I know just enough of the composition of the elixir to place its original source in Egypt, and to number among its ingredients the royal jelly of certain species of bees. To attempt to re-create the formula from this knowledge has been an exercise in futility that has kept me from fully pursuing other areas of interest. I have recently concluded that my Asian friend may not be alone in possessing the formula that I require. I believe that there are other beings to whom what I call the 'Elixir Vitae' is as common as cheap gin to a Stewpony laborer.

"What I've discovered concerns the materials that my man Persano brought to show you. Allow me to explain the curious circumstances surrounding their discovery and we shall see if you infer the same conclusions as do I.

"There are places in the Egyptian desert where entire cities of antiquity lie buried under shifting sands, and modern towns where children play with the bones of kings and wild dogs tear at the bodies of the high priests of the old gods. A strange place indeed, a place which I believe holds the origins of the Elixir Vitae.

"I have made mention of my Asian colleague. Through the subtlest of hints and the wildest of coincidences, I have concluded that he may well have walked the earth long ago, in the identity of a pharaoh of the ancient kingdom. With that in mind, I gathered some of my most puissant aides (and those that can travel publicly without causing undue alarm) and set about to explore my 'friend's' ancestral home.

"I will spare you the details of our being driven off our chosen course by one of the sandstorms endemic to the region. There is much to discover yet in Africa; Burton and Speke's finds pale in comparison to what we stumbled across. The veil of sand was torn asunder, letting us be the first humans in many hundreds of years to find traces of the City of Pillars. Few of the pillars still stand; most were buried, save for a few feet sticking out of the sand.

They were carved of basalt and were a good fifteen feet in diameter. On the top of each of the nine that we saw was a shallow depression containing metal objects similar to the one Persano showed you. Each cylinder had one of the curious star-stones that you have also seen partially covering it. An interesting and incomprehensible arrangement; if the towers were as tall as I suspected they were, what earthly purpose could have been served by placing these objects on their top? I meditated on this for some time while Persano attempted to quell the fears of our bearers, who seemed convinced that we were in the presence of a great evil. Perhaps most curious was the fact that the star-stones were firmly bolted to the pillars with stout iron bands. Someone had taken a great deal of care at some point to ensure that the stones remained in place.

"What has this to do with elixirs of longevity, bees and such, you may ask? On the surface, nothing, and were it not for the avarice of one of our bearers, I would have never deduced the connection myself.

"We had set up camp a short way from the site. Persano, who serves as a personal guard, and I moved our tent some distance farther yet, as is my wont. The desert night was deathly quiet until I was awakened by a horrendous buzzing—the sound of an army of locusts or bees, the air literally vibrating from the beat of their wings. The noise was far deeper and more resonant than that of any insect I have ever heard before. Persano and I stayed where we were, straining our eyes for a glimpse of what was transpiring at the camp. Unfortunately we could see nothing but a shimmering in the night sky.

"As Ra began his journey we were able to see only too clearly what had happened in the night. The camp had been razed; no trace of life remained. Examination of one of the pillars showed that someone—one of the bearers, no doubt; my men are unquestionably loyal—had pried loose one of the star-stones. It lay in the sand not a dozen yards from where he'd removed it. Of the man—

or any of his companions—there was no sign, save for rather ominous reddish stains that dried onto the sands.

"We returned to England, bearing the three objects that Persano showed you. It is quite plain that the cylinder is no less than a device for communication across the gulf of Time and Space. Equally clear is that the stone or the proximity of the stone interferes with the transmission. What do you make of it, Mr. Holmes?"

My friend stared for a minute at our guest, and it seemed to me that there was some silent struggle taking place between these two great minds, almost as though they were peering into each other's thoughts. Finally Holmes spoke.

"You are a brilliant man, Doctor. Your deductions seem to be correct on all counts. I suspect that this object is a communication device of some sort, obviously created by a science far beyond ours. From your description of events I can conclude only that it transmits a signal of some sort through the ether, a signal that is answered by *something* in a rather alarming fashion. There must be some properties to the stone that interfere with this signal, and judging from the events you have related, it would seem more than prudent to keep the stone in proximity to the cylinder at all times."

"My thoughts exactly, Mr. Holmes." Nikola's large dark eyes fairly gleamed with excitement. "My theory is that whatever beings answered this signal took our bearers, not as a matter of malice, but likely from scientific curiosity. That the terrified and ignorant fools may have struggled or attempted to attack them explains the traces of blood we found. Imagine, if you will, the benefit of conversing with these beings, of learning their science, which is obviously so far in advance of ours. If the vast gulfs of space mean nothing to them, is it not reasonable to suppose that they have found means to turn aside the threats of time and death?"

"I suppose nothing, Doctor," Holmes said sharply. "I draw conclusions based on logical inferences; to do anything less is anathema to my methods. It may well be as you say, that whatever visited your camp came from somewhere other than our earth. But to ascertain the motives of something that is by definition *alien* is another matter entirely. Still, the prospect of establishing communication with another sentient race is an intriguing one. What do you suggest?"

Nikola smiled—not a pleasant thing to see. There was no warmth or humor in the expression; it was more akin to an automaton aping human emotion. "I have a relatively secluded building in Limehouse that will be perfect for our experiment. My intent is to summon these 'ethernauts,' as I must call them, and then to effect a dialogue. It's clear that there will be no little danger, but it seems that whatever forces these beings use to traverse the gulfs are nullified when the stone is placed against the cylinder; therefore, we will be able to quickly terminate the interview if we're unable to make ourselves understood.

"Mr. Holmes, you possess a remarkable ability to deduce meaning from the most opaque of clues. I'm asking you to employ this skill in an attempt to communicate with beings from another world!"

Since such talk was the sort of madness one might expect from a pair of opium eaters stumbling and pointing at their hallucinations, to see my friend nodding in assent seemed the height of madness until I reflected on the sight of that strange worm turning its dead features toward us in its vial. Nikola handed Holmes a card with the address of where our experiment was to take place, and left us to confer.

"A most unusual man," Holmes murmured. "I should expect we will hear a good deal more of him and his celestial friend over the years. Watson, this should be a most interesting game. I needn't point out that the stakes are rather high . . ."

We sent our driver off, having no idea how long we would be at Nikola's warehouse. From the looks of it, the doctor was as versed in matters of thrift as he was the sciences. A more unprepossessing structure could hardly be imagined, even in the slums of Limehouse. The building was a wood frame that looked to have collapsed and been rebuilt numerous times. Soot-smudged and grim, it stood in back of a row of ramshackle houses packed with Chinese laborers.

My friend Burke writes little vignettes today that laud the charms and quaint customs of this district and its peoples. I wish to assure my readers that his fond memories lend this deplorable slum an aura that it in fact has never possessed.

We heard the faint tap of a cane's ferrule just moments before Persano appeared. "Gentlemen, my apologies for the subterfuge. As my employer no doubt explained, in matters where the prize may be eternal life, some manners must be laid aside."

Holmes nodded grimly and indicated that Persano should lead the way. The warehouse door was sealed with a massive padlock, for which he produced a large key.

"The doctor used to conduct his experiments here. In an impoverished neighborhood there is no shortage of volunteers—"

"And where is Nikola?"

"He'll be joining us very shortly. Here we are!"

The room still contained a good deal of scientific apparatus, including long tables covered with beakers and tanks, most of which were now empty. A few of the tanks still held evidence of Nikola's vocation of vivisection. The spiders and toads of gargantuan size were bad enough, but I also saw only too clearly what Persano had meant by "volunteers." What atrocities had been performed on these poor people is best left unsaid; my most fervid hope is that his work was confined to experimentation on the deceased and not the living.

A lone table stood off to one side of the room, on which the star-stone and metal cylinder sat. Behind the table stood a curious representation of the human form, wrought cunningly from metal. A clockwork man! If these uncanny items were what the doctor had left behind, what sort of madness and marvels must his laboratory have contained when fully operational?

I glanced at Holmes and there was a look of alarm on his face. Persano was idly examining some of the equipment on one of the tables. Holmes signaled for me to be silent and nodded toward the door by which we had entered.

His cryptic gestures became quite clear as, with a grinding of metal, the clockwork man came to "life." There was no sign of the puppeteer who pulled the electrical strings of this grotesque marionette, but its purpose was all too clear. With a deft motion it grasped the star-stone and removed it from the cylinder.

"Watson, Persano! Out of here as you value your lives!" Holmes's shout startled us both as we stared at the mechanical man, who had now again assumed lifeless rigidity. Holmes grabbed my arm, pulling me along. Persano started to follow us and then stopped and shouted, "Cowards! They will be here soon, the ethernauts; they can grant us eternal life!"

"Ignore him, Watson, he has no conception of the forces at work here. This is yet another of Nikola's experiments . . ."

We stumbled into the chill night, Holmes turning and locking the door behind us. We ran across the street and watched as madness descended . . .

A shimmering funnel, of a color that we could not discern, appeared in the night sky, somehow blocking out the stars. The funnel seemed to bisect the walls of Nikola's warehouse without rending the wood asunder. From within the funnel came a buzzing and whirring as of the wings of a million locusts . . .

Then, as quickly as it had begun, it was over. The night sky resumed its normal properties. We stood quietly smoking for over an hour, watching, waiting—for what, I am not entirely sure. Finally Holmes said, "It was a brief visit; I expect that Mr. Persano's interview was less than satisfactory. Shall we go in? I believe the danger is well passed. Nikola's no doubt here somewhere, watching to see how this all plays out. It would be a shame to disappoint him."

The vast room was undisturbed. Persano was alive, after a fashion . . . We found two more of the remarkable worms, and no doubt Holmes has them still bobbing and nodding in jars of formaldehyde. The cylinder and star-stone we took with us also; surprisingly, their owner never called upon us for their return.

Persano never spoke an understandable word again. From time to time he would scream out strange sounds that were completely beyond even the most capable of linguists to decipher. The cries sounded like an attempt to reproduce sounds never intended for the human throat. Persano died in a madhouse some months later; what he saw remains a mystery that he took with him to the grave.

We did have opportunity to study the worms at leisure. They were no doubt parasites, though of several rather unusual aspects. Their ichor, upon examination, indicated a diet of metal, yet their aspect shares commonalties with certain worms native to Africa and known for boring into a human or animal host. Is it possible that their host organisms are beings of living *metal*?

Whatever the aspect of the ethernauts, the sight of them drove the sanity from Persano. Indeed, while Holmes commented earlier on our inability to discern the motives of a truly *alien* mind, he neglected to offer any speculation as to how terrible the aspect of such a being might be and how even a strong-willed man like Persano might be blasted into madness by the sight.

The events following that awful night were rather anticlimatic. We saw no more of Dr. Nikola, though I have reason to suspect that my friend may have had some further communication with him, perhaps on unrelated matters. As I synopsize these most unusual events of nearly thirty years ago, I cannot help but marvel at some of the things that have come to pass. Nikola's Chinese colleague made his terrible presence felt in London, just as the doctor implied that he would. Nikola himself disappeared into the maw of the Great War, though I suspect that this vanishing is merely temporary. Can such a man as Nikola be truly gone for good? I think it unlikely. We struggle along in a hideously ruined world now, a world growing ready for the advent of a leader capable of promising and demonstrating great marvels. I suspect that the doctor will make an appearance on the world stage sooner rather than later. I do not know if he ever successfully replicated the formula which he sought, but he has had many years in which to conduct his research and recruit new allies in his pursuits.

My friend Holmes has long since retired to an isolated farm in Sussex, where he raises bees. I learned enough of my friend's methods to find the reasons for his avocation elementary. I can only hope his scientific experiments are successful, and that he is never tempted to move the star-stone from its place of proximity to the metal cylinder.

The Mystery of the Hanged Man's Puzzle

PAUL FINCH

Neither Holmes nor Watson had really wanted to attend.

Watson went as far as to say he didn't think they should. And he had good reason for that. One might argue that they were honor-bound to attend, that it was in some ways incumbent on them—after all, this was the net result of much of the work they had done together—but in the particular case of Harold Jobson, the blame rested entirely with the Metropolitan police; neither the good doctor nor his friend had been at any stage involved. Despite this, a letter from the aforementioned gentleman had arrived at 221B Baker Street on a bright May morning in 1897, in the form of a *personal* invitation. Even then, Holmes might not have been tempted. But there was something about the Jobson case . . . something odd and inexplicable. And then there was the letter itself, and its curious, rather ominous wording. And at the end of the day, Newgate was only a quarter of an hour's carriage ride away.

*   *   *

Jobson smiled across the table at them. He had broad, strong features and a chalky-white complexion, which under his mop of jet-black hair, looked almost ghostly. "I knew you'd come," he said quietly.

"Then you're quite the prophet," Holmes replied.

Jobson shook his head. "It's just that I read people well. I knew the great Sherlock Holmes would never be able to resist a matter of national, even international, importance."

"You made that case well in your letter. Can you enlighten us further?"

"I can, but I won't. Instead, I have something for you." Jobson fished a folded scrap of paper from his trouser pocket, opened it, then turned and sought the warders' permission. Both officers examined the item closely before exchanging bewildered shrugs and passing it over the table.

At first glance, Holmes, too, was unable to make head or tail of it. It was a crude, pencil-drawn grid pattern, consisting of ruled lines; most were connected, forming a vague network, though there was no symmetry or identifiable configuration; most of the lines finally tapered down and merged at the right-hand side. Lying roughly in the center, though perhaps slightly to the left, at a point otherwise unreferenced, there was a small circle in red ink.

"What is this?" Watson finally asked.

"That's for Mr. Holmes to fathom out," their host replied. "In giving it to you, Holmes, I'm giving the world a chance. Of course, I owe the world precious little . . . so it's only a *slim* chance. By my approximation, you have, at the most, two or three days to solve the puzzle."

"And if I fail?" Holmes wondered.

Jobson leaned forward over the table, his smile becoming a ghastly sickle-shaped grin. "If you fail . . . there'll be a calamity the like of which you have never imagined. I, of course, won't be here to see it. But in that respect, I'll be among the lucky ones."

"I'd have thought someone in your position would be seeking to make peace with his fellowmen, not leave them a legacy of hatred," said Watson.

"It isn't *my* legacy, Dr. Watson," the felon replied. "Don't be lulled into the cozy misapprehension that in destroying me, the state is destroying its prime foe." He glanced up at the clock on the gray brick wall. It read five minutes to nine. "Quite the opposite, in fact. In roughly five minutes' time, your troubles will only just be *starting*."

A moment later, Holmes and Watson were out in the passage. With a loud clang, the cell closed behind them. Twenty yards to their left, the door stood open to a brightly lit, whitewashed chamber, in the middle of which a slender gentleman in funereal black was putting the last delicate touches to a noose.

"Well, Holmes . . . did he have anything to say?" came a gruff voice.

It was Lestrade. The inspector had arrived in company with two of the other detectives who'd worked on the Jobson case, but it was still a surprise to see him. The Scotland Yard man was currently, and rather notoriously, involved in the hunt for a large male crocodile that had gone missing from the zoological garden at Regent's Park . . . an investigation which had already been the object of several humorous cartoons in *Punch*. It represented a considerable change of pace from his previous and more earnest hunt for Harold Jobson, the vicious murderer of five people.

Holmes shook his head. "For once, Lestrade, both you and I are at an equal loss."

"Some vague ramblings," Watson added. "Didn't make a lot of sense."

The policeman harumphed, then adjusted his collar. In honor of the day, he was wearing one of his higher, stiffer ones. "I daresay the fellow *is* insane . . . but it was a despicable crime. He's going to the only fate he deserves."

"No doubt," Holmes said, turning on his heel and striding away. "No doubt at all."

And that was true. Harold Jobson's crime had been quite despicable.

In the dead of night, in an apparent drugged stupor—nobody could conceive that he'd gone about his heinous act while of sound mind—he'd broken into the Russell Square home of the wealthy chemist and professor Archibald Langley, intending to burglarize the property. At some point during the course of the crime, he came across two of the maids while they slept in their ground-floor room, and brutally bludgeoned them to death with his crowbar. He then went upstairs, where he attacked Professor Langley's butler, Henry, who had risen from his bed, thinking he'd heard a noise. The loyal Henry was also slain, his skull battered to a pulp. Still not sated, Jobson made his way into the bedroom of the chemist's nineteen-year-old daughter, Laura, hauled her from under her blankets, and bound her to a chair with a bellpull cord. He then went next door into Professor Langley's bedchamber and did the same to him. What happened after this was uncertain. Very possibly, Jobson tortured the poor souls, seeking to learn the whereabouts of valuables in the house. Whether or not he did this, he left an hour later empty-handed . . . but only after he'd de-liberately started a fire in the sitting room, which very quickly swept through the rest of the building, entirely gutting it, and burning the still-bound captives beyond recognition as human be-ings. It was to be hoped that Professor Langley and his daughter had been killed first; the evidence, however, suggested otherwise.

As they rode back to Baker Street, Holmes mulled over the dark details of the crime. Even now, with the knowledge of the full confession obtained by the police, it made little sense.

"Why should a fellow," he said, "in the process of committing a crime for which he can expect at most several years' penal servitude, for no obvious reason then go on and make it far, far worse . . . both for his victims and himself?"

Watson shrugged. "Why try to understand the irrational? It can't be done."

"I'm afraid I disagree." For a moment, Holmes was lost in thought. "Often the most irrational acts seem rational to the perpetrator. Yet in this case, though we know a little about Jobson's background—he came from a good family, for example, but regarded himself as a failure, and in later life took to drugs and drink—we've learned remarkably little about his true motives."

"Well, it's typical of Lestrade not to have done a more thorough job, I suppose."

Again, Holmes shook his head. "On the contrary. On this occasion, I think the inspector performed his office excellently. The felon was arrested within a day of committing his atrocity, and a watertight prosecution case was presented."

"Yes, but as you said . . ."

"Ah!" Holmes half smiled. "I don't think Freudian psychoanalysis is really Scotland Yard's field just at the moment, Watson . . . though maybe we should make it ours. What do you make of the rumors that Jobson belonged to some kind of cult or sect?"

"I honestly wouldn't know."

Holmes pondered. "The mentality of the cultist is often the hardest to understand. Still"—and he took out his watch and saw that it read two minutes past nine—"that's one cultist we needn't worry about any longer."

Holmes spent much of the rest of that day engrossed in the puzzle. When he wasn't taking measurements of its lines and making odd calculations, he was at the lab table setting up chemical tests on the paper and the ink. No conclusion of value was drawn.

"Isn't it possible that Jobson was simply trying to inconvenience you?" Watson wondered. "Setting you a meaningless and insoluble problem in order to frustrate you?"

Holmes considered as he gazed down on Baker Street and puffed on his pipe. "But why should he? I never had any contact with the man."

"This forthcoming calamity he spoke about. Perhaps he was just trying to cause a panic . . . his last revenge against society, so to speak?"

Again Holmes thought about this, but shook his head. "In which case he should have gone to the newspapers. Of all people, he must have known that *I* was the least likely to spread it around."

"Well, it confounds me," Watson admitted, getting back to the *Times*.

"And me." Holmes lifted the slip of paper from his desk, looked it over one last time, then folded it and slid it into his jacket pocket. "Perhaps we should approach this from a different angle. Come, we're off to Southwark."

"Southwark?"

"Jobson lived on Pickle Herring Street. I saw it in the trial transcripts. It wasn't an address I was likely to forget."

Pickle Herring Street ran alongside that bustling reach of the Thames known as the Pool of London. It was hemmed in on its north side by a dense forest of sails, masts, and rigging, which extended all the way from Cotton's Wharf to the immense new construction that was Tower Bridge. Little of the grandeur of that marvel of engineering filtered down into the shadowy recesses below it, however. At this point, Pickle Herring Street, which stank somewhat appropriately of whelks, shrimps, and strongly salted fish, gave out to a series of narrow, straw-matted passages, winding off into a gloomy warren of ale shops and dingy lodging houses.

In one of these alleyways, a squalid, rat-infested place, Holmes and Watson found the former habitation of Harold Jobson. It was little more than a lean-to shelter, its broken windows patched up with rags, its single inner room now open to the elements, the door having been torn from its hinges, and anything of value within long ago pillaged.

"I don't understand," said Watson as they stared into the dank interior. "Jobson was educated. He boasted of his comfortable family background. How did he descend to this?"

Holmes pursed his lips. "Who can say? The pressure of living sometimes becomes too much for a man . . . he simply drops out of society. Then there is the cult factor. I've heard of such things before. Acolytes are so mesmerized by their new calling that they surrender everything they have. Either way, Watson, I doubt there's anything of use to us here."

They made their way back by what seemed to Watson a circuitous route, Holmes taking each left-hand turn as they came to it. A few moments later, perhaps inevitably, they were covering ground they'd already covered before.

"You realize we've just come 'round in a wide circle?" Watson ventured.

"I do," Holmes replied quietly. "Do you think the fellow behind us does?"

"Behind us . . ."

"I'd rather you didn't look 'round."

They continued to stroll, but Watson was puzzled. These riverside cut-throughs were thronging with laborers of every sort; riggers, ballast heavers, coal whippers, lightermen, all hurrying back and forth. How his friend had managed to pick *one* out as a potential foe was beyond him.

"The one with the loose nail in his shoe," Holmes added by way of explanation. "It keeps clicking on the cobbles, and it has been doing so for some time."

Watson concentrated, and now indeed he did hear a faint and regular clicking amid the clatter and din of the docks. "Surely he wouldn't have come in a circle, too, unless he was following us?"

"My thoughts exactly," said Holmes, rounding a corner and abruptly stepping into a narrow ginnel, dragging Watson with him.

A moment later, they'd moved through it into a derelict hovel, where they waited. Seconds passed, then there was a hurried pattering of feet as someone came urgently into the ginnel behind them. Clearly, the stalker was anxious for his prey not to elude him. The feet went on past the entrance to the hovel, the loose nail clicking all the way, then halted and backtracked. The owner of the feet, a burly, brutish-looking fellow in a shabby three-piece suit, with a dirty bowler hat pulled down on his broad, fat head, came warily in. He froze when he felt the muzzle of Watson's revolver against his lower back.

"That's far enough, sir," said the doctor.

The man made a sharp move toward his jacket pocket, but Holmes stepped smartly up to him. "Keep your hands where we can see them, if you please."

"What is this?" the man asked, his accent pure Bow. "You trying to rob me or something?"

"We might ask you the same question," said Watson.

"Then again we might not," Holmes added. "I doubt a common thief would be so careless as to follow his intended prey for several minutes along public thoroughfares when he has all these alleys and doorways to skulk in. So tell us, who are you?"

The fellow grinned, showing yellow, feral teeth. "Wouldn't you like to know."

Holmes eyed him, recognizing the stubborn surliness of the foot soldier rather than the officer in command. "What's your connection with Harold Jobson?" he asked.

At this, there was a sudden nervous look about the fellow. "Jobson?" he said. "Dunno him. Never 'eard of him."

"If you've never heard of him, why are you trembling?"

"I never 'eard of him, I tell ya!" the fellow suddenly bellowed, driving one hamlike elbow backward, catching Watson hard in the midriff. Winded, the doctor gasped and twisted in pain. He managed to hang on to the collar of the man's jacket, but dropped his revolver. Holmes went down to retrieve the weapon, in which time, their captive made his escape, hurling himself sideways, tearing free of his jacket and scrambling out through the door and away along the ginnel.

Watson made to follow, but Holmes bade him stay where he was and get his breath back. There was no sense in making a scene, he said; after all, the fellow could complain that he'd done nothing wrong but that *they* had waylaid him at gunpoint . . . and he'd be telling the truth. Watson groaned and rubbed at his chest. "That chap's plainly frightened of something," he observed.

Holmes nodded as he rifled the pockets of the discarded jacket. "Yes, and whatever it is . . . he was more frightened of that than he was of your trusty Webley."

He made a thorough search of the garment, but found only one or two items of interest: a particularly nasty lock knife, its blade at least six inches long and honed to razor sharpness, its hinge well oiled so the weapon could be drawn and flicked open at a moment's notice; and a small, leather-bound notebook, with two entries in it. Both were written in pencil, in a spidery hand. They read:

> Randolph Daker, 14 Commercial Road
> Sherlock Holmes, 221B Baker Street

Watson was shocked. "Good grief. The cad's been onto you all day."

Holmes nodded. "Not just me, though. Randolph Daker of Commercial Road . . . anyone we know?"

Watson shook his head. "I doubt it. Commercial Road's up in the East End."

"Perhaps we should pay it a visit?"

"Good Lord . . . I thought *this* neighborhood was dangerous."

That afternoon they took a cab to the City, then proceeded on foot through the teeming slums of Cheapside and Whitechapel.

Both men were already familiar with this neighborhood; it wasn't ten years since the so-called Ripper had terrorized these hungry, crowded streets. The shocking depredations had brought the crime and squalor in the district to worldwide attention, but little, it seemed, had changed. The roadways were still filthy with mud and animal dung, the entries still cluttered with rubbish. The housing was of the poorest stock: sooty brown-brick tenements, damp, dismal, decaying, leaning against one another for mutual support. The inhabitants, and there were a great many of them—families vastly outnumbered dwellings in this part of London—were exclusively of the gaunt and needy variety. More often than not, rags passed for clothes, and beggary and drunkenness were the day's chief occupations.

"It's an absolute disgrace," Watson muttered. "I'd have thought the Housing of the Working Classes Act would have resolved all this."

Holmes shook his head. "Goodly intentions are no use without goodly sums of money, Watson. The property tax doesn't provide funds even remotely sufficient to ease *this* level of degradation."

Saddened by what they saw, but, inevitably, more concerned with the job at hand, they pressed on, and an hour later, entered Commercial Road. Number 14 was a tall, narrow, terraced house, set back behind a fenced-off garden, now straggling and overgrown. The house's lower windows bore no glass, but had boards nailed across them. Only jagged shards were visible in the upper windows.

"It looks derelict," said Watson.

"It may *look* derelict, but someone's been in and out recently," Holmes replied. He indicated a path leading from the gate to the front door. It was unpaved, but had been beaten through the undergrowth by the regular passage of feet. Several stems of weeds were freshly broken.

They approached the door, which they noticed was standing

ajar by a couple of inches. Holmes pushed it open. Beyond, the house was filled with shadow. A nauseating odor, like fish oil or stagnant brine, flowed out.

The detective raised his voice: "Would Mr. Randolph Daker be at home?"

There was no reply. Holmes glanced at Watson, shrugged, and went in. The interior of the building was unimaginably filthy. A litter of rotten food, abandoned clothes, and broken furniture strewed every floorway. The wallpaper, what little there was left of it, hung in torn-down strips; here and there, there were smeared green handprints on it. The smell intensified the farther in they ventured. "Hello?" Watson called again. Still, nobody answered.

At length, they found themselves in what might once have passed for a sitting room. It was cluttered with the same foul wreckage as the rest of the house. Watson was about to call out a third time when Holmes stopped him. The doctor could immediately tell that his friend's catlike senses had alerted him to something. A tense second passed, then there came a faint shuffle from somewhere close by. An object fell over. There was a grunt, brutish and animalistic . . . and a figure came shambling into view from the doorway connecting to the kitchen and scullery.

It wore a cheap, ill-fitted suit, which had burst at many of its seams. Tendrils of what at first looked like seaweed protruded through them. The same vile matter hung from the figure's hands and face, and now, as it lurched slowly into the open, it was clear that this was not part of any disguise. Whoever the wretched creature might once have been, his head was now a bloated mass of barnacles and marine-type growths. Vitreous, octopus-like eyes rolled amid thick folds of polyp-ridden flesh. Warty lips hung open on a bottomless, fishlike mouth.

Holmes and Watson could only stand stock-still, gazing at the apparition. It tried to speak to them, but only meaningless blubberings came out. Recognizing its inability to communicate, it gave a sharp, keening squeal, then lumbered forward, deformed hands outstretched. It was almost upon them when Watson came to himself. "Back, Holmes, back! Don't let it touch you!"

The two friends retreated, and unable to reach them, the monstrosity, which suddenly seemed to be ailing, slumped down to its knees, then fell forward onto its face. Its shoulders heaved three times as it struggled to breathe, then it lay still.

A stunned silence followed, finally broken by Holmes: "Randolph Daker, esquire, unless I'm very much mistaken."

Watson knelt beside the body and pulled his gloves on. He was still reluctant to touch the thing, even with his hands protected.

"Have you ever seen the like of this before?" the detective asked him.

The doctor shook his head. "Some kind of fungal infection, but . . . it's so advanced."

"Is he dead?"

Watson nodded. "He is now." He glanced up. "What on earth is going on here?"

"We must root around," Holmes replied. "Uncover anything we can that links this fellow Daker with Harold Jobson."

They began to search the premises, and immediately saw through the scullery window that the house's rear yard had been adapted into a makeshift stable. A flimsy plank roof had been set up. Below it, up to its fetlocks in dung and dirty straw, stood a thin, bedraggled horse.

"Daker was a carter," said Watson.

"In which case, he must have kept records," Holmes replied. "Keep searching."

Within moments, Watson had found a wad of dockets held together by a bulldog clip. "Receipts," he said.

Holmes came over to him. "Find the most recent one."

Watson leafed through them. The faint writing, poorly scribbled in pencil, was just about legible. "The last job he did was on

April twenty-second, when he was to 'collect sundry items for Mr. Rohampton' . . . Tibbut's Wharf, Wapping."

Holmes was already making for the door. "Not twenty minutes from here. Most convenient."

"Oh yes . . . now I remember," said the pier master at Tibbut's Wharf, a bearded giant in an old seaman's cap. "That was the American chap, wasn't it?"

"American?" said Holmes with interest.

The pier master nodded, then tapped his fingers on his desk. "Mr. Rohampton. He came in himself and made the booking. There were several crates and three passengers. They arrived on the morning tide on April twenty-second, on the *Lucy Dark*, a private charter from . . ." His memory faded. "Now, where was it . . . place called Innsmouth, I think? Does that ring a bell?"

"Innsmouth, Massachusetts?" Holmes asked.

"No, no, no." The bearded chap shook his head. "Innsmouth, America."

"I see. Well, your powers of recall do you credit."

The pier master leaned back on his stool. "I couldn't very well forget it. The passengers were all parceled up in bandages. Head to foot, they were. I assume this bloke Rohampton's a doctor of some sort, and these were his patients?"

"Very possibly," Holmes replied. "What else can you tell us about him."

"If you'll wait one moment . . ." The pier master opened a register and ran a thick-nailed finger down his various lists. "I think I've got a business address for him."

Burlington Mews was a side street off Aldgate. Though it was part of the moneyed business district, much of the property down there was currently "to let." Only one unit was in fact occupied; Rohampton's Tea & Ginger. For a quaint-sounding company, its windows were partially shuttered, its decayed frontage smothered in grime. Only dusty blackness lay beyond its mullioned panes.

Holmes made to enter straightaway, but Watson held him back. "I say . . . aren't we rushing into this, rather?"

Holmes considered. "Jobson said we have two or three days . . . at the most. We've already dithered for the better part of *one* day. I think it's best if we press on as hard as we can."

"Holmes?" Watson said. "Is everything all right? You seem . . . anxious."

Again, the detective considered. It was one of those very rare moments when he appeared to be at a loss for words. "I've always, as you know, Watson, been a firm believer that every event has its cause and effect . . . is explicable, no matter how bizarre the circumstance, in scientific terms."

Watson nodded.

Holmes regarded him gravely. "That doesn't mean there aren't worlds of strangeness that you and I have yet to encounter." And he went inside.

More curious now than ever, Watson followed.

It was a small suite of offices, paneled in drab, dark wood, and extremely cramped. Even though the May day without was fine and bright, little sunlight filtered inside. No candles burned, no flames flickered in the grate. As well as the pervading gloom, there was also a distinct chill, an air of dankness. For all that, Burgess, the clerk who attended the visitors, seemed perfectly at ease in the environment. He was a short but thickset man, with only a few strands of hair combed over his otherwise bald pate, and a smug look on his pale, rough-cut face. When he approached, he did so with a pronounced limp; one of his legs appeared to be much sturdier than the other.

Holmes introduced himself, then offered a gloved hand. The clerk shook it. The detective at once took note of the fellow's fingers. They were coarse and callused, the nails broken and dirty.

The one thing that didn't besmear them, however, was ink. Neither, Holmes noted, were there any ink stains on the blotter on the clerk's desk, nor any writing on the ledger that was open there. While the clerk lumbered off to find his employer, the detective glanced farther afield. It didn't surprise him to observe a fine sheen of dust covering the nearby wall of book spines, and strands of unbroken cobweb over the shelves where the stationery was stored.

"Gentleman!" came a cultured American voice.

They turned and, for the first time, beheld Julian Rohampton. He came lithely out from the dim rear section of his premises. There was at once an aura of the school sports captain about him. He was tall, of impressive build, and had a shock of fine golden hair. At first glance, he was exceedingly handsome, though up close he had a white, curiously waxen pallor and a silky, almost solid texture to his flesh. When he smiled, only his mouth seemed to move. His eyes remained deep set and startlingly bright.

"Mr. Rohampton?" said Holmes.

"The same. And you are the famous Sherlock Holmes?"

"I am. This is my friend Dr. Watson."

"I'm honored," said Rohampton. "But what fascinating murder case can have brought you here?"

"No murder case," Holmes replied, ". . . as far as we're aware."

"We're looking into—" Watson began, but Holmes cut him short.

"We're looking into a theft. Our client has recently imported goods from America, and somewhere in transit between Tibbut's Wharf and his home in Greenwich, certain of these goods have gone missing. I learned from the pier master that you yourself recently brought items into the country via Tibbut's Wharf. I take it you haven't experienced similar problems?"

Rohampton thought for a moment, then shook his head. "Not as I'm aware. It's not that I make a habit of shipping in goods, you understand. The recent cargo was mainly botanical specimens. They were intended for an associate of mine. He certainly hasn't complained that anything was missing."

"I'm glad," Holmes said. "Of course that doesn't mean that no attempt at theft was made. The passengers who accompanied your imports, I take it they reported nothing unusual?"

Rohampton gave him a quizzical look. "Passengers? There weren't any passengers. At least, if there were, they have no connection with *my* business."

"I see." Holmes sniffed. "In which case, that concludes the matter." He made a move back to the door. "Thanks for your assistance. Please don't let us trouble you any further—"

"Wait gentlemen, please," Rohampton entreated. "It's no trouble to have such lauded guests. Won't you stop for a drop of sherry?"

Burgess had reappeared from the rear chambers, now carrying a tray on which sat a dark bottle and three crystal goblets.

"Well," said Watson, eyeing the tipple thirstily . . .

"Thank you, no," Holmes put in, quite firmly. "We have a lot of work ahead of us. It wouldn't do to get too light-headed."

Rohampton made an amiable gesture. "Whatever you wish. Good day to you, then."

"Oh . . ." Holmes said, before leaving, "there is one minor thing. Would it be possible to speak to your associate . . . the gentleman who received the shipment, just to ensure the consignment was untampered with?"

"Surely," said Rohampton. "His name is Marsh, Obed Marsh. Here, let me write it down for you. He's a former sea captain turned botanist . . . interesting fellow."

He took a pen from his upper breast pocket and, tearing a strip from the blotter on the clerk's table, scratched out a quick address. His mouth curved in a rictal grin as he handed it over . . . again, that grin failed to travel to his eyes. "If anything *is* missing, you'll let me know? Obviously it won't do to be stolen from, and not realize it."

"Of course," said Holmes.

Five minutes later, they were seated in a cab and bound across the City for Liverpool Street. The piece of paper they had been given read *2 Sun Lane*, which both knew as a small cul-de-sac directly behind the railway station.

"Curious chap," said Watson as they rode. "Did you notice, his facial expression hardly changed once?"

"I also noticed that he is little given to work," Holmes replied.

"How do you deduce that?"

"Come, Watson. There was minimal evidence in that office that any work is done there. And if that fellow Burgess is a clerk, then he's recently made it his new calling in life. That limp of his suggests he's more familiar with the ball and chain than the accounts book."

"So what about Obed Marsh?"

Holmes rubbed his chin. "He, I am uncertain about. But I fancy Mr. Julian Rohampton was rather too ready to give us his address, wouldn't you say?"

The cabbie let them down at the mouth of the court in question, took his fare, and drove off. For a moment, they stood and stared, and listened as well. Sun Lane was little more than a grubby access way. Various bins and sacks of rubbish were stacked along it. It was hemmed in by high brick walls, and at its far end, a single door connecting with some rear portion of the railway station stood locked and chained. Nothing moved down there, though it echoed to the racket of shunting locomotives and tooting whistles.

"And a botanist lives *here*?" said Holmes tightly. "I think not."

He ushered Watson to one side, and they took shelter behind a clutter of old tea chests. Moments later, a curtained carriage appeared at the end of the street. The two men watched in silence as the coachman sat there, unmoving, a scarf about his face. A moment passed, then the curtain twitched and a sinister object poked out . . . something like a hefty gun barrel, though it consisted not of one muzzle, but nine or ten, all bound tightly together in a tubular steel bundle.

Watson seized Holmes by the wrist. "Good Lord," he whispered. "Good Lord in Heaven . . . that's a Gatling gun!"

"No doubt fresh from America with whatever else our cold-eyed friend imported," said Holmes quietly. "Little wonder they lured us to a cul-de-sac."

"Great Scott!" Watson breathed. Only now was the nature of those they confronted beginning to dawn on him. "What . . . what do we do?"

"I suggest we lay low for a moment."

Both men held their ground and waited. Minutes passed, during which the team of horses became uneasy and began to paw the ground. The coachman himself stirred, and started to glance around as though confused. At long last, a pedestrian arrived, sloping along, hands in pockets. Holmes and Watson immediately recognized him as the bowler-hatted fellow who'd attempted to follow them on Pickle Herring Street. Rather conspicuously, he was still without his jacket. He shuffled about for a moment when he reached the carriage, then leaned back against the nearby wall. To Holmes's eye, the fellow's posture gave him away . . . he was tense, in fact alarmed.

"Yes," mumbled the detective. "Something should have happened by now, shouldn't it, my friend? Well . . . don't let us disappoint you." Calmly, he produced a police whistle from his pocket and blew three sharp blasts on it.

The effect was instantaneous. The coachman whipped his team away without hesitation, the carriage bouncing on the cobbles as it tore around the corner into Bishopsgate. It barely gave whoever was manning the machine gun time to flick the curtain back over it, let alone the bowler-hatted chap time to climb aboard. *He* now found himself entirely alone and in full view of anyone who happened along. In a panic, he turned and began to run in the opposite direction.

Holmes tapped Watson on the arm, and they rose and followed. Moments later, they were threading through the crowds on the forecourt of Liverpool Street station. Not twenty yards ahead, the bowler-hatted chap had stopped at one of the ticket barriers, where he handed over some change, then bullocked his way through, glancing once over his shoulder, his brutish face a stark purple red in color. If he'd spotted either Holmes or Watson, he didn't betray it, but hurried off down a flight of steps toward the platforms.

"Where did that man just buy a ticket to?" Watson demanded of the clerk on the barrier.

The clerk shook his head. "Nowhere, sir. It was a platform ticket. Only cost tuppence."

"Two platform tickets," Holmes replied, handing over fourpence.

Moments later, they were hastening down the steps in pursuit. At the bottom, they gazed left and right. Thankfully, their prey was still distinctive in his hat and shirtsleeves. He was just in the process of descending another flight of steps.

"He's going to the underground railway," Watson said, surprised.

Holmes didn't reply. A hideous idea had suddenly occurred to him, one which he instinctively wished to put aside, but now found that he couldn't.

They followed the bowler-hatted man onto the westbound platform of the Metropolitan Line, and there, briefly, lost him in the gaggle of commuters. It was the end of the day, after all . . . the station was now at its busiest. They'd fought their way down to the first-class section before they caught sight of him again. To both their amazement, the fellow, having reached the very end of the platform, slipped down onto the rails directly behind the train, and vanished into the wall of wafting steam.

"What the devil . . . ," Watson began.

"Hurry!" Holmes said.

They, too, jumped down, and a moment later found themselves stumbling along the rails, pressing on into the tunnel, which was smoky and hot and echoing and reechoing with the furious crashes and bangs of the underground railway system. Several yards farther on, just as Watson was about to call time on the pursuit, fearing that they were endangering their lives, they saw an open area to the left-hand side, with a dull glow filtering into it from a high skylight. They entered and stopped for a moment, breathing hard and surveying the ground. It was thick with dust and strewn with rags and litter. The fresh footprints of their quarry, however, led clear across it and ended beside a wide, rusty grating, which sat open against the wall. Below this, iron ladders dropped into darkness. The smell that exhaled from that forbidding aperture was as vile and as cloying as either man had ever known.

Watson put a handkerchief to his nose. "You don't suppose he's *really* gone down there?"

Again, Holmes didn't answer. Watson glanced around, and found his friend staring down at the scrap of paper that Jobson had given them.

"Holmes?"

"Watson," the detective finally whispered, ". . . Harold Jobson deceived us. But only slightly. He didn't leave us a puzzle. He left us a map."

"A map?" Watson was astonished. He gazed at the paper for a moment, then down into the foul recesses below the grating. "Not . . . not of the sewers, surely?"

Holmes indicated the numerous tenuous lines on Jobson's paper, and the way they all seemed to reach a common confluence at the right-hand side of the page. "These are the interceptory sewers built by Bazalgette some thirty years ago . . . they divert the city's waste eastward from the main sewers, and studiously avoid the Thames." When he mentioned the river, he indicated a thicker central line with a downward loop that was suddenly reminiscent of the point where the River Thames curved around the Isle of Dogs. Holmes indicated two pencil-scrawled blobs, also at the right-hand side of the map. "Here is the Abbey Mills pumping station in Stratford . . . and here the sewage treatment works at Beckton."

"But what does the red circle signify?" Watson wondered.

Holmes couldn't suppress a shudder. "Well, it lies to the left; in other words, to the west of the city center. If I am correct, this straight line passing through it will be one of the mains that brings fresh water from the drinking reservoirs at Surbiton and Hampton. Watson . . . this circle, whatever it indicates, is located at a point *after* the water is passed through the filters."

Watson felt a crawling between his shoulders. "Jobson said there'd be a calamity . . . *dear God, would that be a water-borne calamity?*"

Holmes's skin had paled to an ashy gray.

"We must send for Lestrade straight away," Watson insisted.

Holmes struggled with this, then shook his head. "There's no time. Come . . . we have a map."

He bent down as though to climb under the grating, but Watson stopped him. "For God's sake . . . you can't mean to venture into the sewers?"

Holmes glanced up at him. "What choice do we have?"

"In the name of heaven . . . you'll need waders, a safety lamp, some sort of lifeline—"

"Watson . . . this may be the gravest case you and I have ever embarked on," Holmes replied, staring at his friend. "Personal safety cannot even enter the equation."

Subterranean London was a multilayered labyrinth of lost sewers, underground railways, pipes, tunnels, culverts, and conduits of every description, a sprawling network of forgotten passages comprising centuries of buried architecture, level upon level of it, from the medieval to the very modern. It was so vast and deep that no known maps covered it in its entirety. It was also hellishly black, and constantly swimming in a foul miasma from the rivers of excrement and industrial and chemical ooze that meandered back and forth through its slimy entrails.

Once down there, Holmes made a torch by tying pieces of rag around a broken stave, and bade Watson do the same, though even then they proceeded with utmost caution, wading warily westward along arched passages of ancient, sweating brickwork. Everything they saw was caked in the most loathsome detritus. Strands of putrid filth hung in their faces; the squeaking of rats was all around them; there was a continuous rumble and groan from the streets above. Persistently, Watson advised against the foolhardiness of such an enterprise, warning about the dangers of Weil's disease, hepatitis, bubonic plague. "And these naked flames," he added worriedly. "They're a perilous option on our part. Suppose we encounter firedamp?"

"That's a chance we must take," Holmes replied, again consulting the map as they approached a junction. "If we turn right here, I believe we'll be cutting north onto the Piccadilly branch."

"Holmes!" Watson protested. "This is a deadly serious matter. Suppose there's a sudden downpour? These pipes get flooded!"

Holmes looked up. "Watson . . . I am perfectly aware of the risks we are taking. Believe me, I wouldn't have brought myself, let alone my dearest friend, into such danger if I wasn't absolutely convinced of its necessity."

"But, Holmes—"

"Watson, I can't force you to accompany me. If you wish to return to the surface and hunt down Lestrade, then by all means do so. You'd be serving a useful purpose. But I *must* continue."

He was wearing his most no-nonsense expression. It was at once plain how utterly serious he was. Finally, Watson shook his head. "And a fine thing that would be . . . for dearest friends to abandon each other in their hour of need." He smiled bravely.

Holmes smiled back, then gripped his companion by the shoulder. "This maze may appear daunting, but Jobson's map is not too difficult to follow. He must have been this way many times himself, to be able to draw it from memory while sitting in the death cell. If *he* can manage it, I fancy we can."

They plodded on for another fifteen minutes, making turns both left and right, occasionally passing under manholes and ventilation grilles beyond which the upper world was briefly visible. The overwhelming stench of rottenness and sewage became slowly bearable, but that didn't lessen the visual horrors in London's dark and fetid bowels. Here and there, gluts of offal were heaped, having been jettisoned from the slaughterhouses; the carcasses of cats and dogs lay decaying, enriching the already poisonous waterways in the most rancid and sickening fashion.

"I doubt anything they could put in the drinking water could be worse than this brew," Watson commented as they sloshed into a low-roofed, egg-shaped passage, which seemed to run endlessly in a roughly northwesterly direction. "Where is this place you mentioned, anyway? Innsmouth? I've never even heard of . . . GOOD GOD, LOOK OUT . . ."

With a reptilian hiss and a ferocious snapping of gigantic jaws, something came barreling out of the noisome darkness in front of them.

"HOLMES!" Watson shouted again, then he was dealt a blow to the chest, which sent him reeling backward.

The torch flew from his hand and extinguished itself in the thrashing water, but not before it cast a fleeting glow on ten to twenty feet of gleaming leathery scales, on a colossal tail swishing back and forth, on an immense saurian-like head filled with daggers for teeth.

Holmes, too, had fallen back, though he maintained his balance and held his light out before him. Its wavering flame reflected in two hideous crimson orbs, but also on a stout iron chain, which was connected at one end to a plate in the tunnel wall, and at the other to a thick ring clamped around the monster's neck. Gasping and choking, Watson scrambled back to his feet, then dug his revolver from his overcoat pocket.

"I wouldn't," Holmes advised. "Not unless you want to deprive Inspector Lestrade of his next triumph."

Watson had already taken aim with the weapon, but now lowered it. "You . . . you think that's the animal missing from the zoo?"

"I'm certain of it," said Holmes. "Unless there's a breeding population of *krokodilos* down here in the London sewers, which I seriously doubt."

He ventured forward to get a closer look. Watson went with him. The brute was now entirely visible, a squat, broad monstrosity, so large it was only half submerged in the brackish fluids. It filled the passage from one side to the other, and now simply sat there, its mouth agape and steaming in a defiant show of menace . . . though a show was about *all* it could manage. By the torchlight, it could be seen that the chain holding the thing was only three or so feet in length and already pulled taut; it meant the savage beast could successfully block access to the tunnel but was unable to advance and pursue those it turned away.

"Whoever went to the trouble of procuring this guard dog must be very committed to their privacy," Holmes mused.

"It's a miracle it didn't kill us both," said Watson. "We were virtually on top of it."

"Yes . . . mind you, reptiles draw their energy from sunlight." Holmes glanced up at the low roof. "This creature hasn't had that opportunity for several days. Fortunately for us, it's rather sluggish at the moment."

"It'll still tear us to pieces if we try to get past it."

"That's true, Watson."

"Do you think there's another way?"

"It wouldn't be logical for whoever's hiding down here to only block off one access route, unless the other one was very well hidden."

Watson raised his revolver again. "In which case, we've no option."

"Did you shoot many crocodiles in India?"

"Not even one."

"That doesn't surprise me." Holmes pushed the revolver down. "I doubt a small-caliber firearm like yours will do more than injure this creature. On the other hand, what it *will* do is alert our real foe. I fancy these sewers would make marvelous echo chambers."

Reluctantly, Watson pocketed the Webley.

"There *will* be another way, however," Holmes said. "I'm sure our bowler-hatted friend hasn't chanced this animal's jaws. Let's backtrack a little."

They retreated for several yards, until Holmes cast his light on a small grid placed among the arched bricks of the ceiling. Like everything else down there, it was thick with grime, and at the most only two feet wide by one foot high. Holmes examined it carefully.

"This is an overflow pipe," he said after a moment.

"Connecting with what?"

"The Walbrook, I imagine."

"The Walbrook?" Watson was startled. "But that river hasn't been seen for centuries."

"Then this is truly a voyage of discovery," Holmes replied.

He thrust his long fingers through the grating and tugged at it experimentally. It came loose almost at once. "As I thought," he said. "This has been forced open sometime quite recently." The bolts that had once secured the grid in place had clearly been broken . . . amid the coat of rust, their jagged edges still shone with the luster of clean cast iron. "Which hopefully means our passage through will be unobstructed."

"It isn't likely to stay that way," observed Watson, giving his friend a leg up. "Not when my bulk gets jammed inside it."

Despite Watson's misgivings, the next few moments were relatively comfortable. The connecting line to the Walbrook was no more than a tube, but it was smoothly cylindrical and, as Holmes had predicted, clear of debris. Though it was something of a squeeze, it took them only a minute or two to forge its ten or twelve feet, then jump down again into the brown, foaming waters of the subterranean river. Thigh-deep, they pressed on, having to duck under bars and buttresses, but at last emerging into a tall vaulted chamber that was something like a cathedral side chapel. Torrents of water poured into it from various high portals. The vast bulk of the flow then plunged away down a steep, circular shaft.

"What do you think *that* is?" Watson wondered. He indicated a narrow wooden door on a dry ledge.

"Possibly a relief room," Holmes replied. "Where the flusher crews take a rest." A moment passed, then he glanced at their "map." "At least that may be what it *once* was used for. According to Harold Jobson, it now has a different purpose entirely."

Watson glanced over Holmes's shoulder and saw again the circle of red ink. Whatever it signified, they were now upon it.

The door was not locked. Immediately beyond it, however, there was a small antechamber, in which a grim warning awaited. There was a second door, and beside it three iron hooks had been hammered into the wall, presumably for equipment. Now, however, two dead bodies hung there.

Holmes and Watson approached them with trepidation. At first glance, the bodies resembled Egyptian mummies. They were swathed in linen bandages, their heads as well as their torsos, though most of the bindings were now loose and filthied. In both cases, the left arm had been unwrapped. Watson examined the exposed limbs. On the insides of both elbow joints, the black bruises of old puncture wounds were visible. The doctor had seen similar wounds on drug addicts, though these were larger and less numerous. More shocking to him was the fact that in either case, the fingers of the victim appeared to be webbed, and that hard patches of shiny, mottled skin occupied areas of the wrists and upper arms, which looked distinctly like scaling. Baffled, he made to uncover the first body's head.

Holmes stopped him. "I shouldn't," he said quietly. "It might be more than you can stomach at this moment. In any case, our *real* business awaits us through here." He indicated the next door.

With a crackle of grit, they were able to force it open, and found themselves at the head of a concrete ramp, which led down into a long, spacious chamber now lit by numerous candles. Possibly, the room had once been used for storage—the ramp suggested that wheelbarrows and the like were taken in and out—but now it had been customized into something like a laboratory. Several items of furniture were in there, mainly tables and sideboards, all laden with bottles and test tubes. Beside them, a variety of opened boxes and crates lay scattered. The next thing Holmes saw caused him to nudge Watson's shoulder. The doctor glanced up and spotted a large cast-iron pipe branching across the ceiling from one side of the chamber to the other, snaking through a canopy of dust-laden cobwebs. Coupled together by bored-socket-and-spigot joints, it bespoke of masterly and care-filled engineering, which suggested only one thing . . .

"The water main," said Holmes. "And so vulnerable. What would you say . . . ten feet up? One would only need a ladder and a hammer and chisel, and one could penetrate it with ease."

But Watson had spied something else, something even more astonishing. Wordlessly, he drew Holmes's attention to a figure at the extreme northern end of the chamber. At first the fellow had been invisible in the dim light, hidden behind an array of connected tubes and vessels, but now, as their eyes attuned to the gloom, they could make him out more clearly. He hadn't yet noticed them, and appeared to be working feverishly beside a truckle bed on which another of the mummified patients lay under a thin blanket. The fellow was in late middle age, and wore his facial hair in a long, graying beard. He also wore round-lensed spectacles.

"Holmes . . ." said Watson in disbelief. "Holmes . . . that's Professor Langley. Good God! He's dead . . . he was burned to a crisp!"

"*Someone* was burned to a crisp," Holmes replied. "Evidently not Langley."

Langley—if it *was* Langley—was dusty and unshaven, and stripped to his grimy shirtsleeves. He appeared gaunt and sallow-faced with lack of sleep. He was currently operating a hand pump, attached to a rubber tube, which ran from an embedded syringe in the patient's arm to a complex construction of valves, pipes, and glass jars set up on a low table beside him. With each depression of the pump, a thick stream of blood visibly jetted into the topmost jar. Several of the lower jars were already filled. At the base of the device, a thin, transparent substance was dripping into a flask.

"He's transfusing blood," said Watson. "But into what? It looks like a distillation unit."

Holmes rubbed his chin. "He's taking something *from* the blood. Some essence, perhaps . . ."

"How remarkable you are, Holmes," came a rich American voice behind them.

Both men turned sharply to find the ramp blocked, not only by Rohampton, but by the brutish fellow in the bowler hat and by the clerk, Burgess, who had detached the Gatling gun from its tripod and now cradled it in his arms so that it was trained squarely on them; a full ammunition belt, partially fed into its firing mechanism, was draped over his arm.

Watson went for the revolver in his pocket, but Rohampton shouted a warning. "Don't even think about it, Doctor!" He tapped the machine gun's heavy muzzle. "You're a former military man. You know what this weapon can do."

"In God's name, Rohampton!" Watson cried. "What horrors are you engaged in here?"

"Horrors, Doctor? How very judgmental of you."

"Judgmental? When you're draining people's blood to the last drop!"

Rohampton gave an almost sad smile, then shouldered his way past the two intruders, walking down the ramp into the center of the lab. The bowler-hatted man followed. Burgess brought up the rear, indicating with the Gatling that Holmes and Watson should go first, pushing them down ahead of him.

"These people . . . as you call them," the American said, "are volunteers. They have willingly surrendered their lives for a greater good." He glanced across the room, to where Professor Langley now watched events from behind his racks of flasks and tubes. "Keep working, Langley!"

"But if they've seen *this* much . . ." the professor protested.

"Trent!" Rohampton said sharply. "Remind our friend the professor why it is so important that he keep his mind on the task at hand."

The bowler-hatted man wove his way across the lab, then drew the curtain back on a small alcove at the other side. Beyond it was a chilling sight. A hospital operating table was propped upright against the dank bricks of the alcove wall, and strapped to this by several belts was a young girl. She still wore the bedraggled tatters of nightclothes, and her fair hair hung in tangled, dirty knots. She gazed at Holmes and Watson pleadingly, but was unable to speak owing to a tight gag pulled across her mouth. Clearly, this was Laura, Professor Langley's daughter.

Directly in front of her there sat an open barrel, stuffed with a green, spongy herbage. Rohampton now approached it, stripping off his frock coat as he did. He took a rubber apron from the wall, along with two heavy-duty industrial gauntlets, and put the entire assembly on. Then he gingerly dipped one gloved hand into the barrel.

"You see this, Holmes?" he said, lifting up a handful of the green material. "Devil's Reef Moss. It's virtually unique. It grows only in one particular place off the New England coast. Don't ask me why, I'm not the scientist here . . ."

Holmes watched carefully. Something about that handful of rank vegetation touched a deep primal fear within him. "Presumably it's toxic?"

"Oh, it's much worse than that," Rohampton replied, gazing at the moss as if fascinated. "But then why am I telling you? You've seen the results for yourself."

"Randolph Daker," said Holmes.

The American opened his hand and wiggled his fingers, making sure to return every scrap of moss to the barrel. "That's correct. Daker . . . the only weak link in our chain. Inevitably, he'd seen something of what we were about, yet what was he? A common carter, a ruffian, a drunkard . . . likely to gossip the first time he got into his cups. We couldn't allow that, Holmes . . . so we spiced those cups."

"Rather glad we didn't sample your sherry," said the detective.

Rohampton smiled. "Yes . . . very intuitive of you. Of course, the moss is quite slow acting. Eventually we became concerned that even infected as he was, Daker might still blab."

"So you dispatched one of your followers to put him out of his misery?"

"That's right."

Holmes glanced at the fellow called Trent. "He wasn't terribly efficient."

Rohampton began to strip off his gauntlets. "These are the tools we must work with, I'm afraid. When one recruits at short notice, and can offer in return only vague promises of wealth and power . . . one is lucky to draw on anything more than the sweepings of the streets. Harold Jobson was a case in point. He and several others successfully orchestrated the kidnap of Professor Langley and his daughter, replacing them in their burning home with two drunken derelicts snatched from the backstreets . . . and then Jobson went and allowed himself to be captured." The American shook his head with feigned regret.

"You are aware, I suppose," said Holmes, "that it was Jobson who led us to you?"

Rohampton made a vague gesture, as if it hardly mattered. "He took his death sentence with a pinch of salt. I think he expected to be rescued virtually up till the final day. Only then did his ambition switch from survival to revenge." Rohampton gave a cold chuckle. "As if anyone in my position has the time or inclination to save the necks of fools."

Watson, meanwhile, was staring at the bandaged form lying on the truckle bed. All the while Langley had continued pumping out its blood. By the lifeless manner in which its arm now lay by its side, it was evident that this patient, too, had expired. "These so-called volunteers?" he said distastefully. "Who are they?"

Rohampton was now removing the apron. He moved back into the lab, beating brick dust from his dress shirt. "Their names are unimportant. Suffice to say this . . . they were chosen from among the ranks of my native townsmen."

"Innsmouth," said Holmes.

For the first time, the American seemed surprised. "You know it?"

"Only stories," the detective replied. "About the tainting of the Innsmouth bloodline some fifty years ago . . . and how the townsfolk have been degenerating ever since."

"Degenerating?" If it was possible for the white, rigid features of Julian Rohampton to grimace with rage, they did so now. "Some would call it *evolving.* Into a higher life-form."

"If it's so high a form," Holmes asked, "why do you hide behind that waxen mask?"

There was a moment of silence, Watson gazing from man to man, bewildered. His gaze settled on Rohampton when the American suddenly hooked his fingers into claws and began to attack his own face. In strips and gobbets, he tore away what had clearly been a finely crafted disguise. Beneath it, the flesh was a pallid gray blue in tone. More horrible yet, it was patterned with scales and fishlike ridges. The lips and eyebrows were thick and rubbery, the nose nonexistent. Down either cheek, lines of gills were visible.

Watson could scarcely believe the abomination before him. "Good . . . Lord!"

Rohampton wiped off the last fragments, then removed his blond wig. "Behold, Dr. Watson, the Innsmouth look! When Obed Marsh returned to us from the South Seas, he brought more than just a new wife. He'd intermarried with a race of beings in every way superior. When the bloodlines were fully mingled, Innsmouth became the cradle of a truly new civilization. As the generations passed and we natives of the town slowly transformed, a cosmic awareness began to dawn on us . . . of the Deep Ones, of their culture and science and beliefs, and of our destiny to be as one with them. In time, I will join their teeming ranks beneath the waves. *And I won't be alone!*"

Holmes remained dispassionate. He strolled to the nearest table, surveying the many bottles of chemicals there. Rohampton's men watched him warily.

"You're creating a bacillus, I take it?" he said, picking up an open jar. He noted with interest that it had dry salts encrusted around its rim. When he sniffed it, he detected picric acid, as he'd suspected.

"Put that down, Mr. Holmes," said Rohampton firmly.

Holmes turned to face him. "Distilling an infectious agent from the life fluids of your own people . . . is that what you're about?"

"You know I am." Even now, Rohampton couldn't resist boasting. "I'm tapping the genetic core of my race. Courtesy, of course, of Professor Langley's biochemical genius."

Watson glanced again at the pipe running overhead. One would only need a ladder and a hammer and chisel, Holmes had said.

"And you intend to impregnate London's water supply with this thing?" he blurted out.

"The loyal Watson gets there in the end," said Rohampton, so amused that he hadn't noticed that Holmes had still not put down the picric jar.

"It's . . . it's inhuman," Watson stammered.

The monstrous thing smiled, now fully and broadly. "Certainly it's inhuman. But tell me, is that necessarily to the detriment? Has humanity made such a work of art of this planet that a scheme to transform it into something better should be decried?"

"To transform humanity?" Holmes scoffed, sensing rather than seeing the rusty iron plate set into the tabletop quite close to him.

"Don't be too quick to jeer, Holmes," Rohampton retorted. "Loud and filthy as she is . . . London is still is the crossroads of world commerce. Once *she* falls, the rest will follow."

"A grand conquest indeed," said Holmes, reaching toward the iron plate with the acid jar. "And all achieved from a hole in the ground, with a few bottles of solvent . . ."

Professor Langley realized what the detective was doing first, and ducked beneath the table.

"HOLMES!" Rohampton warned.

". . . and a flash of inspiration!"

The moment the picric crystals met the exposed iron, they detonated.

There was a dazzling flash, a crunching *bang*, then glass was flying and the dank laboratory was filled with smoke. Rohampton and his men covered their eyes. Holmes went down, flung backward by the force of the blast, but he was up again just as quickly. With all his strength, he turned over the smoking, wreckage-strewn table, sending it toppling against the distillation unit, which fell heavily to the floor and burst apart in a welter of fresh-drawn blood.

Watson, meanwhile, took the opportunity to drag his revolver from his pocket. With a soldierly impulse, he turned first to Burgess, who was wielding the Gatling gun, took aim, and squeezed off a shot. The report crashed and crashed in the deep chamber, but the bullet flew straight, hitting the thug in the left shoulder, sending him staggering backward into the curtained alcove, dropping his deadly weapon. Automatically, Watson turned and pumped two shots at Trent. This second hireling had now snatched up an iron bar. The first bullet punched into his throat, however, the second into his chest. He dropped without a sound, his eyes rolled white in his brutal face.

But in the brief space of time afforded by the chemical explosion, only so much resistance had been possible . . . and now Rohampton dashed forward. He'd already grabbed up the Gatling gun, and with an angry roar, he swung its hefty stock into Holmes's side, then up against his temple, knocking him half senseless to the floor. Ten yards to his left, he sensed Watson falling to a crouch, his revolver leveled.

"Drop it, Doctor!" the hybrid roared, the Gatling gun trained firmly on Holmes. "Drop it . . . or your friend is dead!"

Instantly, Watson realized he had no choice. He only had three shots left, to the several dozen still visible in the machine gun's ammo belt. "Don't shoot," he said, releasing the grip of the Webley so that it swung upside down from his finger. As gently as he could, he lowered it to the floor.

A moment passed, then Rohampton backed away a couple of yards, turned, and surveyed the destruction. His eyes flickered fleetingly over the body of Trent and the groaning, only semiconscious form of the professor, but when they located the shattered distillation unit, his features twisted into a hideous scowl. "Blast you and damn you, but you haven't won anything yet!"

Holmes, though groggy, had come 'round sufficiently to start edging away across the floor. Watson saw that his face was marked with flash burns and riddled here and there with minor cuts. Worse seemed to be about to follow, however.

"You think I can't re-create all this?" Rohampton barked, round-

ing on them again. "It'll only take days, and this time you god-
damn meddlers won't be alive to interfere!"

He took aim at Holmes and was about to fire, when something
suddenly distracted him . . . a muffled, guttural grunting. All three
of them turned toward the alcove, where Laura Langley still hung
in her bonds, now in a dead faint. She was not the object of their
attention, however; it was Burgess . . . the so-called clerk, now more
like something from a nightmare.

When Watson had wounded him, he'd tottered backward into
the alcove, but only so far as the barrel of Devil's Reef Moss,
which he'd collided with, sought to steady himself against, and inadvertently had slipped into, hands and face first. Now he came
slowly back into view . . . already thickly sprouting with shoots and
fronds and hideous clusters of anemones. A vile stench of salt and
sea caves came off him.

He lurched into their midst, swaying back and forth, gasping
and hissing like a deep-sea diver, yet amid that pulsating mass of
marine parasites, his eyes were still horribly human . . . and with
another gurgling, agonized groan, he rolled them toward his master, who, even after all the things *he* had seen and done, was mesmerized with horror by the sight and stink.

"Get back, Burgess!" Rohampton shouted. "Don't touch me!
Don't you dare!"

Possibly Burgess failed to hear, though more likely he chose
not to . . . for he now blundered blindly toward the only person
he knew who might somehow save him.

"Burgess!" Rohampton screamed, retreating swiftly, swinging the
Gatling gun around. "BURGESS, GET AWAY FROM MEEEEE!"

The weapon fired with a thundering roar, flames and smoke
gouting from its muzzle. The servant was ripped apart where he
stood, each slug blowing bloody ribbons from his tortured flesh.
He hurtled backward, his arms flailing, till he struck the far wall,
which he slowly slid down, a gory trail on the bricks behind him . . .
Rohampton didn't let up, he fired and fired, but in doing so, he

failed to notice Holmes rise to his feet, draw something from under his coat, and spring a blade into view.

It was Trent's lock knife. The detective despised all weapons, and this tool of the gutter was particularly repellent to him . . . even so, in desperate times all needs must. He hurled the knife full-on, just as the hybrid turned back to face him. The blade struck home, slashing deeply into the American's upper left arm. Rohampton gasped and twisted. The Gatling gun slumped down across his knees.

Taking his chance, Watson grabbed up his revolver.

"Don't, Watson!" Rohampton snapped. "I'll kill you both . . . I swear it!" But this time even *he* didn't sound convinced.

His left arm now limp and useless, and running with blood, he was struggling both to support the heavy weapon and to keep it trained on its targets. With urgent pants, he backed away across the rubble-strewn room and up the ramp toward the door.

"You've still won nothing," he said, but his voice was cracking with effort. He came up against the door and back-heeled it open. "We'll breed you out yet!" Then he opened fire again.

Holmes lunged down behind the upended table. Watson went the other way, diving behind a brick buttress. Neither need have bothered, however . . . for the hail of random shots rattled inaccurately around the room, several rebounding and narrowly missing Rohampton himself. Furious, but knowing he had no option, he turned and scrambled out into the sewers.

"Come, Watson!" said Holmes, giving rapid chase.

"Are you all right, old man?" Watson asked, hurrying up the ramp alongside him.

"Never better. But beware . . . friend Rohampton is waging a war for his race. He'll not be taken easily."

The American's trail was easy to follow. Even in the gloom of the sewers, his blood besmeared the brickwork and lay in oily swirls on the brackish waters. Though he took turn after turn, passage after passage, he hadn't got too far when Holmes and Watson came in sight of him again. Once more, he turned and greeted their challenge with blazing gunfire. In the narrower confines of the culvert, the furious volley was far more deadly, and both men were forced to cower in the effluent.

"Gad!" Watson cursed. "*This filth* . . . mind you, he can't hold us off for long. That bandolier must be almost spent."

"He doesn't need to hold us off for long," Holmes replied. "Somewhere along here there'll be a downflow pipe to the Thames. If he reaches that, he's as good as free."

"What do you mean?"

Holmes hurried on. "For Heaven's sake, Watson . . . Rohampton is an amphibian, and the Thames connects with the sea. What I mean is he'll shortly have escaped to a place where nobody can ever reach him!"

The full import of that dawning on him, Watson scrambled frantically in pursuit. They rounded a sharp bend and again were almost shot from their feet. Only ten yards ahead, Rohampton had stopped. Just behind him, there was a breach in the wall where a series of bricks had fallen through. From beyond it came the furious gushing of the downflow pipe.

The hybrid gave a riotous laugh. "Humanity's finished, Holmes!" he roared. "And London dies first!"

And then the noxious waters behind him surged and exploded, and the next thing any of them knew, a colossal pair of jaws had snapped closed on Rohampton's midriff. He gave a piercing shriek, which was instantly cut off as the crocodile guardian tossed itself violently over, sending a wave of slime against Holmes and Watson, and tearing and twisting its hapless catch like something made from rags.

The two men could only watch, rooted to the spot.

For what seemed like minutes, the giant, half-starved reptile rent and ripped at its prey, regardless of his shrieks and gargles, swinging him 'round and 'round, beating him on the brick walls in order to pulp and tenderize him, then tearing and chomping on him again, finally swallowing him down in quivering, butchered hunks. The waters around the animal ran deepest red; bone and gristle were swallowed in dinosaur-like gulps; clothing and shoes vanished, too; even the massive machine gun was bent and buckled in the frenzy of the attack, and almost consumed.

The echoes of the slaughter continued until long after it had finished.

When he was finally able to move, Watson drew slowly backward in shock. "Thank . . . thank God I didn't shoot the thing . . . I suppose."

Holmes, steely as he normally was in these circumstances, was also shaken by what they had witnessed. "Thank God indeed," he whispered.

"Of course, you know what this means," Watson finally added. "No one will believe us. I mean, there won't be a scrap of the blackguard left as proof."

Holmes nodded. "Much as I hate to say it, Watson . . . a price worth paying."

The scaled beast had now sunk back under the stained surface, only its ridged back and beady crimson eyes visible. It watched them steadily, hungrily.

The Horror of the Many Faces

TIM LEBBON

What I saw that night defied belief, but believe it I had to because I trusted my eyes. "Seeing is believing" is certainly not an axiom that my friend would have approved of, but I was a doctor, a scientist, and for me the eyes were the most honest organs in the body.

I never believed that they could lie.

What I laid eyes upon in the murky London twilight made me the saddest man. It stripped any faith I had in the order of things, the underlying goodness of life. How can something so wrong exist in an ordered world? How, if there is a benevolent purpose behind everything, can something so insane exist?

These are the questions I asked then and still ask now, though the matter has been resolved in a far different way from that which I could ever have imagined at the time.

I was on my way home from the surgery. The sun was setting into the murk of the London skyline, and the city was undergoing its usual dubious transition from light to dark. As I turned a corner into a narrow cobbled street, I saw my old friend, my mentor, *slaughtering* a man in the gutter. He hacked and slashed with a blade that caught the red twilight, and upon seeing me, he seemed to calm and perform some meticulous mutilation upon the twitching corpse.

I staggered against the wall. "Holmes!" I gasped.

He looked up, and in his honest eyes there was nothing. No light, no twinkle, not a hint of the staggering intelligence that lay behind them.

Nothing except for a black, cold emptiness.

Stunned into immobility, I could only watch as Holmes butchered the corpse. He was a man of endless talents, but still I was amazed at the dexterity with which he opened the body, extracted the heart, and wrapped it in his handkerchief.

No, not butchery. *Surgery.* He worked with an easy medical knowledge that appeared to surpass my own.

Holmes looked up at me where I stood frozen stiff. He smiled, a wicked grin that looked so alien on his face. Then he stood and shrugged his shoulders, moving on the spot as if settling comfortably into a set of new clothes.

"Holmes," I croaked again, but he turned and fled.

Holmes the thinker, the ponderer, the genius, ran faster than I had ever seen anyone run before. I could not even think to give chase, so shocked was I with what I had witnessed. In a matter of seconds, my outlook on life had been irrevocably changed, brought to ground and savaged with a brutality I had never supposed possible. I felt as if I had been shot, hit by a train, mauled. I was winded and dizzy and ready to collapse at any moment.

But I pinched myself hard on the back of my hand, drawing blood and bringing myself around.

I closed my eyes and breathed in deeply, but when I opened them again the corpse still lay there in the gutter. Nothing had changed. However much I desired not to see this, wished it would flee my memory, I was already realizing that such would never happen. This scene was etched on my mind.

One of the worst feelings in life is betrayal, the realization that everything one has held true is false, or at least fatally flawed. That look in Holmes's eyes . . . I would have given anything to be able to forget that.

His footsteps had vanished into the distance. The victim was surely dead, but being a doctor, I had to examine him to make sure. He was a young man, handsome, slightly foreign looking, obviously well off in the world because of the tasteful rings on his fingers, the tailored suit . . . holed now, ripped and ruptured with the vicious thrusts of Holmes's blade. And dead, of course. His chest had been opened and his heart stolen away.

Perhaps he was a dreadful criminal, a murderer in his own right, whom Holmes had been tracking, chasing, pursuing for days or weeks? I spent less time with Holmes now than I had in the past, and I was not involved in every case he took on. But . . . murder? Not Holmes. Whatever crime this dead man may have been guilty of, nothing could justify what my friend had done to him.

I suddenly had an intense feeling of guilt, kneeling over a corpse with fresh blood on my fingertips. If anyone rounded the corner at that moment I would have trouble explaining things, I was sure, not only because of the initial impression they would gain but also because of the shock I was in, the *terror* I felt at what I had witnessed.

The police should have been informed. I should have found a policeman or run to the nearest station, led them to the scene of the crime. I was probably destroying valuable evidence . . . but then I thought of Holmes, that crazy grin, and realized that I already knew the identity of the murderer.

Instead, something made me run. Loyalty to my old friend was a small part of it, but there was fear as well. I knew even then that things were not always as they seemed. Holmes had told me that countless times before, and I kept thinking, *Impossible, impossible* as

I replayed the scene in my mind. But I trusted my eyes, I knew what I had seen. And in my mind's eye, Holmes was still grinning manically . . . at me.

With each impact of my feet upon the pavement, the fear grew.

Holmes was the most brilliant man I had ever known. And even in his obvious madness, I knew that he was too far beyond and above the ordinary ever to be outsmarted, outwitted, or tracked down. *If his spree is to continue,* I prayed, *please God don't let him decide to visit an old friend.*

I need not have worried about informing the police of the murder. They knew already.

The day following my terrible experience I begged sick, remaining at home in bed, close to tears on occasion as I tried to find room in my life for what I had seen. My thoughts were very selfish, I admit that, because I had effectively lost my very best friend to a horrendous madness. I could never have him back. My mind wandered much that day, going back to the times we had spent together and forward to the barren desert of existence which I faced without him. I enjoyed my life . . . but there was a terrible blandness about things without the promise of Holmes being a part of it.

I mourned, conscious all the time of the shape of my army revolver beneath my pillow.

Mixed in with this was the conviction that I should tell the police of what I had seen. But then the evening papers came, and somehow, impossibly, the terrible became even worse.

There had been a further six murders in the London streets the previous night, all very similar in execution and level of violence. In each case, organs had been removed from the bodies, though not always the same ones. The heart from one, lungs from another, and a dead lady in Wimbledon had lost her brain to the fiend.

In four cases—including the murder I had witnessed—the

stolen organs had been found somewhere in the surrounding areas. Sliced, laid out on the ground in very neat order, the sections sorted perfectly by size and thickness. Sometimes masticated gobs of the tissue were found as well, as if bitten off, chewed, and spat out. Tasted. *Tested.*

And there were witnesses. Not to every murder, but to enough of them to make me believe that the murderer—Holmes, I kept telling myself, Holmes—wanted to be seen. Though here lay a further mystery: each witness saw someone different. One saw a tall, fat man, heavily furred with facial hair, dressed scruffy and grim. Another described a shorter man with decent clothes, a light cloak in one hand and a sword in the other. The third witness talked of the murderous lady he had seen . . . the lady with great strength, for she had stood her victim against a wall and wrenched out the unfortunate's guts.

A mystery, yes, but only for a moment. Only until my knowledge of Holmes's penchant for disguise crept in, instantly clothing my memory of him from the previous night in grubby clothes, light cloak, and then a lady's dress.

"Oh, dear God," I muttered. "Dear God, Holmes, what is it, my old friend? The cocaine? Did the stress finally break you? The strain of having a mind that cannot rest, working with such evil and criminal matters?"

The more I dwelled upon it the worse it all became. I could not doubt what I had seen, even though all logic, all good sense, forbade it. I tried reason and deduction, as Holmes would have done, attempting to ignore the horrors of the case in order to pare it down to its bare bones, setting out the facts and trying to fill in the missing pieces. But memory was disruptive; I could not help visualizing my friend hunkered down over the body, hacking at first and then moving instantly into a careful slicing of the dead man's chest. The blood. The strange smell in the air, like sweet honey (and a clue there, perhaps, though I could do nothing with it).

Holmes's terrible, awful smile when he saw me.

Perhaps that was the worst. The fact that he seemed to be *gloating*.

I may well have remained that way for days, my feigned sickness becoming something real as my soul was torn to shreds by the truth. But on the evening of that first day following the crimes, I received a visit that spurred me to tell the truth.

Detective Inspector Jones, of Scotland Yard, came to my door looking for Holmes.

"It is a dreadful case," he said to me. "I've never seen anything like it." His face was pale with the memory of the corpses he must have been viewing that day. "Different witnesses saw different people, all across the south end of London. One man told me the murderer was his *brother*. And a woman, witness to another murder, was definitely withholding something personal to her. The murders themselves are so similar as to be almost identical in execution. The killing, then the extraction of an organ."

"It sounds terrible," I said lamely, because the truth was pressing to be spoken.

"It was." Jones nodded. Then he looked at me intently. "The papers did not say that at least three of the victims were alive when the organs were removed, and that was the method of their death."

"What times?" I asked.

"There was maybe an hour between the killings, from what we can work out. And yet different murderers in each case. And murderers who, I'm sure it will be revealed eventually, were *all* known to those bearing witness. Strange. *Strange!* Dr. Watson, we've worked together before; you know of my determination. But this . . . this fills me with dread. I fear the sun setting tonight in case we have another slew of killings, maybe worse. How many nights of this will it take until London is in a panic? One more? Two? And I haven't a clue as to what it's all about. A sect, I suspect, made up of many members and needing these organs for some nefarious purpose. But how to find them? I haven't a clue. Not a clue! And I'm

sure, I'm certain, that your friend Sherlock Holmes will be fascinated with such a case."

Jones shook his head and slumped back in the armchair. He
looked defeated already, I thought. I wondered what the truth
would do to him. And yet I had to bear it myself, so I thought it
only right to share. To *tell. Holmes, my old friend* . . . I thought
fondly, and then I told Jones what I had seen.

He did not talk for several minutes. The shock on his face hid
his thoughts. He stared into the fire as if seeking some alternate
truth in there, but my words hung heavy, and my demeanor must
have been proof enough to him that I did not lie.

"The different descriptions . . ." he said quietly, but I could
sense that he had already worked that out.

"Disguises. Holmes is a master."

"Should I hunt Holmes? Seek him through the London he
knows so well?"

"I do not see how," I said, because truly I thought ourselves totally out of control. Holmes would play whatever game he chose
until its closure, and the resolution would be of his choosing. "He
knows every street, every alley, shop to shop and door to door. In
many cases he knows of who lives where, where they work, and
whom they associate with. He can walk along a street and tell me
stories of every house, if he so chooses. He carries his card index
in his brain, as well as boxed away at Baker Street. His mind . . .
you know his mind, Mr. Jones. It is *endless*."

"And you're sure, Dr. Watson. Your illness has not blinded you,
you haven't had hallucinations—"

"I am merely sick to the soul with what I have witnessed," I
said. "I was fit and well yesterday evening."

"Then I must search him out," Jones said, but the desperation,
the hopelessness in his voice told me that he had already given up.
He stared into the fire some more and then stood, brushed himself
down, a man of business again.

"I wish you luck," I said.

"Can you help?" Jones asked. "You know him better than anyone. You're his best friend. Have you any ideas, any reasoning as to why he would be doing these crimes, where he'll strike next?"

"None," I said. "It is madness, for sure." I wanted Jones gone then, out of my house and into the night. Here was the man who would hunt my friend, stalk him in the dark, send his men out armed and ready to shoot and kill if need must. And whatever I had seen Holmes doing . . . that memory, *horrible* . . . I could not entertain the idea of his death.

Jones left and I jumped to my feet. He was right. I knew Holmes better than anyone, and after many years accompanying him as he had solved the most baffling of cases, I would hope that some of his intuition had rubbed off on me.

It was almost dark, red twilight kissing my window like diluted blood, and if tonight was to be like last night, then my old friend was already stalking his first victim.

I would go to Baker Street. Perhaps there I would find evidence of this madness, and maybe even something that could bring hope of a cure.

The streets were very different that night.

There were fewer strollers, for a start. Many people had heard of the previous night's murders and chosen to stay at home. It was raining, too, a fine mist that settled on one's clothes and soaked them instantly. Streetlamps provided oases of half-light in the dark, and it was these I aimed for, darting as quickly as I could between them. Even then, passing beneath the lights and seeing my shadow change direction, I felt more vulnerable than ever. I could not see beyond the lamps' meager influence and it lit me up for anyone to see, any stranger lurking in the night, any *friend* with a knife.

I could have found my way to Baker Street in the dark. I walked quickly and surely, listening out for any hint of pursuit. I tried to see into the shadows, but they retained their secrets well.

Everything felt changed. It was not only my newfound fear of the dark, but the perception that nothing, *nothing* is ever exactly as it seems. Holmes had always known that truth is in the detail, but could even he have ever guessed at the destructive parts in him, the corrupt stew of experience and knowledge and exhaustion that had led to this madness? It was a crueler London I walked through that night. Right and wrong had merged and blurred in my mind, for as sure as I was that what Holmes had done was wrong, it could never be right to hunt and kill him for it.

I had my revolver in my pocket, but I prayed with every step that I would not be forced to use it.

Shadows jumped from alleys and skirted around rooftops, but it was my imagination twisting the twilight. By the time I reached Baker Street, it was fully dark, the moon a pale ghost behind London's fog.

I stood outside for a while, staring up at Holmes's window. There was no light there, of course, and no signs of habitation, but still I waited for a few minutes, safe in the refuge of memory. He would surely never attack here, not in the shadow of his longtime home. No, I feared that he had gone to ground, hidden himself away in some unknown corner of London, or perhaps even taken his madness elsewhere in the country.

There was a sound behind me and I spun around, fumbling in my pocket for my revolver. It had been a shallow pop, as of someone opening their mouth in preparation to speak. I held my breath and aimed the revolver from my waist. There was nothing. The silence, the darkness, felt loaded, brimming with secrets and something more terrible . . . something . . .

"Holmes," I said. But he would not be there, he was not foolish, not so stupid to return here when he was wanted for some of the most terrible murders—

"My friend."

I started, tried to gauge where the voice had come from. I tightened my grip on the pistol and swung it slowly left and right, ready to shoot should anything move. I was panicked, terrified beyond belief. My stomach knotted and cramped with the idea of a knife parting skin and delving deeper.

"Is that you, Holmes?"

More silence for a while, so that I began to think I was hearing things. It grew darker for a moment, as if something had passed in front of the moon; I even glanced up, but there was nothing in the sky and the moon was its usual wan self.

"You feel it, too!" the voice said.

"Holmes, please show yourself."

"Go to my rooms. Mrs. Hudson hasn't heard of things yet; she will let you in and I will find my own way up there."

He did not sound mad. He sounded different, true, but not mad.

"Holmes, you have to know—"

"I am aware of what you saw, Watson, and you would do well to keep your revolver drawn and aimed ahead of you. Go to my rooms, back into a corner, hold your gun. For your sanity, your peace of mind, it has to remain between us for a time."

"I saw . . . Holmes, I saw . . ."

"My rooms."

And then he was gone. I did not hear him leave, caught sight of nothing moving away in the dark, but I knew that my old friend had departed. I wished for a torch to track him, but Holmes would have evaded the light. And in that thought I found my continuing belief in Holmes's abilities, his genius, his disregard for the normal levels of reasoning and measures of intelligence.

The madness he still had, but . . . I could not help but trust him.

From the distance, far, far away, I heard what may have been a scream. There were foxes in London, and thousands of wild dogs, and some said that wolves still roamed the forgotten byways of this sprawling city. But it had sounded like a human cry.

He could not possibly have run that far in such short a time.

Could he?

Mrs. Hudson greeted me and was kind enough to ignore my preoccupation as I climbed the stairs to Holmes's rooms.

*   ★   ★

There was another scream in the night before Holmes appeared.

I had opened the window and was standing there in the dark, looking out over London and listening to the sounds. The city was so much quieter during the night, which ironically made every sound that much louder. The barking of a dog swept across the neighborhood, the crashing of a door echoed from walls and back again. The scream . . . this time it *was* human, I could have no doubt of that, and although even farther away than the one I had heard earlier, I could still make out its agony. It was followed seconds later by another cry, this one cut short. There was nothing else.

Go to my rooms, back into a corner, hold your gun, Holmes had said. I remained by the window. Here was escape, at least, if I needed it. I would probably break my neck in the fall, but at least I was giving myself a chance.

I've come to his rooms! I thought. Fly to a spider. Chicken to a fox's den. But even though his voice had been very different from usual—more *strained*—I could not believe that the Holmes who had spoken to me minutes before was out there now, causing those screams.

I thought briefly of Detective Inspector Jones, and hoped that he was well.

"I am sure that he is still alive," Holmes said from behind me. "He is too stupid not to be."

I spun around and brought up the revolver. Holmes was standing just inside the door. He had entered the room and closed the door behind him without me hearing. He was breathing heavily, as if he had just been running, and I stepped aside to let in the moonlight, terrified that I would see the black stain of blood on his hands and sleeves.

"How do you know I was thinking of Jones?" I asked, astounded yet again by my friend's reasoning.

"Mrs. Hudson told me that he had been here looking for me. I knew then that you would be his next port of call in his search, and that you would inevitably have been forced by your high morals to relay what you had so obviously seen. You know he is out there now, hunting me down. And the scream . . . it sounded very much like a man, did it not?"

"Turn on the light, Holmes," I said.

I think he shook his head in the dark. "No, it will attract attention. Not that they do not know where we are . . . they must . . . fear, fear smells so sweet . . . to bees . . ."

"Holmes. Turn on the light or I will shoot you." And right then, standing in the room where my friend and I had spent years of our lives in pleasurable and business discourse, I was telling the truth. I was frightened enough to pull the trigger, because Holmes's intellect would bypass my archaic revolver, however mad he sounded. He would beat me. If he chose to—if he had lured me here to be his next victim—he would kill me.

"Very well," my friend said. "But prepare yourself, Watson. It is been a somewhat eventful twenty-four hours."

The lamp flicked alight.

I gasped. He looked like a man who should be dead.

"Do not lower that revolver!" he shouted suddenly. "Keep it on me now, Watson. After what you think you saw me doing, lower your guard and you are likely to shoot me at the slightest sound or movement. That's right. Here. Aim it here." He thumped his chest and I pointed the gun that way, weak and shocked though I was.

"Holmes . . . you look terrible!"

"I feel worse." From Holmes that was a joke, but I could not even raise a smile. Indeed, I could barely draw a breath. Never had Holmes looked so unkempt, exhausted, and bedraggled. His normally immaculate clothing was torn, muddied and wet, and his hair was sticking wildly away from his scalp. His hands were bloodied—I saw cuts there, so at least for the moment I could believe that it was his own blood—his cheek was badly scratched in several places and there was something about his eyes . . . wide and wild, they belied the calm his voice conveyed.

"You're mad," I said, unable to prevent the words from slipping out.

Holmes smiled, and it was far removed from that maniacal grin he had offered me as he crouched over the dying man.

"Do not jump to conclusions, Watson. Have you not learned anything in our years together?"

My hand holding the gun was starting to shake, but I kept it pointing at my friend across the room.

"I have to take you in, you know that? I will have to take you to the station. I cannot . . . I cannot . . ."

"Believe?"

I nodded. He was already playing his games, I knew. He would talk me around, offer explanations, convince me that the victims deserved to die or that he had been attacked . . . or that there was something far, far simpler eluding me. He would talk until he won me over, and then his attack would come.

"I cannot believe, but I must," I said, a newfound determination in my voice.

"Because you saw it? Because you *saw* me killing someone you must believe that I *did*, in fact, kill?"

"Of course."

Holmes shook his head. He frowned, and for an instant he seemed distant, concentrating on something far removed from Baker Street. Then he glanced back at me, looked to the shelf above the fire, and sighed.

"I will smoke my pipe, if you don't mind, Watson. It will put my mind at rest. And I will explain what I know. Afterward, if you still wish to take me in, do so. But you will thereby be condemning countless more to their deaths."

"Smoke," I said, "and tell me." *He was playing his games, playing them every second . . .*

Holmes lit a pipe and sat in his armchair, legs drawn up so that the pipe almost rested on his knees. He looked at the far wall, not at me, where I remained standing by the window. I lowered the revolver slightly, and this time Holmes did not object.

I could see no knives, no mess on his hands other than his own smeared blood. No mess on his chin from the masticated flesh of the folks he had killed.

But that proved nothing.

"Have you ever looked into a mirror and really concentrated on the person you see there? Try it, Watson, it is an interesting exercise. After an hour of looking, you see someone else. You see, eventually, what a stranger sees, not the composite picture of facial components with which you are so familiar, but individual parts of the face—the big nose, the close-together eyes. You see yourself as a *person*. Not as *you*."

"So what are you trying to say?"

"I am saying that perception is not definite, nor is it faultless." Holmes puffed at his pipe, then drew it slowly away from his mouth. His eyes went wide and his brow furrowed. He had had some thought, and habit made me silent for a minute or two.

He glanced back up at me then, but said nothing. He looked more troubled than ever.

"I saw you killing a man, Holmes," I said. "You killed him and you laughed at me, and then you tore him open and stole his heart."

"The heart, yes," he said, looking away and disregarding me again. "The heart, the brain . . . parts, all part of the one . . . constituents of the same place . . ." He muttered on until his voice had all but vanished, though his lips still moved.

"Holmes!"

"It has gone quiet outside. They are coming." He said it very quietly, looked up at me from sad, terrified eyes, and I felt a cool finger run down my spine. *They're coming.* He did not mean Jones or the police, he did not mean *anyone*. No *man* scared Holmes as much as he was then.

"Who?" I asked. But he darted from his seat and ran at me, shoving me aside so that we stood on either side of the window.

"Listen to me, Watson. If you are my friend, if you have faith and loyalty and if you love me, you have to believe two things in the next few seconds if we are to survive. The first is that I am not a murderer; the second is that you must not trust your eyes, not for however long this may take. Instinct and faith, that is what you *can* believe in, because they cannot change that. It is too inbuilt, perhaps, too ingrained, I don't know . . ."

He was mumbling again, drifting in and out of coherence. And I knew that he could have killed me. He had come at me so quickly, my surprise was so complete, that I had plain forgotten the gun in my hand.

And now, the denial.

Doubt sprouted in my mind and grew rapidly as I saw the look on Holmes's face. I had seen it before, many times. It was the thrill of the chase, the excitement of discovery, the passion of experience, the knowledge that his reasoning had won out again. But underlying it all was a fear so profound that it sent me weak at the knees.

"Holmes, what are *they*?"

"You ask *what*, Watson, not *who*. Already you're halfway to believing. Quiet! Look! There, in the street!"

I looked. Running along the road, heading straight for the front door of Holmes's building, came Sherlock Holmes himself.

"I think they will come straight for me," Holmes whispered. "I am a threat."

"Holmes . . ." I could say little. The recent shocks had numbed me, and seemed now to be pulling me apart, hauling reality down a long, dark tunnel. I felt distanced from my surroundings, even though, at that moment, I knew that I needed to be as alert and conscious of events as possible.

"Don't trust your eyes!" he hissed at me.

That man, he had been running like Holmes, the same loping stride, the same flick of the hair with each impact of foot upon pavement. The same look of determination on his face.

"Faith, Watson," Holmes said. "Faith in God, if you must, but you *must* have faith in me, us, our friendship and history together. For there, I feel, will lie the answer."

There came the sound of heavy footsteps on the stairs.

"I will get them, it, the thing on the floor," Holmes said, "and you shoot it in the head. Empty your revolver, one shot may not be enough. Do not balk, my friend. This thing here, tonight, is far bigger than just the two of us. It is London we're fighting for. Maybe more."

I could not speak. I wished Jones were there with us, someone else to make decisions and take blame. Faith, I told myself, faith in Holmes.

I had seen him kill a man.

Don't trust your eyes.

He was bloodied and dirtied from the chase, hiding from the crimes he had committed.

I am not a murderer.

And then the door burst open and Sherlock Holmes stood in the doorway lit by the lamp—tall, imposing, his clothes tattered and muddied, his face scratched, hands cut and bloodied—and I had no more time.

The room suddenly smelled of sweet honey, and turning my head slightly to look at the Holmes standing with me at the window, I caught sight of something from the corner of my eye. The Holmes in the doorway seemed to have some things buzzing about his head.

I looked straight at him and they were no more. Then he gave me the same smile I had seen as he murdered that man.

"Watson!" Holmes said, reaching across the window to grasp my arms. "Faith!"

And then the new visitor smashed the lamp with a kick, and leaped at us.

I backed away. The room was dark now, lit only by pale moonlight and the paler starlight filtering through London's constant atmosphere. I heard a grunt, a growl, the smashing of furniture, and something cracking as the two Holmes tumbled into the center of the room. I quickly became confused as to which was which.

"Away!" I heard one of them shout. "Get away! Get away!" He sounded utterly terrified. "Oh God, oh sanity, why us!"

I aimed my revolver but the shapes rolled and twisted, hands at each other's neck, eyes bulging as first one and then the other Holmes presented his face for me to shoot. I stepped forward nonetheless, still smelling that peculiar honey stench, and something stung my ankle, a tickling shape struggling inside my trousers. I slapped at it and felt the offender crushed against my leg.

Bees.

"Watson!" Holmes shouted. I pulled down the curtains to let in as much moonlight as I could. One Holmes had the other pinned to the floor, hands about his neck. "Watson, shoot it!" the uppermost Holmes commanded. His face was twisted with fear, the scratches on his cheek opened again and leaking blood. The Holmes on the floor thrashed and gurgled, choking, and as I looked down he caught my eye. Something there commanded me to watch, held my attention even as the Holmes on top exhorted me to *shoot*, shoot, *shoot it in the face!*

The vanquished Holmes calmed suddenly and brought up a hand holding a handkerchief. He wiped at the scratches on his face. They disappeared. The blood smudged a little, but with a second wipe it, too, had gone. The scratches were false, the blood fake.

The Holmes on top stared for a couple of seconds, and then looked back at me. A bee crawled out of his ear and up over his forehead. And then the scratches on his own cheek faded and disappeared before my eyes.

He shimmered. I saw something beneath the flesh-toned veneer, something crawling and writhing and separate, yet combined in a whole to present an image of solidness . . .

Bees left this whole and buzzed around the impostor's head. Holmes was still struggling on the floor, trying to prize away hands that were surely not hands.

The image pulsed and flickered in my vision, and I remembered Holmes's words: *You cannot trust your eyes . . . instinct and faith, that is what you can believe in . . .*

I stepped forward, pressed the revolver against the uppermost Holmes's head, and pulled the trigger. Something splashed out across the floor and walls, but it was not blood. Blood does not try to crawl away, take flight, buzz at the light.

My pulling the trigger—that act bridging doubt and faith—changed everything.

The thing that had been trying to kill Holmes shimmered in the moonlight. It was as if I were seeing two images being quickly flickered back and forth, so fast that my eyes almost merged them into one, Morphean picture. Holmes . . . the thing . . . Holmes . . . the thing. And the thing, whatever it is, was monstrous.

"Again!" Holmes shouted. "Again, and again!"

I knelt so that my aim did not stray toward my friend and fired again at that horrible shape. Each impact twisted it, slowing down the alternating of images as if the bullets were blasting free truth itself. What I did not know then, but would realize later, was that the bullets were *defining* the truth. Each squeeze of the trigger dealt that thing another blow, not only physically but also in the nature of my beliefs. I *knew* it to be a false Holmes now, and that made it weak.

The sixth bullet hit only air.

It is difficult to describe what I saw in that room. I had only a few seconds to view its ambiguous self before it came apart, but even now I cannot find words to convey the very unreality of what I saw, heard, and smelled. There was a honey tang on the air, but it was almost alien, like someone else's memory. The noise that briefly filled the room could have been a voice. If so it was speaking in an alien tongue, and I had no wish to understand what it was saying. A noise like that could only be mad.

All I know is that a few seconds after I fired the last bullet, Holmes and I were alone. I was hurriedly reloading and Holmes was already up, righting the oil lamp and giving us light. I need not have panicked so, because we were truly alone.

Save for the bees. Dead or dying, there were maybe a hundred bees spotting the fine carpet, huddled on the windowsill, or crawling behind chairs or objects on the mantelpiece to die. I had been stung only once, Holmes seemed to have escaped entirely, but the bees were expiring even as we watched.

"Dear God," I gasped. I went to my knees on the floor, shaking, my shooting hand no longer able to bear the revolver's weight.

"Do you feel faint, my friend?" Holmes asked.

"Faint, no," I said. "I feel . . . belittled. Does that make sense, Holmes? I feel like a child who has been made aware of everything he will ever learn, all at once."

"There are indeed more things in heaven and earth, Watson," Holmes said. "And I believe we have just had a brush with one of them." He, too, had to sit, nursing his bruised throat with one hand while the other wiped his face with the handkerchief, removing any remaining makeup. He then cleaned the blood from both hands and washed away the false cuts there as well. He seemed distracted as he cleansed, his eyes distant, and more than once I wondered just where they were looking, what they were truly seeing.

"Can you tell me, Holmes?" I asked. I looked about the room, still trying to imagine where that other being had gone, but knowing, in my heart of hearts, that its nature was too obscure for my meager understanding. "Holmes? Holmes?"

But he was gone, his mind away, as was its wont, searching the byways of his imagination, his intellect steering him along routes I could barely imagine as he tried to fathom the truth in what we had seen. I stood and fetched his pipe, loaded it with tobacco, lit it, and placed it in his hand. He held on to it but did not take a draw.

He remained like that until Jones of Scotland Yard thundered through the door.

"And you have been with him for how long?" Jones asked again.

"Hours. Maybe three."

"And the murderer? You shot him, yet where is he?"

"Yes, I shot him. It. I shot it."

I had told Jones the outline of the story three times, and his disbelief seemed to be growing with each telling. Holmes's silence was not helping his case.

Another five murders, Jones had told me. *Three witnessed, and each of the witnesses identified a close friend or family member as the murderer.*

I could only offer my own mutterings of disbelief. Even though I had an inkling now—however unreal, however unbelievable, Holmes's insistence that the improbable must follow the impossible stuck with me—I could not voice the details. The truth was too strange.

Luckily, Holmes told it for me. He stirred and stood suddenly, staring blankly at me for a time as if he had forgotten I was there.

"Mr. Holmes," Jones said. "Your friend Dr. Watson here, after telling me that you were a murderer, is now protesting your innocence. His reasoning I find curious, to say the least, so it would benefit me greatly if I could hear your take on the matter. There were gunshots here, and I have no body, and across London there are many more grieving folks this evening."

"And many more there will be yet," Holmes said quietly. "But not, I think, for a while." He relit his pipe and closed his eyes as he puffed. I could see that he was gathering his wits to expound his theories, but even then there was a paleness about him, a frown that did not belong on his face. It spoke of incomplete ideas, truths still hidden from his brilliant mind. It did not comfort me one bit.

"It was fortunate for London, and perhaps for mankind itself, that I bore witness to one of the first murders. I had taken an evening stroll after spending a day performing some minor biological experiments on dead rodents, when I heard something rustling in the bushes of a front garden. It sounded larger than a dog, and when I heard what can only have been a cry, I felt it prudent to investigate.

"What I saw . . . was impossible. I knew that it could not be. I pushed aside a heavy branch and witnessed an old man being operated on. He was dead by the time my gaze fell upon him, that was for sure, because the murderer had opened his guts and was busy extracting kidneys and liver. And the murderer, in my eyes, was the woman Irene Adler."

"No!" I gasped. "Holmes, what are you saying?"

"If you would let me continue, Doctor, all will become clear. Clearer, at least, because there are many facets to this mystery still most clouded in my mind. It *will* come, gentlemen, I am sure, but . . . I shall tell you. I shall talk it through, tell you, and the truth will mold itself tonight.

"And so: Adler, the woman herself, working on this old man in the garden of an upscale London house. Plainly, patently impossible and unreal. And being the logically minded person I am, and believing that *proof*, rather than simply *belief*, defines truth, I totally denied the truth of what I was seeing. I knew it could not be because Adler was a woman unfamiliar with, and incapable of, murder. And indeed she has not been in the country for quite some years now. My total disregard for what I was seeing meant that I was *not* viewing the truth, that something abnormal was occurring. And strange as it seemed at the time—but how clear it is now!—the woman had been heavily on my mind as I had been strolling down that street."

"Well, to hear you actually admit that, Holmes, means that it is a great part of this mystery."

"Indeed," Holmes said to me, somewhat shortly. "My readiness to believe that something, shall we say, out of this world was occurring enabled me to see it. I saw the truth behind the murderer, the scene of devastation. I saw . . . I saw . . ." He trailed off, staring from the window at the ghostly night. Both Jones and I remained silent, seeing the pain Holmes was going through as he tried to continue.

"Terrible," he said at last. "Terrible."

"And what I saw," I said, trying to take up from where Holmes had left off, "was an impersonator, creating Holmes in his own image—"

"No," Holmes said. "No, it created me in *your* image, Watson. What you saw was your version of me. This *thing* delved into your mind and cloaked itself in the strongest identity it found in there: namely, me. As it is with the other murders, Mr. Jones, whose witnesses no doubt saw brothers and wives and sons slaughtering complete strangers with neither rhyme nor reason."

"But the murderer," Jones said. "Who was it? Where is he? I need a corpse, Holmes. Watson tells me that he shot the murderer, and I need a corpse."

"Don't you have enough already?" Holmes asked quietly. I saw the stare he aimed at Jones. I had never been the subject of that look, never in our friendship, but I had seen it used more than a few times. Its intent was born of a simmering anger. Its effect, withering.

Jones faltered. He went to say something else, stammered, and then backed away toward the door. "Will you come to the Yard tomorrow?" he asked. "I need help. And—"

"I will come," Holmes said. "For now, I imagine you have quite some work to do across London this evening. Five murders, you say? I guess at least that many yet to be discovered. And there must be something of a panic in the populace that needs calming."

Jones left. I turned to Holmes. And what I saw shocked me almost as much as any event from the previous twenty-four hours.

My friend was crying.

"We can never know everything," Holmes said, "but I fear that everything knows us."

We were sitting on either side of the fire. Holmes was puffing on his fourth pipe since Jones had left. The tear tracks were still unashamedly glittering on his cheeks, and my own eyes were wet in sympathy.

"What did it want?" I asked. "What motive?"

"Motive? Something so unearthly, so alien to our way of thinking and understanding? Perhaps no motive is required. But I would suggest that examination was its prime concern. It was slaughtering and slicing and examining the victims just as casually as I have, these last few days, been poisoning and dissecting mice. The removed organs displayed that in the careful way that they had been dismantled."

"But why? What reason can a thing like that have to know our makeup, our build?"

Holmes stared into the fire and the flames lit up his eyes. I was glad. I could still remember the utter vacancy of the eyes I had seen on his likeness as it hunkered over the bloody body.

"Invasion," he muttered, and then he said it again. Or perhaps it was merely a sigh.

"Isn't it a major fault of our condition that the more we wish to forget something, the less likely it is that we can," I said. Holmes smiled and nodded, and I felt a childish sense of pride from saying something of which he seemed to approve.

"Outside," said Holmes, "beyond what we know or strive to know, there is a whole different place. Somewhere which, perhaps, our minds can never know. Like fitting a square block into a round hole, we were not built to understand."

"Even you?"

"Even me, my friend." He tapped his pipe out and refilled it. He looked ill. I had never seen Holmes so pale, so melancholy, after a case, as if something vast had eluded him. And I think I realized what it was even then: understanding. Holmes had an idea of what had happened and it seemed to fit neatly around the event, but he did not *understand*. And that, more than anything, must have done much to depress him.

"You recall our time in Cornwall, our nightmare experience with the burning of the Devil's Foot powder?"

I nodded. "How could I forget?"

"Not hallucinations," he said quietly. "I believe we were offered a drug-induced glimpse beyond. Not hallucinations, Watson. Not hallucinations at all."

We sat silently for a few minutes. As dawn started to dull the sharp edges of the darkness outside, Holmes suddenly stood and sent me away.

"I need to think on things," he said urgently. "There's much to consider. And I have to be more prepared for the next time. *Have* to be."

I left the building tired, cold, and feeling smaller and more insignificant than I had ever thought possible. I walked the streets for a long time that morning. I smelled fear on the air, and one time I heard a bee buzzing from flower to flower on some honeysuckle. At that, I decided to return home.

My revolver, still fully loaded, was warm where my hand grasped it in my coat pocket.

I walked along Baker Street every day for the next two weeks. Holmes was always in his rooms, I could sense that, but he never came out, nor made any attempt to contact me. Once or twice I saw his light burning and his shadow drifting to and fro inside, slightly stooped, as if something weighed heavy on his shoulders.

The only time I saw my brilliant friend in that time, I wished I had not. He was standing at the window staring out into the twilight, and although I stopped and waved, he did not notice me.

He seemed to be looking intently across the rooftops as if searching for some elusive truth. And standing there watching him, I felt sure that his eyes, glittering dark and so, so sad, must have been seeing nothing of this world.

The Adventure of the Arab's Manuscript

MICHAEL REAVES

Of the many and varied adventures in which I have been privileged to assist my friend and colleague Sherlock Holmes, there are several which I have not made a matter of public record. The majority of these omissions have been for reasons pertaining to the security of the Empire, or to avoid causing scandal and embarrassment to certain parties involved. To a degree, these considerations apply to the following incidents as well. However, after much discussion, Holmes and I have reached the mutual conclusion that it is in the best interest of the Empire—indeed, of mankind in general—that they be documented, despite the considerable personal grief I anticipate recounting them will cause me.

Let me begin, then, on a day in early October, in the Year of Our Lord 1898. The sun was shining, pale and wan in the northern sky. There was a brisk snap to the air, and the leaves were reflecting the variety of nature's palette. Holmes and I were returning from an interview in Reading. It was not long after the occasion of my second marriage, and I was in a mood of pleasurable anticipation at the thought of rejoining my new wife after dropping Holmes off at the Baker Street residence.

Our route took us near Foubury Gardens, at the sight of which my frame of mind became somewhat darkened by certain memories. They were bittersweet recollections, familiar to me by now, but nonetheless poignant. Only for an instant did they intrude, but it was sufficient to cause me to turn my eyes from the hansom window toward the front, and at this point I became aware of Holmes's measuring gaze upon me.

"There are some wounds left by war that time cannot heal, sad to say," he remarked.

Our relationship had endured long enough that his uncanny ability to divine my thoughts no longer had the power to astonish me, although I would never come to regard it as pedestrian. "As always, your words strike home," I replied. "How did you know my mind was dwelling on my service in Afghanistan?"

My friend waved his fingers in a disparaging gesture. "Your behavior was embarrassingly easy to read. As we passed Foubury Gardens I saw you gaze upon the statue of the Maiwand Lion, which stands as a monument to the Berkshire Regiment massacre in that remote Afghan village in 1880. Your brow darkened, your fingers moved slightly toward the shoulder where you sustained your wound, and your posture straightened to that of a more military bearing—all doubtlessly without any conscious volition on your part. Even someone far less observant of human behavior than I would have had no trouble ascertaining your thoughts— provided they knew, as I do, of your past military service."

I gave what I hoped was a noncommittal nod, and after a moment Holmes returned his interest to the scenery of the passing streets. I felt relieved. There are certain things which, despite all his perspicacity, my friend has not deduced about me, and I felt no shame or lack of friendship was implied by my desiring it to remain that way. There are secrets one cannot share with even the closest of friends. Besides, I told myself comfortably, it was long ago in another land; save for the occasional nostalgic twinge, I had wholly put it behind me. Not even Holmes, after all, could intuit an episode out of the past without some form of suggestive evidence.

All of this being said by my inner self to great confidence and satisfaction, I can now only imagine the irony with which my readers must greet this next scene. For when we returned to Holmes's flat at 221B Baker Street, Mrs. Hudson informed him that a young woman awaited within. She presented Holmes with the lady's card. Holmes glanced at it and handed it to me. The print on the pasteboard rectangle was small and cursive, and I was still trying to squint it into focus as I followed him through the door.

I recognized her immediately, of course. It was as if the twenty intervening years had passed in the space of a heartbeat. She was wearing a twill jacket and walking skirt now instead of the lamb-skin *khalat* in which I had last seen her. There were touches of gray in what had been lustrous black hair, and wrinkles—a legacy of the unforgiving tropical sun as much as years—at the corners of her eyes and mouth. But these did not speak of age so much as of life—the harsh and spartan life of the Afghan hill people.

"Miriam," I said. I was dimly aware of Holmes standing somewhat to one side and watching us both, but that knowledge didn't matter. All that mattered was the shock and the almost painful pleasure of seeing her there. I took a step toward her, as she did toward me, and then we simultaneously remembered that we had an audience, and a very curious one. I glanced at Holmes and coughed into my fist.

"My apologies, Holmes," I said. "It's just that—that is, she and I—"

"I believe not even Lestrade could fail to notice evidence of a past association between you two," Holmes said dryly. He gave

Miriam a slight bow. "Sherlock Holmes, at your service, Miss Miriam Shah."

"I am most gratified to meet you, Mr. Holmes," she replied. Her voice was as strong and melodic as I remembered it. She turned somewhat, and I noticed that she was wearing a single piece of jewelry—an amulet, carved from lapus lazuli into the shape of an open hand, with an eye in the middle of the palm. Even the shock of seeing her again was not strong enough to keep me from silently remarking its uniqueness.

I could not resist speaking, propriety be damned. "Miriam," I said, "how do you come to be here? It is so wonderful to see you again—"

"And you, John," she replied. "I wish I could say that naught but the desire to visit you after all these years has propelled me on this long journey. Unfortunately, that is not the truth."

"Most interesting," Holmes said. "Pray be seated, Miss Shah. I am quite curious to know why a chieftain's daughter has journeyed all the way from the hill regions of northern Afghanistan—specifically, I believe, the vicinity of Mundabad—to see me, especially at the possibility of mortal danger to her soul."

Miriam's expression of surprise was, of course, little different from those I had seen on the scores of other clients who had found their way to Baker Street over the past decade. "You do not fall short of your reputation, Mr. Holmes," she said. "How did you intuit these facts?"

Holmes raised an eyebrow. "My dear lady, I do not 'intuit.' I deduce. I extrapolate. In your case, the process was simple. Your accent alone is sufficient to determine your nationality. In addition, you have until recently been wearing the traditional veil of the Moslem woman, which covers the lower half of the face. The upper half is slightly, but noticeably, more tanned. On the whole, Afghan hill women toil at a greater and harder variety of tasks than those who dwell in the country's more metropolitan areas.

This keeps them exposed to the desert sun longer. There are lines of paler skin on your arms and fingers as well, indicating that you are accustomed to wearing jewelry—a practice which few save the daughters and wives of tribal leaders can afford to do. The obvious fact that you know my friend and colleague places you in the Mundabad region. Finally, the single piece of jewelry you have retained"—he gestured at the amulet nestled in the hollow of her throat—"is, I believe, a talisman known as a *hamsa*, intended to ward off evil."

Miriam nodded and sat, and no more was said until after the tea Mrs. Hudson brought had been poured.

I was, of course, aflame with curiosity as to what had brought her to London, this woman who was quite probably the last person on earth I would ever have expected to see here. I restrained myself—after all, a gentleman cannot press a lady to speak until she is ready—but it took quite an effort on my part. For Miriam Shah had once quite literally saved my life.

Miriam took a long sip of tea and shuddered slightly. "That's better," she said. "I believe I understand now why Englishmen are so driven to expand their empire—it keeps them away from this chill climate."

Then she said to Holmes, "Have you ever heard of the *Kitab al-Azif*?"

Holmes started slightly—a reaction that would have, I think, been unnoticeable to all save myself, who had known him for years. It was one of the few times I have ever seen him register surprise.

"I have read of it. My knowledge is, I must admit, somewhat sketchy. *Kitab* is, of course, Arabic for 'book.' *Al-Azif*, as I understand it, is a term used by Mussulmen; it refers to the buzzing of nocturnal insects, which their superstitious minds take to be the howling of *afrit*, or demons. The consensus is that the book was written by a Yemenite named Abdul al-Hazred, around A.D. 700. The work was subsequently translated several times; first into Greek by Philetas, who renamed it the *Necronomicon*, or 'Book

Concerning the Dead,' and later into Latin by Olaus Wormius. There was also an English translation in the late sixteenth century by the occult scholar Dr. John Dee, who called it the *Liber Logaeth*. There have, I believe, been more recent translations as well. The book's contents are supposed to be a compendium of ancient lore and forbidden knowledge concerning various pre-Adamite beings and creatures, some of extraterrestrial origin, who once ruled the earth and who anticipate doing so again."

"Your information is correct," Miriam replied. Then she was silent for a moment, as if gathering herself. As much to fill the silence as anything else, I interjected, "Surely such a work must be considered the product of a demented mind."

"If al-Hazred was not mad before he wrote this infernal opus, he surely was after he completed it," Miriam said. "Those who have looked through the pages of the *Necronomicon* say it is the most dangerous book in the world because it gives far more than just the knowledge that these Old Ones and Elder Gods exist—it also instructs the reader in various ways to summon them from their places of exile, that they may rule the earth as they did eons ago."

I looked to Holmes, assuming he would immediately dismiss such a bizarre statement as utter claptrap. He was slowly filling the bowl of his pipe with shag, and he did not pause in doing so. Instead he said simply, "Please go on."

Miriam continued, and as I listened, my astonishment at her story became great enough to almost supersede my astonishment at her presence.

"According to legend, al-Hazred had delved deep into forbidden knowledge and ancient, hidden cults. He had visited Irem, the dreaded City of Pillars, and other lost conurbations even more dangerous. He had communicated with the *djinn*, and *afrits*, and nameless beings still more primal and powerful. And all of this he put down on parchment—a lifetime of mind-shattering, soul-blasting experiences.

"It is an uncontested fact that, as each successive translator copied the Arab's work into his own language, he edited out various teachings and sections—perhaps because he considered them to contain knowledge that man was not meant to know, perhaps in the interests of brevity and clarity, perhaps both. For whatever reasons, the few copies of the *Necronomicon* extant today are known to be heavily abridged. Far more text is missing than has been left in. The original Latin edition was over nine hundred pages; the *Liber Logaeth* not even six hundred. These pages were assumed lost; the complete *al-Azif* has not been seen for centuries."

"Until now, I take it," Holmes said. His voice was flat, almost contemplative. He had finished filling his pipe, but he did not light it. He sat quite still, his attentive gaze fixed upon Miriam. "Pray continue."

As Miriam continued to speak, I felt an involuntary shiver caress me, and wondered at it—after all, I was used to the damp chill of a London fall, and normally would have scarcely noticed it. But now I shivered. It felt as if the fire's heat were somehow not penetrating the room, even though I could see it blazing away beyond the hearth.

"Two years ago a large ceramic container was found in a cave far back in one of the many narrow canyons near where my people live. There was some concern among the more superstitious villagers that to open it would be to unleash a plague of demons and ill luck. So it was taken to Kandahar, where it was sold to a *ferengi*."

Holmes put down his pipe and steepled his fingers in front of his face, looking, for a surprising moment, almost as if he were praying. "You said the container was sealed. How did you know what the contents were?"

"There was writing inscribed in the clay. And there was this as well, impressed into the wax seal." From within her jacket she withdrew a folded piece of paper and handed it to my friend, who opened it. On it was drawn some sort of symbol—of its exact configuration I cannot say, but as Holmes held it up to look at it, the paper was poised for a moment in front of the fire, which illumination allowed me a brief, translucent impression of the sketch. It was abstract, and even in that imperfect glimpse seemed somehow *wrong*, as if it represented some sort of spatial anomaly. I can think of no better way to describe it. Before I could ask to see it, Holmes had crumpled it up and thrown it into the fire.

"That is known as the Elder Sign, if I'm not mistaken," he said.

"It is. The writing on the container was *al-Azif*, in Akkadian."

"Ah. Which was the lingua franca of the Arabian world until approximately A.D. 700."

"Just so," Miriam said. "It would appear that al-Hazred felt the book's contents important enough to write down the entire manuscript a second time, for safekeeping."

They were both quiet for a moment. Then Holmes said, "You have followed the *ferengi*—the foreigner—who brought the manuscript to England. Why? I understand the volatile nature of the text, but why have you elected to pursue it?"

She glanced at me, then replied, "I volunteered. I am one of the few from my village who speaks French and English, and I have heard whispers, ever since I can remember, of the ancient and shunned sects, the worshipers of Those Who Came Before." Her hand went to her throat, touching the charm that hung there. *"Mashallah,"* she murmured, then continued: "The existing copies of the *Necronomicon* are kept under lock and key, lest the knowledge it still retains be used to shatter civilization. How much more dangerous, then, must the unexpurgated version be? It must be found, as quickly as possible. That is why I have come to you, Mr. Holmes." She glanced at me again, and smiled. "And I could not resist the opportunity to see you again, however briefly, John."

As might be imagined, my state of mind after hearing all this was complex, to put it mildly. It all sounded like the febrile fantasies that I have seen hashish and opium spin in many an Oriental mind—and not a few Occidental ones as well. But one look at

Holmes's grim expression told me that he considered this no fantasy.

"What can you tell me about the one who acquired the manuscript?"

"He was strong in appearance, tall, with black hair and beard and intense blue eyes. My impression was that he was in his mid-thirties."

"Were there any distinguishing marks—any characteristics or traits that might help one single him out in a crowd?"

She thought for a moment. "Yes. He had a scar on the palm of his left hand—as if a knife had been drawn across it."

"Ah. Most illuminating," Holmes commented. He stood. "Very well, Miss Shah; I shall certainly accompany you on your quest, and I hope I speak for my colleague as well"—this last with a glance in my direction. "If you'll excuse me—I must see to some affairs. I foresee that our inquiry should take no more than a day, perhaps two at most, so we shall need to pack but lightly." So saying, Holmes left the room.

For a moment Miriam and I stood silently together. My mind was a welter of conflicting thoughts and emotions—not the least of which was that my wife was waiting for me at our home. She was, of course, used to—perhaps "resigned to" would be a more accurate phrasing—my sudden departures from London at Holmes's requests. This could not help but be different, however, and I could not predict what her reaction to it might be.

Or if even I would tell her.

Such disloyal thoughts did nothing to quell my inner turmoil. I turned to Miriam, feeling the need to say something to break the silence. "I—I don't believe I ever properly thanked you," I said to her, "for saving my life those many years ago." For in fact she had done no less than that, by ministering to me during the long months of my convalescence in Peshawar, after I was wounded on the front lines. During my prolonged battle with enteric fever, on the many occasions when my life balanced on the edge of death, I would often open my eyes to see a young Afghan woman, daughter of one of the tribal chieftains with whom our forces had established a friendly liaison, bending over me, sponging my forehead or otherwise tending to my needs. Initially there were frequent periods of delirium, and it was Miriam who listened to my ravings, who talked to me and gently guided me back to myself. I truly believe that had it not been for her presence grounding me in reality, I would have been lost in madness. And a life without the mind is no life at all.

During the latter months of my convalescence, we had many long conversations. She was well educated, having attended school in Bombay, and she was intelligent and self-possessed to a degree rarely seen in Afghan women—or any woman in my experience, for that matter. Quite a strong friendship developed between us— more than a friendship, if truth be told. The memory I had retained from it, over all these years, was that sense of deep connection—an intimacy that, in many ways, I had not shared with anyone since then, not even my beloved Mary. We had spoken of so many things, Miriam and I, including matters of the heart. Near the end of my recuperation, I asked her to return to London with me. She declined, saying that as the daughter of a chief, she had responsibilities she could not ignore, even for the sake of love.

We both had our obligations, and so parted, but I had, more than a few times over the intervening years, wondered what might have been had we been less faithful to duty.

And now she stood before me—older, as was I, but still in so many ways the woman I remembered. It stirred things in me which had been quiet for no small time.

"No gratitude is needed," she said, in response to my statement. "For surely your presence in my life did enrich it at least as much as I hope mine did yours. I wish that there were time to speak of such things now. But there is not, and we must act swiftly and decisively, John, if we are to ensure any kind of future at all. If we do not, the world may once again feel the tread of the Great Old Ones."

Her apparent dismissal of our past seemed abrupt, and I felt a vague disappointment. I wanted to ask her more, to investigate more deeply this mysterious and seemingly dangerous imbroglio that evidently revolved around the possession of the Arab's manuscript, but she laid a finger lightly across my lips, enjoining silence. "We will speak of the past later," she told me. "But now you must prepare for the trip, as your friend is doing."

Something in her manner and tone seemed to reassure me, on a subtle level, that despite the obvious gravity of our mission, the favorable outcome of it was not in doubt. But there was, too, a sense of foreboding, a coldness that continued to waft through the room, as if the warm and cheery fire had suddenly gone out. Miriam was on the one hand the woman who had called to the passion of my younger self, years ago and worlds away; now she was older and different, not quite as I recalled her. I could not help but feel a nostalgic sadness for the path not taken. I nodded and moved down the hall to what had once been my bedroom to assemble an overnight bag.

Packing did not take long; I had, over the years, become quite good at throwing the necessary accoutrements for a short trip into a valise. In less than a quarter hour I was ready, save for three items, which I then included. The first was a small bit of stone, the size of my closed fist, the surface of which was dark and pitted. If one looked closely at it, deep colors appeared to shift beneath its surface, somewhat like the black opals of Queensland, Australia. I had happened across it in Afghanistan and kept it as a souvenir all this time. I had come to think of it as a lucky piece, despite the knowledge that Holmes did not believe in such things and would have ridiculed me for it. But a man who has stood upon the field of battle amidst flying bullets and survived, while those all around him died, knows that Dame Fortune smiles or frowns upon those whom she chooses. It seemed appropriate with Miriam here that I bring the lucky stone.

The second item I decided to keep upon my person was a small, teardrop-shaped leather sack, perhaps five inches long and filled with fine lead shot. There was a loop of leather at the narrow end. It was what the underworld element called a cosh, or blackjack. I gripped it for a moment, slipped the loop over my thumb and slapped it experimentally against my open palm, then dropped it into my coat pocket.

Though there was no need to carry it at the moment, in my bag I included, too, my Webley Bulldog revolver, for, while most of my adventures with Holmes had been without any real danger to ourselves, the sense of foreboding I felt now urged me to err on the side of caution. Should a need arise, I would prefer to have a weapon at hand. After all, it was not just Holmes and myself I needed to protect this time.

As I left the room I encountered Holmes in the hall. He looked even more preoccupied than usual, and I made an attempt at jocularity. "So, Holmes, once again the game's afoot, eh?"

He did not return my smile. "It is no game this time, Watson." Before I could ask him what he meant by that, we had rejoined Miriam, and Mrs. Hudson was announcing the hansom's arrival.

As we waited for the cabbie to tuck our bags into the boot, enduring a sudden chilly and damp wind that threatened to blow away our hats, Miriam said, "Mr. Holmes, it seems as if you already have a destination in mind."

"Indeed, madam, I do. We shall take the train to Guilford Station, and a carriage across the river to East Molesy. The man we seek is Professor George Coombs, who maintains a house outside of town."

Miriam looked at Holmes, her expression more one of curiosity than the more common reaction of incredulity. "How can you know this?"

"From your description of him, madam. Professor Coombs is a man with a powerful build, black hair and beard, and blue eyes."

Miriam frowned. "I hazard to say, sir, that there must be more than a few men in England who would answer to that same description."

Holmes gave her the briefest of smiles. "Of course. But not that many who have a knife scar across the palm. The professor received that wound warding off an attack from a hashish cultist while in India some years ago. Assassins, they are called, after the drug that incites them to suicidal madness. Normally they employ strangling cords for their foul work, but I understand that the professor, who was something of a pugilist in his university days, thwarted the initial attack, so that the would-be killer had to resort to a blade. Which obviously also failed, since our Mr. Coombs is still with us."

Miriam looked somewhat doubtful. Of course I knew that Holmes would not have engaged a taxi on this scant evidence; there would be more. It was not long in coming: "Professor Coombs is an archaeologist, attached of late to Lord Richard Penshurst's recent expedition to the Khyber Pass. Penshurst is a gifted amateur, and wise enough to engage properly credentialed assistants when he mounts these forays. According to the *Times*, the group is recently returned with a plethora of items that have been donated to the British Museum."

"Wouldn't it be wiser, then, to check the museum first?"

A quick frown flitted across Holmes's saturnine face, and I suppressed a smile. He did not care overmuch for advice, certainly not from those he considered his intellectual inferiors, a category which included nearly everyone. I have even heard him argue at length with his brother Mycroft, whom he considers perhaps his only superior in mental capacity, though I have my doubts upon that score.

"No, madam, for had such a document as you describe been

delivered to the museum, it would have been on the list of items so donated. Since I have seen this list, and since the manuscript is not upon it, I deem it more likely that the professor has kept it for further study. East Molesy is our destination."

To the southwest from London, an hour or so by train, Guilford is a town with an academic bent, the local college being well thought of in certain circles. Professor Coombs, who was an Oxford man and therefore not attached to the local school, lived on the outskirts of Molesy; his family owned a residential property there, and a professor's salary, even when from private sources, is not so great as all that.

This Holmes explained to us on the train as we steamed through the intermittently sunny English countryside. The colors of autumn were upon the land—reds, yellows, and golds—quite pleasant, if such things mattered to one. Holmes, of course, never evidenced much interest in nature per se, though he did remark upon a cluster of boxy white bee hives crowning a hill we passed. The precise construction of bee society and their hives had always seemed of particular fascination to him. Having seen some men swell up like corpses left three days in the tropical sun from naught but bee stings, I held a certain medical interest in the insects, but nothing to the extent with which Holmes viewed them.

After we had journeyed for a couple of hours, Holmes appeared to doze, and once again I found myself alone, after a fashion, with Miriam. I felt the need to talk to her of our past.

"Miriam—"

"Later, John," she said, as if sensing my thoughts. "We will speak of these things later."

Frustrated to no small degree, I subsided. Perhaps she sensed this as well, for she said with a smile, "Do you remember a peculiar stone you showed me once? You said you found it in a dry watercourse near Khusk-i-Nakhud."

"Yes. A strange bit of rock, evidently meteoric in origin," I said. "Odd you should make mention of it; I fancy it rather a good-luck charm, and have brought it along."

"Do you have it with you now?"

I produced the stone from my pocket. Her face lit with a smile, and she held out her hand. I tendered it to her.

She ran her fingers over it lightly, her eyes half closed; it seemed to be almost a sensual pleasure for her, as if the touch of it roused some pleasant tactile memory. After a moment she sighed, and offered it back to me.

"Keep it," I said.

"I couldn't."

"It would please me if you did. It came from your country, after all."

She smiled, though in her expression was a hint of mystery. "Thank you, John," she said softly. "I will treasure it more than you can know." After a moment, she raised her hands behind her neck, unclasped the charm that hung there, and held it out to me. "A gift for a gift. Please."

"Miriam, you don't have to—"

"Take it, John," she urged me. "It will keep us close together, always, no matter the distance between us."

Touched by the sentiment, I accepted. We said no more, but settled into a comfortable and companionable silence as the train continued.

British railways run like fine clocks, and thus we arrived in due course at Guilford Station just before evening, and engaged a hansom. The clouds that had partially obscured the sun were now thickening, and the threat of rain grew stronger during the trip to Professor Coombs's house, which, as Holmes had said, was in the countryside beyond the town proper. By the time we arrived the rain had sent heralding drops, and we barely attained the porch before the skies opened up with a pounding, wind-lashed downpour. Through the rain I noticed, as we drove up the winding lane, the vague outlines of a small hill or mound in the fields behind the place.

The doorbell was answered by a large, rough-looking butler who, it seemed to me, would be more at home on a wharf loading heavy cargo than working as a man's man. His clothes fit well enough, but he did not look comfortable in them. Since our visit was impromptu and without appointment, and as Holmes has always been somewhat impatient with the social graces, I took it upon myself to introduce ourselves and to inquire if the professor might be persuaded to see us. The butler took our hats and bags, showed us to a modest but well-appointed parlor, and lumbered off to speak to his master.

I have never been, nor do I expect ever to be, in Holmes's league when it comes to observation; however, even I noticed that Miriam seemed anxious, lacing and unlacing her fingers and smoothing and adjusting her garments nervously as we waited. Twice she stood, took a few steps in different directions, then returned to her chair. Her high level of concern over the danger represented by the Arab's manuscript was evident. I would have attempted to reassure her, but something in her manner—her movements seemed oddly formal, almost as though she were performing a series of gesticulations by rote—coupled with her earlier reticence, prevented me from doing so. Holmes seemed to have noticed it as well; he watched her with his usual clinical detachment.

A short time passed, during which the only sounds were the rustling of crinoline and the loud ticking of a grandfather clock. At length the apish butler returned. With him, judging by Miriam's and Holmes's descriptions, was Professor Coombs. I appraised him with my physician's eye. He was tall, well made, and sound of limb from his motions, athletic in appearance, and tanned darkly.

Again, I made introductions. Coombs did not appear to be surprised to learn our identities.

"Mr. Sherlock Holmes and Dr. John Watson. Your reputations

precede you, sirs. I am honored, if a trifle puzzled, by your visit. And Miss Shah." He bowed. "Have we met? You seem familiar."

"We have, sir, after a fashion. Though you would not have seen my face, as I would have been veiled."

"Of course." He sat, as did we, and offered us claret, to which we demurred. "What brings you two gentlemen from London? And you, madam, from the Eastern lands?"

"Come now, Professor," Holmes said. "There is no need to be disingenuous. We are here to speak of the *Kitab al-Azif.*"

Coombs's smile was a flash of white against the darkness of his beard. "You are a direct man, Mr. Holmes, as I have heard. Let me be equally as blunt. What business is it of yours?"

Holmes replied smoothly, "Miss Shah's concerns stem from a worry as to its possible . . . misuse."

Coombs raised an eyebrow. "And is this a concern shared by Sherlock Holmes? A rationalist known for his powers of deduction? You are an Englishman and an intellectual, sir—surely you do not subscribe to such beliefs as the *al-Azif* espouses?"

I expected a quick reply from Holmes affirming this, but I was surprised. "My research into this topic is not yet complete," he replied, his voice even. "However, I am unwilling to dismiss the underlying premise out of hand."

Coombs nodded, tugging at his beard. "You are wiser than I have been led to believe, sir. There are things under God's heaven that seem impossible to any modern nineteenth-century mind yet which are in fact quite real." His expression darkened. "Over the years and in my travels, I have seen some of these things, and I have become a believer, albeit a reluctant one."

Holmes did not speak to this. After a moment, Coombs continued. "Miss Shah may rest easy. I guarantee the manuscript will not be misused. It is part of my personal collection of antiques and *curiosa.*" He rose. "I apologize for seeming brusque, but my schedule today—"

"You have the *al-Azif* here, then?" Miriam interjected.

Coombs looked at her. During his speech she had diminished, but not ceased, her patterns of anxious movement. Coombs now seemed to take note of this. His eyes narrowed, and some wordless communion seemed to pass between them. A look of mingled fear and anger filled his face. I saw Holmes lean forward, watching them intently.

"I had not expected you so soon," Coombs said to Miriam. He raised his voice. "Bradley!"

The butler reappeared. In his oversized hand he held a Webley .38 Bulldog, like the one I had in my valise. *Exactly* like mine, I realized, recognizing with a start the custom ivory grips I had caused to be installed on the revolver some years ago. The thug had evidently searched our baggage.

I have never considered myself primarily a man of action, though certainly my time in Her Majesty's service exposed me to more than my share of turmoil in foreign lands. And, while most of the investigations upon which Holmes and I have ventured have been relatively peaceful, there have been times when a stout heart, aided by a quick wit and quicker movements, have been necessary for survival. So it was that the instant I discerned my weapon in the brute's grip, I slipped my own hand into my jacket pocket and quickly removed the cosh, palming it and holding it thus hidden upon my lap. The butler did not appear to notice my action.

Meanwhile, Coombs spoke to Holmes but kept his gaze upon Miriam. "I'm sorry, Mr. Holmes, but you have involved yourself in matters much more complex than you comprehend. I cannot allow the manuscript out of my keeping. Especially to one such as *her*."

He spoke this last sentence with an expression of disgust akin to that which a white man might voice about a wog with leprosy.

If I live to be a thousand, I shall never forget what transpired next. Miriam—dear, sweet Miriam, who had brought me back from Death's door with her own gentle hands—glared at Coombs, her expression one of concentrated evil and fury that seemed inhuman in its intensity. Then she spoke, uttering a short, harsh two-word expression in a language I did not recognize. The discordant timbre of her voice grated painfully in my ears.

"N'gêb Yalh'tñf!"

Coombs suddenly lurched to one side, clutched at his chest, and collapsed, as a man suffering a fatal cardiac convulsion might.

Bradley, the butler, stepped in and leveled my revolver at the back of Miriam's head. He meant to shoot—I saw his finger tighten on the trigger, saw the hammer begin to cock, the cylinder begin to turn, chambering the round to be fired. This all happened in a kind of measured motion, as if time were somehow stretching. In that elongated moment, the only sound I could hear was the ticking of the grandfather clock, which suddenly seemed loud enough for a timepiece the size of Big Ben.

Then sound and movement rushed back to fill the momentary vacuum. I realized I had leaped to my feet. I heard Holmes yell, "Watson, *no!*" But I had already jumped for the butler and brought my cosh down on the man's arm, just above his wrist. I distinctly heard the bone crack. *That would be the radius,* I found myself thinking.

Bradley howled in pain and dropped the gun. But he was a burly brute and, broken arm notwithstanding, he turned to grapple with me.

I fancy that I can handle myself as well as most civilized men in a bout of fisticuffs, but this was not a boxing ring. This thug was half again my size and obviously a brawler who had never heard of the Marquess of Queensbury. I did not hesitate to employ the cosh again.

The advantage to being a doctor of medicine in a tussle is a good knowledge of anatomy. My next strike deadened the ulnar nerve and paralyzed the butler's left arm; even so, I had to duck as he nearly took my head off with a haymaker punch thrown by his broken right. My third strike with the cosh was to his right temple. It stunned him, but it took another hit to his skull to complete the process. Bradley fell, unconscious.

Holmes knelt next to Coombs, who was trying to talk. I looked about anxiously for Miriam, but saw no sign of her. She had apparently fled the room while I was dealing with the butler.

I stepped to Holmes's side; he was cradling the fallen professor's head in one hand. Coombs looked up at us, and his eyes were filled with a fear I had never before seen, not even in the eyes of men dying on the front lines. "B-behind the house," he managed. "In the cromlech! Hurry!"

These were his final words, for they were followed by the unmistakable sounds of his death rattle.

Holmes whipped about to face me. "Watson! Does she have the stone?"

I was by this time, I admit, in something of a state of shock. "What?"

"The good-luck piece you sometimes carry!" There was an intensity in his expression that I had never seen before or since. "Does she have it?"

"I—yes. What's this all about, Holmes?"

But he was already on his feet and rushing for the parlor door. "Out the rear entrance!" He flung back over his shoulder. "*Hurry,* if you want the world to see another dawn! And bring your revolver!"

Bewildered, and more than a little frightened, I snatched the gun from the butler's limp grasp and followed.

I left the rear entrance of the house a few steps behind Holmes. It was raining with almost tropical ferocity now, and full night was upon us. A flicker of lightning showed me our destination: A cromlech—an ancient burial mound probably dating back to the

Neolithic. Holmes dashed up the winding path and under the shelter of the huge capstone. When I regained his side, he had already struck a match and set aflame a makeshift torch, which was little more than a wooden club with the blunt end wrapped in dry reeds and grasses. By its wavering light I saw it was one of several on the ground before the mound's entrance. Holmes picked up a second torch, ignited it from his, and handed it to me. "Keep your gun ready," he whispered. "And pray it will be effective." With that enigmatic statement he started into the narrow passage.

The ceiling barely allowed us room to walk upright. The walls were drystone, broken occasionally by the darker entrances to several interior burial chambers. The central passage led steeply down, twisting back and forth to mitigate the precipitous descent. I had to swallow more than once to equalize the pressure of my inner ears with that of the tomb's dank atmosphere.

At last we reached a level floor. A few paces farther the passage ended at the entrance to a large cist carved from the subterranean rock. And in that chamber, by the light of our torches, was revealed a scene which my mind at first refused to comprehend.

Miriam stood next to what appeared to be a stone altar, bounded on either side by stelae. Petroglyphs were carved into these stone pillars—sigils that seemed, in the uncertain light, to writhe and dance on the rocky surfaces. Atop the altar lay two tall stacks of ancient parchment, one higher than the other. I could barely make out the faded, cryptic scrawl that represented the thoughts, experiences, and fears of the mad Arab, set down by his own hand centuries ago. I realized that this must be the complete *Kitab al-Azif*; the book of which the *Necronomicon* was but the merest fragment.

Lying on the altar before it was my lucky stone, though I scarcely recognized it. It glowed, pulsing with a chatoyant light that shifted through a dark spectrum of colors I could not name.

Miriam did not notice us at first; she was occupied with chanting phrases in that same ear-smiting language she had spoken up-

stairs only moments ago. My senses reeled as I tried to comprehend this phantasmagorical scene. What was happening could not be happening. The very air seemed to be alive and visible, swirling like fog and smoke on a cold London winter's eve, as those bizarre syllables, utterly inhuman in their cadence, reverberated about us:

"Wyülgn mefh'ngk fhgah'n r'tíhgl, khlobå lhu mhwnfgth . . ."

I realized Holmes was speaking to me, his voice urgent and barely audible over Miriam's chant. "Shoot, Watson, *shoot!*"

I looked about in confusion. Shoot what? What I saw was as bizarre and unbelievable as a Jules Verne fantasy, but there was no immediate threat—

"*Now*, man—before she finishes the spell and it's too late! You *must!*"

I stared at him, realizing with horror that he wanted me to shoot *Miriam*. At that point I knew one of us had gone mad, and I honestly wasn't sure if it was Holmes or myself.

I was paralyzed with bewilderment, and Holmes must have realized that, for he raised his walking stick and lunged toward Miriam.

But she realized he was there before he could cover half the intervening distance. She broke off her chant and fixed him with that same horrifying glare that she had used on Coombs. She uttered the two-word command I had heard before—and Holmes stopped as if he had run into a stone wall.

He fell to his knees.

Dear God, I thought. But it was obvious that no benign deity was being invoked here. I looked from Holmes's trembling form to Miriam, and saw there a cruelty in her features—the feral enjoyment of a cat tormenting a mouse. Miriam, who had nursed me for months, who had brought me back from the pit. Miriam, a woman of foreign soil whom I would have, against all convention, made my wife. She seemed unaware of me; all her attention was on Holmes.

"Holmes! I'm coming!" I shouted.

I took a step forward—and a strange lethargy swept over me. I was still aware of what was taking place, but in an increasingly dreamy, somnambulistic way. I felt somehow removed from it all, to the point of numbed intoxication. The hand holding my revolver dropped, to hang at my side. I was reminded of Mesmer's experiments in concentration and suggestion, but even as they occurred to me they seemed spurious. I began to understand that this tableau before me was really none of my affair; more, that my human mind was completely inadequate even to begin to understand the forces at work here. Better, far better, not to interfere . . .

The luminous, thickening quality of the air was increasing; it seemed to be somehow *coalescing* near one side of the chamber. As if something was taking shape where there had been nothing.

Holmes, with what was obviously a great and wrenching effort, turned to look back at me. His face was going gray. A part of me, dim and far away, realized that I was watching my friend die.

Holmes was dying. And Miriam was killing him.

I cannot explain my next action—there certainly seems no logical reason for what I did. I can only be grateful that my body responded in an atavistic, primitive way to the danger. Had I stopped to think, I would have hesitated—and all would have been lost.

My left hand dug into my pocket, grasped the talisman Miriam had given me, and pulled it out. It, too, seemed to be glowing slightly, but perhaps that was only my imagination. I cast it on the stony chamber floor and ground it to powder under my heel.

As it had done before in Coombs's parlor, reality seemed to snap back. The lassitude enveloping me vanished. I took a deep breath, and raised my revolver.

"Miriam, *stop!*" I shouted.

I clearly saw a moment of surprise, of uncertainty, flash across her countenance. "You can't shoot me, John," she said. "You still love me."

It was true, I realized. I *did* still love her. Even though I knew

she had laid some kind of mental snare for me, even as she continued to somehow cause Holmes's slow death from afar—still I felt love for her.

"Join me, John," she said. Even without the aid of the charm, her voice was alluring, convincing. "The secrets of the Arab can grant us a life beyond earth, beyond flesh, beyond imagining . . . the cosmos can be ours, John; worlds to create, to command, to destroy . . ."

The sound of my weapon firing was perhaps the loudest noise I have ever heard.

Miriam, a look of stunned disbelief on her face, stared at me in shock as she crumpled. Simultaneously Holmes seemed to regain his strength. He and I ran forward. I remember wondering if my medical training could save her, wondering if my loyalty to humanity—to life itself—would let me—

I held the torch high and we saw the answer to that.

Whatever it was, it was no longer Miriam Shah—if in fact it ever had been. Obviously it was not life as we define the word, as its death was unlike the death of any material being. Or so I am given to understand. Mercifully, I do not remember it—my brain has elided that memory, a fact for which Holmes says I should be profoundly grateful. It is he who has supplied the gist of our final few moments in the underground chamber. My last recollection is of pulling the trigger. The sound of the gunshot still reverberates within me.

My next complete memory is of our train ride back to London the next day. Of the time it took us to return to the surface, I remember only brief, intermittent flashes.

"You knew," I said to Holmes. "You knew what she was. You called on me to stop when I prevented Bradley from shooting her."

He nodded gravely. "I had thought to spare you, old friend. I was hoping to deal with her myself, but I confess I underestimated her power. If Coombs's man could have ended it then and there, I was willing to go that route."

I felt utterly drained—grief was there, but it was a distant wave on a distant shore. "How did you know, Holmes?"

For the first time in my association with him, Holmes seemed reluctant to expound upon his deductive abilities. "The most obvious clue was the talisman she wore," he said at last. "No good Mohammedan woman would bear such a thing, for their faith does not permit such charms, and the representation of the human form in their artwork—even so much as a hand—is expressly forbidden by the Prophet. But I had thought it no more than part of her disguise. I would surmise there were magnetic elements in it that somehow gave her mesmeric power over you.

"But what was more informative was her demeanor. Although you have never spoken directly of her, I long ago surmised that you had met someone during your service in the East. The confirmation of that came nearly four years ago, when I happened into a discussion of the Maiwand campaign with a former infantryman who had been a physician's assistant in your ward. Please believe me when I tell you I did not solicit details about your stay there—he volunteered the information that you and an Afghan woman had developed a certain . . . affection for each other."

It was my turn to nod. Affection. At least Holmes allowed me to cling to whatever shreds of self-respect I might still have.

"I could tell that something in her had changed since you knew her. Her attitude was distant, even though she smiled and spoke politely; I ascertained an ulterior motive. She showed no real surprise when I announced our destination, merely questioning the reasoning that led me to the conclusion. It was obvious she already knew the identity of Professor Coombs."

"Then why involve us at all? Why not proceed directly to his house?"

"She needed two things from us. The first was the meteorite

stone you carried. The vibratory rate of the elements that compose it was a necessary part of the ritual. The second was a means to combat any opposition the late professor might have mounted against her. He had anticipated some kind of attempt to claim the manuscript, even though he wasn't sure what form it would take."

"This still seems like madness to me," I said wearily. "Magic books . . . a woman possessed by an ancient spirit . . ."

"Not magic, Watson. My researches have made clear to me that the powers of the Old Ones were based on science, albeit science far in advance of ours. There are theories that concern the possibilities of different realities stacked side by side with our own, like a deck of cards. And these realities, by invocation of certain forces, might be merged. I believe that is what the thing that had assumed Miriam Shah's identity was attempting—to sunder the boundary between our world and another." He paused, then added, "I believe her personality had been completely subsumed by the other consciousness. Perhaps you can console yourself by knowing that the animus of the woman you knew was already gone."

I nodded. I understood—I even believed it, absurd as it all sounded. Still, I felt none the better for knowing that I had killed, not Miriam, but instead a being which had usurped her identity for its own foul purposes. Holmes tells me that the strange vortex that had started to form in the chamber while the thing—I cannot call it "Miriam"—was performing the rite had vanished when the ritual was interrupted. But even the knowledge that we had saved our world from infestation by an enemy from *outside* was cold comfort. The bullet had ripped through my own heart as surely as it had hers.

Perhaps Holmes was right in his theory that Miriam's essence had been extinguished before she came to London. But I will still take with me to my own grave the expression of hurt and betrayal on her face as the bullet fired by my hand drained the life from her on that damp cavern floor.

As I fought for composure a flash of recollection came to me:

an image of Holmes standing before the altar, torch held high, staring down at that abominable stack of pages. "And what of the Arab's manuscript, Holmes? What did you do with it?"

He did not speak for a moment. Then he said, "Ancient parchment burns quite well."

Something odd in the tone of his voice made me glance at him. He was looking out the window. There was nothing to see but the English countryside, a sight that, I knew, usually interested him not in the slightest.

"You destroyed it, then," I said.

Again the hesitancy. For a moment fear nearly stilled my heart. Then he looked back at me and smiled. "Yes, Watson," he said, and this time it was the voice of the Sherlock Holmes I knew and trusted. "I put the torch to it. Within seconds there was nothing left of the *Kitab al-Azif* but ashes. And the world is the better for it."

I felt immense relief. After all, Holmes prized knowledge above all else, no matter what its source. How long could even his formidable will have resisted such a temptation? He had done the sensible thing, the sane thing, by destroying it.

Holmes looked out the window again. I peered over his shoulder. We were once again passing the bee hives.

"Remarkable creatures, bees," Holmes murmured. "Each one a part of a greater whole. Every action, every movement and communication orchestrated, ritualized—almost preordained. Fascinating . . ."

The Drowned Geologist

CAITLÍN R. KIERNAN

10 MAY 1898

My Dear Dr. Watson,

At the urgent behest of a mutual acquaintance, Dr. Ogilvey, lately of the British Museum, I am writing you regarding a most singular occurrence which I experienced recently during an extended tour of the Scottish lowlands and the east English coast south on through north Yorkshire. The purpose of my tour was the acquisition of local geological specimens and stratigraphic data for the American Museum here in Manhattan, where I have held a post these last four years. As one man of science writing openly to another, I trust you will receive these words in the spirit in which they are intended; indeed, the only spirit in which I presently know how to couch them: as the truthful and objective testimony of a trained observer and investigator who has borne witness to a most peculiar series of events, which, even now, many months hence, I am yet at a loss to explain. I fear that I must *expect* you to question the veracity of my story, and no doubt my sanity as well, if you are even half the man of medicine and of science that your reputation has led me to believe. As to why Ogilvey has suggested that I should entrust these facts to you, sir, in particular, that will shortly become quite clear. Moreover, if my voice seems uncertain and strained at times, if my narration seems to falter, please understand that even though the better part of a year has passed since those strange days by the sea, only by the greatest force of will am I able to finally set this account down upon paper.

My travels in your country, which I have already mentioned, began last June with my arrival in Aberdeen after a rather uneventful and regrettably unproductive month spent studying in Germany. Moving overland by coach and locomotive, alone and availing myself always of the most convenient and inexpensive modes of transportation for my often unorthodox purposes, I wandered throughout the full length of June and July, on a course winding crookedly ever southward, across rugged bands of Paleozoic and Mesozoic strata, usually exposed best, as my luck would have it, along the most inaccessible coastal cliffs and beachheads. So it was that by mid-August, on the morning of the twelfth to be precise, I had worked my way down to Whitby and taken up residence in a small hotel overlooking the harbor.

After the long weeks I'd spent on the road and often on foot, making my way across the rugged countryside, even these modest accommodations seemed positively luxuriant, I can assure you. To have a hot bath at the ready and cooked meals, a roof to keep the rain off one's head, such little things become an extravagance after only a little time without them. I settled into my single room on Drawbridge Road, excited at the prospect of exploring the ancient, saurian-bearing shales along the shoreline, but also relieved to be out of the dratted weather for a time. A fortnight earlier, I had cabled Sir Elijah Purdy, a fellow of the Geological Society of

London and a man with great experience regarding the Liassic strata at Whitby and the fossil bones and mollusca found therein, and he was to meet me no later than the afternoon of the fourteenth, at which time we would begin our planned weeklong survey of the rocks. Meanwhile, I was to examine specimens in the small Whitby Museum on the Quayside, perusing what type specimens of ammonites and reptilia resided in that institution's collection.

I will endeavor not to bore you with a travelogue, for I know from Ogilvey that you are familiar with the village of Whitby, with its quaint red roofs and whitewashed walls, the crumbling abbey ruins at East Cliff, & etc. And I had, by the time, I must confess, taken in more than my share of maritime scenery, and had little interest or patience remaining for anything save the fossil shells and bones, and fossiliferous strata, which I had come so many thousands of miles to see.

After a good night's sleep, despite a terrible storm toward dawn, I dressed and went down to breakfast, where there was some considerable excitement and discussion among other guests and the proprietor regarding a Russian schooner, *Demeter,* which had run aground only a few days prior at Tate Hill Pier. As I have said, I was quite beyond caring about ships and scenery at this point, and paid little attention to the conversation, though I do recall that the circumstances of the ship's grounding were somewhat mysterious and seemed the source of no small degree of anxiety. Regardless, my mind was almost entirely on my work. I finished my eggs and sausages, a pot of strong black coffee, and set off for the museum. The morning air was not especially warm nor cool, and it was an easy walk, during which I hardly noticed my surroundings, lost instead in my thoughts of all things paleontological.

I reached the quayside shortly before eleven o'clock and was met, as planned, by the Reverend Henry Swales, who has acted now for many years in a curatorial capacity, caring for the museum's growing cabinet. Though established originally as a repository for fossils, in the last several decades the museum's mission has been significantly expanded to encompass the general natural history of the region, including large assemblages of beetles, botanical materials, lepidoptera, and preserved fishes. Reverend Swales, a tall, good-natured fellow with a thick gray mustache and the eyebrows to match, eagerly directed his Yankee guest to the unpretentious gallery where many wall-mounted saurians and other fossils are kept on display for the public. I listened attentively as he related the stories of each specimen, as a man might relate another man's biography, the circumstances of their individual discoveries and conservation. I was taken almost at once with a certain large plesiosaur which had preserved within its rib cage the complete skeleton of a smaller plesiosaur, and much of the afternoon was passed studying this remarkable artifact, making my sketches, and losing myself ever deeper in my fancies of a lost, antediluvian world of monstrous sea dragons.

Eventually, the Reverend Swales returned and reminded me that the museum would be closing for the day at four, but I was welcome to stay later if I wished. I did, as I'd only just begun to scratch the surface of this marvelous collection, but didn't wish to abuse the reverend's hospitality. After all, I had many more days to pore over these relics, and my eyes were beginning to smart from so many hours scrutinizing the plesiosaurs and ichthyosauria.

"Thank you," said I. "But that really won't be necessary. I'll return early tomorrow morning." He reminded me that the museum did not open until eight, which I assured him was entirely agreeable. I tidied my notes and left Reverend Swales to lock up for the night.

Leaving the quayside behind, I decided to take a leisurely stroll toward the seaside, as it was still early, the weather was fine, and I'd little else to occupy my time except my books and notes. My route took me north along Pier Road, with the dark brown waters of the narrow River Esk flowing swiftly along on my right-hand side. High above the river, of course, rose East Cliff and the venerable ruins of the old abbey.

Though earlier it had interested me not even in the least, I found myself gazing, fascinated, at the distant, disintegrating walls, the lancet archways, perhaps somewhat more disposed to appreciate "local color" now that some small fraction of my desire to examine Whitby's famous saurians had been sated by the day's work. I knew little of the site's history, only that the original abbey had been erected on the cliffside in A.D. 657, destroyed two centuries later by Viking raiders, and that the ruins of the present structure were the remains of a Norman abbey built on the same spot at some later date. I thought perhaps there had been some saint or another associated with the abbey, that I had read that somewhere, but could not recollect the details. However, as I proceeded along the Pier Road, those towering ruins began to elicit from me strange feelings of dread, which I was, then and now, sir, completely at a loss to explain, and I decided it was best to occupy myself with other, less foreboding sights. So it was that in short order, I came to West Cliff, there above the beach, where the old cobbles of Pier Road turn sharply back to the south again toward the village, forming something like the crooked head of a shepherd's staff.

I must apologize if I have drifted into the sort of tedious travelogue I earlier promised to avoid, but it is important to impress upon you, at this point in my account, my state of mind, the odd and disquieting effect the abbey had elicited from me. I am not someone accustomed to such emotions and generally regard myself as a man not the least bit dogged by superstition. I told myself that whatever I felt was no more than the cumulative product of light and shadow, compounded by some exhaustion from my long day, and was only what most any other rational man might feel gazing upon those ruins.

At West Cliff, I was at once distracted from my intended goal, the Liassic shales themselves, by the extraordinary sight of a schooner run aground on the eastern side of the quay, across the Esk, and quickly realized that I was, in fact, seeing the very schooner, the *Demeter*, which I'd heard discussed with such excitement and foreboding over breakfast. I assure you, Dr. Watson, that the dead Russian ship cut a peculiar and lonely spectacle, cast up as she was on the jagged shingle of Tate Hill Pier, at the foot of East Cliff and the old graveyard. Her pathetic, shattered masts and bowsprit at once put me in mind of the tall spines of some pre-Adamite monster, not an odd association, of course, for someone in my profession. The tangled rigging and torn canvas hung loose, sagging like some lifeless mass of rawhide and sinew, flapping in the ocean's breeze.

And once again, that unaccustomed sense of dread assailed me, though even stronger than it had before, and I admit to you that I considered turning at once back toward the comfort of the inn. However, as I have said, I count my freedom from baser beliefs and superstitions as a particular point of pride, and knowing there was nothing here to fear and determined to have a look at the alum beds, not to be deterred by such childish thoughts or emotions, I began searching for some easy access to the beach below me, where I might better examine the rocks.

Within only a very few minutes I'd located a spiral, wooden stairway affixed to the cliff near the wall of the quay. However, the years and ravages of the sea had done much damage to the structure and it swayed most alarmingly as I carefully descended the slick steps to the sands below. Having finally reached the bottom, I paused briefly and stared back at the rickety stairway, sincerely hoping that I might find an alternate means of reaching the top again. The tide was out, revealing a broad swath of clean sand and the usual bits of flotsam, and I rightly supposed that I still had a good hour or so to look about the foot of West Cliff before setting out to discover such an alternative became a pressing concern.

Almost at once, then, I came across the perfectly preserved test of a rather large example of spiny echinodermata, or sea urchin, weathered all but entirely free of the alum shales which had imprisoned it for so many epochs, and deposited on the sand. I brushed it off and examined it more closely in the sunlight, unable to place either its genus or species, and suspecting that it might perhaps be of a form hitherto unrecognized by paleontologists; I deposited my prize in my right coat pocket and continued to scan the steep rocks for any other such excellent fossils. But, as the evening wore on, I failed to spot anything else quite as interesting, all my additional finds consisting in the main of broken pieces of ammonoid and mussel shells embedded in hard limestone nodules, a few fish bones, and what I hoped might prove to be a small fragment from one of the characteristic hourglass-shaped flipper bones of an ichthyosaur. I glanced out to sea, and then back to the dark gray rocks, trying to envision, as I had so often done before, the unimaginable expanse of time which had transpired since the stones before me were only slime and ooze at the bottom of an earlier and infinitely more alien sea.

"You are a geologist?" someone asked at that point, a man's voice, giving me a start, and I turned to see a very tall, gaunt man with a narrow, aquiline nose watching me from only a few feet away. He was smiling very slightly, in a manner that I thought oddly knowing at the time. For all I guessed, he might well have been standing there for an hour, as I have a habit of becoming so intent upon my collecting that I often neglect to glance about me for long stretches.

"Yes, sir," I said. "A paleontologist, to be more precise."

"Ah," he said. "Of course you are. I would have seen that for myself, but I'm afraid the wreck has had me distracted," and the man motioned in the direction of the quay, the Esk, and the stranded *Demeter* beyond. "You are an American, too, and a New Yorker, unless I miss my guess."

"I am," I replied, though by this point I confess that the stranger was beginning to annoy me somewhat with his questions. "Dr.

Tobias Logan, of the American Museum of Natural History," I introduced myself, holding out a hand which he only stared at curiously and smiled that knowing smile at me again.

"You're hunting the sea monsters of Whitby," he said, "and, I gather, having blasted little luck at it."

"Well," I said, taking the urchin from my pocket and passing it to the man, "I admit I've had better days in the field."

"Extraordinary," the tall man said, carefully inspecting the fossil, turning it over and over in his hand.

"Quite so," replied I, relaxing a bit, as I'm not unaccustomed to explaining myself to curious passersby. "But, still, not precisely the quarry I had in mind."

"Better the luck of Chapman, heh?" he asked, and winked.

I realized at once that he was referring to the discovery of William Chapman in 1758 of a marine crocodile on the Yorkshire coast, not far from where we were standing.

"You surprise me, sir," I said. "Are you a collector?"

"Oh no," he assured me, returning the urchin. "Nothing of the sort. But I read a great deal, you see, and I'm afraid few subjects have managed to escape my attention."

"Your accent isn't Yorkshire," I said, and he shook his head.

"No, Dr. Logan, it isn't," he replied, and then he winked at me once again. The man turned and peered out at the sea, and it was at this point that I realized that the tide was beginning to rise, the beach being appreciably more constricted than it was the last time I'd noticed.

"I fear that we shall certainly be getting our feet wet if we don't start back," I said, but he only nodded his head and continued to stare at the restless, gray expanse of the sea.

"We should talk at greater length sometime," he said. "There is a matter, concerning an object of great antiquity, and uncertain provenance, that I should very much appreciate hearing your trained opinion on."

"Indeed," I said, eyeing the rising tide. "A fossil?"

"No, a stone tablet. It appears to have been graven with hiero-glyphics resembling those of the ancient Egyptians."

"I'm sorry, sir, but you'd surely be better off showing it to an archaeologist, instead. I wouldn't be able to tell you much."

"Wouldn't you?" he asked, cocking an eyebrow and looking thoughtfully back at me. "I pried it from those very strata which you've spent the last hour examining. It's really quite an amazing object, Dr. Logan."

I believe I must have stared at the man for some time then without speaking, for I am sure I was too stunned and incredulous to find the words. He shrugged, then picked up a pebble and tossed it at the advancing sea.

"Forgive me," I said, or something of the sort. "But either you're having me on or you yourself have been the victim of someone else's joke. You're obviously an educated man, so—"

"So," he said, interrupting me, "I know that these strata are too old by many millions of years to contain the artifact I've told you I found buried in them. Obviously."

"Then you *are* joking?"

"No, my good man," he said, selecting another pebble to fling at the tide. "Quite the contrary, I assure you. I was as skeptical as you when first I laid eyes upon the thing, but now I am fairly con-vinced of its authenticity."

"Poppycock," I said to him, though I had many far more vul-gar expressions in mind by this point. "What you're proposing is so entirely absurd—"

"That it doesn't even warrant the most casual consideration of learned men," he said, interrupting me for the second time.

"Well, yes," I replied, somewhat impatiently, I'm afraid, and then returned the urchin to its place in my coat pocket. "The whole idea is perfectly absurd, man, right there on the face of it. It runs contrary to everything we've discovered in the last one hun-dred years about the evolution and development of life and the rise of humanity."

"I suspected," he said, as though I'd not even spoken, "at first, that someone might have planted the artifact, you see, that perhaps I had stumbled upon a prank aimed at someone else. Someone who, unlike me, makes a habit of collecting shells and rocks and old bones on the seashore.

"But I was able to identify—oh, what is it that you geologist fellows say? The positive and negative impressions—yes, that's it. The positive and negative impressions of the tablet were pressed quite clearly, unmistakably, into the layers of shale immediately above and below it. I have succeeded in recovering them as well."

"I'm sure you did," I said doubtfully.

"But, even more curiously, this isn't the first such inappropriate artifact, Dr. Logan. Two years ago, a very similar stone was found by a miner up the coast at Staithes, where, as you surely know, these same shales are mined for their alum. I have seen it myself, in a private cabinet in Glasgow. And there was a third, discovered in 1865, I think, or 1866, down at Frylingdales. But it seems to have vanished and, regrettably, only a drawing remains."

The man stopped talking then, for a moment, and gazed toward the walls of the quay. From where we were standing, one could just make out the splintered foremast of the ill-fated *Demeter* and he presently motioned toward it.

"There are dark entities afoot here in Whitby, Dr. Logan. Ay, darker things than even I'm accustomed to facing down, and I assure you I'm no coward, if I do say so myself."

"The tide, sir," I said, for now each wave carried the sea within mere feet of where we stood.

"Indeed, the tide," he said in a distracted, annoyed way, and nodded his head again. "But perhaps we can talk of this another time, before you leave Whitby. I will be glad for the chance to show you the tablet. I will be here another week, myself. I would rather prefer, though, if you kept this matter between us."

"Gladly," I assured him. "I have no particular wish to be thought a madman."

"Even so," he said, and with that enigmatic pronouncement at once began the perilous ascent up the rickety stairs to the Pier Road. I stood there a bit longer, watching as he climbed, expecting those slippery and infirm planks to give way at any second, dashing him onto the rocks and sand at my feet. But they held, and seeing that the sea had already entirely engulfed the beach to the west of me, and having only the high and inaccessible quay wall to the east, I summoned my courage and followed him. By no small stroke of luck, I also survived the climb, though the structure swayed and creaked and I was quite certain that my every footfall would be my last.

By now, Dr. Watson, I have but little doubt that you must have begun to understand why Ogilvey has urged me to write you. I have read in the press several accounts of the extraordinary Mr. Holmes's death in Switzerland, and I hope that the remarkable possibility, which I will not explicitly suggest here, but rather let stand as an unstated question for your consideration, will bring you no further pain. I have been made well aware of the great friendship that existed between you and Mr. Sherlock Holmes, and had not my reason been so vexed and controverted by the bizarre events at Whitby last August, I would have preferred to keep the encounter forever to myself. I would never have been led to reflect at such length on the identity of the man on the beach, a man whose appearance and demeanor I think you might recognize.

But I should continue my story now, and must continue to hope that you see here anything more than the ravings of an overtaxed mind and an overindulged imagination.

By the time I had at last finished my climb and regained secure footing at the crumbling summit of West Cliff, storm clouds were moving swiftly in from the southwest, darkening the murmuring waters of the Esk and creating an ominous backdrop for the abbey ruins. Fearing that I might lose my way among the unfamiliar streets should I attempt to discover a shorter route back to the hotel, I hurried instead along Pier Road, retracing my steps to the inn on Drawbridge Road. But I'd gone only a little way when the wind and thunder began and, in short order, a heavy, chilling downpour. I had neglected to bring an umbrella with me, thinking that the day would remain pleasant and clear, and not having planned on the walk down to the beach beforehand. As a result, I was now treated to a most thorough and proper soaking. I must have made for a dreary and pitiful sight, indeed, slogging my way down those narrow, rain-swept avenues.

When at last I reached the hotel, I was offered a hot cup of tea and a seat at the hearthside. As tempting as the latter was, I told the innkeeper that I preferred instead to retire at once to my room and acquire some dry clothes and rest until dinner. As I started up the stairs, he called me back, having forgotten a message that had been left for me that afternoon. It was written on a small, plain sheet of stationery and read, as best I can recall:

Toby, will call again first thing in the morning. Please await my arrival. Reached Whitby earlier than expected. I have *much* to relate re: unusual fossils found in Devon Lias and now in my care. Are you familiar with Phoenician (?) god Dagon or Irish Daoine Domhain? Until the morrow,

Yrs., E. P.

Though rightly intrigued and excited at the prospect of the new Devon fossils which Purdy had mentioned, I was quite completely baffled by his query regarding Phoenician gods and those two words of unpronounceable Gaelic. Deciding that any mysteries would readily resolve themselves in the morning, I retired to my room, where I at once changed clothes and then busied myself until dinner with some brief notes on the urchin and other specimens from West Cliff.

I slept fitfully that night while the storm raged and banged at the shutters. I am not given to nightmares, but I recall odd scraps of dream where I stood on the shore at West Cliff, watching as the *Demeter* sailed majestically into the harbor. The tall man stood somewhere close behind me, though I don't think I ever saw his face, and spoke of my wife and child. I finally awoke for the last time shortly after dawn, to the smell of coffee brewing and breakfast cooking downstairs, and the comforting sound of rain dripping from the eaves. The storm had passed, and despite my rather poor sleep, I recall feeling very rested and ready for a long day prospecting the seaside outcrops with Purdy. I dressed quickly, and armed with my ash plant and knapsack, my hammer and cold chisels, I went down to await my colleague's arrival.

However, at eleven o'clock I was still waiting, sipping at my second pot of coffee and beginning to feel the first faint twinges of annoyance that so much of the day was being squandered when my time in Whitby was to be so short. I am almost puritanical in my work habits and despise the wasting of perfectly good daylight, and could not imagine what was taking Purdy so long to show.

The terrible things that soon followed, I must tell you, occurred with not the slightest hint of the lurid or sensational air that is usually attached to the macabre and uncanny in the penny dreadfuls and gothic romances. There was not even the previous day's vague sense of foreboding. They simply happened, sir, and somehow that made them all the worse. It would be long weeks before I would begin to associate with the events the singular trepidation, indeed the genuine horror, which would gradually come to so consume my thoughts.

I was reading, for the second time, a long article in an Edinburgh paper (the paper's name escapes me now, as does the precise subject of the article), when a young boy, possibly eight years of age, came in and announced that he'd been sent to retrieve me. A man, he said, had paid him sixpence to bring me to West Cliff, where there had been a drowning in the night.

"I'm sorry, but I am not a medical doctor," I told him, thinking this must surely be a simple case of mistaken identity, but no, he assured me at once, he'd been instructed to bring the American Dr. Tobias Logan to the beach at West Cliff, with all possible haste. As I sat there scratching my head, the boy grew impatient and protested that we should hurry. Before I left the hotel on Drawbridge Road, however, I scribbled a quick note to Purdy and left it with the proprietor, in case he should come in my absence. Then I quickly gathered my belongings and followed the excited boy, who told me his name was Edward and that his father was a cobbler, through the narrow, winding streets of Whitby and once again down to West Cliff.

The body of the drowned man lay on the sand and clearly the gulls had been at him for some considerable time before he was discovered by a beachcomber. Yet, despite the damage done by the cruel beaks of the birds, I had no trouble in recognizing the face of Elijah Purdy right off. Several men had crowded about, including the constable and harbormaster, none of whom, I quickly gathered, had paid the boy sixpence to bring me to West Cliff.

"First that damned Russian ghost ship," the constable grumbled, lighting his pipe. "Now this."

"A foul week, to be sure," the harbormaster muttered back.

I introduced myself at once and then kneeled down beside the tattered earthly remains of the man whom I had known and of whom I'd been so fond. The constable coughed and exhaled a great, gray cloud of pipe smoke.

"Here," he said. "Did you know this poor fellow?"

"Very well," I replied. "I was to meet him this very morning. I was waiting for him when the boy there fetched me from the inn on Drawbridge Road."

"Is that so now?" the constable said. "What boy is that?"

I looked up and there was, to be sure, no sign of the boy who had led me to the grisly scene.

"The cobbler's son," I said, and looked back down at the ruined face of Purdy. "He said that he was paid to summon me here.

I assumed you'd sent for me, sir, though I'm not at all sure how you could have known to do so."

At that, the harbormaster and constable exchanged perplexed stares and the latter went back to puffing at his pipe.

"This man was an associate of yours, then?" the harbormaster asked me.

"Indeed," said I. "He is Sir Elijah Purdy, a geologist from London. He arrived in Whitby only yesterday. I believe he may have taken a room at the Morrow House on Hudson Street."

The two men looked at me and then the constable whispered something to his companion and the two nodded their heads in unison.

"You're an American," the constable said, raising an eyebrow and chewing at the stem of his pipe.

"Yes," I said. "I'm an American."

"Well, Dr. Logan, you may be certain that we'll get straight to the bottom of this," he assured me.

"Thank you," I said, and it was at that moment that I noticed something odd, about the diameter of a silver dollar, clutched in the drowned man's hand.

"Murders here in Whitby do *not* go unsolved."

"What makes you think he was murdered?" I asked the constable, prying the curious, iridescent object from Elijah Purdy's grasp.

"Well, for one, the man's pockets were filled with stones to weight the body down. See there for yourself."

Indeed, the pockets of his wool overcoat were bulging with shale, but on quick inspection I saw that they all contained fossils and explained to the man that in all likelihood, Elijah Purdy himself had placed the stones there. One of his vest pockets was likewise filled.

"Ah," the constable said thoughtfully, and rubbed at his mustache. "Well, no matter. We'll find the chap what did this, I promise you."

In no mood to argue the point, I answered a few more questions, told the constable that I would be available at the inquest, and made my way back up the rickety stairway to Pier Road. I stood there for a short time, surveying the scene below, the men arranged in a ring around the drowned man's corpse, the dark sea lapping tirelessly at the shore, the wide North Sea sky above. After a bit I remembered the object I'd taken from Purdy's hand and held it up for a closer inspection. But there was no doubt of what it was, a small ammonite of the genus *Dactylioceras*, a form quite common in sections of the English Liassic. Nothing extraordinary, except that this specimen, though deceased, *was not fossilized,* and the squidlike head of the cephalopod stared back at me with silvery eyes, its ten tentacles drooping limply across my fingers.

I fear that there is little else to tell, Dr. Watson, and glancing back over these few pages, I can see that there is not nearly so much sense in what I've written as I'd hoped for. I returned to the hotel, where I would spend the next three days, making one more visit to the Reverend Swales's museum, only to discover my enthusiasm for work had dissolved. After the inquest, during which it was determined that Sir Elijah Purdy's drowning was accidental, having occurred while he collected fossils along the beach and that no foul play was involved, I packed up my things and returned home to Manhattan. I delivered the very recently dead *Dactylioceras*, preserved in alcohol, to the curator of fossil invertebrates, who greeted the find with much fanfare and promised to name the surprising new species for the man from whose grip I had pried it. One final detail, which will be of interest to you, and which forms the primary reason of this writing, is a letter which I received some weeks after coming back to the States.

Posted from Whitby on the twelfth of September, one month to the day after my arrival there, it carried no return address and had been composed upon a typewriter. I will duplicate the text below:

Dear Dr. Logan,

I trust that your trip home will have passed without incident. I have written to offer my sincerest apologies for not having attended to the matter of your friend's untimely death, and for not having found the time to continue our earlier conversation. But I must implore you to forget the odd matter of which I spoke, the three tablets from Whitby, Staithes, and Frylingdales. All are now lost, I fear, and I have come to see how that outcome is surely for the best. Dark and ancient powers, the whim of inhuman beings of inconceivable antiquity and malignancy, may be at work here and, I suspect, may have played a direct role in the death of Sir Elijah. Take my words to heart and forget these things. To worry at them further will profit you not. Perhaps we will meet again someday, under more congenial circumstances.

S. H.

Whether or not the letter's author was, in fact, your own associate, Mr. Sherlock Holmes, and if that was the man I spoke with at West Cliff, I cannot say. Any more than I can explain the presence in the waters off Whitby of a mollusk believed vanished from the face of the earth for so many millions of years or the death of Elijah Purdy, an excellent swimmer, I have been told. Having never seen the tablets firsthand, I can profess no reliable opinion regarding them, and feel I am better off not trying to do so. I have never been a nervous man, but I have taken to hearing strange sounds and voices in the night, and my sleep and, I am very much afraid, peace of mind are beginning to suffer. I dream of—no, I will not speak here of the dreams.

Before I close, I should say that on Friday last there was a burglary at the museum here, which the police have yet to solve. The Whitby ammonite and all written records of it were the *only* things stolen, though some considerable vandalism was done to a number of the paleontology and geology offices and to the locked cabinet where the specimen was being kept.

I thank you for your time, Dr. Watson, and, if you are ever in New York, hope to have the pleasure of meeting you.

Dr. Tobias H. Logan
Department of Vertebrate Paleontology
American Museum of Natural History
New York City, New York

(Unposted letter discovered among the effects of Dr. Tobias Logan, subsequent to his suicide by hanging, 11 May 1898.)

A Case of Insomnia

JOHN P. VOURLIS

Holmes couldn't sleep. Not that this was unusual—he required no more than three to four hours on any given night. While London slumbered, he would prowl the gaslit neighborhoods of the city, past the breadmakers at the foot of Baker Street already at work, observing the late-night revelers staggering home from Soho in their drunken stupor as he continued down Regent Street, through Mayfair, past the ladies of the evening in Shepherd's Market still hoping to squeeze the last few pounds out of the night before lying down in their own beds as the sun rose. Through Piccadilly, Edgware, Marylebone, and finally home again to the flat we shared. This was the route Holmes's sleeplessness followed—which he often detailed for me over a morning pipe.

As a man of medicine, I pondered the root of his affliction. Holmes's mind was an engine of perpetual thought, constantly at work on some problem that required wakefulness. Sleep seemed a nuisance to him, a luxury he had little use for. So it was no real surprise to me that Thursday in March when he came striding into my chambers at half-past seven in the morning, the *Daily Press* in hand, and said, "Watson, I simply cannot sleep!"

"What about the *Valeriana officinalis* I prescribed for you?" I said.

"Useless. It's been three days now, and I haven't so much as closed my eyes. And I am not alone in my suffering," he continued, shoving the newspaper into my hands. "Read there, page three, column seven, near the bottom."

I scanned the paper, searching for the item.

"There." He pointed, jabbing his finger like a dagger at the headline.

" 'Plague of Insomnia,' " I read aloud. " 'Citizens of northern town of Inswich suffer third month of sleeplessness. Town rife with wild rumors of cause. What began as a few isolated cases has become a full-blown epidemic . . .' Holmes, you're not suggesting a connection between your restlessness and theirs?"

"Of course not," Holmes replied. "But when I couldn't sleep this third night, I went to an apothecary on Hadry Street."

I knew the man. His shop was in Islington, and he was really nothing more than a glorified opium peddler. I grew more concerned for my friend's condition. He noted this in my expression, of course, and went on to clarify himself.

"It became apparent that I required something a bit stronger than your roots and herbs."

I looked at Holmes with disapproval, but he brushed straight past it. "He prescribes a tincture of Turkish poppy and cannabis," he continued. "However, when I requested a dram of this medicine, he explained that he'd been out of supply since before the New Year. I found this very curious indeed, as he has never failed to satisfy my need on any prior occasion, and I asked him how such a thing had transpired. He then related to me that a large shipment had been sent north, and that his usual suppliers had failed to refill his inventory ever since, due to exceedingly high demand and the accompanying inflation of price."

"Sent to Inswich, I'll wager."

"Correct, Watson," Holmes replied, rubbing his eyes. "Now pack your things. We have a train to catch."

As I readied myself to depart with him for Inswich, I could sense his rising agitation, akin to those Thoroughbreds at Aston waiting with impatience at the starting line for the race to begin. "Do hurry along," he said, picking up a few of his own things, including the revolver he sometimes carried.

"Are you expecting difficulties?" I asked.

"I *expect* nothing," he replied.

At the Marylebone station, we purchased our tickets for Barrington, the stop nearest Inswich, an otherwise rather isolated hamlet. I picked up the *London Mail* from a smoke shop to occupy myself on the arduous seven-hour journey.

As he stood restless beside me, Holmes brought to my attention a fellow passenger some distance down the tracks.

"Isn't that Dr. Mashbourne?" he said.

I looked up from where I had given the man at the shop a half-pence for the paper and saw our old acquaintance, Arthur Mashbourne, doctor of medicine at Charing Cross. We made our way through the morning crowd to greet him.

I recalled Mashbourne as a thin man of enormous appetites, ruddy of complexion, who now gave the appearance of having been squeezed into his trousers and jacket like ground meat stuffed into casings of sausage. Pleasant enough a gentleman when engaged in dinner or drink, he would, if deprived of either for too long, become so single-minded in their pursuit as to be most gently described as "off-putting."

"Gentlemen! What a pleasure to see you," he said, clasping our hands with vigor. "And where might you be traveling?"

"To Inswich, with you," said Holmes.

"How did you know my destination?" asked the startled Mashbourne. "One of your clever deductions, I suspect. Let's hear it."

"Merely the ticket in your breast pocket," Holmes replied, and without pausing asked, "What do you make of this rash of insomnia they're having up there? That *is* the reason for your journey?"

"Yes. I go to see a patient, an old friend who has contracted this sleeplessness. A most unusual epidemic, from what little I've gathered. It's the subject of your inquiry as well, then?"

"Indirectly, yes," I said. "It seems they have cornered the market on a certain soporific which our friend Holmes means to acquire."

"You're having trouble sleeping as well, Holmes?" asked Mashbourne, concerned.

"I go to satisfy my curiosity," he said, frowning at me, "not my craving for sleep."

I decided it was better not to dispute this point of fact, and an awkward moment passed before our train pulled in and the conductor called for all to board.

It was unavoidable that we share a berth with Mashbourne. Closing our compartment, we made ourselves as comfortable as possible for the passage to Inswich. I looked to my paper as Holmes took out his pipe and began filling it. Mashbourne removed his coat and produced a silver flask, offering it around.

"Brandy?" he said.

"No, thank you," I replied.

"Holmes?"

Holmes was deep in thought and made no effort to respond.

"I find that when I have trouble sleeping, brandy can be of use," the doctor said, taking a swig.

"Yes, for some," I said, "though I prefer pestled valerian in a warm chamomile tea."

"That could be equally effective," said Mashbourne, taking another draft, "though not as pleasurable."

We changed trains at King's Cross for the remainder of the trip north. As we reboarded, I asked Mashbourne, "Do you have any theories as to what could cause such a curious epidemic?"

"I shall require more facts before making a diagnosis," he replied.

"Facts we have," said Holmes perfunctorily. "The town: Inswich. The time of year: spring. The weather: rainy. The duration of the epidemic: three months. That would put its inception sometime around mid-January."

"Are you suggesting this is a seasonal disorder?" said Mashbourne, clearly engaged on the problem now. "Perhaps a respiratory condition, such as pleurisy?"

Holmes let out a "humph" and drew at his pipe, leaving Mashbourne and me to continue the discussion of various pulmonary distresses.

The train from King's Cross picked up speed, belching black smoke into the blue morning sky. As the city gave way to the countryside, I buried my head in my newspaper, reading of the previous day's events. Mashbourne made a pillow of his coat and was soon fast asleep, the brandy having served its purpose.

Holmes, meanwhile, continued to puff on his pipe and occasionally emitted another "humph." At each grumble, I looked up from my reading, thinking he was about to expound on some facet of the case. But he never did, and I was left to ponder in silence what possibilities he might be eliminating.

As morning moved into afternoon, we adjourned to the dining car for supper, where Holmes turned the conversation once more to Inswich. As Mashbourne devoured his roast beef, bread pudding, and apple sausages, Holmes recounted all manner of facts and figures about the town, speaking of the place with such passion that one would scarcely realize he had never set foot there. But it was all digesting in that exceptional mind of his, just as surely as the tremendous quantities of food that now filled Mashbourne's stomach.

The population of Inswich was small, recounted Holmes, barely three hundred people. The town had been founded by a Roman general as a way station on the road to and from London. The town square had been built on the site of an ancient druidic temple, third century A.D. Before the railway had come to Barrington, a town some ten miles or so to the east, Inswich had had a population of several thousand, with produce and livestock as the chief exports, shipped south to market via canal. But that day had passed, and the town had fallen into decline, until now the few residents remaining tended the various great estates that dotted the north of England, or farmed their own meager plots of land.

We arrived in Barrington at half-past four, with the sun hidden by drab gray clouds. Leaving the platform, we secured a small coach for the final leg of our journey to Inswich, which would last another three-quarters of an hour.

"If you gentlemen are of a mind," said Mashbourne, "I may secure you lodging at Carthon, my friend's estate, not far from here, where I shall be a guest."

"No thank you, Doctor," said Holmes before I could accept. "We shall take lodging in Inswich. I should like to find a central location which can afford us the greatest ease of access to the townspeople."

"Very well," said Mashbourne. "But you must dine with me this evening. I should very much like you both to meet the Lady Carthon, a most exquisite hostess."

We parted company with the doctor in Inswich, agreeing to call at Carthon at eight bells, then set about securing ourselves lodging at the Black Hart, a small inn located at the center of the town—a prime spot, observed Holmes, from which we could conduct all necessary business.

Entering a low-ceilinged anteroom meagerly lit by several sputtering oil lamps, we found no one at hand to attend us. I clapped the bell, and a haggard figure stirred from the shadows. Rising from a rocking chair, an elderly woman of perhaps seventy appeared: hair gray as slate, one eye brown, the other clouded milky white with cataract.

"Two rooms?" she asked in a tired, creaky voice.

"Yes, madam, thank you," I replied.

"And how many nights?" she asked.

"I will be quite surprised if we are unable to conclude our business this very evening," said Holmes.

"You'll find no reason to stay here longer, sir," agreed the woman. "We have little to boast of."

"We understand that the entire town has suffered from sleeplessness these last three months," said Holmes.

"It's in all the London papers," I hastened to add, fearing that my friend's peremptory manner might distress our hostess.

"Yes, well, there is that," she said softly.

"Are you so afflicted yourself?" inquired Holmes.

"I am indeed," she replied, but before she could continue, one of the lamps flickered out, and she hurriedly moved to it, her hands shaking as she struck a match and rekindled the wick.

"Are you all right, madam?" I asked, concerned that we might have inadvertently frightened the poor woman.

"You'll pardon me, sir," she replied nervously, "but the night has become a thing to dread 'round here."

"Indeed?" I said. "And why might that be?"

" 'The devil is driven from light into darkness and is banished from the world,' " she replied, as if that somehow answered my question.

"Job, chapter eighteen, verse eighteen," said Holmes.

She nodded, offering nothing further, but handed over two keys. "Seven and eight, up the stairs to the right," she continued. "And would you be wanting tea this evening?"

"No, madam, we are expected at Carthon," I said.

"Best get there before dark," she replied.

"Thank you, we shall do our best," I replied.

She nodded, then turned back to her chair, bidding us good evening.

I found her brief biblical quotation to be quite nonsensical, wondering how a roomful of lamps would suffice to keep away the devil, should he actually decide to come to Inswich, and said as much to Holmes as we made our way up the stairs.

"No doubt we've just witnessed the result of sleeplessness mixed with religious fervor," he said sardonically.

I thought no more of it for the moment. After all, we were merely here to track down Holmes's sleeping medicine, and in the morning we would be on our way back to London. We deposited our belongings in our quarters, both of which, like the lobby, were lit with sputtering lamps, as were several other open rooms we passed.

We found no doctor to speak with, Inswich being no doubt too small to attract a resident physician, but we did locate the local dentist, who offered certain information regarding Holmes's much-sought-after apothecary's tincture.

The dentist, it seems, had been approached by an ever-increasing number of townspeople over the last three months in a high state of anxiety over their inability to get any meaningful rest, "On ac-count of a night creature." Some sort of wild animal that he said was terrorizing the local populace.

Not putting much stock in the stories he heard—"A load of superstitious rubbish," he said—yet with no other clear course of action available, he had ordered a large quantity of sleep medicine from his brother-in-law, an apothecary in London, and prescribed it to nearly every man, woman, and child in the town.

"Once I determined that neither rotting teeth nor indigestion was the cause of their sleeplessness," he told us, "I decided that putting them all to sleep was the only way to keep them from overrunning my premises."

But though the tincture had provided some relief for the first night or two, the symptoms had quickly returned. This of course led to even greater anxiety, and the demand for larger doses, which quickly resulted in the depletion of his brother-in-law's entire supply.

"Treating the symptom, not the cause," said Holmes in my ear.

When Holmes inquired of the man whether he had any of the medicine left, even a single dram, that he might purchase, he was told the last of it had gone to Carthon House some weeks ago.

"Perhaps we should investigate this night creature," I said half in jest as we left the dentist, noting that we had several hours before we were expected for dinner.

Despite his disappointment regarding the tincture, Holmes required no more prodding than this, though his fatigue was now punctuated regularly by enormous yawns and a frequent rubbing of his tired eyes, for his natural curiosity was now aroused. So he and I took a stroll through the little town, making stops at the smoke shop, the general store, a small pub, and the town hall—in which was located the magistrate's office, but no magistrate. The tired woman on duty informed us that "his lordship" was away on holiday.

We interviewed a dozen or so citizens about their experiences of sleeplessness, and as we talked with them, it became clear that it wasn't only the old innkeeper who feared the night. A rather homely woman of fifty reported that something had been trying to enter her bedroom window, scraping at the glass, rattling the latch, awakening her consistently whenever she neared slumber. Upon rising from her bed and opening the shutters, however, she would invariably find nothing there, only a "bad odor" floating about.

A young mail clerk reported seeing "a giant shadow, like a bat, only enormous," swoop down on him as he made his way home late one evening. He avoided the fell creature, he said, by rushing into a well-lit pub.

Another swarthy fellow, a butcher, looking haggard and worn down, said that he was awakened several times each night for the last month by the feeling that someone or something was sitting on his chest, intent on strangling him. Upon awakening and turning up his lantern, he could find nothing about. I dismissed his story as mania brought on by a continual lack of sleep, such deprivation no doubt resulting in hallucinations.

"I recently read an article by a Dr. Breuer," I remarked to Holmes as we moved on in our search, "in a journal of the medical college in Vienna, regarding a type of hysterical condition of the mind which can, under some circumstances, manifest itself throughout an entire community."

"I have read the very same article, Watson," said Holmes. "But that is the symptom, and we search for a cause. Once we have that, a cure should be forthcoming."

None of those we interviewed had stated that they had actually *seen* the creature—that is, until we happened upon one young mother, dark circles around her eyes, who attested that her child had seen the thing enter his bedroom, and had ever since insisted that he sleep in his mother's bed. I must say that I was forced to suppress a smile at this last accounting, though Holmes appeared to find it not the least bit amusing.

He asked to speak with the boy.

"Can you tell me what you saw, sir?" said Holmes, conversing with him as if he were quite the grown man, and not the eight-year-old child he was.

The young boy looked at his mother, uncertain whether to speak, until she nodded her approval. "I went to bed like I always do," he said, "and Mummy left a candle burnin'."

"To keep the night creatures away," said the young woman, rather embarrassed, and by way of explaining herself, "Me mother is a superstitious woman, and she's lately insisted I not leave the boy to sleep in the dark on account of this animal that's been prowlin' about."

"But I wanted to see it," the boy said. "To see if it were real, so I put out the light. I waited up a long time, and I think I fell asleep maybe, but then I heard the door open, and saw it. It sniffed 'round a sec, but our dog Jeffery took to barkin' like mad, and scared it right off."

"And could you describe this creature for me?" asked Holmes.

"Oh, he can do better than that," said his mother. "Show him, son."

The little boy reached into his pocket and pulled out a scrap of paper, which he carefully unfolded and handed to Holmes. Holmes studied it closely before handing it to me to examine as well. It was an impressive drawing, very realistically done, with a charcoal stick I assumed, of a quite hideous, winged creature with a snarling dog's face—certainly a most disturbing picture to have come from the mind of a child.

"He draws it all day long," said his mother.

I felt rather skeptical that anyone so young could render such a monstrosity in considerable detail, especially based on his own alleged experience, and chose to believe instead that one of the superstitious townsfolk must have been telling this child fairy tales.

"Your son is quite the artist," I said, politely patting the boy on the head.

"Yes, he is," said Holmes, turning to the boy. "May we keep this, young man?"

The boy looked again to his mother, who nodded to Holmes. "By all means, sir."

"Well, it is all most curious," I said as we left the boy and his mother. "But we will have to continue our investigations tomorrow, I'm afraid, as it's half-past six now and we must be at Carthon by eight."

"Punctual as always, eh, Watson?" remarked Holmes.

"Etiquette demands the attempt."

After returning to the Black Hart and changing into more suitable dinner attire, we returned to the town square to search for a means of transport. There we found that the central area now contained an enormous bonfire, nearly twenty feet high, which lit the night for a great distance all around. A dozen or so men huddled in small groups tended the monstrous blaze. Once again Dr. Breuer's article on mass hysteria came to my mind, and I would have remarked on it to Holmes, but the conflagration seemed hardly unusual after all that we had seen and heard this day.

I asked the men where we might find transport, and one

pointed out a small open transom parked nearby. Its driver was a middle-aged chap with a gap in his teeth and a single thick brow like a long black caterpillar extending across both his eyes. He seemed extremely reluctant to ferry us to Carthon at first, asking why we should want to take such a long ride, then offering excuses as to his horses being tired and it being awfully near to his own dinnertime. A guinea from my waistcoat quickly transformed his hesitation into compliance.

He opened the side door on his small vehicle and assisted us in boarding. "Who am I to tell such fine gentlemen where to go and when? Right this way, sirs."

As we made the journey, our talkative driver continued nervously chatting—about the weather, the price of sheep and cattle, his mother-in-law in Barrington—but made no mention of insomnia. He likely would have gone right on expounding to us ad infinitum had not Holmes asked him, "Have you been sleeping well of late?"

"No one sleeps well in Inswich, sir," the man solemnly replied.

"And what do you suppose might be the cause?" I asked casually, presuming a reluctance to reply on his part.

"I'm sure I don't know, sir," he answered. "I'm just a carriage man, y'know. 'Course, I do hear the odd bit, tales of beasts that prowl the night and the like."

"We've heard the same stories," I said.

"Old wives' tales, don't y'agree?" said the driver.

"Yes, of course, most assuredly," I replied.

"Do you recall when these stories began?" Holmes asked.

"It was back in January, I believe, not long after the moon went clipped."

"Went *clipped*?" I asked.

"Yes, sir. There's the moon, then it's clipped."

"The lunar eclipse," said Holmes, rather excited. "December twenty-seventh, was it not, Watson?"

"Yes. I believe so," I said, trying to recall the precise date.

"That's right," said the driver. "It was all black for a long minute or two, and the old women went to church afterward, and fell down on their knees to pray for our souls. Wuhn't long after I heard the missus tell me to leave a light on afore bed so's to keep the devil hisself away."

The discussion went no further, though I had no doubt Holmes's mind was hard at work. Save for the clacking of the horses' hooves and the turning of the transom wheels, we traveled on in silence. We arrived at Carthon House just before eight. A long stone driveway, with tall regal oaks lining both sides like sentries, led up to the magnificent estate, an enormous mansion ablaze with lights in nearly every window, of which the front prospect alone featured over a hundred—a welcoming beacon in the stark, moonless night.

"Extraordinary," I remarked.

"Will you be wanting me to stay, sirs?" asked our driver as we disembarked.

"No, thank you," said Holmes.

The man nodded, turned his transom around, and disappeared quickly back into the night.

"He seemed rather in a hurry to leave, did he not?" I remarked to Holmes.

"Did you notice the lump beneath the breast pocket of his long coat?" replied Holmes. "Unless I am mistaken, it was a revolver— quite at the ready by the way his right hand checked for its presence every minute or two."

"Perhaps there really are beasts about?" I said, again in jest.

"That *is* one possibility," said Holmes.

I simply shook my head in disbelief at him for not dismissing these tales of nocturnal fright out of hand.

As we climbed the stairs to the mansion's entrance, the great door opened and Dr. Mashbourne appeared, accompanied by a footman.

"Splendid, splendid," said Mashbourne as the footman took our coats and hats. "You're right on time as always, Dr. Watson."

Holmes grinned at me with that tight-lipped sour grin of his as we entered Carthon house.

The interior was every bit as magnificent as the exterior. A great chandelier hung over the ornate foyer, spilling light from dozens of candles.

"Must be the devil to keep that in good order," I said, motioning as we walked through.

"That's not even the largest of them," said Mashbourne, "as you'll see when we reach the dining hall."

He led us into the drawing room and called for one of the servants to bring us some sherry. As we drank, I discussed with Mashbourne our various encounters in Inswich and the stories of the creature that haunted the townsfolk's nights.

"A creature, you say? What sort of creature?"

Holmes took out the scrap of paper with the young boy's drawing on it, and showed it to Mashbourne. He studied it closely, and I felt as I watched him that he was taking the whole thing rather too seriously.

"How long can a person continue without sleep?" asked Holmes.

"I've had single cases of some days," I interjected, "even a week—*you* well know—though I daresay I've never encountered such a prolonged and widespread case as this, not even in the journals."

"Nor I," concurred Mashbourne, handing the drawing back to Holmes. "Have you formulated a hypothesis yet, Mr. Holmes?"

"Yes," replied Holmes, to my plain surprise.

"And what would that be?" said a gentle, soft voice behind us.

We turned, and there beheld a stunning woman of thirty years or so, with golden hair, shimmering blue eyes, and skin of translucent alabaster. She wore a pale dress the color of eggshells, with a high closed collar, and a delicate silver chain with a small black stone hanging 'round her neck. Like the myriad lights that filled her home, she gave off a veritable glow of warmth.

Even Holmes was silent, leaving it to Mashbourne to break the spell and make introductions.

"Lady Carthon, these are my good friends Dr. John Watson and Mr. Sherlock Holmes. They are quite famous in London—"

"For solving many a notorious crime," she said, completing his sentence. "I'm familiar with the reputation of the good Mr. Holmes. And what brings you two gentlemen to our humble Inswich?"

"A rumor that the place was overrun with beautiful women," I said.

She laughed so easily as to make me blush. "You're quite charming, Dr. Watson, really," she replied.

"You flatter me, madam," I replied, bowing my head, pleased that I had elicited such a pleasant response from so fair a lady.

The butler arrived, summoning us to dinner. We followed Lady Carthon like anxious suitors as she glided elegantly into the dining hall.

Once seated, we were indulged with the most excellent of meals, consisting of several courses, one following immediately upon the other. Mashbourne was in heaven. He said very little, merely nodding his understanding at what conversation there was, or grunting his approval of the variety of foods brought before us. As Holmes seemed lost in thought again, it was left to me to converse with Lady Carthon.

"Do you live here alone?" I asked, somewhat too forthrightly, I feared.

"Yes, alone," she answered, betraying no embarrassment at my directness.

"And your husband?" I asked, noting the wedding band on her left hand. "Is he away traveling?"

"My husband was killed in Egypt, a year ago January," she replied. "He was a captain in Her Majesty's Royal Army. A most wonderful man."

"My deepest sympathies, madam," I said, chastened by her reply. "It must be difficult managing this large estate without him."

"Thank you, sir," she said, "but I manage well enough."

"Most assuredly," I replied. "You must entertain often."

"Oh, not often. I do have my dear friend Dr. Mashbourne call upon me occasionally, to deliver little tidbits of news from London, as well as personable guests such as yourself."

Mashbourne nodded and smiled, his mouth too full to speak.

"Are you aware that the entire town of Inswich is suffering a sleep affliction?" interjected Holmes.

"Yes, of course I'm aware of it."

"And tell me, madam," continued Holmes, "do you sleep well yourself?"

She paused for a moment, then answered, "No, not well at all."

Dr. Mashbourne cleared his throat. "Emily is the patient I mentioned to you on our journey north. Her husband and I served briefly together in Egypt."

"Yes," said Holmes. "You were not long in the service, if I remember correctly."

"Eighteen months," said Mashbourne.

"And how long has this sleepless condition persisted?" said Holmes to Lady Carthon.

"Quite some time," she replied.

"Yet you only called upon Dr. Mashbourne quite recently?"

"It was of little concern before."

"And now?" said Holmes.

"It's become increasingly troublesome," Lady Carthon replied.

"Do you remember the last time that you actually slept through the night?" said Holmes.

"It was January, I suppose."

"Are you telling us, Emily, that you have not slept in three whole months?" said Mashbourne.

"How are you able to function?" I asked, incredulous. "Are you not perpetually exhausted?"

"Do you have any idea what it is that is keeping you awake?" Holmes continued, in a relentless manner I did not condone.

She seemed rather overwhelmed by this barrage of questions, for it seemed she was unsure how to reply.

"Have you heard the stories the townspeople tell, of a creature that haunts their sleep?" asked Holmes after a moment.

She hesitated again, then finally answered. "I have."

"And what do you make of them?"

"I find them to be most disturbing."

"You believe them?" I asked.

"That is why she has a light burning in every room, is it not, madam?" said Holmes.

"Yes," she said. "I'm sure this must all sound quite silly to gentlemen from London, but I assure you it has been most frightening for me."

"Please do explain," said Holmes.

"It all began one night in late December," she said, recomposing herself. "There was a total lunar eclipse. Many among the townspeople were unnerved by it, especially when the local priest, a sadly superstitious old man, I'm afraid, packed up his belongings and left us the very next day. I myself did not share their fears, having studied the stars somewhat, and stayed awake well into the night to witness the event. Afterward, I went to the drawing room for a glass of brandy, and as I made my way down the dark hallway, I suddenly felt a *presence*—very close by. It was a black shadow of a thing, and I felt it brush my neck. It frightened me very badly, of course, and I'm afraid I screamed quite loudly. My maidservant, Estella, came running out of her room with a lantern to see what all the ruckus was about, and as she approached, the thing simply disappeared.

"I was quite shaken, as you might expect, and allowed myself even a second glass of brandy, after which I returned to bed, believing by then that I had hallucinated the entire incident. But when I doused the lamp in my bedroom, I felt the *presence* return. I immediately relit the lamp, and once again the thing vanished, so I kept a light burning all through the night. I slept quite poorly, as you might guess, waking often to check that the lamp remained lit.

"The next evening, before retiring, I had my servants check the entire mansion for any open windows, unlocked doors, making sure they were all bolted shut. Once I was assured that all was secure, I doused my light and climbed into bed. It was only a moment later when I once again sensed the *presence*, and immediately lit the lamp.

"I then woke all the servants and instructed them to search the house. They found a single open door, with strange scrapings around the outside latch, like claw marks.

"This same ritual went on for the better part of a week, and each night a different door or window was found open. Finally, I instructed my servants to light a lamp in every room of the house and keep them lit all night, believing this to be the only way to scare off the invader."

As she told her tale, Lady Carthon's hand went several times to the stone on her necklace, and I saw it clearly for the first time then. It was an oddly shaped amulet, like a long teardrop, with flattened edges and a strange black color that oddly reflected no light.

"Your husband," said Holmes, pressing on, "he gave you that necklace?"

She nodded, looking transfixed at the stone that hung from it. "It was an anniversary gift. Sent to me from Egypt. It arrived only a week or two after he died."

"Were you told any of the circumstances of his death?" asked Holmes.

"Really, Holmes!" I said, quite forcefully.

"It's all right, Doctor," she said gently. "I was told he was murdered by grave robbers while on patrol somewhere near the Great Pyramids. But Arthur could tell you more. He was there."

"I'm sure we can discuss this later," I said, hoping to spare the poor woman any further discomfort.

"Yes, of course," said Mashbourne, "after dinner."

"You miss him terribly, don't you?" said Holmes.

"I would give anything to have him back with me," she answered, tears welling up in her eyes, the song now gone from her voice.

She suddenly looked tired, quite pallid and gaunt. As if the light that was the life in her pale blue eyes had been momentarily snuffed out, leaving only a glassy, vacant stare that reflected the black teardrop's empty darkness. I was quite taken aback by this change, as was Mashbourne. Only Holmes maintained his cool detachment.

"Have you tried any medicines to induce sleep?" I asked.

"Any number of them, Doctor. *Valeriana,* passionflower, warm milk, chamomile tea, a short walk before dark, a hot bath before bed. Lately I have even ordered special elixirs from an apothecary in London. Nothing has helped."

I looked at Holmes, whose expression revealed nothing.

"You must try some of my brandy," said Mashbourne, pulling the silver flask from his waistcoat. "It puts me to sleep even at the noon hour."

She smiled at him with such a sad affection that it put a lump in my own throat. "I *have* tried it, Arthur," she said.

"Yes, you're right. You have," he said softly. Then he turned to us and spoke forcefully, "We *must* uncover the mystery behind this."

"I should think one night's sleep in this house and I will have the answer," said Holmes.

Lady Carthon rose from her chair, and we rose with her. With a warm, sad smile, she said, "My sweet champions. I feel most fortunate to have you as my guests this evening."

"It has been our pleasure, I assure you, madam," I said.

She bid us good evening, leaving instructions with a servant to turn down two more beds, and departed from us for the night.

We watched her leave in silence. When she was gone, Holmes turned to Mashbourne. "The circumstances of the lady's husband's death, if you please."

Mashbourne cleared his throat with a swallow of wine, then began. "As Emily has said, Captain Carthon was on patrol with his men in the desert near the Great Pyramids. I was assigned to his regiment as physician. Carthon's men reportedly came upon a group of grave robbers one evening making off with a large quantity of antiquities from a recently uncovered burial sight. There was a brief but bloody skirmish, and the robbers were apprehended.

"Now, as Captain Carthon related to me in secret after he had secured the pilfered treasures with the royal governor, he'd come across something amongst the many items that he fancied would make an excellent gift for his wife. He showed me the necklace we all saw her wearing this evening. What followed, oddly, were several nights of unrest among the soldiers of the regiment."

"Sleeplessness, you mean?" asked Holmes.

"Yes," Mashbourne said, "but not to this degree. It lasted no more than a week. Then one night while out on patrol again, Carthon was murdered. Some said it was the grave robbers come back for their loot, but I was certain it had to have been a wild animal of some sort, for I examined the body, and it had been very badly mutilated.

"It was my unfortunate task, since I was returning to England, to deliver the unpleasant news, along with some of her husband's effects, to Lady Carthon."

"And the necklace was among those items?" asked Holmes.

"No," said Mashbourne. "I believe he sent that to her earlier, before he was killed."

I could see Holmes's mind working again. "You said earlier that you were on to something," I said to him. "Care to share it yet?"

"I have a theory, which I plan to put to the test tonight," was all that Holmes offered.

"Come now," said Mashbourne, clearly annoyed. "Is there no small crumb you might leave for us as a trail to follow your reasoning?"

"A crumb would leave you most unsatisfied," he said, pushing back his chair. "Now, I'm afraid I must leave you, gentlemen. Sleep well." As he reached the doorway, he turned again to us. "And keep a light on. If you encounter anything unusual this evening, any unnatural sounds or the like, come find me at once. I'm certain I shall be awake." Then he was gone.

"He is a singularly peculiar fellow, is he not, Watson?" said Mashbourne.

"That he is," I replied.

After cigars and a bit of Mashbourne's brandy, we, too, retired for the night, a servant leading us upstairs and delivering us to our rooms.

"Good evening, Dr. Mashbourne," I said as I left him.

"Good evening, Dr. Watson. I'm sure that I, for one, shall sleep soundly tonight. This day has truly exhausted me."

He closed himself inside his room.

I shut my own door and found that a robe and pajamas had been laid out for me on what looked to be a most comfortable bed. A pitcher of water sat on a nightstand nearby, and I helped myself to a glass before dousing the light and climbing beneath the covers.

As I lay there, my eyes growing accustomed to the dark, I ruminated over Holmes's last words, wondering as to what sort of unnatural sounds he referred. I listened carefully, surveying the night around me, and as my ears grew accustomed to the silence, I heard the sounds of the wind blowing through the trees outside, of an unlatched shutter banging softly in some distant part of the house.

★   ★   ★

I awoke to a crash. Attempting to rise, I found myself paralyzed, save for my eyes, which were wide open but useless in the utter darkness. I tried to maintain calm, convincing myself that the paralysis must be gone momentarily, that I most certainly must be dreaming. But then I heard a key twisting in the lock—*had I bolted my door?*—and sensed someone enter the inky blackness of my room.

I cursed myself at that moment for having ignored Holmes's advice and dousing my light. Dark foreboding, a sense of malevolent evil, gripped me then. My heart began to race. I struggled vainly to get up—my arms and legs tingling, sweat forming on my brow, my breath sorely entering and leaving my chest—but still I was unable to rise.

I heard footsteps, coming nearer to my bedside. I told myself it was just a servant, looking in on me, or perhaps someone sleepwalking, but the panic in my heart rose to a crescendo, and something *leaped up onto my chest!* Cold hands grasped at my throat, strangling me. I gasped for air, trying to cry out for help as the breath left my lungs beneath the weight of my assailant.

Just as the darkness was about to swallow me, the door to my room crashed open with such force that it fell from its hinges, and blessed light poured in from the hallway.

A *creature*—for I know not what else to name it—was revealed by the light, crouched menacingly over me! No child's fairy story was this, but a roughly bipedal, forward-slumping beast, with a vaguely canine cast, a doglike face with pointed ears. The texture of its flesh was a kind of unpleasant rubberiness. This nameless blasphemy stared at me with glaring red eyes, its scaly claws around my throat, its flat nose and drooling lips expelling the thing's acrid, fetid breath upon me. Fanged teeth set all askew in its gaping maw were poised to rend me, when it howled its hatred at the sudden brightness, stretched out hideous black wings, and releasing me, flew directly toward the blazing doorway where Holmes stood, a lantern in one hand and his revolver in the other.

Holmes fired off a shot, striking the beast in the chest. The force merely knocked the creature backward a step, before it leaped again at him, wailing with fury. I saw Holmes empty his revolver point-blank into the beast, sending it toppling over dead at his feet.

"Watson! Are you all right?" he said.

I had managed to prop myself up on one elbow, the paralysis waning. "I don't know," I replied, still badly shaken, and examined myself for wounds. I'd been bruised about the shoulders and neck, but otherwise remained mercifully unscathed.

"Can you stand, old man?"

"Yes, I believe so," I said, making a poor show of it, my legs trembling.

Movement on the floor caught my eye then, and I watched with Holmes in wonder as the dead thing slowly melted into a sulfurous oozing tallow, seeping through the floorboards until it was gone.

"What in God's name was that?" I asked Holmes.

"Nothing of this world," he said. "Now come, this way."

I followed him to Mashbourne's room, where, from the glow of Holmes's lantern, I could see the poor man lying sprawled on the floor, his sleeping gown covered in blood. I moved quickly to his side, checking his wrist for a pulse. Finding none there, I moved to his neck, withdrawing in horror when I saw that his throat had been torn open.

"He is beyond help," I said to Holmes, then leaped to my feet. "Lady Carthon!"

We raced down the long dark central corridor, all the while my heart dreading what we might find once we reached her room.

"Why are all the candles out?" I asked, my voice cracking.

"I put them out," said Holmes. "To test my theory."

I looked to him with confusion, but he offered nothing further. When we reached the door to Lady Carthon's chamber, we found it partially open, and the room swathed in darkness. As we entered, I feared that she, too, had fallen prey to this night creature. But when Holmes swept his lantern across the room, the beam fell upon Lady Carthon, lying motionless upon her bed, her hand dangling over the edge, and several glass vials lying on the floor close by.

"Dear God," I said as I raced to her side, taking up her hand and feeling for her pulse.

Holmes picked up one of the vials and examined it closely, running a finger along the open edge and putting it to his lips.

"The apothecary's tincture," he said. "From the number of empty vials here, I'd say she's swallowed quite a bit of it."

"A suicide?" I asked.

"It would appear so," he replied.

I could feel no pulse on her wrist, and moved my hand to her neck. And there, thankfully, I felt the faint beating of her heart.

"She lives!" I said with a mixture of relief and apprehension that she still might succumb, and tried to rouse her, shaking her shoulders quite vigorously.

"Lady Carthon! Lady Carthon! Wake up!"

Holmes grabbed a pitcher of water nearby and splashed some on her face. Finally, she stirred.

"Oh God," she said softly. "What has happened?"

"You have taken too much sleep medicine," I said gently, trying not to frighten her.

She looked at me, quite puzzled.

"Do you remember anything?" asked Holmes.

"I remember preparing for bed, as I always do, hoping this would be the night when I finally found sleep. But as I was removing my necklace, my thoughts went to my husband, wishing it was he who had removed it, wishing he were here still, holding me in his arms, and I knew right then I would remain restless another night. I broke down, I think, and took all that remained of the sleeping drug."

"And then?" said Holmes.

"Nothing. Just the darkness. The horrible, unending darkness. I couldn't find my way out of the darkness." She looked up at us then, seeing the blood that covered my hands and my night-clothes. "Dr. Watson, what's happened? Where is Arthur?"

I could not bring myself to speak, leaving it to Holmes.

"Dead," was all he said.

She began to sob. "This is all my fault."

"I think not," said Holmes. "He was not murdered by your hand."

"It came for me," she said, shaking her head from side to side. "In the night. From those hideous dreams."

"What do you mean?" I said. "The creature came for you?"

"It wanted something from me. That night in January, when the moon went dark. *I knew that it wanted something, but God help me, I could not comprehend what.* A key, I think. An opening. A door-way to some other place. I could not understand what it wanted. I felt its thoughts, but its language was foreign to me. I begged it to leave me be. But it would not give me a single night's rest. Each time I tried to close my eyes, each time I allowed myself to be in darkness, it came haunting me again. I warned people. I told them to keep their lights on at night, to avoid the darkness. It feared the light. Hated the light. It came from the darkness, you know, from the void. It traveled a great distance, searching . . ."

"Searching for what?" I asked.

"I do not know," she said softly.

"Well, it can search no more," said Holmes, taking up the neck-lace from where it lay at her bedside. "We have put an end to it."

We dressed quickly, leaving Carthon on foot as the sun was rising. Looking back at the mansion, we found it a much different place in the day. It had a sadness, a solemnity, which neither sunlight nor lamplight could ever hope to hide. The glowing beacon of light that lit up the previous evening was gone, a dream turned nightmare, and now in the daytime the illusion was replaced by stark, unpleasant reality.

As we walked back to Inswich, I asked Holmes to recount what he had done after he left Mashbourne and me the previous night, and how he had happened to come to my rescue so quickly.

"After I bid the two of you good night," he said, "I followed Lady Carthon to her room, making sure she had put herself safely away for the evening. When you and Mashbourne adjourned to your rooms, I began to put out the lights, moving from the far eastern side of the manor to the west. I was hoping to call out this thing, to confront it, to ascertain whether it really existed at all. That is when I heard it—"

"The beast that nearly killed me?" I asked.

"Yes," he replied. "I heard a terrible crash, from Mashbourne's room. I lit my lantern and raced to him, but it was too late. Then I went immediately to summon you. Finding the door locked, I proceeded to shoulder it open."

"And I am most grateful that you did, my friend."

"I'm sorry, Watson. I had not expected you both to put out your lights. I had instructed you not to."

"Force of habit, old man," I said. "Not your fault at all."

"I should have anticipated that possibility," he said. "I should have been more forceful in my instructions. Perhaps it was my own fatigue, but I did not think the beast would act so murderously."

"I still don't understand why you believed the stories of this creature. They sounded most preposterous to me."

"I could only conjecture, Watson," he replied.

"But how could you even guess?" I said, trying to comprehend his reasoning.

"First, there was the fact that no one could offer any other cause, or medical explanation, for such a widespread epidemic of sleeplessness. A hysterical condition did not seem out of the question at first. No doubt the lady's warnings put everyone on edge. And the soporific had me a bit confused as well, I must admit, for it seemed that when it was first administered, the citizens did sleep through the night, but their symptoms soon returned. And after hearing tales of a creature from so many, seeing the child's drawing, and sensing the carriage driver's dread of this place, I began to suspect there was more truth than superstition to these stories.

"But it was Mashbourne himself who finally convinced me. He saw the body of Captain Carthon. He said it did not look to him like he was murdered by grave robbers, but mutilated by some wild animal."

"And you think it was the same creature that killed Mashbourne?"

"The very same."

"But why?"

"For this," said Holmes, pulling Lady Carthon's necklace out of his pocket.

"The necklace?" I said.

"Not the necklace," said Holmes. "The stone on the necklace."

I looked at what he held in his hand. In the daylight, it seemed merely a black rock, the obsidian trinket of some long-dead Egyptian. Yet when I stared at it awhile, Holmes had to call my name loudly to regain my attention.

"This is the key that Lady Carthon spoke of?" I asked.

"I believe so, Watson," he said. "As I listened to her talk about the creature, about what it seemed to be after, I recalled something I had read in a dark text, rarely mentioned, written by a mad Arab, about objects that act as windows on the void, objects older than this earth, which lay buried in lightless crypts built by long-forgotten pharaohs."

"Not forgotten long enough," I said, still transfixed by the black stone. "So this is what got Captain Carthon murdered?"

"Undoubtedly," said Holmes. "And more might have died if Lady Carthon had not discovered the creature's weakness, and warned the whole town to always keep a light on."

"How did it know to come to Inswich at all? And why did it

take so long to get here?" I asked, trying to fit the remaining pieces of the puzzle together.

"No doubt it could sense where the stone was. But it seems it was only able to travel such a great distance in total darkness," said Holmes.

"The eclipse," I said, finally understanding everything.

"Correct," said Holmes.

"So what will you do with the thing?" I asked. "Turn it over to the Royal Society?"

"No, Watson. That would be too dangerous. I'm afraid this is beyond our abilities to reason, beyond science's understanding. I think perhaps that I must drop it in some deep well, and hope to never hear from it again."

At the Black Hart, the innkeeper was asleep in her rocking chair, quietly snoring. We went to our rooms and collected our things, then left sovereigns on the counter as payment, without disturbing the good woman.

Outside, we found our chatty driver, asleep atop his transom. Holmes nudged him awake.

"Apologies, guv," he said. "I musta dozed off." Recognizing us, he added with surprise, "I see you're safely back from Carthon. Where can I take you, gentlemen?"

"To the station at Barrington, my good man," said Holmes, flipping him a sovereign. "And an extra guinea if you get us there before the nine o'clock to London leaves."

He eagerly jumped down from his perch, taking our bags and securing them to the rear of the open carriage as we climbed up. In a moment we were off.

"Barrington's a nice spot," he said. "Me mother-in-law lives there."

He continued talking the entire length of the ride back to town, but I was too lost in my own thoughts to pay him any heed. Upon our arrival, Holmes asked him to stop at the local constabulary.

"Has some crime been committed?" the man asked.

"No," I said quickly. "Just an unfortunate accident."

We found the constable, a short, stout man of fifty, quietly snoring away at his desk. Once he was sufficiently recovered from the embarrassment of being found asleep at his post, Holmes related to him the episode of the previous evening, carefully omitting the more fantastic elements, substituting a rabid dog for the otherworldly beast, and ending it all by explaining that there was a body to be found at Carthon House.

We made the nine o'clock train with time to spare and settled in for the long journey home. Later that day, Holmes would make arrangements for Lady Carthon to spend time convalescing at a sanitarium outside London. The unpleasant task of notifying Mashbourne's next of kin he left to me.

As we departed the station, I turned to see my friend fast asleep, his arms crossed, his chin resting comfortably upon his chest, his breathing slow and measured. I envied him his quietude. After what I had seen at Carthon, it would be some time before I could sleep as soundly.

The Adventure of the Voorish Sign

RICHARD A. LUPOFF

It was by far the most severe winter London had known in human memory, perhaps since the Romans had founded their settlement of Londinium nearly two millennia ago. Storms had swept down from the North Sea, cutting off the Continent and blanketing the great metropolis with thick layers of snow that were quickly blackened by the choking fumes of ten thousand charcoal braziers, turning to a treacherous coating of ice when doused with only slightly warmer peltings of sleet.

Even so, Holmes and I were snug in our quarters at 221B Baker Street. The fire had been laid, we had consumed a splendid dinner of meat pasties and red cabbage served by the ever-reliable Mrs. Hudson, and I found myself dreaming over an aged brandy and a pipe while Holmes devoted himself to his newest passion.

He had raided our slim exchequer for sufficient funds to purchase one of Mr. Emile Berliner's new gramophones, imported by Harrods of Brompton Road. He had placed one of Mr. Berliner's new disk recordings on the machine, advertised as a marked improvement over the traditional wax cylinders. But the sounds that emerged from the horn were neither pleasant nor tuneful to my ears. Instead they were of a weird and disquieting nature, seemingly discordant yet suggestive of strange harmonies which it would be better not to understand.

As I was about to ask Holmes to shut off the contraption, the melody came to an end and Holmes removed the needle from its groove.

Holmes pressed an upraised finger against his thin lips and sharply uttered my name. "Watson!" he repeated as I lowered my pipe. The brandy snifter had very nearly slipped from my grasp, but I was able to catch it in time to prevent a disastrous spill.

"What is it, Holmes?" I inquired.

"Listen!"

He held one hand aloft, an expression of intense concentration upon his saturnine features. He nodded toward the shuttered windows which gave out upon Baker Street.

"I hear nothing except the whistle of the wind against the eaves," I told him.

"Listen more closely."

I tilted my head, straining to hear whatever it was that had caught Holmes's attention. There was a creak from below, followed by the sound of a door opening and closing, and a rapping of knuckles against solid wood, the latter sound muffled as by thin cloth.

I looked at Holmes, who pressed a long finger against his lips, indicating that silence was required. He nodded toward our door, and in a few moments I heard the tread of Mrs. Hudson ascending to our lodging. Her sturdy pace was accompanied by another, light and tentative in nature.

Holmes drew back our front door to reveal our landlady, her hand raised to knock. "Mr. Holmes!" she gasped.

"Mrs. Hudson, I see that you have brought with you Lady Fairclough of Pontefract. Will you be so kind as to permit Lady Fairclough to enter, and would you be so good as to brew a hot cup of tea for my lady. She must be suffering from her trip through this wintry night."

Mrs. Hudson turned away and made her way down the staircase while the slim young woman who had accompanied her entered our sitting room with a series of long, graceful strides. Behind her, Mrs. Hudson had carefully placed a carpetbag valise upon the floor.

"Lady Fairclough." Holmes addressed the newcomer. "May I introduce my associate, Dr. Watson. Of course you know who I am, which is why you have come to seek my assistance. But first, please warm yourself by the fire. Dr. Watson will fetch a bottle of brandy with which we will fortify the hot tea that Mrs. Hudson is preparing."

The newcomer had not said a word, but her face gave proof of her astonishment that Holmes had known her identity and home without being told. She wore a stylish hat trimmed in dark fur and a carefully tailored coat with matching decorations at collar and cuffs. Her feet were covered in boots that disappeared beneath the lower hem of her coat.

I helped her off with her outer garment. By the time I had placed it in our closet, Lady Fairclough was comfortably settled in our best chair, holding slim hands toward the cheerily dancing flames. She had removed her gloves and laid them with seemingly careless precision across the wooden arm of her chair.

"Mr. Holmes," she said in a voice that spoke equally of cultured sensitivity and barely repressed terror, "I apologize for disturbing you and Dr. Watson at this late hour, but—"

"There is no need for apologies, Lady Fairclough. On the contrary, you are to be commended for having the courage to cross the Atlantic in the midst of winter, and the captain of the steamship *Murania* is to be congratulated for having negotiated the crossing successfully. It is unfortunate that our customs agents delayed your disembarkation as they did, but now that you are here, perhaps you will enlighten Dr. Watson and myself as to the problem which has beset your brother, Mr. Philip Llewellyn."

If Lady Fairclough had been startled by Holmes's recognizing her without introduction, she was clearly amazed beyond my meager powers of description by this statement. She raised a hand to her cheek, which showed a smoothness of complexion and grace of curve in the flattering glow of the dancing flames. "Mr. Holmes," she exclaimed, "how did you know all that?"

"It was nothing, Lady Fairclough, one need merely keep one's senses on the alert and one's mind active." A glance that Holmes darted in my direction was not welcome, but I felt constrained from protesting in the presence of a guest and potential client.

"So you say, Mr. Holmes, but I have read of your exploits and in many cases they seem little short of supernatural," Lady Fairclough replied.

"Not in the least. Let us consider the present case. Your valise bears the paper label of the Blue Star Line. The *Murania* and the *Lemuria* are the premiere ocean liners of the Blue Star Line, alternating upon the easterly and westerly transatlantic sea-lanes. Even a fleeting glance at the daily shipping news indicates that the *Murania* was due in Liverpool early this morning. If the ship made port at even so late an hour as ten o'clock, in view of the fact that the rail journey from Liverpool to London requires a mere two hours, you should have reached our city by noon. Another hour at most from the rail terminus to Baker Street would have brought you to our door by one o'clock this afternoon. And yet," concluded Holmes, glancing at the ormolu clock that rested upon our mantel, "you arrive at the surprising hour of ten o'clock *post meridian*."

"But, Holmes," I interjected, "Lady Fairclough may have had other errands to perform before coming to us."

"No, Watson, no. I fear that you have failed to draw the proper inference from that which you have surely observed. You did note, did you not, that Lady Fairclough has brought her carpetbag with her?"

I pled guilty to the charge.

"Surely, had she not been acting in great haste, Lady Fairclough would have gone to her hotel, refreshed herself, and left her luggage in her quarters there before traveling to Baker Street. The fact that she has but one piece of luggage with her gives further testimony to the urgency with which she departed her home in Canada. Now, Watson, what could have caused Lady Fairclough to commence her trip in such haste?"

I shook my head. "I confess that I am at a loss."

"It was but eight days ago that the *Daily Mail* carried a dispatch marked Marthyr Tydhl, a town situated on the border of England and Wales, concerning the mysterious disappearance of Mr. Philip Llewellyn. There would have been time for word to reach Lady Fairclough in Pontefract by transatlantic cable. Fearing that delay in traveling to the port and boarding the *Murania* would cause intolerable delay, Lady Fairclough had her maid pack the fewest possible necessities in her carpetbag. She then made her way to Halifax, whence the *Murania* departed, and upon reaching Liverpool this morning would have made her way at once to London. Yet she arrived some nine hours later than she might have been expected to do. Since our rail service remains uninterrupted in even the most severe of climatic conditions, it can only have been the customs service, equally notorious for their punctilio and their dilatory conduct, which could be responsible."

Turning once more to Lady Fairclough, Holmes said, "In behalf of Her Majesty's Customs Service, Lady Fairclough, I tender my apologies."

There was a knock at the door and Mrs. Hudson appeared, bearing a tray with hot tea and cold sandwiches. This she placed upon the table, then took her leave.

Lady Fairclough looked at the repast and said, "Oh, I simply could not."

"Nonsense," Holmes insisted. "You have completed an arduous journey and face a dangerous undertaking. You must keep up your strength." He rose and added brandy to Lady Fairclough's tea, then stood commandingly over her while she consumed the beverage and two sandwiches.

"I suppose I was hungry after all," she admitted at last. I was pleased to see some color returning to her cheeks. I had been seriously concerned about her well-being.

"Now, Lady Fairclough," said Holmes, "it might be well for you to go to your hotel and restore your strength with a good night's slumber. You do have a reservation, I trust."

"Oh, of course, at Claridge's. A suite was ordered for me through the courtesy of the Blue Star Line, but I could not rest now, Mr. Holmes. I am far too distraught to sleep until I have explained my need to you, and received your assurance that you and Dr. Watson will take my case. I have plenty of money, if that is a concern."

Holmes indicated that financial details could wait, but I was pleased to be included in our guest's expression of need. So often I find myself taken for granted, while in fact I am Holmes's trusted associate, as he has himself acknowledged on many occasions.

"Very well." Holmes nodded, seating himself opposite Lady Fairclough. "Please tell me your story in your own words, being as precise with details as possible."

Lady Fairclough drained her cup and waited while Holmes filled it once again with brandy and a spot of Darjeeling. She downed another substantial draft, then launched upon her narrative.

"As you know, Mr. Holmes—and Dr. Watson—I was born in

England of old stock. Despite our ancient Welsh connections and family name, we have been English for a thousand years. I was the elder of two children, the younger being my brother, Philip. As a daughter, I saw little future for myself in the home islands, and accepted the proposal of marriage tendered by my husband, Lord Fairclough, whose Canadian holdings are substantial and who indicated to me a desire to emigrate to Canada and build a new life there, which we would share."

I had taken out my notebook and fountain pen and begun jotting notes.

"At about this time my parents were both killed in a horrendous accident, the collision of two trains in the Swiss Alps while vacationing abroad. Feeling that an elaborate wedding would be disrespectful of the deceased, Lord Fairclough and I were quietly married and took our leave of England. We lived happily in Pontefract, Canada, until my husband disappeared."

"Indeed," Holmes interjected, "I had read of Lord Fairclough's disappearance. I note that you refer to him as your husband rather than your late husband still, nor do I see any mourning band upon your garment. Is it your belief that your husband lives still?"

Lady Fairclough lowered her eyes for a moment as a flush rose to her cheeks. "Although ours was somewhat a marriage of convenience, I find that I have come to love my husband most dearly. There was no discord between us, if you are concerned over such, Mr. Holmes."

"Not in the least, Lady Fairclough."

"Thank you." She sipped from her teacup. Holmes peered at it, then refreshed its contents once again. "Thank you," Lady Fairclough repeated. "My husband had been corresponding with his brother-in-law, my brother, and later, after my brother's marriage, with my brother's wife, for some time before he disappeared. I saw the envelopes as they came and went, but I was never permitted to so much as lay eyes on their contents. After reading each newly delivered letter, my husband would burn it and crush the ashes beyond recovery. After receiving one very lengthy letter—I could tell it was lengthy by the heft of the envelope in which it arrived— my husband summoned carpenters and prepared a sealed room which I was forbidden to enter. Of course I obeyed my husband's command."

"A wise policy," I put in. "One knows the story of Bluebeard."

"He would lock himself in his private chamber for hours at a time, sometimes days. When he disappeared, in fact, I half expected him to return at any moment." Lady Fairclough put her hand to her throat. "Please," she said softly, "I beg your pardon for the impropriety, but I feel suddenly so warm." I glanced away, and when I looked back at her I observed that the top button of her blouse had been undone.

"My husband has been gone now for two years, and all have given him up for dead save myself, and I will concede that even my hopes are of the faintest. During the period of correspondence between my husband and my brother, my husband began to absent himself from all human society from time to time. Gradually the frequency and duration of his disappearances increased. I feared I knew not what—perhaps that he had become addicted to some drug or unspeakable vice for the indulging of which he preferred isolation. I inferred that he had caused the construction of the sealed room for this purpose, and determined that I should learn its secret."

She bowed her head and drew a series of long, sobbing breaths, which caused her graceful bosom visibly to heave. After a time she raised her face. Her cheeks were wet with tears. She resumed her narrative.

"I summoned a locksmith from the village and persuaded him to aid me in gaining entry. When I stood at last in my husband's secret chamber I found myself confronting a room completely devoid of feature. The ceiling, the walls, the floor were all plain and devoid of ornament. There were neither windows nor fireplace, nor any other means of egress from the room."

Holmes nodded, frowning. "There was nothing noteworthy about the room, then?" he asked at length.

"Yes, Mr. Holmes, there was." Lady Fairclough's response startled me so, I nearly dropped my fountain pen, but I recovered and returned to my note taking.

"At first the room seemed a perfect cube. The ceiling, floor, and four walls each appeared absolutely square and mounted at a precise right angle to one another. But as I stood there, they seemed to—I suppose, *shift* is the closest I can come to it, Mr. Holmes, but they did not actually move in any familiar manner. And yet their shape seemed to be different, and the angles to become peculiar, obtuse, and to open onto other—how to put this?—*dimensions.*"

She seized Holmes's wrist in her graceful fingers and leaned toward him pleadingly. "Do you think I am insane, Mr. Holmes? Has my grief driven me to the brink of madness? There are times when I think I can bear no more strangeness."

"You are assuredly not insane," Holmes told her. "You have stumbled upon one of the strangest and most dangerous of phenomena, a phenomenon barely suspected by even the most advanced of mathematical theoreticians and spoken of even by them in only the most cautious of whispers."

He withdrew his arm from her grasp, shook his head, and said, "If your strength permits, you must continue your story, please."

"I will try," she answered.

I waited, fountain pen poised above notebook.

Our visitor shuddered as with a fearsome recollection. "Once I had left the secret room, sealing it behind myself, I attempted to resume a normal life. It was days later that my husband reappeared, refusing as usual to give any explanation of his recent whereabouts. Shortly after this a dear friend of mine living in Quebec gave birth to a child. I had gone to be with her when word was received of the great Pontefract earthquake. In this disaster a fissure appeared in the earth and our house was completely swallowed. I was, fortunately, left in a state of financial independence, and have never suffered from material deprivation. But I have never again seen my husband. Most believe that he was in the house at the time of its disappearance, and was killed at once, but I retain a hope, however faint, that he may somehow have survived."

She paused to compose herself, then resumed.

"But I fear I am getting ahead of myself. It was shortly before my husband ordered the construction of his sealed room that my brother, Philip, announced his engagement and the date of his impending nuptials. I thought the shortness of his intended period of engagement was unseemly, but in view of my own marriage and departure to Canada so soon after my parents' death, I was in no position to condemn Philip. My husband and I booked passage to England, on the *Lemuria* in fact, and from Liverpool made our way to the family lands in Marthyr Tydhl."

She shook her head as if to free it of an unpleasant memory.

"Upon arriving at Anthracite Palace, I was shocked by my brother's appearance."

At this point I interrupted our guest with a query.

"Anthracite Palace? Is that not an unusual name for a family manse?"

"Our family residence was so named by my ancestor, Sir Llewys Llewellyn, who built the family fortune, and the manor, by operating a network of successful coal mines. As you are probably aware, the region is rich in anthracite. The Llewellyns pioneered modern mining methods which rely upon gelignite explosives to loosen banks of coal for the miners to remove from their native sites. In the region of Marthyr Tydhl, where the Anthracite Palace is located, the booming of gelignite charges is heard to this day, and stores of the explosive are kept at the mine heads."

I thanked her for the clarification and suggested that she continue with her narrative.

"My brother was neatly barbered and clothed, but his hands shook, his cheeks were sunken, and his eyes had a frightened, hunted look to them," she said. "When I toured my childhood home I was shocked to find its interior architecture modified. There was now a sealed room, just as there had been at Pontefract. I was not permitted to enter that room. I expressed my concern at my brother's appearance but he insisted he was well and introduced his fiancée, who was already living at the palace."

I drew my breath with a gasp.

"Yes, Doctor," Lady Fairclough responded, "you heard me correctly. She was a woman of dark, Gypsyish complexion, glossy sable hair, and darting eyes. I disliked her at once. She gave her own name, not waiting for Philip to introduce her properly. Her maiden name, she announced, was Anastasia Romelly. She claimed to be of noble Hungarian blood, allied both to the Habsburgs and the Romanovs."

"Humph," I grunted, "Eastern European nobility is a ha'penny a dozen, and three-quarters of them aren't real even at that."

"Perhaps true," Holmes snapped at me, "but we do not know that the credentials of the lady involved were other than authentic." He frowned and turned away. "Lady Fairclough, please continue."

"She insisted on wearing her native costume. And she had persuaded my brother to replace his chef with one of her own choosing, whom she had imported from her homeland and who replaced our usual menu of good English fare with unfamiliar dishes reeking of odd spices and unknown ingredients. She imported strange wines and ordered them served with meals."

I shook my head in disbelief.

"The final straw came upon the day of her wedding to my brother. She insisted upon being given away by a surly, dark man who appeared for the occasion, performed his duty, and then disappeared. She—"

"A moment, please," Holmes interrupted. "If you will forgive me—you say that this man disappeared. Do you mean that he took his leave prematurely?"

"No, I do not mean that at all." Lady Fairclough was clearly excited. A moment earlier she had seemed on the verge of tears. Now she was angry and eager to unburden herself of her tale.

"In a touching moment, he placed the bride's hand upon that of the groom. Then he raised his own hand. I thought his intent was to place his benediction upon the couple, but such was not the case. He made a gesture with his hand, as if making a mystical sign."

She raised her own hand from her lap, but Holmes snapped, "Do not, I warn you, attempt to replicate the gesture! Please, if you can, simply describe it to Dr. Watson and myself."

"I could not replicate the gesture if I tried," Lady Fairclough said. "It defies imitation. I cannot even describe it accurately, I fear. I was fascinated and tried to follow the movement of the dark man's fingers, but I could not. They seemed to disappear and reappear most shockingly, and then, without further warning, he was simply gone. I tell you, Mr. Holmes, one moment the dark man was there, and then he was gone."

"Did no one else take note of this, my lady?"

"No one did, apparently. Perhaps all eyes were trained upon the bride and groom, although I believe I did notice the presiding official exchanging several glances with the dark man. Of course, that was before his disappearance."

Holmes stroked his jaw, deep in thought. There was a lengthy silence in the room, broken only by the ticking of the ormolu clock and whistling of the wind through the eaves. Finally Holmes spoke.

"It can be nothing other than the Voorish Sign," he said.

"The Voorish Sign?" Lady Fairclough repeated inquiringly.

Holmes said, "Never mind. This becomes more interesting by the moment, and also more dangerous. Another question, if you please. Who was the presiding official at the wedding? He was, I would assume, a priest of the Church of England."

"No." Lady Fairclough shook her head once again. "The official was neither a member of the Anglican clergy nor a *he*. The wedding was performed by a woman."

I gasped in surprise, drawing still another sharp glance from Holmes.

"She wore robes such as I have never seen," our guest resumed. "There were symbols, both astronomical and astrological, embroidered in silver thread and gold, green, blue, and red. There were other symbols totally unfamiliar to me, suggestive of strange geometries and odd shapes. The ceremony itself was conducted in a language I had never before heard, and I am something of a linguist, Mr. Holmes. I believe I detected a few words of Old Temple Egyptian, a phrase in Coptic Greek, and several suggestions of Sanskrit. Other words I did not recognize at all."

Holmes nodded. I could see the excitement growing in his eyes, the excitement that I saw only when a fascinating challenge was presented to him.

He asked, "What was this person's name?"

"Her name," Lady Fairclough voiced through teeth clenched in anger, or perhaps in the effort to prevent their chattering with fear, "was Vladimira Petrovna Ludmilla Romanova. She claimed the title of Archbishop of the Wisdom Temple of the Dark Heavens."

"Why—why," I exclaimed, "I've never heard of such a thing! This is sheer blasphemy!"

"It is something far worse than blasphemy, Watson." Holmes leaped to his feet and paced rapidly back and forth. At one point he halted near our front window, being careful not to expose himself to the direct sight of anyone lurking below. He peered down into Baker Street, something I have seen him do many times in our years together. Then he did something I had not seen before. Drawing himself back still farther, he gazed upward. What he hoped to perceive in the darkened winter sky other than falling snowflakes, I could hardly imagine.

"Lady Fairclough," he intoned at length, "you have been remarkably strong and courageous in your performance here this night. I will now ask Dr. Watson to see you to your hotel. You mentioned Claridge's, I believe. I will ask Dr. Watson to remain in your suite throughout the remainder of the night. I assure you, Lady Fairclough, that he is a person of impeccable character, and your virtue will in no way be compromised by his presence."

"Even so, Holmes," I objected, "the lady's virtue is one thing, her reputation is another."

The matter was resolved by Lady Fairclough herself. "Doctor, while I appreciate your concern, we are dealing with a most serious matter. I will accept the suspicious glances of prudes and the smirks of servants if I must. The lives of my husband and my brother are at stake."

Unable to resist the lady's argument, I followed Holmes's directions and accompanied her to Claridge's. At his insistence I even went so far as to arm myself with a large revolver, which I tucked into the top of my woolen trousers. Holmes warned me, also, to permit no one save himself entry to Lady Fairclough's suite.

Once my temporary charge had retired, I sat in a straight chair, prepared to pass the night in a game of solitaire. Lady Fairclough had donned camisole and hair net and climbed into her bed. I will admit that my cheeks burned, but I reminded myself that in my medical capacity I was accustomed to viewing patients in a disrobed condition, and could surely assume an avuncular role while keeping watch over this courageous lady.

There was a loud rapping at the door. I jerked awake, realizing to my chagrin that I had fallen asleep over my solitary card game. I rose to my feet, went to Lady Fairclough's bedside and assured myself that she was unharmed, and then placed myself at the door to her suite. In response to my demand that our visitor identify himself, a male voice announced simply, "Room service, guv'ner."

My hand was on the doorknob, my other hand on the latch, when I remembered Holmes's warning at Baker Street to permit no one entry. Surely a hearty breakfast would be welcome; I could almost taste the kippers and the toast and jam that Mrs. Hudson would have served us, had we been still in our home. But Holmes had been emphatic. What to do? What to do?

"We did not order breakfast." I spoke through the heavy oaken door.

"Courtesy of the management, guv."

Perhaps, I thought, I might admit a waiter bearing food. What harm could there be in that? I reached for the latch only to find my hand tugged away by another, that of Lady Fairclough. She had climbed from her bed and crossed the room, barefoot and clad only in her sleeping garment. She shook her head vigorously, drawing me away from the door, which remained latched against any entry. She pointed to me, pantomiming speech. Her message was clear.

"Leave our breakfast in the hall," I instructed the waiter. "We shall fetch it in ourselves shortly. We are not ready as yet."

"Can't do it, sir," the waiter insisted. "Please, sir, don't get me in trouble wif the management, guv'ner. I needs to roll my cart into your room and leave the tray. I'll get in trouble if I don't, guv'ner."

I was nearly persuaded by his plea, but Lady Fairclough had placed herself between me and the door, her arms crossed and a determined expression on her face. Once again she indicated that I should send the waiter away.

"I'm sorry, my man, but I must insist. Simply leave the tray outside our door. That is my final word."

The waiter said nothing more, but I thought I could hear his reluctantly retreating footsteps.

I retired to make my morning ablutions while Lady Fairclough dressed.

Shortly thereafter, there was another rapping at the door. Fearing the worst, I drew my revolver. Perhaps this was more than a misdirected order for room service. "I told you to go away," I commanded.

"Watson, old man, open up. It is I, Holmes."

The voice was unmistakable; I felt as though a weight of a hundred stone had been lifted from my shoulders. I undid the door latch and stood aside as the best and wisest man I have ever known entered the apartment. I peered out into the hall after he had passed through the doorway. There was no sign of a service cart or breakfast tray.

Holmes asked, "What are you looking for, Watson?"

I explained the incident of the room-service call.

"You did well, Watson," he congratulated me. "You may be certain that was no waiter, nor was his mission one of service to Lady Fairclough and yourself. I have spent the night consulting my files and certain other sources with regard to the odd institution known as the Wisdom Temple of the Dark Heavens, and I can tell you that we are sailing dangerous waters indeed."

He turned to Lady Fairclough. "You will please accompany Dr. Watson and myself to Marthyr Tydhl. We shall leave at once. There is a chance that we may yet save the life of your brother, but we have no time to waste."

Without hesitation, Lady Fairclough strode to the wardrobe, pinned her hat to her hair, and donned the same warm coat she had worn when first I laid eyes on her, mere hours before.

"But, Holmes," I protested, "Lady Fairclough and I have not broken our fast."

"Never mind your stomach, Watson. There is no time to lose. We can purchase sandwiches from a vendor at the station."

Almost sooner than I can tell, we were seated in a first-class compartment heading westward toward Wales. As good as his word, Holmes had seen to it that we were nourished, and I for one felt the better for having downed even a light and informal meal.

The storm had at last abated and a bright sun shone down from a sky of the most brilliant blue upon fields and hillsides covered with a spotless layer of purest white. Hardly could one doubt the benevolence of the universe; I felt almost like a schoolboy setting off on holiday, but Lady Fairclough's fears and Holmes's serious demeanor brought my soaring spirits back to earth.

"It is as I feared, Lady Fairclough," Holmes explained. "Both your brother and your husband have been ensnared in a wicked cult that threatens civilization itself if it is not stopped."

"A cult?" Lady Fairclough echoed.

"Indeed. You told me that Bishop Romanova was a representative of the Wisdom Temple of the Dark Heavens, did you not?"

"She so identified herself, Mr. Holmes."

"Yes. Nor would she have reason to lie, not that any denizen of this foul nest would hesitate to do so, should it aid their schemes. The Wisdom Temple is a little-known organization—I would hesitate to dignify them with the title religion—of ancient origins. They have maintained a secretive stance while awaiting some cosmic cataclysm which I fear is nearly upon us."

"Cosmic—cosmic cataclysm? I say, Holmes, isn't that a trifle melodramatic?" I asked.

"Indeed it is, Watson. But it is nonetheless so. They refer to a coming time 'when the stars are right.' Once that moment arrives, they intend to perform an unholy rite that will 'open the portal,' whatever that means, to admit their masters to the earth. The members of the Wisdom Temple will then become overseers and oppressors of all humankind, in the service of the dread masters whom they will have admitted to our world."

I shook my head in disbelief. Outside the windows of our compartment I could see that our train was approaching the trestle that would carry us across the River Severn. It would not be much longer before we should detrain at Marthyr Tydhl.

"Holmes," I said, "I would never doubt your word."

"I know that, old man," he replied. "But something is bothering you. Out with it!"

"Holmes, this is madness. Dread masters, opening portals, unholy rites—this is something out of the pages of a penny dreadful. Surely you don't expect Lady Fairclough and myself to believe all this."

"But I do, Watson. You must believe it, for it is all true, and deadly serious. Lady Fairclough—you have set out to save your brother and if possible your husband, but in fact you have set us in play in a game whose stakes are not one or two mere individuals, but the fate of our planet."

Lady Fairclough pulled a handkerchief from her wrist and dabbed at her eyes. "Mr. Holmes, I have seen that strange room at Llewellyn Hall at Pontefract, and I can believe your every word, for all that I agree with Dr. Watson as to the fantastic nature of what you say. Might I ask how you know of this?"

"Very well," Holmes assented, "You are entitled to that information. I told you before we left Claridge's that I had spent the night in research. There are many books in my library, most of which are open to my associate, Dr. Watson, and to other men of goodwill, as surely he is. But there are others which I keep under lock and key."

"I am aware of that, Holmes," I interjected, "and I will admit that I have been hurt by your unwillingness to share those volumes with me. Often have I wondered what they contain."

"Good Watson, it was for your own protection, I assure you. Watson, Lady Fairclough, those books include *De los Mundos Amenazantes y Sombriosos* of Carlos Alfredo de Torrijos, *Emmorragia Sante* of Luigi Humberto Rosso, and *Das Bestrafen von der Tugendhaft* of Heinrich Ludvig Georg von Feldenstein, as well as the works of the brilliant Mr. Arthur Machen, of whom you may have heard. These tomes, some of them well over a thousand years old and citing still more remote sources whose origins are lost in the mists of antiquity, are frighteningly consistent in their predictions. Further, several of them, Lady Fairclough, refer to a certain powerful and fearsome mystical gesture."

Although Holmes was addressing our feminine companion, I said, "Gesture, Holmes? Mystical gesture? What nonsense is this?"

"Not nonsense at all, Watson. You are doubtless aware of the movement that our Romish brethren refer to as 'crossing themselves.' The Hebrews have a gesture of cabalistic origin that is alleged to bring good luck, and the Gypsies make a sign to turn away the evil eye. Several Asian races perform 'hand dances,' ceremonials of religious or magical significance, including the famous *hoo-la* known on the islands of Oahu and Maui in the Havai'ian archipelago."

"But these are all foolish superstitions, remnants of an earlier and more credulous age. Surely there is nothing to them, Holmes!"

"I wish I could have your assuredness, Watson. You are a man of science, for which I commend you, but 'There are more things in heaven and earth, Horatio, than are dreamed of in your philosophy.' Do not be too quick, Watson, to dismiss old beliefs. More often than not they have a basis in fact."

I shook my head and turned my eyes once more to the wintry countryside through which our conveyance was passing. Holmes addressed himself to our companion.

"Lady Fairclough, you mentioned a peculiar gesture that the dark stranger made at the conclusion of your brother's wedding ceremony."

"I did, yes. It was so strange, I felt almost as if I were being drawn into another world when he moved his hand. I tried to follow the movements, but I could not. And then he was gone."

Holmes nodded rapidly.

"The Voorish Sign, Lady Fairclough. The stranger was making the Voorish Sign. It is referred to in the works of Machen and others. It is a very powerful and a very evil gesture. You were fortunate that you were not drawn into that other world, fortunate indeed."

Before much longer we reached the rail terminus nearest to Marthyr Tydhl. We left our compartment and shortly were ensconced in a creaking trap whose driver whipped up his team and headed for the Anthracite Palace. It was obvious from his demeanor that the manor was a familiar landmark in the region.

"We should be greeted by Mrs. Morrissey, our housekeeper, when we reach the manor," Lady Fairclough said. "It was she who notified me of my brother's straits. She is the last of our old family retainers to remain with the Llewellyns of Marthyr Tydhl. One by one the new lady of the manor has arranged their departure and replaced them with a swarthy crew of her own countrymen. Oh, Mr. Holmes, it is all so horrid!"

Holmes did his best to comfort the frightened woman.

Soon the Anthracite Palace hove into view. As its name would suggest, it was built of the local native coal. Architects and masons had carved the jet-black deposits into building blocks and created an edifice that stood like a black jewel against the white backing of snow, its battlements glittering in the wintry sunlight.

Our trap was met by a liveried servant who instructed lesser servants to carry our meager luggage into the manor. Lady Fairclough, Holmes, and I were ourselves conducted into the main hall.

The building was lit with oversized candles whose flames were so shielded as to prevent any danger of the coal walls catching fire. It struck me that the Anthracite Palace was one of the strangest architectural conceits I had ever encountered. "Not a place I would like to live in, eh, Holmes?" I was trying for a tone of levity, but must confess that I failed to achieve it.

We were left waiting for an excessive period of time, in my opinion, but at length a tall wooden door swung back and a woman of commanding presence, exotic in appearance with her swarthy complexion, flashing eyes, sable locks and shockingly reddened lips, entered the hall. She nodded to Holmes and myself and exchanged a frigid semblance of a kiss with Lady Fairclough, whom she addressed as "sister."

Lady Fairclough demanded to see her brother, but Mrs. Llewellyn refused conversation until we were shown to our rooms and had time to refresh ourselves. We were summoned, in due course, to the dining hall. I was famished, and both relieved and my appetite further excited by the delicious odors that came to us as we were seated at the long, linen-covered table.

Only four persons were present. These were, of course, Holmes and myself, Lady Fairclough, and our hostess, Mrs. Llewellyn.

Lady Fairclough attempted once again to inquire as to the whereabouts of her brother, Philip.

Her sister-in-law replied only, "He is pursuing his devotions. We shall see him when the time comes 'round."

Failing to learn more about her brother, Lady Fairclough asked after the housekeeper, Mrs. Morrissey.

"I have sad news, sister dear," Mrs. Llewellyn said. "Mrs. Morrissey was taken ill very suddenly. Philip personally drove into Marthyr Tydhl to fetch a physician for her, but by the time they arrived, Mrs. Morrissey had expired. She was buried in the town cemetery. This all happened just last week. I knew that you were already en route from Canada, and it seemed best not to further distress you with this information."

"Oh no," Lady Fairclough gasped. "Not Mrs. Morrissey! She was like a mother to me. She was the kindest, dearest of women. She—" Lady Fairclough stopped, pressing her hand to her mouth. She inhaled deeply. "Very well, then." I could see a look of determination rising like a banked flame deep in her eye. "If she has died there is naught to be done for it."

There was a pillar of strength hidden within this seemingly weak female. I would not care to make an enemy of Lady Fairclough. I noted also that Mrs. Llewellyn spoke English fluently but with an accent that I found thoroughly unpleasant. It seemed to me that she, in turn, found the language distasteful. Clearly, these two were fated to clash. But the tension of the moment was broken by the arrival of our viands.

The repast was sumptuous in appearance, but every course, it seemed to me, had some flaw—an excessive use of spice, an overdone vegetable, an undercooked piece of meat or game, a fish that might have been kept a day too long before serving, a cream that had stood in a warm kitchen an hour longer than was wise. By the end of the meal my appetite had departed, but it was replaced by a sensation of queasiness and discomfort rather than satisfaction.

Servants brought cigars for Holmes and myself, an after-dinner brandy for the men, and sweet sherry for the women, but I put out my cigar after a single draft and noticed that Holmes did the same with his own. Even the beverage seemed in some subtle way to be faulty.

"Mrs. Llewellyn." Lady Fairclough addressed her sister-in-law when at last the latter seemed unable longer to delay confrontation. "I received a telegram via transatlantic cable concerning the disappearance of my brother. He failed to greet us upon our arrival, nor has there been any sign of his presence since then. I demand to know his whereabouts."

"Sister dear," replied Anastasia Romelly Llewellyn, "that telegram should never have been sent. Mrs. Morrissey transmitted it from Marthyr Tydhl while in town on an errand for the palace. When I learned of her presumption I determined to send her packing, I can assure you. It was only her unfortunate demise that prevented my doing so."

At this point my friend Holmes addressed our hostess.

"Madam, Lady Fairclough has journeyed from Canada to learn of her brother's circumstances. She has engaged me, along with my associate, Dr. Watson, to assist her in this enterprise. It is not my desire to make this affair any more unpleasant than is necessary, but I must insist upon your providing the information that Lady Fairclough is seeking."

I believe at this point that I observed a smirk, or at least the suggestion of one, pass across the face of Mrs. Llewellyn. But she quickly responded to Holmes's demand, her peculiar accent as pronounced and unpleasant as ever.

"We have planned a small religious service for this evening. You are all invited to attend, of course, even though I had expected only my dear sister-in-law to do so. However, the larger group will be accommodated."

"What is the nature of this religious service?" Lady Fairclough demanded.

Mrs. Llewellyn smiled. "It will be that of the Wisdom Temple, of course. The Wisdom Temple of the Dark Heavens. It is my hope that Bishop Romanova herself will preside, but absent her participation we can still conduct the service ourselves."

I reached for my pocket watch. "It's getting late, madam. Might I suggest that we get started, then!"

Mrs. Llewellyn turned her eyes upon me. In the flickering candlelight they seemed larger and darker than ever. "You do not understand, Dr. Watson. It is too early rather than too late to start our ceremony. We will proceed precisely at midnight. Until then, please feel free to enjoy the paintings and tapestries with which the Anthracite Palace is decorated, or pass the time in Mr. Llewellyn's library. Or, if you prefer, you may of course retire to your quarters and seek sleep."

Thus it was that we three separated temporarily, Lady Fairclough to pass some hours with her husband's chosen books, Holmes to an examination of the palace's art treasures, and I to bed.

I was awakened from a troubled slumber haunted by strange beings of nebulous form. Standing over my bed, shaking me by the shoulder, was my friend Sherlock Holmes. I could see a rim of snow adhering to the edges of his boots.

"Come, Watson," said he, "the game is truly afoot, and it is by far the strangest game we are ever likely to pursue."

Swiftly donning my attire, I accompanied Holmes as we made our way to Lady Fairclough's chamber. She had retired there after spending the hours since dinner in her brother's library, to refresh herself. She must have been awaiting our arrival, for she resopnded without delay to Holmes's knock and the sound of his voice.

Before we proceeded further Holmes drew me aside. He reached inside his vest and withdrew a small object which he held concealed in his hand. I could not see its shape, for he held it inside a clenched fist, but I could tell that it emitted a dark radiance, a faint suggestion of which I could see between his fingers.

"Watson," quoth he, "I am going to give you this. You must swear to me that you will not look at it, on pain of damage beyond anything you can so much as imagine. You must keep it upon your person, if possible in direct contact with your body, at all times. If all goes well this night, I will ask you to return it to me. If all does not go well, it may save your life."

I held my hand toward him.

Placing the object on my outstretched palm, Holmes closed my own fingers carefully around it. Surely this was the strangest object I had ever encountered. It was unpleasantly warm, its texture like that of an overcooked egg, and it seemed to squirm as if it were alive, or perhaps as if it contained something that lived and strove to escape an imprisoning integument.

"Do not look at it," Holmes repeated. "Keep it with you at all times. Promise me you will do these things, Watson!"

I assured him that I would do as he requested.

Momentarily we beheld Mrs. Llewellyn moving down the hallway toward us. Her stride was so smooth and her progress so steady that she seemed to be gliding rather than walking. She carried a kerosene lamp whose flame reflected from the polished blackness of the walls, casting ghostly shadows of us all.

Speaking not a word, she gestured to us, summoning us to follow her. We proceeded along a series of corridors and up and down staircases until, I warrant, I lost all sense of direction and of elevation. I could not tell whether we had climbed to a room in one of the battlements of the Anthracite Palace or descended to a dungeon beneath the Llewellyns' ancestral home. I had placed the object Holmes had entrusted to me inside my garments. I could feel it struggling to escape, but it was bound in place and could not do so.

"Where is this bishop you promised us?" I asked of Mrs. Llewellyn.

Our hostess turned toward me. She had replaced her colorful Gypsyish attire with a robe of dark purple. Its color reminded me of the emanations of the warm object concealed now within my own clothing. Her robe was marked with embroidery of a pattern that confused the eye so that I was unable to discern its nature.

"You misunderstood me, Doctor," she intoned in her unpleasant accent. "I stated merely that it was my hope that Bishop Romanova would preside at our service. Such is still the case. We shall see in due time."

We stood now before a heavy door bound with rough iron bands. Mrs. Llewellyn lifted a key which hung suspended about her neck on a ribbon of crimson hue. She inserted it into the lock and turned it. She then requested Holmes and myself to apply our combined strength to opening the door. As we did so, pressing our shoulders against it, my impression was that the resistance came from some willful reluctance rather than a mere matter of weight or decay.

No light preceded us into the room, but Mrs. Llewellyn strode through the doorway carrying her kerosene lamp before her. Its rays now reflected off the walls of the chamber. The room was as Lady Fairclough had described the sealed room in her erstwhile home at Pontefract. The configuration and even the number of surfaces that surrounded us seemed unstable. I was unable even to count them. The very angles at which they met defied my every attempt to comprehend.

An altar of polished anthracite was the sole furnishing of this hideous, irrational chamber.

Mrs. Llewellyn placed her kerosene lamp upon the altar. She turned then, and indicated with a peculiar gesture of her hand that we were to kneel as if participants in a more conventional religious ceremony.

I was reluctant to comply with her silent command, but Holmes nodded to me, indicating that he wished me to do so. I lowered myself, noting that Lady Fairclough and Holmes himself emulated my act.

Before us, and facing the black altar, Mrs. Llewellyn also knelt. She raised her face as if seeking supernatural guidance from above, causing me to remember that the full name of her peculiar sect was the Wisdom Temple of the Dark Heavens. She commenced a weird chanting in a language such as I had never heard, not in all my travels. There was a suggestion of the argot of the dervishes of Afghanistan, something of the Buddhist monks of Tibet, and a hint of the remnant of the ancient Incan language still spoken by the remotest tribes of the high Choco plain of the Chilean Andes, but in fact the language was none of these and the few words that I was able to make out proved both puzzling and suggestive but never specific in their meaning.

As Mrs. Llewellyn continued her chanting, she slowly raised first one hand then the other above her head. Her fingers were moving in an intricate pattern. I tried to follow their progress but found my consciousness fading into a state of confusion. I could have sworn that her fingers twined and knotted like the tentacles of a jellyfish. Their colors, too, shifted: vermilion, scarlet, obsidian. They seemed, even, to disappear into and return from some concealed realm invisible to my fascinated eyes.

The object that Holmes had given me throbbed and squirmed against my body, its unpleasantly hot and squamous presence making me wish desperately to rid myself of it. It was only my pledge to Holmes that prevented me from doing so.

I clenched my teeth and squeezed my eyes shut, summoning up images from my youth and of my travels, holding my hand clasped over the object as I did so. Suddenly the tension was released. The object was still there, but as if it had a consciousness of its own, it seemed to grow calm. My own jaw relaxed and I opened my eyes to behold a surprising sight.

Before me there emerged another figure. As Mrs. Llewellyn was stocky and swarthy, of the model of Gypsy women, this person was tall and graceful. Swathed entirely in jet, with hair a seeming midnight blue and complexion as black as the darkest African, she defied my conventional ideas of beauty with a weird and exotic glamour of her own that defies description. Her features were as finely cut as those of the ancient Ethiopians are said to have been, her movements filled with a grace that would shame the pride of Covent Garden or the Bolshoi.

But whence had this apparition made her way? Still kneeling upon the ebon floor of the sealed room, I shook my head. She seemed to have emerged from the very angle between the walls.

She floated toward the altar, lifted the chimney from the kerosene lamp, and doused its flame with the palm of her bare hand.

Instantly the room was plunged into stygian darkness, but gradually a new light, if so I may describe it, replaced the flickering illumination of the kerosene lamp. It was a light of darkness, if you will, a glow of blackness deeper than the blackness which surrounded us, and yet by its light I could see my companions and my surroundings.

The tall woman smiled in benediction upon the four of us assembled, and gestured toward the angle between the walls. With infinite grace and seemingly glacial slowness she drifted toward the opening, through which I now perceived forms of such maddeningly chaotic configuration that I can only hint at their nature by suggesting the weird paintings that decorate the crypts of the Pharaohs, the carved stele of the mysterious Mayans, the monoliths of Mauna Loa, and the demons of Tibetan sand paintings.

The black priestess—for so I had come to think of her—led our little procession calmly into her realm of chaos and darkness. She was followed by the Gypsy-like Mrs. Llewellyn, then by Lady Fairclough, whose manner appeared as that of a woman entranced.

My own knees, I confess, have begun to stiffen with age, and I was slow to rise to my feet. Holmes followed the procession of women, while I lagged behind. As he was about to enter the opening, Holmes turned suddenly, his eyes blazing. They transmitted to me a message as clear as any words.

This message was reinforced by a single gesture. I had used my hands, pressing against the black floor as I struggled to my feet. They were now at my sides. Fingers as stiff and powerful as a bobby's club jabbed at my waist. The object which Holmes had given me to hold for him was jolted against my flesh, where it created a weird mark which remains visible to this day.

In the moment I knew what I must do.

I wrapped my arms frantically around the black altar, watching with horrified eyes as Holmes and the others slipped from the sealed room into the realm of madness that lay beyond. I stood transfixed, gazing into the Seventh Circle of Dante's hell, into the very heart of Gehenna.

Flames crackled, tentacles writhed, claws rasped, and fangs ripped at suffering flesh. I saw the faces of men and women I had known, monsters and criminals whose deeds surpass my poor talent to record but who are known in the lowest realms of the planet's underworlds, screaming with glee and with agony.

There was a man whose features so resembled those of Lady Fairclough that I knew he must be her brother. Of her missing husband I know not.

Then, looming above them all, I saw a being that must be the supreme monarch of all monsters, a creature so alien as to resemble no organic thing that ever bestrode the earth, yet so familiar that I realized it was the very embodiment of the evil that lurks in the hearts of every living man.

Sherlock Holmes, the noblest human being I have ever encountered, Holmes alone dared to confront this monstrosity. He glowed in a hideous, hellish green flame, as if even great Holmes were possessed of the stains of sin, and they were being seared from within him in the face of this being.

As the monster reached for Holmes with its hideous mockery of limbs, Holmes turned and signaled to me.

I reached within my garment, removed the object that lay against my skin, pulsating with horrid life, drew back my arm, and with a murmured prayer made the strongest and most accurate throw I had made since my days on the cricket pitch of Jammu.

More quickly than it takes to describe, the object flew through the angle. It struck the monster squarely and clung to its body, extending a hideous network of webbing 'round and 'round and 'round.

The monster gave a single convulsive heave, striking Holmes and sending him flying through the air. With presence of mind such as only he, of all men I know, could claim, Holmes reached and grasped Lady Fairclough by one arm and her brother by the other. The force of the monstrous impact sent them back through the angle into the sealed room, where they crashed into me, sending us sprawling across the floor.

With a dreadful sound louder and more unexpected than the most powerful thunderclap, the angle between the walls slammed shut. The sealed room was plunged once again into darkness.

I drew a packet of lucifers from my pocket and lit one. To my surprise, Holmes reached into an inner pocket of his own and drew from it a stick of gelignite with a long fuse. He signaled to me and I handed him another lucifer. He used it to ignite the fuse of the gelignite bomb.

Striking another lucifer, I relit the kerosene lamp that Mrs. Llewellyn had left on the altar. Holmes nodded his approval, and with the great detective in the lead, the four of us—Lady Fairclough, Mr. Philip Llewellyn, Holmes himself, and I—made haste to find our way from the Anthracite Palace.

Even as we stumbled across the great hall toward the chief exit of the palace, there was a terrible rumbling that seemed to come simultaneously from the deepest basement of the building if not from the very center of the earth, and from the dark heavens above. We staggered from the palace—Holmes, Lady Fairclough, Philip Llewellyn, and I—through the howling wind and pelting snow of a renewed storm, through frigid drifts that rose higher than our boot tops, and turned about to see the great black edifice of the Anthracite Palace in flames.

The Adventure of Exham Priory

F. GWYNPLAINE
MACINTYRE

My friend Sherlock Holmes was never quite the same after his return from the dead. I refer, of course, to that long interruption in his detective career, after he vanished from the brink of the Reichenbach Falls and was presumed dead: an illusion which he maintained for a period of three years until the moment when he removed his disguise in my study in Kensington.

Yet the man who returned was transformed. Before his seeming death, Holmes had been disposed to occasional bouts of melancholy. After his return, I found him to be increasingly saturnine and grim: his periods of good humor became fewer and briefer. Of late, whenever Sherlock Holmes played his violin, he no longer performed barcaroles and waltzes, showing a newfound preference for the darker motifs of Beethoven and Wagner.

One evening in April of 1901, I was detained in my Harley Street consulting surgery with an urgent case. In consequence, I did not return to our rooms in Baker Street until well past sunset. I found Holmes clad in his old smoking jacket, seated near the sideboard with an expression of doom on his countenance whilst he peered at a strange ill-shapen object clutched between his long fingertips.

"Hallo, Watson," said my friend, gesturing for me to sit across from him. "I see that you have been draining a patient's mastoid infection."

"*Two* infections," I said, astonished. "But how did—"

"Never mind that, Watson. Come, what do you make of this?" As I seated myself, Holmes pressed the strange object into my hands.

It was a carved piece of stone, roughly nine inches long, of some black mineral resembling basalt. The object was highly polished and deeply curved—concave on one side, convex on the other—yet so thoroughly weathered as to suggest that this artifact was of an immense age. At one edge, the stone was broken and jagged. "It appears to be a fragment off the rim of a large bowl or dish," I ventured.

"Exactly so, Watson. Observe that the rim's curvature is uniform: this was part of a *circular* object, not an elliptical one. By measuring the fragment's arc, I have established that this was once part of a dish some thirteen feet in diameter. And the object is exceedingly weathered, yet the broken edge is still sharp, and the jagged surface at the edge is still dark and glossy . . . so the original object is ancient, but this piece was broken off quite recently. What else do you see?"

I brought the fragment closer to the electrical lamp. The convex surface of the black stone was incised with weird hieroglyphs and runes. Then I turned over the broken stone so as to view the dish's inner surface. And now I felt a sudden revulsion as I saw that the concave side of the bowl was crusted with a dark russet-colored stain resembling *coagulated blood*.

"Holmes," I said. "Wherever did you get this?"

"Sent to me in the morning post," said he calmly. "The parcel bore a postmark from Anchester, which my gazetteer identifies as a village of the Welsh Marches. It was enclosed with a most intriguing letter, concerning—wait, there is the door."

Our housekeeper had brought us a visitor: a man above the middle height, sallow-faced and exceedingly distraught. His hair was dead white, his countenance haggard. His clothes were well tailored and immaculate, yet they hung from his frame as if there were a scarecrow within them.

The visitor's face was an astonishment. He appeared to suffer from some congenital deformity, to a degree I had never encountered in my medical studies. His cranium was exceedingly narrow, with a receding forehead and chin, watery green eyes, and a flattened nose. Above his celluloid collar, there were several rows of oddly deep creases in the sides of his neck. The skin of his face and hands was peeling, as if from some cutaneous disease, and his fingers were strikingly short in proportion to his hands. "Came up to London as soon as I could, in spite of the engine change," he gasped, in a breathless whisper which put me in mind of a fish out of water. The visitor spoke in a cultured voice which betrayed no regional accent. "And then the cab horse lost a shoe in Great Portland Street, so I got out and ran the rest of the way. Which one of you is Mr. Sherlock Holmes?"

"I have that honor, sir," said my friend. "And it is clear to me that you are Jephson Norrys. Your family are from Cornwall, yet you reside in the Welsh Marches. You are a man of some prosperity, but in recent months you have been keenly agitated."

The newcomer had been pale, yet now he turned ashen. "Black magic!" he exclaimed. "You must have read my letter, but how could you have known my—"

"Simply a matter of deduction," said Sherlock Holmes, pointing to our visitor's waistcoat. "Your watch chain bears an ivory pin, in the shape of a black cross upon a white field: that is the flag of Cornwall. But the ivory is yellowed with age, indicating that the pin came to you as an heirloom . . . from your father perhaps, but at any rate from a Cornish forebear. If you had traveled here to London from Cornwall, your railway journey would have ended at the Great Western terminus in Paddington Station . . . but you mentioned Great Portland Street, which is in the opposite direction. The nearest railway station in that neighborhood is Euston . . . and the shortest route from Euston to Baker Street, along the Marylebone Road, passes through Great Portland Street. I need hardly consult my *Bradshaw's Railway Guide* to know that most of the rail lines arriving at Euston Street station originate in Birmingham. Yet you mentioned an engine change, so your journey must have commenced *before* Birmingham: perhaps as far west as Shrewsbury, on the Welsh border. If you had traveled from as far away as Wales to get here, your journey would have required *two* engine changes . . . but you mentioned only one. So! East of Shrewsbury, yet west of Birmingham, eliminates all territory excepting the Welsh Marches. I have just received an urgent letter from Jephson Norrys of Anchester, and you are evidently he."

"As for the rest, sir," I suggested to Norrys, "your shirtfront and your suitings are expensive and new: tailored for a man of your own height but of wider girth, for they hang slackly on your body. You have clearly lost a great deal of weight in recent weeks, due to some nervous condition."

Jephson Norrys mopped his brow with a handkerchief. "Yes! It's true, as you say. Mr. Holmes, I was told that you are the only man in England who can help me. Will you take my case?"

Sherlock Holmes nodded. "Your letter fascinates me." Turning to myself, he remarked: "I may have need of a good medical man for some business in Anchester. What say you, Watson? Can I rely on you to suspend your Harley Street practice for some few days?"

I looked at our visitor, and I confess that my selfless desire to assist Jephson Norrys was mingled with my selfish urge to study his medical symptoms more closely. "I will gladly throw in with you," I replied.

"Thank the heavens for that," said our trembling visitor. Then the gaze of his watery eyes fell upon the dark basalt fragment which Holmes had left on the sideboard. "You have examined what I sent you, then?" asked Norrys, indicating the black stone. "Mr. Holmes, I'll wager you've never seen such an object before."

"On the contrary," said Sherlock Holmes. He reached into his pocket and drew forth a hexagonal object roughly six inches across, and set this on the sideboard alongside the ancient fragment.

It was a dish of some sort, graven from black basalt and weathered with age. Along the outer rim of the six-sided dish, I beheld a weird series of hieroglyphs and runes from some alien script. The inner surface of the dish was flecked and caked with what appeared to be *coagulated blood* . . .

"Wherever did you get this, Holmes?" I asked him.

"That bloodstained dish has been in my possession these past ten years," said my friend Sherlock Holmes. "Perhaps it is time that I told you, Watson, of my encounter with the Reichenbach Horror."

The next few hours contained much activity. I sent a telegram to one of my Harley Street colleagues, urging him to take charge of my patients until my return. "It would be well for us to go armed, Watson," said Holmes as he packed a valise. I retrieved my Webley Bulldog revolver and some of the recently invented 6.25-grain cordite cartridges while the housekeeper summoned a hansom to fetch us to Euston Street station. Holmes and Norrys and I caught the late train to Birmingham, securing a first-class compartment for ourselves.

Jephson Norrys showed symptoms of extreme exhaustion, so I gave him a sleeping draft. Before he quaffed this, Norrys pressed a loose-leaf memorandum book into my friend's hands. "Read this, please. It will explain much," said Norrys, in that peculiar gasping voice. As he fell deeply into slumber in a corner of our compartment, I stethoscoped him and was astonished to discover that his cardiac rate was in the bottom range of human limits. A man in such a state of nervous agitation should exhibit a heartbeat like a trip-hammer . . . yet the slow pulse of Jephson Norrys indicated a metabolism more appropriate to some cold-blooded amphibian. Still, his respiration was regular, and Norrys seemed safe for the moment. As he slept, his mouth opened and closed silently, suggesting the respiration of a fish.

Holmes looked at me ruefully. "Watson, old friend, how long have you known me?"

"This past January, when Queen Victoria died, also marked twenty years since you and I first clasped hands at St. Bart's," I reminded him.

"And yet I fear that you have never truly known me." Holmes drew a black perfecto from his cigar case while the train carried us through the dark network of railway tunnels northwest of London. "You may recall, Watson, our encounter with the Sussex Vampire. I remarked at the time that I disbelieved in ghosts or supernatural agencies. I implied that I have *always* disbelieved."

For a long moment, Sherlock Holmes merely lighted his uncut cigar and paused reflectively. "What do you recall of my encounter at the Reichenbach Falls?"

"There were two different versions of the truth," I said. "You and Professor Moriarty went over the precipice together, and died. Later, it transpired that only Moriarty fell, and you chose to counterfeit your own death."

"And now I must present a third version," said Holmes, while our express train rattled through Watford without stopping. "Neither I nor Moriarty went over the falls. At the brink of the falls, Moriarty brandished a pistol and urged me toward a nearby footpath. At gunpoint, he ushered me downhill to the waterfall's lowest cataract. Here we encountered a cliff face of solid granite, curtained with overgrown vines. Moriarty urged me forward, and I discovered that the solid cliff was actually two separate walls of rock, with a narrow passage between them concealed by a membrane of vines. Passing between the vines, and still held at gunpoint, I found myself entering a cavern . . . utterly dark, except for the weird glow of phosphorescent lichens oozing from the cavern's walls. Moriarty followed at my heels. It was clear to me that he knew in advance of this place's existence, and had brought me here for some grim purpose."

Sherlock Holmes extended his cigar case to me. I accepted a torpedo cigar and took out my cigar cutter as Holmes resumed his narrative: "Inside the cavern, three robed and hooded figures stood awaiting us. Moriarty addressed them in a tongue unknown to me, although I fancy it resembled ancient Chaldean. Moriarty pointed at me, and by his gestures and intonations, I grasped his general meaning: 'Here is the man whom I agreed to give you.'

"But then, in the half dark, one of the hooded figures reached out with inhumanly long limbs and snatched Moriarty's revolver while another of the figures pinioned my enemy's arms. I heard Moriarty cry out in English: 'No! Not me, too! Your master promised that I would go free if I gave you this man!'

"Something coshed me. I awoke in darkness, with a throbbing headache, and found myself lying supine on cold stone. Something unseen was probing my face: weird tendrils pressed against my features, oozing across my eyelids and my mouth. Watson, my nostrils detected an odor of utter obscenity. From nearby in the darkness, strange chittering voices assailed my ears with high-pitched cries: '*Tekeli-li! Tekeli-li!*' Beneath these sounds, I heard the low whimpering moans of a human voice: Moriarty's voice. Did I say a *human* voice? Watson, in that dark cavern I heard something in Moriarty's voice which told me that his mind had cast off the moorings of sanity, and was no longer human. Beneath Moriarty's anguished tones, in counterpoint, I heard a damp rapid noise which sounded like dozens of tongues, lapping some unknown liquid repast."

I shuddered, and nearly burned myself attempting to light my cigar. "Great heavens, Holmes!"

"Heaven had no embassy in that dark place, Watson. I had the sense to lie still, hoping my eyes would grow accustomed to the darkness. They did not. Yet by a little whiles, the procession of tendrils across my face slowed and became less frequent while the tongue-lapping sounds attained their hideous crescendo. *Something* was giving less attention to me, and more heed to the consumption of that unknown liquid. The fingers of my right hand touched something in the dark: something cold and hard, with sharp corners. It came away easily in my hand, yet it was heavy enough that it might serve as a weapon.

"The unholy tendrils had ceased their explorations now, and all hands—or rather, all tongues—seemed to be devoting full attention to their liquid refreshment. Moriarty's voice had gone silent. Slowly, carefully, I slipped the heavy object into my pocket and I crept toward light: the one thin gleam in all that stygian dark. The chittering cries were well behind me as I crawled into another chamber of the cavern, lined with more of those luminescent fungi. I looked back for one instant, and against the eerie glow of the fungoids I beheld the shadowed outlines of an immense silhouetted figure with a weird star-shaped head. I turned 'round from this, and dared not look back a second time. As soon as I could see well enough to risk standing erect, I fled uphill along the slope of the cavern, and soon reached the familiar curtain of vines and the outer world beyond. It was nightfall when I emerged, but at least I had the light of a full moon. Watson, believe me when I tell you that I ran from that place at all speed."

From his pocket now, Holmes withdrew the hexagonal dish. "*This* is the object which I found in the cave beneath the Reichenbach Falls. At my first opportunity, I had this dish treated with carbolic acid, to disinfect it and eliminate the stench. But I have never cleaned off these stains, intending to have them analyzed. Nine different chemists—all sworn to secrecy—have examined the stain on this dish."

"Is it blood, Holmes?" I asked. "*Human* blood?"

"There is the stain of human blood, yes. But there is also a second stain . . . a layer of coagulated blood from a species unknown. It has some traits of human blood, yet it more closely resembles the blood groups of aquatic vertebrates. The blood is both man-like and fishlike."

I shuddered again, and looked at Jephson Norrys while he slept. His mouth opened and closed silently.

"Come, Watson, have a look at this." Sherlock Holmes drew forth a folded sheet of foolscap. "Here is the letter which our friend Norrys sent me. You are in this as deep as I am, so you ought to read it."

For brevity's sake, I shall not divulge the full text. Suffice it to say that Norrys was the landholder of Exham Priory, a medieval estate in Anchester. In recent months he had grown aware of curious incidents in the priory, combined with peculiar changes in his own health.

Holmes was examining the loose-leaf notebook which Norrys had given him. On its cover, I recognized the royal emblem of Her late Majesty Victoria's Diamond Jubilee, of four years past. "Whatever else our friend Norrys might be, he is clearly a patriotic Englishman," said Holmes. "You see, Watson? This memorandum book is one of the innumerable pieces of merchandise—most of them worthless cheapjack—which greedy souvenir merchants foisted upon the British populace in 1897 as mementos of the Jubilee. Look here." From a slipcase inside the notebook's cover, Sherlock Holmes withdrew a hand-colored square of pasteboard. It bore two photographic studies, side by side, like a stereopticon. The first image depicted Victoria Regina in her youth, with Prince Albert and some of the royal children. The second image showed our late queen as she was in '97, in her widow's weeds, wearing the crown of the Empire.

"Observe, Watson," said my friend. "This pasteboard portrait of Her Majesty was included with the notebook during its manufacture, to justify the notebook as a Jubilee souvenir. The pasteboard is creased and dog-eared, yet still in its original slipcase. Clearly, Jephson Norrys has taken this card out of its case many times to gaze upon the likeness of his monarch and then returned the portrait to its rightful place in the notebook despite its long wear. The notebook's leather cover is split and stained, yet the gilt of the royal Jubilee emblem is like new: it has been lovingly polished and cleaned, even though it has no pecuniary value. Our man Norrys is a loyal subject of the Crown, come what may. Hmm! Let us see what he wanted us to find in these pages."

Holmes began reading the loose-leaf book which Norrys had lent him, and he passed each page to me in turn. Pasted into the notebook's frontispiece was a tintype photograph, dated to Jubilee month of 1897. The portrait displayed a clear-eyed handsome man in a Norfolk jacket, and I felt a shiver through my spine when I realized that this was Jephson Norrys. I glanced at the slumbering deformity in the corner of our compartment: he seemed barely human now. How could any man have degenerated so thoroughly in so short a time?

The papers were all written in the same hand, which I took to be that of Norrys . . . yet, as I viewed the pages in their sequence, the handwriting gradually devolved from a neat schoolboy cursive into a clumsy scrawl. It took much the length of our railway journey for me to peruse the lot. In brief, Norrys had been a respectable Cornishman of good family and prospects until he was summoned to Anchester to assist his uncle Habakuk Norrys in the management of Exham Priory. The eleventh Baron Exham had quit this estate during Stuart times and fled to the Virginia colony without explanation: the priory had been Crown property ever since, until the elder Norrys had purchased it in 1894. The priory was not electrified, nor even gas-fitted, and Habakuk Norrys had begun the sorely needed task of renovation . . . until he acquired some peculiar malady which seemed to be progressively deforming him. Now the same ailment had afflicted Jephson, and it was steadily worsening.

I looked back at the letter posted to Holmes and scanned again its last paragraph. Several days earlier, with a paraffin-lantern and an electric torch, Jephson Norrys had descended into the subcellar of Exham Priory to discover the source of certain "eldritch sounds" (as he deemed them) which he had heard there at night: the rapid scrabbling of clawed feet, and eerie intonations like the chanting of obscene acolytes. The cellar was dark in full daylight. During his descent, Norrys had stumbled on the limestone staircase: his torch and lantern were extinguished, and he fell headlong down the staircase. In the darkness (Norrys wrote), his outflung hand touched something cold as stone, and circular and damp. A fragment of this broke away in his grasp. Without light, he made his way up the staircase as rapidly as his deformity permitted, and fled to one of the outbuildings on the priory's grounds. He sought aid from the residents of the neighboring village: they spurned him, and the local constabulary refused to enter the priory. The district magistrate declined to take action.

The testament of Jephson Norrys ended in a demented scrawl that was barely legible: *I had thought that the sounds might be rats in the walls: now I know they are something far worse. The whispering voices in the subcellar seemed human at first; I had feared that they might be burglars, or tramps, or smugglers evading the Welsh tariffs. But now I have seen the blood-caked dish, and I know: the lurkers in the priory's cellar* have no right to call themselves human . . .

"Come, Watson!" said Sherlock Holmes briskly. "Here we are at Birmingham, and the engine change for Anchester. I'll collect our luggage while you see to wakening our companion."

★   ★   ★

It was past midnight when the spur line brought us to an obscure railway station in northwestern Shropshire. A single brougham stood vigil in the cab rank, and—although the cabman glanced sharply at Norrys—Holmes persuaded him to convey us to Anchester. As the cabman took up his reins, Holmes returned the memorandum book to Norrys, who concluded his narrative:

"My agony grows steadily worse, gentlemen. Each morning, I waken to find myself slightly less human. At night, my desperate efforts at sleep are invaded by queer dreams: nightmares, in which I hear dark voices whispering obscene promises." Norrys trembled, and there was a dampness in his eyes. "The police will not help me; my telegrams to the Home Office receive no reply. Mr. Holmes, Dr. Watson: you two are my very last hope."

"What do you hope to achieve?" I asked as gently as I could. "Your medical condition may well be irreversible, and—"

"I want the voices in the dark to go away," Norrys quavered. "The voices and . . . and the sound of the rats in the walls!" Norrys clamped his hands over his ears, although his ears by now had dwindled to mere vestigial slits on his scaled flesh. "My life is nothing to me now. I have not entered the priory these last three days . . . yet I can still hear the whispering voices, and the rats in the walls!"

Our cab stopped abruptly, and the cabman informed us that he "warn't going no nearer that there priory." We paid him and alighted on a Shropshire country road, lined with high bushes of yellow gorse. Looming ahead of us was a dark tower, weirdly silhouetted in the moonlight, which Norrys assured us was our destination. Holmes switched on his battery lamp whilst I slid back the safety catch on my revolver.

Jephson Norrys had difficulty keeping up with us: he walked with a shambling gait, as if his legs were determined to fuse together and had to be forcibly separated with each stride.

The priory was a moss-crusted dilapidation at the edge of a limestone precipice. The grass all around the verge of the estate was blighted and yellow, and the night beasts which are so common to the countryside of England's Salopian region—the bats, the owls, the voles—were strangely absent. I saw some broken headstones on the priory's outermost grounds. Norrys produced an old brass ring with several warded church keys, and he used these to unlock the outer gate, then the inner gate, and then he finally unlatched the door leading into the priory itself.

A strange odor assailed us. Motioning for me to keep my weapon ready, Holmes led the way through the priory's antechamber to a half-open doorway. Here we beheld a crumbling limestone stairway, descending into the depths of the priory's cellars. To Norrys, I gently suggested: "Perhaps you should wait here . . ."

Jephson Norrys shook his head grimly and clenched the remnants of his teeth. "I will see this thing through, Doctor."

We began our descent. I felt a maddening certainty that we were *not alone in the cellar*. All around us in the dark were muffled sounds, like the scurrying of tiny unseen creatures. I fancied I heard voices whispering nearby me, plucking at my mind as though seeking entrance. Voices accosted me, proclaiming themselves as denizens of many centuries and climes. I understood only some few of them. A voice speaking French introduced himself to me as Montagny, a courtier of Louis XIII. Another sentience, speaking in baroque dialects of English, professed to be the disembodied intellect of James Woodville, a merchant of Cromwell's time. My grasp of Latin was sufficient to perceive another voice which claimed to be the mind of Titus Sempronius, *quaestor palatii* of the Roman Empire. All of these voices, and others, beseeched me to heed them.

"Can you hear it, Watson?" There was awe in my friend Sherlock's voice. "A parliament of minds! There seem to be many intelligences here: a harvest of intellects, gathered from several millennia. I recognize one voice's speech as predynastic Chinese, and another employs a Greek dialect. Like shadows out of time, projected into our midst. 'Pon my word, Watson, this is astonishing!"

"How is it possible, Holmes?" I asked while we descended the staircase.

"Perhaps these voices somehow transcend time itself. Watson, have you read the works of Henri Bergson, or Loubachevskii? They postulate a fourth dimension of space, enabling instantaneous communication across vast gulfs of distance and vast intervals of time. I wonder if—"

"*You always did talk too much, Holmes,*" said a harsh voice, somewhat louder and nearer than the others.

In the pale glow of Holmes's battery lamp, I beheld a strange man. He was exceedingly tall and thin, round-shouldered, with a high-domed forehead and a protuberant face punctuated by two deeply sunken eyes. As there was something fishlike in the appearance of Jephson Norrys, there was much in *this* man that seemed reptilian. He stood midpoint along the flight of steps on the limestone staircase beneath us, glowering malevolently upward at Holmes.

"Dr. Watson, I have the honor of presenting Professor Moriarty," said my friend Sherlock Holmes. "Although it had been my understanding that Moriarty long ago gave quits to this earthly realm, and changed his forwarding address to the realm of the dead."

"Merely a temporary inconvenience, I assure you, Mr. Holmes," said Moriarty. From the darkness behind him, there came the chanting unison of many unseen throats:

> *Tekeli-li, tekeli-li!*
> *Tch'kaa, t'cnela ngöi!*
> *Tekeli-li, teka'ngai,*
> *Haklic, vnikhla elöi . . .*

I raised my revolver, but Holmes's hand on my arm restrained me. "Steady on, Watson. Professor Moriarty has been killed at least once already . . . or perhaps twice, if those rumors I encountered in Kowloon are accurate." Gesturing for Jephson Norrys to draw closer, Holmes spoke: "Come, Moriarty! What is your un-holy interest in this man?"

"None whatever," Moriarty replied. "Norrys is merely the tenant of this place. It is the priory itself which we covet. Of all places on Earth, this priory's subcellar is uniquely suited to our needs. By *we*, of course, I mean myself and the Elder Gods."

Behind Moriarty, the chanting grew louder.

"I have long suspected, Moriarty, that I am your true prey," said Sherlock Holmes. "This unfortunate fellow Norrys was merely your bait. Now that I am here, will you release Jephson Norrys and restore him to his manly condition?"

Moriarty spread his long spidery hands, palms upturned. "You wrong me, Holmes. I am innocent of any crime against Norrys. The taint which you behold is in his blood. The Norrys bloodline is obliquely descended from the house of de la Poer, the ancestral heirs to this estate . . . and the inheritors of its curse. By returning to these ancient grounds, first Habakuk Norrys and then his nephew Jephson have awakened the long-dormant taint in their ancestral blood."

"Tekeli-li!" said the voices, as if in agreement with Moriarty.

"What do you want of me?" Sherlock Holmes asked.

"That's better," said Moriarty, rubbing his thin hands together. "You will join me, Holmes, in a long journey . . . a one-way pas-sage, without a return ticket. A voyage to Yith."

"Where's that when it's at home, then?" asked Jephson Norrys.

Moriarty waved a hand airily. "Yith is the home of the Old Ones, countless millions of miles from here . . . yet, when the stars are right, and the dimensions of space can be bent to the Elder Gods' whim, Yith lies only a few inches beyond Shropshire's realm in this cellar." Beckoning us to draw nearer, Moriarty pointed into the darkness behind him at the base of the stairs. *"This way."*

And now a most peculiar violet-colored glow appeared at the foot of the stairs. It began as a single point of light, then it rapidly swelled and enlarged until it formed a glowing sphere, then it suddenly flattened into a hexagon of violet-colored light in mid-air. The hexagon's vertical axis expanded until it became coffin-shaped.

A wind sprang up in the still air of the priory's cellar. I felt a breeze rush headlong past me down the stairway toward the hexagon of light. The wind clutched at my sleeves, at my coattails and cravat. A piece of lichenous moss suddenly tore loose from the wall near my elbow: I saw the moss whirl through the air, borne on the current of wind, until it was suddenly and awfully pulled *into* the violet-colored aura, where it vanished. In a paroxysm of horror, I observed that the peculiar glowing hexagon was a *vortex* of some sort . . . siphoning air and life from this catacomb to some hideous place.

And now I heard the voices again. Beneath the strange alien chant, I heard the whispers of human dialects: French, Latin, Old English, and others . . . beckoning within my mind.

"D'you hear them, Watson?" said Holmes beside me. I saw the look on his face, and I shuddered. Sherlock Holmes was trembling with a rapture that seemed nearly spiritual. "Hear them, Watson! All the minds that have preceded me into this place: intellects out of time, from Earth's past and Earth's future. Some snatched un-willingly, some abducted, yet all of them awaiting me on the far side of that vortex . . . and gloriously sentient! Think of all the se-crets . . . all the mysteries which their abducted wisdom can reveal to us! Come, Watson! Let us visit to Yith, and pay a call on the Old Ones."

"No, Holmes!" I cried. "It's a trick! We daren't . . ." And then, as I spoke, I heard one other whisper joining the alien chorus. This voice was gentle, and fair, and familiar . . . and I heard her sweet words easily above the growing howl of the wind.

"John," said the beckoning voice. *"Darling John, here I am . . ."*

I knew that voice, though I have not heard it for these past

seven years. The voice came from the center of the vortex. I knew I must not turn toward it. I knew I must not raise my head to see. And yet . . . *I looked.*

Within the glowing hexagon I beheld my dear departed wife, Mary, exactly as I had known her before her last consumptive illness carried her off. With all my intellect, I knew the truth: *she was dead, she is buried in Nunhead Cemetery.* No power in the universe could restore life to my beloved Mary Morstan and convey her, smiling and complete, to the other side of the unearthly portal from which she now stood beckoning me. *And yet she was there . . .*

Suddenly a memory from my university days broke the surface of my consciousness. I recalled one of my professors demonstrating a peculiar rhizomatous flower, native to certain American swamps. Insects are lured to the deadly leaves of this plant by the sweet nectar which it exudes from its flowers to entice unsuspecting prey. It is *Dionaea muscipula*, or Venus's-flytrap. But why was I suddenly reminded of . . .

Sherlock Holmes had a death grip on my arm. I felt him pulling me, step-by-step, down those limestone stairs toward the beckoning vortex. I tried to resist him, as I tried to resist the enticements of my departed wife, whom I knew to be not my wife at all. *"Come to me, John . . ."* she whispered. *"Hurry to me, for the vestibule between the worlds cannot stay open much longer."* And I knew that I could not resist . . .

"I am coming, Mary." The words escaped my lips, despite myself.

Somewhere far away, yet very close, I heard Moriarty's laughter.

"Can't you see it's a trap?" Someone rushed past me on the stairs. I saw Jephson Norrys fling himself headlong at Moriarty. For a moment they grappled at the brink of the grim vortex: Moriarty within it, Jephson still outside it on the bottom stair of the subcellar. I saw the two men struggle, yet it was clear that Moriarty was the stronger. Laughing dementedly, he gripped Norrys by the throat and bent him easily backward, threatening to snap his spine. With Moriarty's hands 'round his throat, I saw Jephson Norrys gasping for air like a fish out of water while the wind of the vortex clutched and tore at Norrys's coat.

Something fell from his pocket. I saw that it was Norrys's memorandum book. It struck the staircase, and the gray limestone split it open. I saw loose-leaf pages scattered by the wind, whirling in spirals of air. I saw the tintype photograph of Jephson Norrys in his younger days, snatched by the gale force and sucked into the vortex. I saw something else fall from the memorandum book. In the dim glow of the battery lamp, I saw a glimpse of color . . .

Moriarty saw it, too. I saw him release his grip on Jephson Norrys, who fell sprawling while Moriarty looked toward the foot of the limestone staircase. As Norrys fell, I saw Moriarty's face change. His features softened; his expression of leering cruelty became almost wistful. I saw the face of a man who had suddenly glimpsed something precious which he feared was lost forever. I saw Moriarty bend, and reach down to pick it up . . .

With an oath, Jephson Norrys struggled to his feet and lunged forward. With all his strength, he snatched Moriarty and plunged pell-mell with him into the mouth of the vortex. I heard a strangled cry. And then, abruptly, the edges of violet-colored aura contracted. Of a sudden the jaws of the vortex snapped shut . . . with Moriarty and Norrys within. I heard a hideous crunching sound, and then *something* flew past my head and landed on the limestone steps above me.

In the gleam of the lamp, I saw *Jephson Norrys's hand* with some few inches of his severed forearm in a bloodstained coat sleeve. The broad paddled mass of his finlike appendage pointed accusingly toward the bottom of the staircase. The rest of Norrys, and the whole of Moriarty, had quite vanished. The interdimensional vortex had closed while Jephson Norrys's arm was inside the aperture . . . and his hand had been *neatly sheared off.*

The whispering voices fell silent. But now I heard again the muffled scurryings, like the sounds of unseen rats within the walls.

And from somewhere nearby, in the dark, it resumed: the faint whisper of *"Tekeli-li . . ."*

"Really, Holmes," I ventured, "I see no point in our tarrying here."

"Just a moment, Doctor." My friend reached down with one of his long arms to retrieve something, then we ascended the stairs with all speed, and soon—not soon enough for my tastes—we were in the moonlit graveyard of the priory. Not until we were well past that shunned place and safely on the road to Anchester did Holmes consent to speak.

"Evidently, Bergson and Loubachevskii were correct," said Sherlock Holmes, pausing briefly to light his pipe before we continued down the road. "It *is* possible to bridge the gulf between distant points in the dimensions of space. Some unknown factor in the cellar of that priory enables it to serve as the terminus for a viaduct between Earth and elsewhere: perhaps the limestone deposits, or some peculiar mixture of the minerals which have seeped through them for centuries. Moriarty spoke of the stars being 'right' for his intentions: but the stars in the heavens move constantly, and bring their gravitational fields along with them . . . which may explain why Moriarty could keep the viaduct open for only such a brief time."

We walked in silence for a moment whilst I lighted a cigar, and then Sherlock Holmes spoke again: "That vortex, Watson, is the most fiendish thing I have ever encountered, with the possible exception of the giant rat of Sumatra. Something within that vortex seemed to promise us *the thing we most desired*, although the promise was certainly false. I was offered a chance to commune with intellects nearly the equal of my own. Watson, I heard you cry out the name of your late beloved wife, so I can guess what you were offered. I can but hope that Jephson Norrys has found some measure of peace, and that he entered the vortex of his free will. As for Moriarty, I believe that he found his final temptation on *this* side of that hideous gulf between the worlds."

"What do you mean, Holmes?"

"The Elder Gods, or whatever they were, made an unholy bargain with Moriarty," said Sherlock Holmes. "They have snatched away his humanity, and given him darker things in return. But there is one thing that the Elder Gods cannot offer. It is something which Moriarty gave up willingly, before our encounter at the Reichenbach Falls. And yet it is something which Moriarty clearly desired, and he repented having lost it. Did you mark the expression of longing on his face? Permit me one deduction, Watson: I deduce that, in those final moments in the vortex, Moriarty was suddenly reminded of what he had lost when he squandered his humanity, his life, his very soul."

We were nearing an inn, where two coach lamps stood sentinel in the front window. Now Sherlock Holmes held something in his outstretched hand, and by the light of the coach lamps I saw in his grasp what had fallen from Jephson Norrys's pocket. It was the object which had momentarily distracted Moriarty, and which he had sought to retrieve: the hand-tinted Jubilee portrait of Queen Victoria.

"For one moment, Professor Moriarty remembered what it meant *to be an Englishman*," said Holmes, pocketing the pasteboard as we approached the inn. "That is what Moriarty gave up in his bargain with the Old Ones . . . and not even all the infinite realms of the Elder Gods could make up for that loss. Come, Watson! I hear piano music in the saloon bar, and voices singing . . . not 'Tekeli-li' this time, but rather 'Knocked 'Em in the Old Kent Road' . . . so it is elementary to me that this tavern is open all hours, and we shall find glad company within. Would a pint of bitter go welcome?"

Death Did Not Become Him

DAVID NIALL WILSON AND
PATRICIA LEE MACOMBER

It has been many years since the events I now record took place, and even as I run through them in my mind, I'm uncertain if I should continue. There is a question of privacy involved, to be certain. There is more. I fancy that when all is said and done, these words will one day find their way into the hands of others. Still, my purpose over the years has never been to further my own reputation, and certainly I've been brutally honest when it comes to others.

Let me begin by mentioning the most glaring oddity of all. In this case, when my friend Mr. Sherlock Holmes admitted his newest client to 221B Baker Street, it was none other than myself, half-crazed and shaking like a scared dog.

Upon my arrival in the neighborhood, the clock in the church tower had chimed eleven. It was later than I had thought, and far too cold for a sane man to be about. All but one light was out in Holmes's flat and I assumed him to be asleep. It did not matter. The burden of that night was too much to bear alone, and at the very least I needed the comfort of my old friend's solid intellect.

I paced, until my shoes threatened to wear ruts in the sidewalk. I wanted desperately to turn around and return to my own home, have a brisk shot of brandy, and slide between the cool sheets of my bed. What I most emphatically did not want was to see my relationship with Holmes tainted by the appearance of insanity. Still, there was nothing for it but to plunge ahead, and I finally dashed for the door in desperation, wanting to reach it before my traitorous feet turned away yet again. Before I could raise my hand to the door knocker, the door swung inward, and I found myself stumbling to a clumsy halt, staring into the grinning countenance of Mr. Sherlock Holmes.

"Do come in, Watson," Holmes said with a twinkle in his eye that set my cheeks burning with embarrassment. "Another few paces and you'll wear the leather from your soles." As he took in my own expression, Holmes grew more serious, and he closed the door quickly behind us, taking my coat.

"I'm terribly sorry about the hour, Holmes," I blurted, "But the matter simply can't wait."

"I gathered from the odd slant of your hat and the mismatching of buttons that this was a matter of some importance," he replied. He turned and disappeared into his study, and I hurried to catch up with him. When I reached the dimly lit room, he was already in his chair, legs stretched out before him and fingers pressed together under his chin. "So tell me what brings you out so late on a cold night."

"I've come to offer you a new client, Holmes."

"But you've come alone. Who, then, would your client be?"

I watched him for a moment, steepling his fingers and staring at me, eyes twinkling. I knew he had already deduced my reply, but I made it anyway. "It is I, Holmes. This time, it is I who seeks your aid."

The skin around his eyes drew taut and his lips pursed. "Very well, Watson. Why don't you sit down, take a brandy, and tell me your story."

I sat back, closed my eyes, and let the events of the evening flow back into my consciousness, telling the tale as best I could. I knew any detail I left out, or forgot, might prove the one thing Holmes needed to see through it all as nonsense, so I was careful. The brandy helped. This is the tale I told.

It was but a few hours before when a knock came at my door. It was later than I was accustomed to accepting callers. I immediately assumed it to be you, Holmes. Who else would call on me at such an hour? My heart quickened at the thought of adventure, and I hastened to open the door.

The man who met my gaze was gaunt, tall, and weathered as if he'd spent long years on the deck of a ship, or working a farm. His complexion was dark, and his coat clung to him like a shroud. I could make out two others standing directly behind him in the gloom.

"Dr. Watson," he asked, his voice sharp and edgy.

"You have me at a disadvantage," I countered. "I'm Watson, and you are? My God, man, do you know the time?"

"I am well aware of the time," the man answered. "My business with you cannot wait."

The man held forth a sheet of paper, pressing it toward my nose as if I could read it in the dark. "Did you sign this?" he asked sharply.

"I can't see what it is from here," I said. "Step inside Mr. . . ."

"Silverman," he said, stepping hurriedly through the doorway. "Aaron Silverman. My companions are Mr. Sebastian Jeffries and . . . well, read the paper, and you may see who else accompanies me."

I knew I should have told the men to return by daylight, but I'd invited them in, and the deed was done. I glanced at the other two, who remained silent. The first was a white-haired old chap with ruddy features and wide, bulging eyes. His cheeks were overly full, making his lip drape oddly downward. I didn't know him. The third wore a dark coat, as did Silverman, and a hat pulled down to hide the features of his face.

I glanced back to the paper and began to read. It was a death certificate. I had signed it only a week before, pronouncing one Michael Adcott dead of a knife wound to the back. Mr. Adcott had been out too late in the wrong part of town, and apparently someone had fancied his wallet.

"What has this to do with any of you?" I asked bluntly.

"Mr. Jeffries," the first man explained, "is my solicitor. I should say, he is my cousin's solicitor. I'm not certain if you would have been told, but there was a sizable fortune—a tontine—involved in the death. Michael was one of only two surviving members of the tontine, and upon the declaration of his death, the courts moved to deliver the tontine's assets to a Mr. Emil Laroche.

"I knew of no tontine," I said, "but I see no way I can help you in such a matter. Mr. Adcott died, and as I understand such arrangements, that would indicate that the courts were in the right."

"So you say," Silverman said, "and yet, you would be—for the second time this week—mistaken."

I blinked at him. "Mistaken? How—"

Silverman held up a hand, then turned to his third companion. "Michael?"

My heart nearly stopped. The man removed his hat slowly, staring at me through eyes I'd seen glazed and closed so few days in the past. He didn't seem to see me, not really, and yet he reacted to Silverman's words with perfect understanding. The dazed, haunted expression of those eyes burned into my mind, and I had to shake my head to clear the sensation of—something—something dark and deep. Something *wrong*.

"This is quite impossible," I stated. "There is no way this can be the same Michael Adcott that I examined earlier in the week. That man had sustained a direct stab wound to the back, penetrating a lung, and he lay dead in the street at least an hour before I arrived on the scene. There was a constable on the spot—Johnston was his name."

"And yet," Silverman said, holding up one hand to silence me, "Michael Adcott stands and breathes before you, a very alive, and suddenly destitute, man. Only your intervention, Dr. Watson, can prevent a horrid miscarriage of justice."

This was a strange situation, to be certain, but I fancy that I've acquitted myself well in any number of odd happenings over the years. Without hesitation, I stepped closer and stared at the man before me. He wavered back and forth, as if his legs barely held him upright, and I squinted, trying to find some fault between my memory of the dead man and the one who'd disturbed my evening.

"Impossible," I muttered, stepping back. "Preposterous."

Silverman eyed me coldly. "And yet, a fact that is difficult to deny, I suspect," he said shortly.

At this, the plump man, who'd remained silent until that moment, stepped forward, fumbling a monocle from his breast pocket and perching it on the bridge of his nose with a palsied hand. The lens teetered, and I was nearly certain it would drop from its perch before he could steady it, but miraculously the man got it under control. He lifted a small sheaf of papers, bringing them closer so he could glance at them through the lens.

"It would seem," he spoke, the words slow and forced, "that we have a situation before us requiring the utmost in haste and discretion."

"You would be Mr. Jeffries," I stated, not waiting for an answer. "I would expect, sir, that of all gathered here, you would be first to note the absurdity of the claim laid before me. Dead men do not pry themselves from the grave, no matter the fiscal windfall it might provide themselves or others. This man cannot be Michael Adcott."

Jeffries glanced up from his papers quickly, nearly sending the monocle flying. "I assure you, Dr. Watson, that he is. I have served the Adcotts for the past twenty years as solicitor, and I know my client when he stands before me."

"Which would lead me to believe, sir, that you have mistakenly pronounced Mr. Adcott dead." Silverman folded his hands in front of him and peered down his nose at me.

I must say that I would rather admit to an error in judgment than to the possibility of the walking dead. All evidence and proof aside, I needed them gone just then.

"Return here tomorrow at four sharp and I'll have the answers you seek," I told them, shoving the papers at Silverman and marching them forward.

Holmes had grown contemplative; his eyes were focused, but not, I think, on any point in the reality we shared. Leaning forward in my chair, hands on my knees, I gazed at him anxiously and finished.

"With the house again empty and my heart still beating a savage rhythm in my chest, I could think of only one thing to do, and that was to bring the matter to you."

Holmes eyes shifted, and he rose suddenly. "And well you did, my dear Watson, well you did indeed."

He was already walking toward the door, wearing an uncharacteristically distracted expression. "I must see to some things, Watson," he said suddenly. "And you must rest, old friend. When the sun has risen a little higher in the sky, we shall see what we can find."

"But, have you no thoughts on this matter?" I cried.

"Thoughts are often all that we have, Watson. There is nothing that I can say for certain, but I do have—thoughts. That is for tomorrow. Go and get some rest."

With that, he opened the door, and I could think of nothing to say or do, other than to stumble out into the night and off toward home, wondering if my old friend now thought me daft. The sky was already stained a deep bloodred with the sunrise.

Silverman glanced furtively to either side, then slipped through a massive wooden door and into the depths of the squat, monolithic building beyond. The exterior was dingy brick; even the soot and grime seemed soiled, and there was an oily sheen to the place, gleaming sickly in the early-morning light.

He carried a case under one arm, and he'd come on foot. No coach waited outside that door, nor did anyone spot his entry. There had been precious little traffic through those doors in recent years, and what there was, men tended to ignore. Such knowledge was best left to others, or to no one at all. It was a dark place, and the screams of those who'd entered and never been freed echoed through the air surrounding the place like a hum of electricity. So it seemed to some.

The Asylum of St. Elian had been closed for reasons never released to the public. There were rumors of dark experiments, of torture and sin, but they were not often repeated, and usually died before reaching the level of greatness. There was nothing good in the building, and if it hadn't required actual contact with the place, most would have been happy to wield one of the hammers that would bring it down.

Silverman had found no trouble at all in renting a portion of the fading edifice, and with Jeffries handling the legalities and paperwork, had managed to do so with near anonymity, the solicitor having been granted the right to sign on Silverman's behalf. The laboratory of St. Elian's, and the ward nearest that foul place, had come under Silverman's control easily and without contest. Even the homeless and the drunks had avoided the place. It was empty and lifeless as a tomb, and that suited Aaron Silverman just fine.

Now he made his way down the dark main corridor and fumbled a large skeleton key from one pocket of his jacket, balancing the leather case precariously under one arm. He'd cleaned up as much as was possible—or necessary—but the old lock ground its metal tumblers together in a sound near to disbelief at the intrusion of his key. St. Elian's hadn't welcomed him gladly.

Once inside, Silverman wasted no time. He moved about the room, bringing the dim lights to life and placing the wooden case carefully on a bench just inside the door. The laboratory was much as he'd found it. There had been a great deal of equipment left behind when the building closed, and none had felt the urge to return and clear it away. The thought of the use it might have seen was enough to slap away even the greediest of fingers. Silverman had carted in, late at night and under cloak of the deep London fog, the last remaining bits of what he'd dragged from his father's home—his inheritance.

Despite the hum and glow of the lamps, shadows clung like swamp lichen to every surface and bit of furniture. Silverman shivered; then, irritated with himself, he drew forth a box of matches and lit the large oil lamp on the table beside his case. Turning up the wick, he watched as the flame licked upward, flared, and settled. Standing in the pool of light this created, he felt a little of the spell of the unease lifting and drew a deep breath.

There was little time, and there was no room for delays, or hesitation. Silverman flipped open the case and stared down at the contents. The interior was lined in rich velvet. In slots manufactured to accommodate their exact shape and size, a line of six vials rested. The first three were empty. In the next two slots, a greenish liquid roiled. It was not quiescent, as it should have been, sitting still on the table. It swirled and curled toward the edges of the vials, reaching up the sides and falling back down—as if trying to escape. The sixth and last of the vials contained a flat red powder. Silverman stared for a few moments longer, as if mesmerized.

Then, recovering his senses, he reached for the next full vial and drew it forth, along with the sixth vial, containing the powder.

With one deft movement of his thumbs, he uncapped both vials. Inside the first—green, liquid and light—the solution ceased its movement. He tilted the second, angling the lip of it toward the first, tapping gently, mentally ticking off grains of the powder. The green liquid devoured it, changing color slightly, then regaining its normal appearance, almost as though the powder had been—digested. He recapped both vials, and returned the powder to its place in the wooden case.

To the right of the case, farther along the bench, sat an open carton. Silverman carefully laid the vial down beside the box and reached inside, drawing forth a small leather bag. It might have been easier to work had he unpacked his things, but there was something about the old laboratory, and the asylum walls surrounding it, that made even Silverman want to avoid deeper connection with the place than was absolutely necessary. The less he unpacked, the less he'd have to pack when his work was done.

Silverman opened the bag and pulled out a small kit. The kit contained a syringe, a bottle of alcohol, and a small pouch of glittering blades and tools. He grabbed the syringe, which sported a hideously long needle, picked up the vials once again, and turned toward the door.

At that precise moment, a low moan echoed through the corridors beyond that door, and Silverman froze. The sound was deep, rolling up from the stone bowels of the asylum and rising to a banshee wail that reverberated and echoed back onto itself, forming waves of sound without rhythm or reason. The sound was drenched in pain.

Silverman staggered, bringing one hand to his brow to brush away the sweat and nearly poking out his own eye with the syringe. He cried out, ducking away from this own hand, and cursed softly.

"Damn you," he said softly. "It's too soon. I should have hours." He stared at the doorway, and the dark, shadowed hall beyond. "I should have hours," he whispered.

The moans rose again, louder than before, and there was a deep metallic clang. He could almost believe the solid stone floor shook.

Under his breath, Aaron Silverman began to pray. He prayed in the ancient Hebrew the words he'd committed to memory, the charm his father had brought to him from the mind and faith of his grandfather and his grandfather's father. He thought of the ancient, torn shred of canvas, soiled and worn, the spidery lettering etched into that cloth. With his eyes closed, he could see those letters burning brightly—as if they had a life of their own. He could sense the madness behind the verse, could almost see the wild, skewed eyes. He had heard them described so many times they seemed part of his own memory, and not that of his father's father.

Silverman spoke slowly and very softly, trying not to blend his voice with that other—that horrible, hate-filled sound.

Entering the hall, he took a single deep breath, released some of the pressure he was putting on the vial before he crushed it in his hand, puncturing his skin. Fresh sweat broke out on his brow at the thought of that green, glowing slime slipping into his veins. He had a sudden image of the case in the laboratory behind him, the vials and the thick velvet. This led to further memories, journals, and stories—stories that would be impossible to believe—were the proof not waiting one floor down in a stone room barred with iron.

Silverman shook it off and stepped into the hallway, moving quickly and purposefully toward the sound. Nothing mattered but the vial in his hand, the syringe that would empty it, and the words. He had to speak the words, had to repeat them from memory, just as he'd learned them, or it would all be for nothing. The madness that echoed through the halls would become his own, and the money . . . all that money . . .

There were dim lights strung along the hall, leading down a wide stone stair, and into the shadows below. Silverman took the steps at a trot, ignoring the sounds, which had grown to a constant shriek of madness and a grinding rattle of metal. As he went, he grasped the syringe tightly and plunged it into the lid of the vial. His footsteps grew quicker, and the heaving of his breath threatened to steal the words from his lips, but he couldn't wait any longer. It had to be now, and it had to be quick.

He hit the bottom step, stumbled, righted himself, and hurried down the hall. The sounds were close now, immediate and maddening. To his right, barred doorways loomed, cells that had lain empty for long years, their iron doors latched and rusted. He passed the first two cells without a glance, but as he came abreast of the third, he slowed, backing toward the center of the hall. Fingers gripped the bars of that third cell, long and sinewy—strong. The bars shook again.

Silverman took a step closer, raising the syringe like a dagger over his head. The words flowed from his lips, but he had no more control of them now than he did of the tremble in his wrist, or the rubbery sensation that threatened to deny him the use of his legs. He slipped toward the barred door, and suddenly a face slammed into it, too-wide eyes glaring at him, framed in wild, unkempt hair. The skin was sallow and pale, and the bars shook harder than they had before, threatening to tear loose from the stone of the walls.

With a cry, Silverman plunged the syringe down and slammed it into the flesh of one of the arms groping through the bars, fingers wide to seek his throat. He felt the needle bite and brought his free hand down on the plunger, jamming it home with a grunt and stepping back, leaving the needle deeply embedded in its target, watching in horror as the arm was jerked inward, catching the syringe on the bar and snapping it off near the center of the too-long needle. Green liquid glittered in the air, splashing the walls and floor in droplets that glowed and hissed. Silverman stepped back farther with a gasp. His heart slammed too quickly—too violently—in his chest, and he feared it would stop. He couldn't get breath to slip past the knot in his throat, and only the intervention of the wall at his back prevented his toppling to the stone floor.

The screams tore through the air at inhuman volume. Silverman slapped his palms to his ears and closed his eyes. Nothing could have blocked that sound, but he muted it, and blessedly, within moments, the sounds began to fade. The screams receded slowly to wails, the wails to moans. Silverman's eyes snapped open wide, and he pushed off the wall, moving toward the bars of the cell. His voice rose instantly, returning to his chant, bringing the ancient Hebrew to life through his voice, and trying to imagine that he was in control of the situation.

He stepped closer. The light was very dim, and the bony wrists and yellowed, skinny arms no longer groped between the bars. In fact, the cell's occupant had retreated to the far wall and slid down to a sitting position on the floor, knees drawn up and head back.

Silverman spoke more clearly, enunciating carefully. There was no reaction within the darkened cell. No motion, no sound. Silverman grew calmer, gaining confidence, and he stepped to within an inch of the bars, staring down fixedly at the man cowering against the back wall. The final words of the chant tumbled from his lips, resonant and strong. For just an instant, as the hall fell silent, Michael Adcott raised his head, staring into the eyes of his captor. The captive man's eyes blazed with something beyond insanity, beyond rage or pain.

But only for a second. Then those eyes were dead. Blank. Nothing more reflected in their dull black depths but the dim light of the torches in the hall. Silverman watched a moment longer, letting his breathing catch a normal rhythm and straightening his jacket, running one hand back through sweat-soaked hair.

Reaching into one pocket, Silverman retrieved a ring of keys and inserted a large iron skeleton key into the cell's huge old lock.

"Come along, then," he said, his voice cracking once, then steadying again. "Come along, Michael. We have work to do, and I've had enough nonsense for one day."

Adcott didn't move. Not until Silverman's fingers gripped his upper arm and tugged. Then, with slow, mechanical movements, he levered himself from the floor, leaned against the wall for support, and found his feet. The man did not turn to Silverman, nor did he answer. When Silverman turned toward the door of the cell, Adcott followed as if drawn in the other man's wake.

It was nearly three o'clock by the time Holmes made his way to the door of my flat. He stood outside the door, and when I invited him in, he shook his head impatiently.

"Your coat, Watson, and hurry. Timing is crucial, and we have several places to be before evening."

I didn't hesitate. Long years as Holmes's companion have removed several layers of my natural hesitation. There were only two choices: follow as best I could, or be left behind and miss whatever was to come. My coat over one arm, my hat in the other hand, I slipped out the door, and Holmes pulled it tight behind me.

Just as I was turning to go, I saw him bend at the waist, reaching down to run a finger along one of the cracks in the sidewalk. Straightening, he removed a bit of paper from his pocket and carefully folded whatever he'd scraped from the ground inside. I thought to ask what he was doing, then thought better of it. *All in its time,* he'd say. Why force the words?

There was a carriage waiting at the curb, and Holmes slipped inside. I followed, and without a word from Holmes, the driver was off. I should have liked to ask where we were bound, but experience told me the words would be wasted. Holmes had the predatory, hunter's gleam in his eye I'd seen so many times before, and I knew he'd speak to me only when he was ready. I contented myself with slipping into my coat and leaning back to watch the streets as we passed.

The carriage headed into the center of the city, and it was only a short time before we pulled to the curb. A quick glance out the window confirmed my suspicions. We had pulled up in front of the morgue.

"Why have we come here?" I asked in surprise. "I've told you the man was in my flat, alive and standing as you, or I."

"If, indeed, the man you saw was the same Michael Adcott you pronounced dead," Holmes replied, exiting the coach and motioning the driver to wait, "then I would expect without doubt to find that body here. The fact you met a man you believe might be Adcott does not mean the Adcott for whom you signed the death warrant is not dead."

He fell silent then, leaving me to follow the trail of his thoughts to their obvious conclusions. A brother? A close cousin? Why hadn't it occurred to me? My ears were burning with the sudden realization I'd acted the fool, but I followed Holmes into the morgue entrance nevertheless. What had I been thinking? That dead men walk?

It was late in the day, and it was unlikely that many would be walking the halls of that dark place, but Holmes entered with familiarity and confidence. There was nothing to do but to follow.

It took a good bit of cajoling on Holmes's part, but the clerk behind the desk, a dour little man with too-thick glasses and a perpetual frown that creased his brow with deep wrinkles, finally agreed to escort us to where the body of Michael Adcott had been stored. The body was, he assured us, right where it had been left, tagged and recorded.

"I sent you a report earlier this very day, Mr. Holmes, did you not get my message? Do you think he's up and walked away, then?" the man asked. His voice was grave, but now there was a twinkle in his eye that had not been present as he argued with Holmes at the front desk. "They do that, you know. One day here, the next up and gone, and days later wives and mothers, daughters and friends, are here, telling how they've met the corpse on the road and asking after the remains. Sometimes, they're just not there."

I didn't much appreciate the clerk's levity, but Holmes paid the man no mind at all.

"You saw the man, then," Holmes asked, watching the clerk's face with keen interest. "You verified the information you sent personally?"

The old man cackled. "If he's in my book, Mr. Holmes, he's in my morgue. There are papers that must be filled out to remove a corpse, and permissions to be granted. No such papers have passed my desk for the late Mr. Adcott, and if there are no papers, there is no reason to look. He is here."

"Then let us wish him Godspeed on the road to the next world," Holmes replied. "Let us see Mr. Adcott for ourselves, and then we shall see what we can make of the rest of this business."

Unfortunately for my own sanity, the remains of the late Mr. Michael Adcott were indeed missing from their slab. No note, no papers of explanation or permission. The numbers and documentation lay neatly in place, but no body accompanied them. The small man was less talkative now, and a sight less sure of himself.

"Perhaps he's been moved?" I suggested.

The man shook his head, not turning to meet my gaze, only staring at the empty spot where a dead man should be. "There were no papers. No one moves without paperwork. No one."

"And yet," Holmes observed mildly, "Mr. Adcott seems to have been in the mood for an afternoon stroll."

"Shall we search for him?" I asked, ready to button up my sleeves and get to the task at hand.

"There's no time," Holmes said, his expression shifting in an instant to the old, familiar intensity of the hunt. "I didn't really expect he would be here, but without knowing . . ." He trailed off, and I followed him out the door. Without a word, he was back in the cab and holding the door impatiently, as I made to enter.

At just that moment, there was a cry from down the street, and I turned, startled. A young man darted from around the corner of the morgue, tousled hair waving about a roguish face and a scrap of paper clutched tightly in grubby fingers. I recognized him at once, as did Holmes, who rose and exited the carriage, calling to the driver to hold.

Wiggins was the leader of a group of ragged urchins Holmes had called on a number of times in the past. Holmes claimed there was more work to get from one of the little beggars than a dozen of London's finest, and I'd had occasion to see the truth in this. As always, though, Wiggins's arrival was a surprise to myself.

"Mr. Holmes," Wiggins cried, coming to a halt and holding out the paper. "We've found him, sir, as you asked."

Holmes didn't say a word, but took the paper from the boy's hand, eyes blazing. He read quickly, then folded the paper and slipped it into one of the pockets of his coat. "The others are posted?" he asked quickly.

Wiggins nodded. "He'll not slip past, sir. Count on it."

"I do," Holmes replied, almost smiling. Shillings changed hands and Holmes had turned away and reentered the carriage before I could ask what was written on the paper, or who the "irregulars" were watching.

I knew better than to ask. I'd seen that expression on Holmes's face too many times. He was on the trail of something, and until that thing was in his grasp, he'd not share it with anyone. Best to keep to his side, watch his back, and wait until he was ready to speak. The carriage took off without a word from Holmes, and I realized suddenly that he'd already anticipated our next stop. Either the note Wiggins had brought him had confirmed his suspicions, or it was related to another matter.

I watched out the curtained window as we passed deeper into the city, trying not to think of the scrap of paper in Holmes's pocket, or the pallid face of Michael Adcott, staring at me from heavily lidded eyes.

★   ★   ★

Silverman walked briskly down the street, hands pressed deeply into the pockets of his coat. At his heel, Michael Adcott followed more slowly, his gait forced and clumsy. Silverman paid his companion no mind. They had to meet Jeffries at the court before the last of the judges left his chambers, and that left little time indeed. Time was slipping through his fingers too quickly, and things he'd expected to have accomplished had evaded him.

The doctor—Watson was his name—was a problem. The man should have seen what was obvious, feared what was less so, and signed off on the paperwork by now. Without that signature, they would be forced to let a court decide Michael's state, and at the very least, he'd be found unfit to speak on his own behalf. That wouldn't do. Michael Adcott would not be speaking to anyone, and that was another problem.

For the moment, things were under control. The serum—alone—was not enough. That much had been clear in the sketchy notes that had been included with the case that lay waiting in the laboratory at St. Elian's. Only fate—a bottle of wine—and a loose tongue had given Aaron Silverman the information he needed.

"There was a time," his father had said, head drooping toward the table and fingers loosely gripping his wineglass, "when we had ways to deal with our problems. There are things we know." The old man had glanced up to see that his son knew the *we* in question. "We have always harbored our secrets, Aaron. There was a time when we kept them less guarded—when a rabbi could walk the streets with the respect of those around him. They knew. I know."

Several glasses of wine later, and a lot of cajoling and flattery on Aaron's part, and those secrets had begun to surface. Men from clay. The Cabala. Patterns of words and form, rhythm and breath, that emulated the formation of the first man. A mad Arab poet who spoke as if he were in another place and time and stared into distances that were not there. Those words, copied onto the canvas corner of a tent and guarded, studied—shifted over the years and recombined. Al-Hazred, the man had been called, and though he'd been mad, he'd been a prophet as well—a prophet of power. At first the notion had seemed ludicrous. A clay monster controlled by he who gave it life, born of the proper words, the proper earth—the prayers—the faith of the rabbi, and the vision of a madman.

Sworn to secrecy, Aaron had left his father's home and set out to find a use for his new secret. Money wasn't everything, he reminded himself often, but no money was certainly something to be avoided. Money was power, and if you were not the one with the power, you were under that man's thumb. Aaron Silverman would feel the pad of no man's thumb.

A chance encounter had landed the wooden case in his hands, won from a drunken, reeling fool at poker. The man had wagered it against a five-pound note, holding it close to his chest and announcing drunkenly that the secrets to life itself were contained within, and that this being the case, it certainly qualified as collateral against a five-pound note. The case had been found floating, he claimed, off the shore of the island of Eucrasia after the explosion that destroyed its culture and its ruler. It had been handed from man to man since, and nothing was known of its contents save that they came from the laboratory of one Dr. Caresco Surhomme. Silverman, who knew of Caresco's work, had agreed impatiently, the four threes in his hand itching to be slapped to the tabletop, and he'd walked away with all the other man's money, and the wooden box. He could still hear the fellow's words, echoing in his mind.

"You'll find more than you bargain for in there. I'm glad to be rid of it. God bears a very heavy burden my friend—don't be too quick to shoulder it."

It had taken years of poring over corresondence and articles, diatribes about and against Caresco and fictions written about the man and his work, to realize what it was that he possessed. It had taken another five years to analyze the serum and attribute it to one small corner of Caresco's work. The reversal of aging. The shaving away of the ravages of time. Taken to the extreme, and with certain additions of Silverman's own devising, reversing the process of death.

Silverman shook his head to dislodge the memories of what had come before. More important to see to the needs of the moment. He led Michael around a corner and disappeared into the fog. Jeffries would know what to do, and they would have to set about whatever it was with haste. Both the serum, and the incantations and amulets his father had reluctantly provided him, were proving less stable than he'd anticipated. The row in the cell earlier had been a near miss that Silverman didn't want repeated.

The asylum brooded over the street beneath, giving off a sensation of density, immovable and old as time. When the carriage stopped in front of that place and Holmes stepped out, tipping the driver, I was sure he had lost his mind. The Asylum of St. Elian had been deserted since I was a young man, still pursuing the degrees and education that would lead me to a career in medicine. The stories I'd heard had seemed laughable enough at the time, but when I was faced with the reality of the place, they came back to me full force, flickering across the years of my memory with chilling speed.

Holmes didn't hesitate. He moved from carriage to door with forceful steps, reached up, and rapped his knuckles against the door sharply. I stared at him, then at the building before us. I would have bet my last pound that no one had passed through that door in ten years. Holmes knocked again, then turned to me with a purpose.

"No one seems to be about, Watson. We must hurry."

"Hurry where?" I inquired.

Holmes was already trying the door. It was, of course, locked, but I noted with amazement and some alarm that Holmes had pulled a small tool from his pocket and inserted one end into the lock. A few deft movements of wrist and finger, and I heard the sound of tumblers sliding into place. The latch gave way, and Holmes pulled the door open, slipping inside. There was nothing to do but to follow him into the shadows, and to pray that most of what I'd heard back at university was the hogwash it had seemed. The heavy door closed behind us with a loud *click*. Holmes fiddled with it for a moment, then turned away.

"Locked," he whispered.

There was no light, but Holmes moved quickly and easily, making his way to the first set of doors to his left. He pulled out a box of matches, lighting one and holding it up as we entered the room. It was a crude, antiquated sort of laboratory. On one of the benches, a few crates lay open, packing material and other items strewn about as if opened and gone through quickly and without much care.

I moved up beside Holmes, glancing over his shoulder as the light from the first match flickered, then died. The quick glimpse had been enough.

"Medical equipment," I said softly.

"As I suspected," Holmes replied, turning to the other bench. He lit another match, and this time he slipped along the wall and found the light switch, flicking the power to on.

"Someone will see," I hissed.

My friend ignored me, and with a quick turn about the room, I realized my error. There were no windows. We were encircled in stone as surely as if entombed. The light was dim, but Holmes made use of it quickly, making his way to a wooden case flung open on one of the bench tops.

The case held two vials, and I saw that Holmes had looked past the greenish, glowing liquid and the other—full of something that looked like sand. He plucked it from the case and held it to the dim light. Then he removed the folded paper he'd brought away from the doorstep of my flat and opened it. He held the two objects together, and I saw that what was on the paper was a bit of clay. Red clay, unlike anything near the city. The dust, or sand, in the vial had the same reddish hue.

"Watson, have you heard of a man named Caresco?"

I started violently, nearly toppling into the nearest of the benches. "Caresco is dead." I replied, a bit more calmly. "His island was buried in volcanic ash. That Caresco?"

Holmes held up a hand, and I fell silent. The greenish contents of those vials had taken on a new reality for me. I had heard of Caresco and his hellish experiments, and I knew the end he'd reached. Playing God with the human anatomy, enslaving the mind. Seeking a cure for death and time.

"I know of Caresco as well," Holmes assured me. "I was fairly certain his work was tied up in this, but there is more—something vital that we are missing."

He returned the card to the case and began pacing the room, rooting through the remaining cases and tossing paperwork and equipment aside without a thought. Clearly, he had no intention of trying to keep our illegal entry a secret. Holmes turned and lifted the vial in his hand so that I could see it more closely.

"Clay?" he asked. I didn't believe that he expected an answer, so I remained silent as he replaced the vial and continued to stare into the case.

Then, just as I was certain he would turn in disgust and leave that accursed place, Holmes laid hand on a small leather-bound volume. Pulling it nearer to the light, he flipped open the covers, which had nothing upon them but a few characters rendered in Hebrew. Holmes's brow furrowed, and he flipped the pages rapidly, grunting under his breath.

I glanced over his shoulder as he flipped through the pages. The script was coarse, and though I'm no linguist, I saw what seemed to be alternating lines of Hebrew and some antiquated form of Arabic. There were notes scribbled in the margins. I could make out none of it, but Holmes seemed to be devouring it all.

"There's no time to waste, Watson," he said at last, replacing the book where he'd found it and tidying up the room just enough so that a cursory glance would show no evidence of our presence. "We must hide ourselves."

We moved none too soon. Holmes had just switched off the lights, and dragged me down the hall and through another door, when we heard the grate of an iron key turning slowly in the lock. We could just make out the cursing voice of Aaron Silverman through the solid wood, growing louder as he pushed the door inward and stepped inside.

"I curse the day I first laid eyes on you," he was saying.

There were two sets of footsteps, and I guessed that the second set must belong to Michael Adcott. There was no answer to Silverman's ranting diatribe, but the echo of shuffling feet followed his hard, sharp strides into the hall. The door closed once more, and Silverman moved into the laboratory, shoving things about roughly. I held my breath, but he seemed to notice nothing amiss.

"I suppose there's nothing to do but to put you back in your cell and go in search of Watson," he said at last. "There is more than one way to get a paper signed, and if Jeffries can't straighten this out without the good doctor's authorization, then authorization he shall have."

Only silence was his answer, and the two sets of footsteps moved closer to us once again, passing into the hall and by our door, moving into the gloomy interior of the old asylum. Holmes hesitated only for a moment, then followed. I trailed behind, moving a bit more slowly, dragging the fingertips of my right hand along the wall beside us as we went. I didn't want a chance misstep to alert Silverman to our presence. Indeed, I had no idea what Holmes planned to do, and I wanted to be as ready as possible for any circumstance.

We followed the pair down into the bowels of that wretched structure, and at last I felt Holmes's hand on my arm and came to a stop. Just ahead, around a final corner, there was a stationary glow, as if a torch, or a lantern, was being held. I could still hear Silverman's muttering voice, and I heard as well the clatter of keys on a ring. Holmes was moving ahead again, very slowly now, and I followed, keeping well back, not wanting to cause my companion to stumble.

Silverman's words came into clearer focus. He was so agitated that his voice quavered. If I'd been seeing him in my office, I'd have prescribed a stiff brandy, and a few hours' rest, but Silverman was as far from being prepared to rest as a man could be.

"I'll find him, don't you worry," he was saying. "I'll make him sign those papers, show him the error of his ways. He saw you, plain as the nose on his face, walking about. Alive. No reason he shouldn't sign, and by the Gods he will."

There was more. His lips never ceased their motion, the words flowing in an endless stream. There was the solid *click* of a key turning in a lock, and the creaking of rusted hinges, followed by the shuffling of feet. I started to inch forward, not wanting to miss a word of what was being said, but I felt Holmes's hand gripping my shoulder tightly, and I grew still.

He leaned in close and whispered into my ear: "Something is afoot, Watson. Listen!"

I did—and there were two voices. The second, far from coherent, began as a low moan, shivering up from some deep darkness I could not equate with human consciousness. I heard the scrape of shoes on the stone floor, but they weren't measured steps. The sound was random and wild, quickly drowned out by the wailing voice. It rose from a moan to a banshee screech so rapidly that I was physically stunned by the blast of sound. There was a crash, and a loud cry, followed by a volley of crazed curses.

"Now, Watson," Holmes hissed. "We must hurry."

Without looking back, Holmes rounded the corner and stopped. I came up short behind him and stared over his shoulder.

Aaron Silverman was shoving Michael Adcott toward the door of the cell frantically, cursing with each breath, fighting to avoid the other's flailing arms. Adcott's hands were clasped to Silverman's head, fingers twined in his thin, wispy hair, ripping, then gripping again, and ripping more, tufts drifting about the two in a slow-motion counterpoint to their struggle.

"Get in that cell, damn you," Silverman screeched.

Adcott either didn't hear the words or ignored them. Backpedaling, he rammed Silverman into the stone wall, spun to the side, and began slamming his own head into the stone with such force it made me sick to watch. Silverman, momentarily stunned, took a step toward Adcott, then seemed to think better of it. He reached into a pocket and pulled out a wrinkled sheet of paper. With trembling voice, he began to read, or, at least I believe he was reading. The words were unfamiliar to me, and his entire frame was shaking with such frustrated rage that he couldn't hold the paper still enough to read.

Adcott stilled, just for a moment. The man turned toward Silverman, who stood between Holmes, myself, and Adcott, providing a face-on view. To the day of my own death—may it be more lasting and complete than poor Michael's—I will never shake the image of those eyes from my mind. They flared with inner light so intense that I could imagine worlds within, arms flailing and voices crying out for salvation. Those eyes were windows straight to hell, and in that second, they burned full force into the soul of Aaron Silverman.

Silverman began to back away. He tried to continue the chant, but the words failed him, and his voice faltered, then fell silent. Adcott was moving with quick purposeful strides that slipped from a walk to a full sprint in seconds, propelling his slight frame with alarming speed toward his tormentor. The madness of moments before had blossomed into an intense concentration of anger.

"My God," I whispered.

Adcott hit Silverman at a full run. One of Michael's hands

gripped the other man by the throat and drove him backward into the stone with a sickening crunch. Silverman tried to speak, but no words or air made it past the iron grip at his throat. His legs buckled, and as Adcott continued to drive forward, squeezing ever harder, Aaron Silverman fell to his knees, eyes bulging.

In a voice so clear and pure that it washed over the scene like the water of a mountain stream on a flame, Adcott spoke. He spoke three short words, and as he spoke them, Silverman struggled a final time, eyes widening farther, if that was possible, and then went absolutely limp, the life crushed from his body.

Adcott staggered back. The effort of concentration had drained him, and the otherworldly rage and strength with which he'd propelled himself vanished. He turned, noticing us for the first time, and raised a hand toward Holmes, as if asking for something. Seconds later, I saw Michael Adcott die for the second time in a single week, and I nearly fainted away on the spot.

Holmes had me by the arm and headed toward the door before I had my wits fully about me, and we were out and into the waiting carriage without a word, closing and locking the doors of St. Elian's behind us firmly. Holmes stared out into the night, and I collapsed into the seat and my own thoughts as the carriage hurried into the fog.

We were seated in Holmes's study, sipping brandy and watching the fire that very night. Holmes was staring into the flames, not offering any explanations, and at last I'd had all I could stand of it.

"Holmes," I said, "back in that laboratory, you said there was something we were missing. I'm familiar with Caresco's work, and the abominations he is purported to have created. I have heard that he managed to reverse aging in some subjects, though at the cost of the mind—this is beyond me. I never heard that he had cheated death, and in any case, Adcott showed none of the madness reported of the earlier experiments. A great number of very learned men have pored over the bits and pieces that remain of his notes—they found the research to be an abomination, and the process beyond repair. Was Silverman a mad genius?"

"He was not," Holmes replied, turning to me at last, steepling his fingers and taking a long breath. "Aaron Silverman was a Jew."

I stared at my friend, wondering if something in the night's business had addled his brains. He returned my gaze with his usual frank, half-amused expression firmly in place. I waited, and, finally, cracked.

"What in the world," I asked slowly, "can that possibly have to do with this mess?"

For the first time since we'd left that accursed asylum, Holmes smiled.

"How much do you know of Jewish history?" he asked. I shrugged, and he continued. "There are legends," he said. "Legends that trail back to the Holy Land itself, and that are known to only a select few. When you first spoke to me, I was nearly certain that Adcott must have a twin that no one had been aware of, or a cousin who bore a striking resemblance to the dead man whom they were trying to pass off as Adcott to win the funds from the tontine. There were obvious answers, but very quickly, the obvious answers caved in, one by one.

"I then began to explore the less obvious, and there was something that bothered me from the start. Silverman's name. I knew it was familiar to me, but Aaron is hardly an uncommon name, nor is Silverman, so I set out to see if I could find what it was that itched at my mind.

"My search led me to the local temple, and the rabbi, an old friend, was very helpful. He remembered the name of Aaron Silverman immediately, but the Silverman he remembered had been dead for many years. Silverman was a rabbi, or had been. He migrated to London about fifty years ago and made a home here, but even among his fellows he was shunned. Rabbi Silverman had spent years in the Arabian desert, studying and fasting. He came away from that study—changed. He had scrolls and teachings that were unfamiliar to the others already settled here, scrolls dealing with legendary creatures and the Cabala. Scrolls dealing with the Golem. It is reported that he had a scrap of cloth that contained verses from al-Hazred himself, inscribed in blood. Bits of a larger work."

"The *Necronomicon*?" I asked dubiously. "That work has long been passed off as legend. And what in the world is a Golem, Holmes, and what has it to do with Michael Adcott?"

"The Golem was an instrument of revenge," Holmes continued. "It was a creature formed of clay and brought to life by the will, faith, and rage of a rabbi. It would serve the purpose of that rage, and only the rabbi himself could control it."

"And Adcott?" I asked, not certain I wanted the answer. "He was no man of clay."

"No," Holmes agreed. "He was a man brought to a sort of hellish, painful un-life by the science of Caresco Surhomme and the diabolical research of Aaron Silverman. It was the incantations, and the clay, Watson, clay from another place—another time. Clay inherited from Silverman's father, Aaron Silverman Senior— Rabbi Silverman. The substance in that sixth vial was the very clay of which I speak. When I found a bit of it on your doorstep, I was intrigued. When I saw the vial, I was certain.

"Through the power invested in the clay, Silverman was able to exercise enough control of Adcott's reanimated form to lead it about in public. You'll recall that Adcott never spoke, not at your first meeting, nor at any time thereafter."

"But he did," I said at last. "He spoke, right at the end. What do you suppose he said, and what enabled him to do what he did?"

"He spoke in Hebrew," Holmes answered at once. "The words were very clear, and, I suspect, appropriate. I believe that Adcott's soul managed to make use of the same power that the elder Silverman would have used to animate clay. He used his will, and his faith, and he spoke the only words that could bring him peace.

"He said, 'It is done.' "

I stared at Holmes for a long time, watching for doubt, or belief, anything in those wise eyes that would prove a clue to the mind beyond, but he had turned his gaze to the fire once again, and grown silent.

"I wonder," I said, rising and retrieving my coat, suddenly very tired and ready for my own home, and my bed, "who got the money."

Holmes didn't look up as I departed, but I sensed the smile in his answer.

"To the living go the spoils, Watson. Always to the living."

Shaking my head, I opened the door and made my way into the late-evening fog.

Nightmare in Wax

SIMON CLARK

PROLOGUE

Thunder tears the air asunder. Half of Europe, it seems, is afire. Nations shrink back before a Pentecostal wind. Today, the London Times *brings news of the sinking of the* Lusitania *by the Hun. Over a thousand innocent lives lost. While yet more newsprint carries the dreadful litany of tens of thousands of our soldiers consumed by the war—this war to end all wars. In the midst of global conflict, the cases of my friend Mr. Sherlock Holmes might appear of little importance now. Last night, however, I was roused from bed by three visitors. I will not identify them for obvious reasons; although two of them would be widely known from king to barrow boy. Suffice to say: one gentleman holds a very senior post in His Majesty's government, the second a high rank in the army, while the third is a leading light in the clandestine and anonymous world of our secret service.*

Clad in dressing gown and slippers, I invited them into my sitting room.

The military gentleman said: "Dr. Watson. We apologize for calling

on you at this time of night, but you will appreciate the fact that we are
here on business of a most important nature that concerns not only the se-
curity of the Empire but the preservation of all nations."

"I understand, gentlemen," I replied. "How may I help you?"

The military man said, "We have two matters to put to you. Firstly,
do you know the whereabouts of Sherlock Holmes?"

I shook my head. "I understand he is traveling."

"Do you know where?"

Again I shook my head. "I'm afraid not."

"Has Mr. Holmes contacted you?"

"I received a telegram from him perhaps three weeks ago."

"Are you able to divulge the contents of the message?"

"Normally not. But as it's you, gentlemen . . ." I cleared my throat.
"Holmes simply wrote, 'Watson, the game is afoot.' "

"I see . . ."

The third gentlemen then spoke. "Thank you, Dr. Watson. That
brings us to our second matter. We have brought with us a phonograph
recording made several years ago, which my agents retrieved, from a Home
Office vault. We should be grateful if you would listen to this recording
and identify the voices you recognize."

Assembling the phonographic equipment with its horn speaker and
wax cylinders took but a few minutes. Then the intelligence officer wound
the clockwork motor before pushing a brass lever that set the audio mecha-
nism in motion.

The chimes of midnight from the church across the square died on the
air as the wax cylinder yielded the sound of a man's voice to the hushed
room. This, then, is what I heard.

Now, pray . . . are you in the mood for a little sport? Perhaps you
might care to guess my name? What's that you say? Is it a name of
some importance? Will history have even recorded that name? Or,
as with countless billions of men and woman who have swarmed
upon the surface of this planet like so many maggots, will it be
forever lost to the four winds?

You require a clue?

A certain amateur detective who can perform tricks with clues with all the cack-handed dexterity of a Barbary ape juggling apples, described me as "the organizer of half that is evil and nearly all that is undetected in London." Evil? The man's interpretation of the word is unutterably blunt. I admit I have the ability to acquire that grubby medium called money and to exert my will on men without the handicap of conscience. Moreover, the term *evil* is merely a rather clichéd insult directed by the weak against the strong. And you will be patently aware that the strong are not forgotten by history. Some might accuse Rome's Julius Caesar of evil, but he will never slip from memory. The seventh month of the year is named after him. His successor, Augustus, a powerful man of scant conscience, made posthumous claim to the following month, August. Perhaps one day my name will be similarly honored in the calendar.

Ah . . . Do you have my name yet? That same aforementioned detective also bestowed upon me the title "the Napoleon of Crime." A laughably inaccurate one, I should add. Napoleon ultimately lost, whereas I shall be the victor. Still, you may have guessed by now. No?

Dear, oh dear. Then I'll delay no longer because I only have precisely one hour to preserve this account of my singular endeavor for posterity. My name is Professor James Moriarty. Never one to fail to exploit the cream of new technology, I am recording my voice on a phonograph. These wax cylinders will preserve this verbal testament for all mankind. After all, I don't wish anyone hearing this to believe that I merely somehow stumbled upon the greatest discovery made by man through sheer luck. Believe me, luck is for fools. Effort mated with intelligence brings success, not mere chance. What I have uncovered is the result of twenty-five years of painstaking labor and applied thought. Indeed the purpose of my criminal career, as the ignorant might term it, has merely been to fund important research work; although I have to admit that devising all those nefarious strategies did reward me with a modicum of entertainment. I daresay I could have netted the required capital via legitimate commerce, but how deadly dull those long years would have been. Indeed, I would never have had the opportunity to engage in those cerebral duels with that aforementioned detective, one Sherlock Holmes (a name, I daresay, soundly forgotten by history).

Now here I am, Professor Moriarty, sitting alone in a most elegantly appointed carriage that is drawn by a privately chartered locomotive. It is the first day of November, 1903. On the throne of England and commanding the British Empire is that idiot wastrel King Edward VII.

No doubt during the pauses between my words you can hear that *clickety-click* of iron wheels against track. Isn't it an evocative sound? A symphony for the traveler! The time is ten minutes before midnight. We are passing through a forbidding moor that is ill lit by a gibbous moon. In a short while . . . *there* . . . did you hear it? The train's whistle? The driver has signaled that we are but a few miles from a most singular destination. Even now I see ocean away to my right.

Yet what unfurls beyond the windows on this fiercely cold winter's night is of far less importance than what lies on the desk in front of me. In this snugly warm carriage is the product of twenty-five years of the most demanding labor imaginable. If through the medium of these wax cylinders you could *see* what this singular object is, you might not immediately be moved to excitement. "It is merely a book," you might say. Ah, but what a book. Not just any book. Hear that? That whispery sound? Like the voices of a million ghosts revealing secrets from beyond the grave? Ah . . . That sound you hear, my friends, is the pages of this great and glorious tome. And if you could see the title—that strange and darkly powerful title that has filled many a man with dread—*you* still might not understand its importance. But I proclaim here and now that this, indeed, is the Book of books. It is the bridge between worlds . . . it is the *Necronomicon*.

My diaries reveal in intricate detail the background to my research. However, to toss you a little information in easily digestible morsels will help you to understand what I am about to accomplish tonight. Twenty-five years ago a large body of antique volumes came into my possession from some ruffian who wanted little more in exchange for them than the price of a few quarts of gin to souse his bloated liver. From the blood-spattered trunk they arrived in, one can deduce without difficulty how the ruffian came by them. No matter. I examined the volumes, intending to sell them on to collectors. However, these were no ordinary books. For the main part they related to occult matters in a number of disparate cultures.

Now, these volumes did tickle my curiosity delightfully. Moreover, there were several journals in the excitable hand of a certain Father Solomon Buchanan. A man of God who was clearly far more interested in what lay in pagan tracts than can ever be found in the Gospels. I quickly grasped the core of the man's fascination with these apparently disparate cultures. From the Americas to Europe to Africa to the Orient, he'd studied pagan mythology and arcane writings in search of a common element universal to all cultures across the globe, yet a common element that was a deeply held secret, and known only to an inner sanctum of priests, witch-doctors, and shamans. Now, this was something of immense interest, because if the most powerful individuals guard certain information with the utmost rigor, it means just one thing: that *information* confers *power* on its keeper. And isn't power the most sublime asset of all?

On the table before me in my study all those long years ago, I carefully laid out drawings that Father Buchanan had made of statues from Mesopotamia, tomb paintings from Egypt, ritual masks from the Tehucan people of Central America, cremation jars from Ban Na Di in India, and a bronze cauldron that belonged to a priest of China's Shang Dynasty. To an uneducated eye the drawings would merely be of museum pieces; however, even though these depictions of archaeological artifacts came from each corner of the globe and were many thousands of years old, they all contained a representation of the same being: one that is squat, bulbous, some might say toadlike. Yet it has little in the way of facial features save for a vertical slitlike mouth above which sit toadlike eyes. In each representation hooded priests worship before it. While scattered before this object of veneration are severed human limbs and heads.

This is one example of multitudinous deities that are common to disparate cultures. Ergo, at some point in man's history fabulous creatures occupied our world. There are suggestions in Buchanan's journals that there was a mingling of human and inhuman blood. Moreover, these creatures were worshiped as gods, the masters of humanity.

Night after night I pored over Father Buchanan's writings. He enthused about a secret book, the *Necronomicon*. He recounted ancient testimonies of men driven mad after encountering abominable unhuman races that dwelled in the sea or in subterranean lairs. Strange words leaped out at me from the text—Cthulhu, Dagon, Y'golonac, Shub-Niggurath, Daoloth. Soon I realized that the priest had discovered not only a hitherto unknown race of beings that had long ago penetrated our world, but that these Old Ones possessed a source of enormous occult power. A power capable of being accessed—and exploited—by a man of knowledge and courage. Now, twenty-five years later, I, Moriarty, am within barely fifty minutes of achieving just that. The power of steam and electricity barely—

Now, this isn't right . . . the train is slowing . . . it's not scheduled to stop here. Through the windows all I see is moorland. The train is still ten minutes from its destination . . . now . . . now . . .

Forgive me for that pause. The train has indeed come to halt. Ah, here is my trusted assistant, Dr. Cowley.

"What's the delay, Cowley? We must be at Burnston by twelve-fifteen."

"We're continuing immediately, Professor. We've paused to allow one of the engineers to be brought on board."

"What on earth is an engineer doing here? He should be at the drainage site."

"I'm sorry, Professor, but there appears to have been a problem."

"Problem, what problem, Cowley? I was telegrammed that the area had been successfully drained."

"I—I'm not sure of the details, Professor. But the engineer's waiting in the next—"

"Bring him in, then. Let's hear what he has to say."

Ah, this is most irritating. Nevertheless, I will keep the clockwork running on the phonograph in order to record my conversation with the man that Dr. Cowley is in the process of collecting from the next carriage. Ha, the sound of the locomotive . . . we are in motion once more. I should be dreadfully annoyed if we weren't in Burnston on time.

And now here is the engineer, a bespectacled man of fifty-five, I should say, in his Norfolk jacket and muddy boots.

"Sit down, there's a good fellow. And don't be distracted by this apparatus. You'll have seen phonograph recording equipment before?"

"Indeed I have, sir."

"I am keeping an aural record of a scientific experiment. Every sound you utter will be preserved on the wax cylinder here as it turns. Don't worry, it won't bite."

"I understand, sir."

"Now, I need to know the nature of the problem that has taken you away from your work in order to stop this train."

"Well, sir, I thought you should—"

"Ah, first of all, your name? For the benefit of record."

"Of course, sir. My name is Victor Hatherley."

"You're the hydraulic engineer?"

"I am."

"Then, for our audience perhaps you will briefly explain the nature of the contract of works I awarded to your company earlier this year?"

"If you wish, sir."

"I do wish, Hatherley. Now lean forward. Speak clearly."

"The firm of engineers with which I am employed has been contracted to drain a parcel of low-lying hinterland that lies on the Yorkshire coast. Five years ago a storm in the North Sea flooded the village of Burnston. Since that time the village has lain at the bottom of a lagoon of saltwater that averages some twelve feet in depth. My colleagues and I erected sea defenses in order to isolate the lagoon, which we then proceeded to drain with the aid of steam pumps."

"And now the village of Burnston has been reclaimed from the ocean?"

"Indeed it has, sir."

"So what problem has brought you all the way out here to stop my train?"

"The men wish to discontinue work at the site."

"Then fire them."

"We require a number of men to serve the pumps, otherwise seepage through the subjacent soil results in fresh flooding."

"And why, pray, do the men refuse to earn the wages I am paying them?"

"The navvies aren't happy, they say—"

"Speak up. The phonograph can't record murmurs."

"The professional men continue their duties, but the navvies are afraid to enter the village."

"I daresay there are a few human bones, Hatherley, moldering in the silt; after all, I gather that a hundred and fifty villagers were lost when the place was flooded."

"The men aren't afraid of skeletons, sir."

"Then what, pray, is the problem?"

"They discovered bodies in the buildings when the water levels dropped far enough for them to enter."

"Well, then?"

"The people they found in the houses . . . they were still alive."

Our friend Hatherley is now drinking tea in another carriage. The absurdity of these artisans. They fear their own shadows. I, Professor Moriarty—please: take a fix on that name—will not be afraid to enter the drowned village, for I know that is where the greatest treasure of all lies. It was in Burnston that Father Solomon Buchanan discovered an ancient pagan temple beneath the parish church . . . a temple dedicated to the worship of the Old Ones described in the *Necronomicon*.

In a little while I will enter the temple. I will conduct the solemn rites that I have painstakingly reconstructed from a thousand fragmentary ancient texts. Then we shall see what we shall see . . .

I am continuing to record my account of events on the phonographic device. I have raised the blind of the carriage as the train pulls into a rather ad hoc station built by the hydraulic engineers to serve the drainage site. The time is fourteen minutes past midnight. Now, what do I see before me? Some quarter of a mile away I spy in the moonlight the rolling silver of the North Sea. Between ocean and land is a rampart of earth and rocks that has been raised by the navvies to sever the lagoon from the tides. The lagoon, you will recall, was formed quite recently when the village of Burnston was engulfed during a storm. I see men toiling by the light of hurricane lamps. Horses drawing carts mounded with yellow gravel to renew the roadway. Sparks rising from the chimneys of steam engines that drive pumps to expel seawater from the inundated village.

Of the village itself, I see houses without roofs. Loathsome mud still oozes across streets to the height of the windows. There's the village inn, the Mermaid, with its sign still festooned with sea-weed. And here is the church of St. Lawrence, covered with a white leprous rash of barnacles. It is in this location that Father Buchanan uncovered a pagan temple beneath the nave. Carved there on the walls are symbols that evoke the Nameless One. In a few moments I shall leave the carriage to conduct a momentous ritual within the ancient temple. With that I shall access power of unimaginable—ah, it is Cowley again; here to interrupt my soliloquy. His face is as purple as a beet.

"Cowley, can you not see I am making a phonograph recording?"

"I beg your pardon, Professor."

"Go on."

"Those individuals that the navvies found in the houses . . ."

"Oh yes, pixies for the pixilated, no wonder."

"No, Professor. These individuals are attacking the navvies."

"Ridiculous."

"They are devouring the men!"

"Away with you, man."

"No, Professor, sir. Can't you hear the screams? The men are being eaten alive. I've seen it myself. Their attackers are grotesque . . . monstrously deformed."

"Shhh. There, perhaps the phonograph can record those sounds. Yes, Cowley, you're not wrong. I can hear screams. Fascinating. You say that people who are deformed in some way inhabit the houses?"

"Worse than deformed, Professor. I'm a medical man and yet I've seen nothing like this. These individuals suffer from some condition that endows them with skin much like that of a fish. They have no eyelids, and possess vast eyes that are perfectly round. They make one nauseated if one looks upon them."

"How intriguing."

"Professor, we must leave at once."

"No. We will not retreat. You have your revolver?"

"Yes."

"Then guard the door, man. I will observe events as they unfold from the carriage."

"But—"

"Do as I order, man."

"Yes, sir."

Now I will continue my observations. Indeed, I see any number of figures emerging from the houses . . . more accurately they slither like seals from the windows; squirming on their bellies across the silt before standing upright. My workmen appear no match for the creatures. The men are being killed and devoured as I watch. And how unusual the gait of these creatures: they move in a queer, swaying way, as if unfamiliar with moving on dry land. The battle is almost over. Now perhaps fifty of the creatures approach the carriage. They make gestures with their limbs—to call them arms would be misleading—there is something tentacular about them. The creatures' heads are rounded, domelike; their eyes resemble those of a cod. Large and round and black. They do not blink. Yes, this moonlight is bright enough to appreciate more detail than perhaps one would wish. Initially, I thought they would attack, but now they have paused some thirty paces from the carriage. They look at me. Perhaps, by some clairvoyant process, they recognize my identity. Perhaps they know I am a friend and ally?

Now they move their limbs again. I see it is a priestly gesture . . . and what's that? I hear voices . . . hissing voices: reminiscent of the exhalation of air from a dolphin's blowhole. There, perhaps this instrument is sensitive enough to pick up the chorus of voices . . .

"Fhe'pnglai, Fhe'glinguli, thabaite yibtsill, Iä Yog-Sothoth, Cthulhu . . ."

An incantation. I recognize it from my translation of the *Necronomicon*. This indeed is a fabulous sight. Unique. An epoch-making event. This should—*tut-tut* . . . another interruption.

"You're the engineer. Hatherley?"

"Yes, sir, I came to warn that—"

"Sit down there, man, and silence please. Can't you see what I am doing?"

Ah, to continue . . . now, a brilliant flash of light. The creatures are evoking that alien power. My God, my good God . . . this will be at my disposal, too. Am I, also, to become the destroyer of worlds?

Ah, but I am quite dazzled by the light. And strange . . . *Strange.* I don't hear the sound of the locomotive, but we seem to be in motion . . . there . . . I've managed to draw shut the carriage's window blind, but I am still quite dazzled by that burst of incandescence . . . most peculiar; the train is moving, yet impossibly it feels as if we're descending. At an incredible rate of speed, too. Those denizens of Burnston must have cast some ineffably exotic and occult influence upon the vehicle.

"Dr. Cowley."

"Yes, Professor?"

"Don't sound so frightened, man. With my presence here, you cannot be harmed."

"But . . . we're falling. What have they—"

"Hush now. Compose yourself."

"I'm sorry, sir."

"Now go to the window. Look out without disturbing the blind more than you can help it. Describe what you see outside."

"Outside, sir?"

"Yes, man, and quickly. I'd do it myself, but the flash of light has left me dazzled. There . . . are you at the window yet, Dr. Cowley?"

"Yes, sir."

"Peep through the gap in the blind as you would spy through a keyhole. On no account open it."

"I understand."

"Mr. Hatherley, remain in that seat. Do not attempt to look out of the window. On no account touch the blinds."

"I understand, sir."

"Excellent. Now, Dr. Cowley, describe exactly what you see."

"Professor . . . oh, my dear God, we're falling . . . We're falling!"

"Describe exactly what you witness. The phonograph must record every single word."

"We're falling into what appears to be a pit, yet I can see stars embedded in its walls. Entire constellations of fabulous complexity. Beneath us are strange lights and patterns; geometric shapes. Weird shapes. I find it disturbing to gaze upon them . . . wait . . . I see now. It's as if the train has drawn up to the very edge of a cliff of enormous height. I'm looking down upon lakes and canals and cities and oceans. We are plunging toward a city that contains a huge purple mountain in its center. The crash will smash us all to pieces."

"It won't, Cowley. We are slowing. We will gently alight in the citadel. Now, *describe*."

"I see fabulous things . . . *fabulous* . . . but frightening . . . as if these are visions induced by an opiate."

"Describe what you see. Delineate. Give me details. Colors. Shapes. Metaphor and simile, if you must."

"It is an exotic city, like something from a dream. It is how I imagined the appearance of Byzantium. We pass through rose-colored mist. I see houses stacked terrace on terrace, one above the other, as they march up toward the mountain of purple. Myriads of chimneys expel fragrant smoke that drifts on star winds. I see ships with golden sails on oceans of emerald. I see towers of ivory reaching to the sky, I see dome on dome on dome stretching into infinity. I see bronze bells the size of battleships set into arches. The bells swing back and forth, ringing out fabulous notes that shimmer with an alien resonance across the city. Bell peals that will never change and *never* decay so long as the cosmos shall retain its cohesion. Through chinks in the window frame I smell the most beautifully exotic traces of incense. Spices, too, from kitchens that were old when the pyramids were new. I hear unearthly music. Magic fluting. Drums beating. I hear singing in the streets. Songs of ineffable beauty. Melodies of numinous power."

"That is our reception party, Cowley. We will be honored guests."

"We are flying low over the city now. I can see people—millions of people thronging the streets. I sense their jubilation, their adoration of us. This is akin to a family reunion. We are not venturing here, Professor. *We are returning!*"

"Indeed we are, Dr. Cowley."

"Now the train glides through the air; I see our line of carriages headed by the locomotive still issuing steam; the train has all the supple grace of a snake gliding through water. Beneath us are bazaars, Oriental marketplaces, Casbahs shaded by silken awnings. Turquoise banners ripple in the perfumed breeze of evening. I see geese white as snow in gardens. Leaping fish in fountains. I see millions of people in the exotic robes of Arabia. Fabrics of gold, crimson, scarlet, jade.

"Now we approach the purple mountain that rises above everything like a god of old. It gleams as if illuminated from within. Oh, I see a transfiguration. No . . . No!"

"Cowley, continue to relate what you see below us."

"But . . . no . . . it's changing, transforming . . . degrading: the entire city is melting into the most obscene—"

"Describe. *Describe.*"

"Monsters. Those aren't men down there. They're creatures with webbed hands, barbel-necked . . . eyes like toads, bulging from the ugliest faces. I know I can have no knowledge of this, but somehow I divine that these beasts are profane. They are man and monster mated into a terrible form . . . please, permit me to close my eyes."

"Dr. Cowley. Tell me what lies below."

"I see the city as a malignant sore on a body. From it ooze

rivers of corruption through which its inhabitants swim up to mock us. I see the mountain grow larger, swelling. Transforming. Features form upon it . . . mouth . . . eyes, hideous eyes . . . that— oh! I cannot look into those eyes. And it speaks . . . the mountain speaks to me . . . I know the meaning, if I don't understand the words. It tells me to cease to hope. It describes what I shall become . . . please!"

Ah, that pitiful sobbing is my assistant, Dr. Cowley. He is quite unmanned. "Stay huddled in the corner if you will, sir. You've served your purpose . . ." So that leaves the engineer and me with our wits still intact. For obvious reasons I shall not trouble to look out of the window yet. For I must sheathe myself in protective incantations from the *Necronomicon* . . . Wait, the book? Where is it?

"Hatherley. What are you doing with my book? Hand it to me at once."

"No, Professor Moriarty. I'll not hand it back."

"My name is not Professor Moriarty. What on earth—"

"Indeed you are, Moriarty. Professor James Moriarty."

"Hatherley. I insist—"

"Come, come, Moriarty. If I know your true identity, surely you can guess mine? Especially if I remove my spectacles and this irritating India-rubber compound from my cheeks."

"Holmes . . . Sherlock Holmes?"

"One and the same, Professor."

"Holmes. Give me the book. If you do not, we will be—"

"Killed? Surely we await a fate far worse than that. Ask your assistant."

"Holmes. You must let me have the book before it is too late."

"This book, the *Necronomicon*? With all its fearsome and blasphemous content? No, this belongs with its true owner."

"Holmes? No!"

"Moriarty, I trust your phonograph etched those sounds upon its cylinder. There's no mistaking the melody of breaking of glass.

Although I daresay it can not record the sound of the book falling down onto a landscape as alien as that one."

"You're a fool, Holmes. Now . . . do you hear that? Hear those screams?"

"I hear screams of frustration and disappointment. Somehow, Moriarty, I have contrived to upset your plans . . . and the plans of whatever monstrosity slithers across that profane world beneath us . . ."

"You don't know what you have done."

"No, not exactly. I believe what we have so nearly encountered is beyond human ken. But that, if I'm not mistaken, is the sound of the train's whistle . . . and now that? That you hear is quite clearly the sound of our carriage wheels running on a more earthly track. Unless, I'm very much mistaken, the train is back on that rather chilly Yorkshire moor."

"Holmes. Damn you . . ."

"And you will gather that the train is running backward—away from Burnston. Ah . . . and don't trouble yourself about your assistant's pistol. I shall retrieve that. There . . . I know it's rude to point at people, especially with firearms, but I think it safer for every one of us if you are prevented from meddling with matters that lie beyond the bounds of human understanding."

"You really think you've won, Holmes? Is that pure arrogance or unalloyed conceit?"

"Perhaps you could define the word *victory*, Professor Moriarty? Then compare that definition to the desired outcome of the players of this singular game of—Moriarty, *don't be a fool!*"

My name is Sherlock Holmes. Today is the third day of November, 1903. The sun is shining over freshly plowed fields as the train steams toward the station at York. With a few moments of my journey remaining before I disembark to make my report to a senior representative of His Majesty's government, I have decided to speak my own postcript into this ingenious mechanical device, which will then be consigned to a secret Home Office vault. You will have listened to these phonograph cylinders and heard a record of Moriarty's folly. Ah, and what of Moriarty himself? He chose to exit the train through the broken carriage window; the very same break that resulted when I tossed that damnable book from the train to whatever monstrosity lay below. One could have assumed that the scoundrel would have broken his neck in the fall, but units of the King's Own Yorkshire Rifles have searched that section of track without success. I can only deduce that Moriarty has managed to slip away once more into that nefarious under-world that conceals him so well. Other units of the regiment are engaged, even as I speak, in eradicating every trace of those part-human horrors that dwelled in the submerged village. Thereafter, the soldiers are instructed to dynamite the seawall and return cursed Burnston to the ocean. And what of Dr. Cowley? All self-hope and peace of mind were forever extinguished in his soul upon looking on those nameless creatures. He took his own life with chloroform. You will appreciate the fact that I did nothing to obstruct his final act.

My friend Watson, who so admirably records my cases, has not been privy to this one for what are, to your ears, obvious reasons. Therefore, I have not been able to employ his delightfully teasing methods of introducing evidence, or his entertaining manner of recording my discussion of pertinent clues, their meaning, and subsequent deduction. Hence, at best, here is a rather more prosaic bundle of sentences in lieu of a full and frank explanation of the case's origins. In all truth, this case has been long and arduous and my methods have been somewhat darker than the norm. More-over, they are not for popular consumption. In short, my former dabbling with cocaine in combination with exotic fungi from the Americas opened the doors of perception far wider than I could have believed possible. These narcotic visions of nameless ones encountered beyond tideless, otherworldly seas set me on the trail of arcane writings. Suffice to say: Moriarty isn't the only obsessive personality to possess a copy of the *Necronomicon* . . . moreover, he wasn't the only one to draw upon its occult power. It was necessary for me to access its recondite properties to return the locomotive from its nightmare destination, and to bring this disturbing case to a satisfactory conclusion.

Ah, the needle has all but reached the end of the cylinder. Now all that remains is for the owner of the voice you hear now, one Sherlock Holmes, to bid you, dear listener, across whatever gulf of time separates us, a most sincere adieu.

EPILOGUE BY JOHN H. WATSON, M.D.

The three gentlemen have left my house with their gramophone and cylinders of wax that document those most singular events. I did as I was asked and identified the voices of Holmes and Moriarty. My three visitors were apparently satisfied, and yet they did not elaborate further on the nature of their mission, or how they will use the information I have given them. Such is the secrecy of wartime. I am alone again with my thoughts and a transcript of the recording. Clearly, if Moriarty had succeeded in harnessing the power that can be accessed via that profane volume, the Necronomicon, *then this would elevate him above the title of "Napoleon of Crime"; Moriarty would have become a veritable Satan. He would be capable of destroying any individual or any nation that opposed him. However, my old friend Sherlock Holmes outwitted the man. Moreover, Holmes rid the world of a book that was so potently evil.*

If I cast my mind back more than a dozen years to that time when Moriarty was poised to literally raise hell, I recall a Sherlock Holmes at his most preoccupied and his darkest. Far be it from me to make deductions, but I dare guess that it was this case that troubled him so.

Now, I confess, those troubles are visited upon me. Perhaps I should have been more candid with my visitors, considering their elevated stations, but some instinct caused me to hold my tongue. It is true that Holmes did telegram me with that single sentence that made my heart leap with excitement: "Watson, the game is afoot!" But only the day after the message arrived he made a telephone call to this very house. The connection was a bad one. The earpiece hissed and stuttered. I couldn't make my old friend Holmes hear me. And all he could do was to try to fight against the storm of noise by repeating over and over:

"Watson . . . I have found Moriarty . . . he has the book again . . . he has the Necronomicon*!"*

CONTRIBUTORS

John Pelan is the author of *An Antique Vintage* and numerous short stories. He is the editor of several anthologies, including *Darkside: Horror for the Next Millennium*, *The Last Continent: New Tales of Zothique*, *The Darker Side*, *Dark Arts*, and with Benjamin Adams, *The Children of Cthulhu*. With Edward Lee, he is coauthor of *Goon*, *Shifters*, *Splatterspunk*, *Family Tradition*, and numerous short stories. His novella *The Colour out of Darkness* is forthcoming. John's solo stories have appeared in *The Urbanite*, *Gothic.net*, *Enigmatic Tales*, and numerous anthologies; a collection, *Darkness, My Old Friend*, is in the works, as are at least two novels. As a researcher and historian of the horror genre, John has edited over a dozen single-author collections and novels of classic genre fiction and is currently working on assembling the selected supernatural fiction of Manly Wade Wellman for Night Shade Books. For his own imprints, Midnight House and Darkside Press, he is editing volumes by Fritz Leiber, John Wyndham, Harvey Jacobs, Cleve Cartmill, and several other authors. At various times he's been a pool hustler, professional darts player, sales trainer, steelworker, bartender, and several other things that you'll be better off not knowing about. Visit his site at *www.darksidepress.com*.

Michael Reaves is an Emmy Award–winning television writer, screenwriter, and novelist. He's written for *Star Trek: The Next Generation*, *The Twilight Zone*, and *Sliders*, among others. He was a story editor and writer on *Batman: The Animated Series*, and on the Disney animated series *Gargoyles*. His screenwriting credits include *Batman: Mask of the Phantasm* and the HBO movie *Full Eclipse*. Reaves's latest books, *Hell on Earth* and a *Star Wars* novel *(Darth Maul: Shadow Hunter)*, have been published by Del Rey. Reaves has had short stories published in magazines and anthologies such as *The Magazine of Fantasy & Science Fiction*, *Heavy Metal*, *Horrors*, and *Twilight Zone Magazine*, and has written comic books for DC Comics. In addition to winning an Emmy, he has been nominated for a second Emmy, an ASIFA Award, and a Writers Guild Award. His prose fiction has been nominated for the British Fantasy Award and the Prometheus Award. In 1999, he was named Alumnus of the Year by his alma mater, California State University at San Bernardino.

Steven-Elliot Altman refers to himself as a "storyteller" and finds himself equally at home writing novels, short stories, screenplays, or advertising campaigns. He recently created an anthology called *The Touch*, which was a Write Aid project to benefit both AIDS and Cancer charities, and it received rave reviews from both *Publishers Weekly* and *Asimov's Science Fiction*. His latest novel, *Deprivers,* due out from Putnam, regards a recently uncovered medical epidemic called Sensory Deprivation Syndrome, whose victims are able to render other people blind or deaf by making simple skin-on-skin contact. His Web site is *www.deprivers.com* and he thought it fit to mention that Lovecraft's work scared the living hell out of him.

Elizabeth Bear has lived in her native New England for most of her life, with the exception of three very hot years spent in the Mojave. The fact that she shares a birthday with Frodo and Bilbo

Baggins, coupled with a tendency to read the dictionary as a child, doomed her to early penury, friendlessness, intransigence, and the writing of speculative fiction. She drinks tea in quantity, participates in giant-breed dog rescue, cooks decent ethnic food, and has so far sold to a few publications—most recently, *The Magazine of Fantasy & Science Fiction*.

Poppy Z. Brite is the author of six novels, two short story collections, and a great deal of miscellanea. Her novel *The Value of X* has recently been published by Subterranean Press, and her novel *Liquor* will be published in Spring 2004 by Crown. She lives in New Orleans with her husband, Chris, a chef. Find out more about her at *www.poppyzbrite.com*.

Simon Clark is the author of several acclaimed novels of horror fiction, including *Nailed by the Heart*, *Darkness Demands*, and *Blood Crazy*. Recent releases include the collection *Salt Snake and Other Bloody Cuts* and an authorized sequel to John Wyndham's classic *The Day of the Triffids*.

David Ferguson is a writer and musician who lives in Athens, Georgia. He and Poppy Z. Brite have been friends and confidants since 1990. He has fronted numerous bands over the years and has published one previous collaboration with Brite.

Paul Finch is a former cop and journalist, but now a full-time writer, living in the north of England with his wife, Cathy, and two children, Eleanor and Harry. He's been the writer for the popular British TV crime series *The Bill* for the last two years. Dark fantasy and horror remain his main interests, with massive collections from Ash-Tree Press and Silver Salamander Press both released this year. Mr. Finch's acclaimed novella *Long Meg and Her Daughters* appeared in the Del Rey anthology *The Children of Cthulhu*.

Neil Gaiman read the Sherlock Holmes books in big bound collections in his school library in Sussex between the ages of ten and twelve, mostly by pretending to have a headache and being sent to the library for a quiet sit-down. He found H. P. Lovecraft in paperback a couple of years later and bought the books with his own money. He has an unpublished chunk of a Sherlock Holmes novel he started when he was about twenty that may be burned when he dies, but that he feels explains the whole beekeeping thing rather well.

He's won the World Fantasy Award, the Bram Stoker Award, most of the comics awards, and lots of other literary awards from all over the world, and still remains humble, lovable, modest, and shy. He is currently saving up for a small tropical island with a hidden shark pool and the kind of giant laser death beam that can be concentrated on any of the major cities of the world. Not for any particular reason.

Barbara Hambly, at various times in her life, has been a high-school teacher, a model, a waitress, a technical editor, a professional graduate student, an all-night clerk at a liquor store, and a karate instructor. Born in San Diego, she grew up in Southern California, with the exception of one high-school semester spent in New South Wales, Australia. Her interest in fantasy began with reading *The Wizard of Oz* at an early age, and it has continued ever since. She attended the university of California, Riverside, specializing in medieval history. In connection with this, she spent a year at the University of Bordeaux, France, and worked as a teaching and research assistant at UC Riverside, eventually earning a master's degree in the subject. While there, she also became involved in karate, making black belt in 1978 and competing in several national-level tournments. She now lives in Los Angeles.

Caitlín R. Kiernan is the Irish-born author of two award-winning novels, *Silk* and *Threshold*, and her short fiction has been collected in *Candles for Elizabeth, Tales of Pain and Wonder, Wrong Things* (with Poppy Z. Brite), and *From Weird and Distant Shores*. She has recently completed her third novel, *Low Red Moon*. Ms. Kiernan lives in Providence, Rhode Island, and is seriously considering giving up writing for a career as a freelance paranormal investigator.

Tim Lebbon's books include *Mesmer, Faith in the Flesh, Hush* (with Gavin Williams), *As the Sun Goes Down, Face, The Nature of Balance, Until She Sleeps*, and the novella collection *White and Other Tales of Ruin*. His novellas *White* and *Naming of Parts* both won British Fantasy Awards for Best Short Fiction, and his short story "Reconstructing Amy" recently won the Bram Stoker Award. He has been published in many magazines and anthologies, including *The Mammoth Book of Best New Horror, Dark Terrors 6, Keep Out the Night, Year's Best Fantasy and Horror, The Darker Side, Cemetery Dance, October Dreams, The Children of Cthulhu,* and *Phantoms of Venice.*

Future books include *Dusk and Dawn*, a fantasy duology from Night Shade Books; *Into the Wild Green Yonder,* a collaboration with Peter Crowther due soon from Cemetery Dance Publications; a new novella from PS Publishing, *Changing of Faces;* and a novella collaboration with Simon Clark for Earthling Publications.

James Lowder has worked extensively in fantasy and horror publishing on both sides of the editorial blotter. He's authored several best-selling fantasy and dark fantasy novels, including *Prince of Lies* and *Knight of the Black Rose*; short fiction for such diverse anthologies as *Historical Hauntings, Truth Until Paradox,* and *Realms of Mystery*; and a large number of film and book reviews; feature articles; and even the occasional comic-book script. His credits as anthologist include *Realms of Valor, The Doom of Camelot,* and *The Book of All Flesh*. He also serves as executive editor for Green Knight Publishing's line of Arthurian fiction.

Richard A. Lupoff says, "I was introduced to Arthur Conan Doyle's Sherlock Holmes as a small child when my older brother, under strong protest, took me to see the Basil Rathbone/Nigel Bruce version of *The Hound of the Baskervilles*. I discovered H. P. Lovecraft on my own when I came across 'The Dunwich Horror' in a paperback anthology when I was eleven.

"Both authors have influenced my own work. My Holmesian tales include 'The Adventure of the Boulevard Assassin' and 'The Incident of the Impecunious Chevalier.' I've actually done more Lovecraft-inspired stories, among them 'The Doom That Came to Dunwich,' 'Facts in the Case of Elizabeth Akeley,' and 'Simeon Dimsby's Workshop,' which will be collected in a volume called *Tentacular Tales*, forthcoming from Fedogan & Bremer.

"These and other pastiches represent only a portion of my work, which includes many science fiction and mystery novels, more than one hundred short stories, film scripts, journalism, criticism, and *The Great American Paperback*, an award-winning illustrated history of mass-market publishing."

F. Gwynplaine MacIntyre spent his formative years in Australia but now lives in New York City and in Minffordd, North Wales. He is the author of the Victorian horror novel *The Woman Between the Worlds* (1994) and author/illustrator of the humor anthology *MacIntyre's Improbable Bestiary* (2001). His science fiction, fantasy, and horror stories have been published in *Weird Tales*, *Analog*, *Isaac Asimov's Science Fiction Magazine*, *Absolute Magnitude*, and many anthologies. He is also an illustrator for *Analog*. Mr. MacIntyre has written one previous Sherlock Holmes story, in which Holmes and Watson cross paths with Aleister Crowley and Ambrose Bierce: "The Enigma of the Warwickshire Vortex" (published in *New Sherlock Holmes Adventures*, 1997).

Steve Perry has sold dozens of stories to magazines and anthologies and written a considerable number of novels, animated teleplays, nonfiction articles, reviews, and essays, along with a couple of un-produced movie scripts. He wrote for *Batman: The Animated Series* during its first Emmy Award–winning season, and during the second season, one of his scripts was nominated for an Emmy for Outstanding Writing—which no doubt caused the subsequent loss of that award. His novelization of *Star Wars: Shadows of the Empire* spent ten weeks on the *New York Times* Bestseller List. He also did the bestselling novelization for the summer blockbuster movie *Men in Black*, and all of his collaborative novels for Tom Clancy's *Net Force* series (seven of them so far) have made the *Times* list. His Matador series of science fiction novels has been called a cult clas-sic. For the past several years he has concentrated on books, and is currently working on his fiftieth novel.

Brian Stableford's final installment of his six-volume "future his-tory" series from Tor, *The Omega Expedition,* was published in De-cember 2002. Other recent publications include *The Eleventh Hour* (Cosmos, 2001), *The Gateway of Eternity* (Cosmos, 2002), and *Kiss the Goat: A Twenty-First Century Ghost Story* (Prime, 2003). *The Curse of the Coral Bride,* the first novel in a projected six-book se-ries of farfuturistic fantasies, will hopefully appear in 2003, but is uncontracted at the time of writing. Brian is currently employed as a 0.25 lecturer in creative writing at King Alfred's College, Win-chester, teaching an M.A. course in Writing for Children.

John P. Vourlis is one of the few people who can say that writing isn't rocket science and actually know what he's talking about. That's because John *was* a rocket scientist, working in Space Pro-pulsion Technology at NASA's Glenn Research Center in Cleve-land. He's also launched his own interactive multimedia software company and now helms an Academy Award–winning special-effects lighting company in Hollywood. John would like to thank Steve Altman, Patrick Merla, and Michael Reaves for their tireless encouragement on this story, and offer highest praise to Mr. Doyle and Mr. Lovecraft for providing important clues, and vital inspiration, in the quest to solve his own mysterious case of insomnia. John is currently cowriting a novel, *Timespanners,* with graphic artist Jaime Lombardo.

David Niall Wilson and Patricia Lee Macomber share their passion for writing and each other in a large, historical home in Hertord (the middle of nowhere), North Carolina. Surrounded by four psychotic cats, an increasingly ill-defined "dwarf" bunny, a fish named Doofish, and their children Billy and Stephanie (all the time) and Zach and Zane (sometimes), they write from a shared desk where it's possible to type and hug at the same time. David has been publishing since the mideighties and has six novels and over a hundred short stories in print, and is current president of the Horror Writers Associtaion. Patricia is the winner of the Bram Stoker Award for editing the on-line magazine *Chiaroscuro,* and has sold a steady string of stories over the past several years while serving as the current secretary of the Horror Writers Association. "Death Did Not Become Him" is David and Patricia's first published collaboration.